Flight To Exile

Chris Reher

Chris Reher

ACKNOWLEDGMENTS

Many thanks to Mallory Moutinho for dispensing sanity.
Also to Carla Levy, to Ghosty, to Tracy and to Craz

Also by Chris Reher:

Sky Hunter - 1

The Catalyst - 2

Only Human - 3

Rebel Alliances - 4

Delphi Promised - 5

Quantum Tangle – Sethran 1

Terminus Shift – Sethran 2

Chris Reher

ONE

Aletha had only the vaguest interest in how she had come to this place. She didn't know who these people were or why she had joined their group here, in a dirt-bare courtyard tucked between untidy rooming houses.

It didn't really matter; at least not as much as her cold feet did. Tonight's damp breeze reaching inland from the sea chilled her more than usual. For some reason she now wore only a simple sleeveless shift and she seemed to be missing her shoes, a fine pair of seal slippers given to her by a friend. What was his name? He always found nice things for her. Where was he? Maybe he could tell her how she came to be here, among these strangers, with cold feet and… ah, she remembered that armed man over there in the shadows. A brutish thug who'd been there, at the wharf. He'd hit Shep with his huge fist and then things had disappeared in a strange fog. Maybe he had her shoes. Maybe she should ask about them.

"I'm telling you," a person on her left interrupted her disjointed thoughts, "once you clean her up some she'll be the envy of the quarter."

Aletha turned her head to stare dully at the speaker, a fleshy-faced, malodorous person dressed in foppish clothes that might have looked elegant and expensive before he had combined them with a broad-brimmed, feathered hat and a generous application of grease on lapel and sleeves. She recognized him no more than she did the three other men and two women at the table. The others, dressed in more practical fashion, observed her critically, clearly doubting his words.

"She doesn't seem bright," one of the women said. She reached across the table to turn Aletha's hand, revealing a small leaf tattooed on her wrist. Her shrewd eyes examined the girl, seeing toned muscle and supple limbs – uncommon among the wives, priestesses and merchants that made up most of the harbor town's female population. She pushed back the tangled mass of dark ringlets obscuring the slave's face. "Island folk, I'll say. She'll be running off the minute you turn your back, and all the hounds of Harlyn won't find her if she don't want to be found. I've got no use for her." She rose from the table and adjusted her waxed straw hat. "Call on me when you've got something worthwhile to sell, trader. I'm looking for working folk, not wet woods tree-dwellers."

Aletha watched the woman leave the courtyard and enter the tavern, aware that she had failed some sort of test. She wondered if someone would come with water or food; her hunger was making her ill and light-headed.

The man at her side spat into the mud of the inn's yard before turning back to the others. "This one won't ever be anyone's maid," he grinned knowingly.

A very thin, very young man leaned forward to study Aletha more thoroughly. Aletha resisted an urge to reach out and tug on his earrings. The elaborate bone and shell masterpieces hanging from his head just begged to be yanked. She stifled a helpless giggle, noted with obvious distaste. "Well, true, she may clean up fine, but the Jedry woman's right. You've got yourself a simpleton here. She'd better clean up really good if you hope to get anything for her."

Aletha stared without comprehension. Didn't these

people realize that she needed to sleep? Just a few minutes would be enough. Her attention drifted to some lively music coming from the direction of the inn's open windows. It would probably be warmer in there. And brighter. Someone in there was laughing; it was the sort of laughter that came easily when people were warm and comfortable. She wondered about the person who had laughed. He sounded kind – no one who laughed like that would deny her their company. If only she had the strength to get up and walk into the tavern!

The trader beside her chuckled at some unseen joke. "Well, now that Jedry's gone, I'll show you what this one's really worth." He shook Aletha's arm, jolting her from her daydreams.

She turned half-closed eyes on him. "Huh?"

"Show'em, girl," he commanded.

She frowned. Didn't he know that she was just too damn tired for this? Her head drooped toward him but he shook her again and this time his fingers dug painfully into her arm.

"Do it!" he snapped. "That thing with the lamp, like you did yesterday."

The thin man looked nervous. "What are you up to, Tellos?" He backed away when Aletha sat up a little straighter, her expression strained as though she searched for a sound in the distance. She raised her hand, palm turned toward the sputtering fish oil lamp on the table, apparently ready to demonstrate something.

"By the Gods!" The buyer jumped up from the bench, earrings rattling in agitation. "She's a Descendant?"

The trader bowed his head as if he had just performed a magic feat of his own. "Indeed. Sit yourself down, you superstitious fool. She's not about to turn you into a rat." He paused for effect, looking around the circle of wary faces. "He's right. This one is the real thing. I've seen it with my own eyes. She's one of them. A Descendant."

"You're mad! A magic user? I want nothing to do with her kind and you'd be well advised to get rid of her. You'll bring ruin on us all." Everyone, including Aletha, watched as yet another potential customer made a hasty exit, fearfully looking over his shoulder as though expecting someone to come after him with murderous intent.

"Are the rest of you idiots as well?" the slaver growled, staring balefully at the remaining group. "This is the best bit of merchandise I've had in years and everyone runs as though the Gods were having a bad day. Can you not see what the likes of her can do for you?"

The second woman at the table stood up. She regarded him scornfully. "Maybe we can, Tellos, but we can also see that you can't keep her drugged like this forever. She's half-dead from your potions already. I don't know how you managed to catch this one but I dare say it wasn't painless, judging from the gash on your face. I'll have nothing to do with this, either."

"Go then," Tellos roared and did not wait for her to leave before turning to the remaining two men. "What of you, then? Start your bidding or go."

"Can anyone bid on this auction?" a new voice made itself heard. Everyone shifted in their seats and peered into the gloom of the courtyard to discover the source of the interruption.

A figure emerged from the shadows and approached the table, moving gracefully but with purpose. He was dressed for travel, armed with curved daggers sheathed near either hand and a crossbow slung over his shoulder, yet he wore no insignia to identify any known mercenary company or clan. In the fitful light of the few nearby lamps they could see that his hair was much darker than was common in these parts and in loosely curling strands hanging to his shoulders. Against his sun-darkened skin, the whites of his eyes seemed to pierce the night. The expression on his face was unreadable.

Tellos scowled at his hired guards who were paid twice their worth to prevent surprises during this transaction. At his signal two of them moved to stand behind him.

The stranger did not even spare them a glance. He tipped his head toward the tavern. "The man in there told me you might be selling what I'm buying," he said, an oddly inflecting accent in his speech.

Tellos put his ire aside and grinned, having read the quality of the mercenary's clothes and weapons. "She's not cheap," he said. "Virgin, most likely."

"Do I look like I run a brothel?"

Aletha barely followed all of this. None of it seemed to have anything to do with her, really. She was reminded of late evening gatherings she had attended as a child where adults talked and argued, happily or not, their words without meaning and of no interest to the little girl huddled sleepily among them. Of course, the adults on those long-ago evenings had been kind and comforting. These here today didn't seem to like her very much. But maybe this newcomer was a little friendlier. She watched silently as he swung a long leg over the bench to sit by her side. He nodded benignly to the others but his expression changed when he looked into her face. Why was he angry with her?

"What's your price?" he said.

"By Dazai's beard, she's a rare find, and you can bet your boat on that. Worth a small fortune if you take her East. There isn't a warlord who doesn't own a witch or two, or covets one. You look like you've seen a few battles on this moon; you know what I mean. Unfortunately, I have urgent business southwards and so I'm forced to let her go for a pittance. Nath here opened the bidding at five long counts." Tellos jerked a thumb across the table. The man called Nath looked up in surprise but whatever comment he had was quickly swallowed.

The stranger sneered. "I could buy the Grand Priestess for that. Two."

Aletha did not follow the bidding. The edges of her vision were gradually turning gray and an annoying numbness had begun to plague her feet and hands. She slumped in her seat, craving sleep.

The mercenary gripped her arm to keep her upright. Roughly, he grasped a handful of her curls to turn her face to the light. Ignoring her weak struggles, he cupped her chin in his hand as if to examine her features more closely. "What proof do you have of her talents?"

Aletha's eyes widened in surprise when a peculiar sensation began to radiate from his hands. The power of his healthy body seemed to enter her weakened one, making her stronger and more alert as if she had received the drink of water she craved so much. Things began to swim back into focus. She was able to see the faces of those around her and feel the hard bench on which she sat. The voices were clear now and their words had meaning. Her senses sharpening, she heard the sound of some nocturnal bird and the creak of leather when the stranger moved. Not caring how he managed to heal her tired body, she leaned closer to him, greedy for more.

He took a quick, hissing breath and released her. When he lowered his head to search his pockets for the required crystal, Aletha saw through the strands of hair that hid his features that he had squeezed his eyes shut as if her illness had somehow drained into him.

"By the Gods..." she murmured, shaking her head to rid herself of the fog in her mind.

Tellos turned abruptly to peer into her no longer glazed eyes. He stood up and hauled her to her feet. "Well, sir," he said. "It's obvious that you don't have a fair offer. I will give you time to think about this opportunity. Let us meet again tomorrow. It's late and the rain returns."

Aletha tried to pull out of his grasp but he had pinched her fingers in a painful lock, unseen by the others. She knew that more pain would come her way if she tried to escape.

The stranger looked up and waved a hand in a careless gesture. His smile was a friendly one but Aletha saw a weariness that had not been there before. "Until then." With fluid grace that seemed out of place on someone of his size, he rose from the table and sauntered back to the alehouse.

* * *

Not long later, Aletha found herself hurried along the narrow streets of the harbor town, one of the trader's burly guards on either side, a third following behind. Her hands were bound and her feet barely touched the ground as she was half-carried along by the thugs.

She remembered these past few days now and knew that the slaver would give her no food or water that wasn't laced with a peculiar substance, the one that made her confused and tired. He was eager to get rid of her, not only worried about her evil magic but also the punishment he risked for harboring a Descendant. So far, the price she would fetch outweighed the hazard of holding her captive even while his guards were paid extra wages for their silence and willingness to handle a magic user. She wondered for how much longer he would take the risk.

Their furtive progress through the damp alleys came to an abrupt halt when a tall man stepped out of a doorway into the spill of light cast by some shop-front torches.

Tellos recognized him. "You! I thought we agreed that the bidding was done for the day. Out of my way or I'll have my guards after you."

"We'll have a fairer fight, then," a low voice intoned behind them. When they turned they saw a second man, someone who was not only similarly attired and armed but who was also a twin of the mercenary.

"Help me," Aletha cried. "I am not a slave. I've been—" The rest of her plea was cut off when one of the guards struck her and she fell to the ground.

Without any apparent effort on their part and no movement anyone could discern, the twins had each thrust a long dagger into a guard, stabbing expertly and with immediate, fatal result. The guards dropped where they stood, at the feet of the last of the thugs who gaped in silent incomprehension. One of the strangers reached out and tapped him on the shoulder, almost playfully, and the guard slumped onto the cobbles, leaving only the frightened and confused trader standing between the twins.

"Gods protect me, Descendants! Take her," Tellos squealed, staring at the corpses that had until recently been his only protection. "Take her, she's nothing to me. Just leave me be."

One of the twins knelt beside Aletha. Although anger played over his dark features and shone like a light from narrowed eyes, his hands were gentle when he untied her hands. "Try to get up," he said.

She let him pull her to her feet and leaned against him when she felt his supporting arms move around her. There was something oddly comforting about his presence and despite the cold and the damp she felt as though it were possible to go to sleep right here in his careful embrace.

His brother stood with a knife to the slaver's throat. "What is her name?" He snatched the ridiculous hat from the slaver's head and tossed it aside.

"What? Her name? I don't know her name!" The trader looked up and down the narrow alley, wondering if he should call for help. But he had seen the unnatural speed with which these demons moved and he dared not. "She's just a slave. I bought her off the South Island boat this morning."

The stranger shoved him against the wall of the alley where he pinned him with an iron forearm. The knife at the trader's throat pierced his skin and his eyes bulged in terror when he saw his own blood flow along the blade. "She's one of them," he said quickly. "That's all I know. One of your own. A Descendant. I saw her practice her dark arts. It's the truth, I swear!"

Aletha tried to find strength where there was none to be found. "Aletha," she whispered her name. She looked up into the mercenary's eyes and for the first time in many days saw compassion and concern on someone's face. "Please don't turn me in."

"I could have done exactly that," Tellos babbled. "I could

have taken her before the emissaries, but I didn't. What harm is there in a man trying to turn a profit? At such risk to his own life? She is a leader of demons. She tried to kill me."

"No!" Aletha sobbed, feeling faint. "I'd never..." her knees buckled beneath her. How could anyone accuse her of such things? She had always been careful to hide her talents as she moved about the city of Phrar, using her gifts to pick the pockets of those who could afford to have their pockets picked. No one was ever about when she practiced the more arcane arts, and few even knew that her abilities went beyond those of a common trickster and fortuneteller. Certainly, none of her gifts could protect her from the likes of Tellos and his thugs.

"She's dying," the twin said. He had lowered his voice but she heard him even through the fog still dulling her senses. "What drug did you use?"

"Just a common mushroom, steeped with herbs. I know nothing about it. Here, I'll show you." The stranger watched suspiciously as Tellos fumbled in his vest pockets to find a small pouch. "This. The emissaries use it."

His assailant did not touch the package. "Chibane? A red mushroom?"

"Yes, perhaps," the trader said eagerly, hoping that these demons would take this information and leave him alone. "It's dried but I'm sure it was red."

The foreigner rolled his eyes in disgust and drove his knife deep into Tellos' neck, cutting off his sudden scream and his life in one swift motion.

Aletha contemplated the lifeless body for a moment and then slumped in a faint.

* * *

Chor picked her up and raced after his twin through the maze of rain-slick alleys and cobbled laneways of Phrar, not entirely sure which way to turn. It seemed as though this town had expanded over the years through the haphazard addition of buildings and roadways wherever the need arose and in complete disregard of logic and forethought. It was not long before a distant alarm sounded; no doubt someone had stumbled upon the dead slaver and his guards.

His twin, Galen, uttered a few ripe curses when he realized that they had arrived in yet another dead end street. Gasping for breath, Chor put Aletha down but kept his arm around her waist. She mumbled something unintelligible and remained standing. He put a hand over her mouth and both twins froze, listening, waiting. Soon footfalls and angry shouts echoed through the deserted streets, sounding like a dozen men bent on retribution.

Chor pulled Aletha into a recessed doorway while Galen shielded them both with his body. Knife in hand, he forced himself into calmness and waited for the posse to round the corner and descend into the alley. When he saw the first of the mob appear he held up a hand and focused his thoughts on his target. The air between them and the intersection blurred. Darkness, fog and random shafts of light coalesced to create some indefinable shape. It only took an instant for the men at the vanguard to glance into the alley, see little but vague shadows, and hurry onward, taking their torchlight and excited voices with them. Exhausted, Galen let the illusion dissipate and slumped against his twin.

"Looks like you got the trick of it," a thin voice cut through the silence of the street.

Galen spun around to squint into murky shadows. "Who's there?" he snapped, dismayed that he had not sensed this presence so close to them. What was happening to his perceptions on this moon? "Step out where I can see you."

A slight figure separated from a pile of empty crates and Galen found himself looking down into the grime-smeared face of a street urchin, a young girl. "I'm thinking it's you that don't want to be seen," she said. "What do you want with Aletha? If you plan to do harm on her I'll have my friends after you. I have friends bigger than you, even. Plenty of them!"

"You know her?" Chor lifted Aletha into his arms again.

"Everyone knows her." The girl tried to peer around the twins. "Is she all right? Aletha? Say something!"

"She is not all right. Can you get us out of here?"

"Course I can. Where'd you want to go?"

"Where there aren't as many questions." Galen looked up, alerted to movements in the dark. "More people coming."

"It's the emissaries, no doubt in my head. Dazai's mercy, don't be using any more of your magic. They can smell that from leagues away."

"Who? How would they—"

"Come away, quick!"

The twins followed her deeper into the alley and finally up a creaking staircase clinging precariously to the side of a warehouse. The door at the top was unlocked and they slipped into the building. Through some cracks in this loft they saw orderly rows of wooden kegs and stacks of crates lined up near the loading doors below. Something down there exuded a heavy, earthy odor, not unpleasant.

"Safe here for a while," the girl said. Busying herself with a candle, she gestured toward a pallet in the corner of the room. "No one knows about this place. Belongs to a friend. He's very rich."

"I'm sure he must be," Galen said doubtfully and lowered Aletha onto the pile of rags that appeared to be someone's makeshift bed. He covered her with a blanket before shrugging off his sodden vest. The urchin ladled some water into a cup, obviously at home in this cozy, if shabby, squatter's hideaway. The snug space was cluttered and in need of a broom, but it boasted a brazier for heat and cooking, and there were some treasured possessions, or perhaps stolen goods, displayed on upended crates. The drizzle outside allowed a little moonlight to slant through a grimy pane set into the wall.

"You live here?" Galen lifted Aletha's head to help her drink some of the water.

"No, just a hiding place. My dad and me have a place

down the way a bit." The girl knelt beside Aletha and gently shook her shoulder. "Aletha? What's wrong with her?"

"Poisoned," Galen said. He tugged her blanket aside to place a hand on the woman's belly and the other on her chest. With a glance at the wide-eyed urchin he shifted it higher, near her throat. His twin touched her temples.

"Hey! What are you about, Mister?"

"Shh." Minutes passed and, although distracted by the child's restlessness, they managed to lend Aletha more of the energy she needed to combat the poison in her body. There wasn't much to spare. They released her and fell back, slumping wearily against the rough wooden wall behind them.

"We need a place to hole up for a while," Galen said, his eyes closed. "Something tells me you know your way around."

"Do I! I'll have you hidden away so good, the damn emissaries wouldn't find you in a hundred years ever. They been looking for her for days. My name's Yala. Yalarian, really, but that name's bigger than I am, Dad says."

Chor pulled Aletha's blanket to her chin and accepted a jug from Yala. After taking a long draught from it, he passed it to his twin. Galen winced when he felt the bite of the cheap liquor. When its warmth reached his tired limbs he took another drink. "I am Galen, and my brother is called Chor. What are these emissaries?"

"How can you be unknowing of them? They're evil hounds, who sniff out the likes of Aletha. She's been hiding from them for years. I been helping her. But you're not so smart. You don't ever use magic when there's emissaries about. You might just as well be running up and down the street, yelling 'Descendants! Over here! Come and get us'. Gods, everyone knows that!"

"My magic doesn't frighten you?" Galen asked, amused. His experience with children was limited to seeing them from a distance, if at all. They were rarely found roaming the Homeworld on their own, and this one seemed especially adventuresome. Short yellow curls tangled by disassociation with brush and comb stood out in all directions and her clothes were a collection of rags topped by a magnificently embroidered vest several sizes too large. Pale and likely undersized for her age, Yala served as a good example of what he had seen so far of the motley population breeding among the wharves in this town.

"Nah, around here no one's ever been done evil to by no demons. Aletha helps us when she can. My dad's got a bad leg and she's made it good as new, almost."

"She's a healer?" Galen asked. Aletha's thin dress seemed hardly appropriate for the weather and certainly not for someone working as a physician. She was small, he thought, although possessing some rather interesting curves. A mop of dark curls surrounded an impish face made alluring by large, gray eyes. Considering that he had nearly purchased her as a pleasure slave, if not a magic user, he had begun to make some assumptions about her occupation in these dreary streets.

"Aye, although for a coin she'll look into your soul and reveal your future."

Galen lowered his head to hide a chuckle. "I see now why the slaver valued her so highly." He had been surprised when his search for Aletha on this moon had led to finding her subsisting as a member of the Phrar's lower caste. But what had he expected? Another pampered queen, perhaps, ensconced in her gilded tower, adored and feared by all whose talents fell short of her superior mind.

He smirked at the disheveled ragdoll on the pallet beside him and imagined her first meeting with the La'il, the perfumed and powerful perfection that ruled the Homeworld. It was something to look forward to.

"The others'll be damn glad when they hear she got clear of that slaver. It was a bad commotion, that's for certain. Only I heard tell it was emissaries who took her, not slavers." Yala shifted her eyes from Aletha to study the twins. "What are you, anyway? Descendants, for sure. But you're not from here. Can I have a look at your crossbow, Mister? Where's your company?"

"This is pretty well it," Galen said. Not for the first time had someone here mistaken him for a member of some roving band of mercenaries or guard for hire. He studied his twin who, in spite of being his mirror image, seemed to be able to strike fear in just about anyone by means of his scowl. Perhaps the crossbow was a little excessive. Their attempts to learn how to use it these past few days had been utter failures. Chor tossed her the weapon. "It's yours."

Delighted, the girl turned the bow to admire its fine design. "We'll be eating well this month!"

"You don't want to keep it?"

"Who would I shoot? Food we can always use."

Galen fished a small crystal from a pocket. "How about this: you don't tell anyone what happened here tonight and I give you this. You'll eat well for another month." He had no expectation that the scamp would be able to keep this secret but he hoped for at least a few days' silence. Enough for the woman to recuperate and for them to journey to the launch site in the mountains where they would make the return jump down to the planet. If nothing else, he thought, the small fortune he offered the child would keep some people fed for a while.

"That sounds like a fine deal." Yala held the crystal into the light of the candle to assess its quality. Her bright eyes shifted to Galen. "You'll look out for her?" she said, for the first time sounding unsure. "She'll be well, I mean? You mean no harm?"

Galen smiled. "None. Just find me a quiet room. Somewhere where they don't ask questions and where she can get well. And some real clothes for her. Then forget you ever met us."

TWO

Aletha woke slowly, aware of the pain before she opened her eyes. A steady thudding noise in her head matched the dull throbbing of her starved and poisoned body. Although it was dimly lit, she saw that this room was a rented one, serving various functions without any hint of permanent occupation. Two beds, some chairs, a table and little else. Wooden walls and floor and rough-hewn beams below the ceiling told her that she was probably somewhere on the harbor side of Phrar. The familiar, comforting sound and smell of the ocean confirmed this. She closed her eyes again, exhausted.

She was not alone. There was someone near the window; another now approached her cot. She felt a confident peace of mind here, a serenity as calming as the sound of the dawn owls gliding among the rooftops. She recognized the creaking sound made by the leather he wore as he bent over her for a moment and then sat on the edge of the bed.

"How do you feel now?" he said, an edgeless accent coloring his speech. She blinked at him tiredly. His face was an interesting collage of angles and panes that might have made his features harsh were it not for the gentler lines of jaw and chin. His eyes were soft, almost lazy, in the way that made women wonder what thoughts went on behind them.

Although he seemed not much older than she, his dark hair was shot through with strands of gray. He smelled faintly of wood smoke and something like herbs or some strange, sweet spice.

"I'll live. Tired. Aching all over." She peered around him at his twin. That one did not seem to care about her state of health. He had not even turned around when his brother had spoken but remained leaning against the window frame, his attention on something outside. She wanted to get another look at his face, remembering the brief glimpses she had had of the twins' remarkable likeness the night before. The gray-streaked hair was the same; on the other twin it was neatly gathered into a short queue. Her eyes moved beyond him when the nearby door caught her attention.

"What the…" Here was a simple wooden door with a flimsy lock, the type to be found in any inn of this sort. Most people would not find it extraordinary. Aletha, however, saw something not meant to be noticed. The lock stood out in the shadowed room as though someone held a lens over it. She could see every scratch on the metal and every shadow cast by the heads of the nails holding it in place. A slow smile tugged at her lips. It seemed that the twins, too, knew a trick or two. The whole lock seemed to be more *there* than any other object in the room and she knew that she was not the only demon here. She turned her attention back to the man sitting on the edge of her cot. "I'll be all right in a few hours. I know some things about healing." She raised her hand to explore her bruised forehead.

"You do? And is that all?"

"Who are you?"

"My name is Galen. My brother is Chor. We are traders. From the north."

Their eyes held, both of them amused by this game.

"I would have taken you for an Inlander. And you trade in slaves? Or are you looking for a fortune teller?"

"Telling fortunes is not our custom. Nor is slavery."

"What customs do you have in the north?" she said. "Is it

your custom to bewitch locks?"

His eyes shifted to the door. "Most people wouldn't notice that. Do all fortune tellers here see as well as you do?"

"Most fortune tellers do well to keep promising wealth and happy marriages to the gullible," Aletha replied, her mood suddenly sour. "True sages are more feared for their talents than paid for them."

He helped her up to lean against the bed's headboard, which she managed with a few winces and groans. Once she was upright, the thin blanket tucked around her frail body, he pulled up a chair and described what had happened after she had blacked out. She had only fragmented recollections of having been hurried through Phrar's back alleys and none of her stay in the warehouse. A smile curved her lips when he told her of Yala's part in her rescue.

"Those weren't frightened peasants back there," he said finally, reaching for a jug of water on a nearby shelf. "You're not a fortune teller and they knew it."

She took a cup from him but simply stared into it as if to find her words there.

"You can trust me," he said. "Why are these emissaries after you?"

"I'm a Descendant. Why else would they be after me?"

"What's a Descendant?"

She frowned. "You don't know? You must have traveled a long way."

"We have."

She considered her answer for a while. "You're right, I'm not a seer. I've never known anyone who can look into the future and it's certainly not something I can do. Sometimes I find bits of, well, I don't know, magic I guess. It helps me understand what they feel, which I suppose makes it seem like I know what they are thinking. It isn't difficult then to imagine things to come for them and make it ring true."

"Clever."

"But there are times when this magic will let me do other things. It isn't much but it frightens people anyway. I try to hide it. I don't know how to explain..." She looked at the door. "I guess I don't have to explain it, do I?"

He shook his head.

"Years ago, many people here were demons like me but they were driven away. All we have now are stories about sorcery and anyone with any knowledge of the magic is hunted, killed. Or sold into slavery. We are the Descendants of the magic users. They were powerful back then, much more than we are."

"There are more here like you?"

"No, not like me. I wasn't born in this town. I was a foundling and raised in the islands, where we aren't hunted. It's just too far for them to bother. Some of the people out there know about the magic. They use it to make themselves stronger or to keep warm. But…" she bit her lip.

"But you can do more, right? For some reason you can use it to heal, or know who's coming down the hall outside." He jerked a thumb at a rodent rustling busily behind the wooden wall. "You can see things, smell things others can't and your ears are also very good. You can probably move things around without touching them."

"Yes!" she whispered. "It scares me. There is no one who can tell me what I am, or why these things are. It's dangerous to even speak of it."

"You'd be killed by these emissaries, whatever they are?"

"No priests in the north, either?" When he gave her only a bland smile she shrugged. "The emissaries are a circle of men whose only mission is to hunt and destroy Descendants. So I hide the things I do. Or most things. I help my friends when I can. People who treat me well and who aren't afraid of me." She dropped her eyes. "But how have I repaid them? When I was taken, those men killed two of my friends. They're dead because they tried to help a demon!"

He shook his head. "Demon! You're not a demon and neither are we. Not even your young friend believes that. It's a talent. A gift."

"A gift! What good is this gift if I can't rely on it? Two

people are dead because of it. Why could I not even notice those men in time to save them? Some talent!"

"Talents need to be practiced."

Aletha closed her eyes against the still throbbing headache. "Look, whoever you are, I have to sleep. I can't think while I'm like this. I need to put myself back together."

He nodded and rose. "While you do that I'll get us something to eat."

"Why are you doing this? Why are you here?"

He walked to the door. "Later. Get well first." He passed his hand over the lock. "You need to leave this town. Soon."

Aletha stared at the door after it had closed behind him. "Advice easier given than followed," she mumbled.

"Why is that?"

She turned her head, the sudden movement sending a new jolt of pain through her skull. She had forgotten about the other man in the room. He had left his post by the window and now stretched out on the second bed.

"Where would I go? What's your name again?"

"Chor," he said in her direction but his eyes were focused on some far distant point. He seemed preoccupied, as if hearing something she could not. He raised a hand to wave it indifferently at the door, which locked again. "You should sleep now," he said, apparently about to do the same.

When he said nothing more, she closed her eyes, not just to find sleep, but to use her gifts to heal her body. Slowly, she felt herself mending, the bruises fading and the terrors of the previous night receding. She fought off the last of the poison before she fell asleep, still wondering about this pair of twins and what might have brought them here.

* * *

She woke to the certainty that a long time had passed. There had been nightmares and a strange aching pain as the effects of the slaver's drug faded, leaving her weak and thirsty. Moments of lucidity had followed restless sleep and at times she had felt someone's hand on her forehead to soothe her dreams.

Aletha turned to see one of the strangers at the table, his brother asleep on the other cot in the room. He looked up from his meal as if he had sensed her wakening.

"How do you feel?" He gestured at a bundle placed at the foot of her bed.

She rose gingerly, annoyed by the wobbly feeling in her knees. The parcel contained new clothes and a few items she recognized. "These are mine," she said when she found sandals, a comb and a small, bejeweled dagger she had stolen somewhere and liked too much to trade.

She turned to find him watching her, his eyes on her legs. "Seen enough?" She gazed at him with an arched eyebrow until he turned his back to her. Quickly, she discarded the thin gown and slipped into blouse and tights, covering them with a long tunic tied at the sides. "I'm not sure I want to know how you knew these would fit me," she said, grateful to be appropriately dressed again.

"Yala brought those. And a few things from your home. She'll fetch what you need but it might not be safe to return there. She said there were some of those emissaries nosing around the harbor."

She came to the table and carefully lowered herself into a chair. "She's a sweet girl. Her father is a decent sort but without a mother she's grown into a reckless little rogue. I don't want her snooping where there are emissaries about." She closed her eyes and gripped the edge of the table when the room suddenly lurched sideways.

"You all right?"

She took a deep, hitching breath and nodded. "It'll be a while before I'm well again. I haven't really eaten in days. I'll need to sleep a lot. And bathe."

"There is a bathhouse out back," he said, grimacing. "Although that's a rather grand term for it. We have to leave this place soon. There is some suspicion about us downstairs. They saw us carry you up here; I'm sure they're... uh... wondering what's going on."

She winked lewdly, amused by his discomfort. "I'm not sure what's going on, either, but something tells me it'd be best to have them thinking exactly what they're thinking." She shrugged. "Right now I'm starving!"

He gestured at the food on the table and tipped his chair back to watch her dig into the bowl of boiled grains, fish and vegetables. "Don't you people here use forks or spoons or something? I don't think I've seen anyone use anything but their hands to eat. And everyone eats from the same bowl."

"I wasn't aware that you folks in the north are so fussy." She nodded when he offered tea.

"We're not from the north, but you knew that," he said as he filled her cup. "We are called adepts. People with a gift for… magic. You'll meet more of us once you're home." He smiled at her astounded expression. "Eat!"

"What do you mean: home?"

"We're taking you home with us. You are needed elsewhere."

"And where's that?"

He looked beyond her to the open window. Through a haze of clouds a wedge of the Homeworld planet was visible within its frame. Its oppressive nearness when in a clear sky was burdensome to Thali moon's citizens and many felt relief when the perpetual cloud cover hid it from sight. To feel it hovering over their heads served as a constant and unwelcome reminder of their exile. Shortly, the planet would move over the sun to blot out daylight for one of the frequent eclipses involving either the Homeworld or the second moon, or even both. "Over there. The planet. Our Homeworld."

She stared blankly at the planet before turning back to him. "Is that meant to be funny?"

"Why would you think it's funny?"

She jumped up and her chair clattered to the floor. Could this man really be a Homeworlder? One of the Old Ones, returned to this moon to spread mischief and terror? "I don't belong there! And if you two are from there I'll have nothing to do with you." She edged around him to the door before she remembered that he had barred it. "You are enemy to Chenoweth."

"Yes, I know that," he said, seeming surprised by her reaction. "Why does that upset you? We mean you no harm, I promise."

"You've locked me in here. That doesn't seem harmless."

He nodded toward the door. "There, open. Leave if you want, but you need to hear what I have to tell you."

She lifted the latch but then left the door closed. "Hear what?"

"Come, sit down, you'll wake Chor up."

"He's no more asleep than we are," she said but after a moment returned to pick up her chair. The stranger slouched casually and she felt none of the violent hostility that had exuded from him when they had faced the slaver and his guards. There was nothing here to fear. "What's your business with that planet?"

"We live there. You belong there, too."

"Not likely! Your people left us in exile. It's because of you that we are locked away up here on this moon."

"We didn't leave you on purpose. We were prevented from coming here by Chenoweth."

Aletha's eyes involuntarily moved the window when he mentioned the second moon above the Homeworld, the icy, distant Chenoweth. "Yes, of course you were. They banished you. How did you two find your way back up here?"

"Chi'ro."

"Chi what?"

"Chi'ro, or sometimes called *chiaro*. You mentioned it this morning when you called it magic."

"Our magic has a name?"

He nodded. "But it isn't magic. It's an element that exists on the Homeworld and on both moons. There is very little of it here on Thali moon. It's like an intense, living energy that rises from the ground but it can't be seen with the eyes. Chi'ro affects some people's brains. Their minds. You and I have the gift to use this energy to suit our purposes. There are many like us on the Homeworld."

"People who can magically visit the moons?" she said, sarcasm evident in her tone.

"Not any more. Coming here was quite a feat, even for us. But at one time this was easy. Not just for the 'magic users', but for everyone. There are places where chi'ro is concentrated in what we call risers, like little clouds of it, coming up from the ground. And back in time there were places so dense with it that the risers reached out to the moon, or to other places on the planet, to form conduits, gateways of sorts. We call those launches. At one time these were stable and led from one place to another. From one moon to another. We used it to travel."

"That's a long way to travel."

He smiled. "It takes only a moment to step through those conduits. It's like space and even time don't exist in there."

Aletha considered the prospect, curious despite her doubts about what this stranger was telling her. "Sounds like magic."

"Well, I guess it does. In any case, a few hundred years ago something happened and Chenoweth cut themselves off from the Homeworld and then cut this place off as well. They found a way to seal all of the launch sites that lead to the moons. It took a long time and much of our resources to find a way to send us here from the planet. We were sent by... by the most powerful mind on the Homeworld. It was difficult for her to open a conduit to let us through and it isn't something she can do very often. It takes up an incredible amount of chi'ro now. I don't know why Chenoweth sealed the launches." He looked to the window. "I don't know much about this place at all. It's a bit of a mystery to us."

"Chenoweth sealed them to keep you out. You should not have come here. You are in more danger than I am, Demon." Her eyes moved to the planet that on clear days seemed close enough to touch. "It's because of your ways that we were trapped up here."

"Tell me your story. We've had no news of you for hundreds of years. This place isn't what I expected."

She shrugged. "It's like you said, Chenoweth severed our worlds from each other. At one time we got along, we were neighbors. My people here on this moon, the Homeworlders down there, and the gods on Chenoweth."

"Gods?"

"Yes, how can you not know about them? They live on Chenoweth now, the Garden of the Gods."

"They used to be over here on this moon?"

She nodded. "For many years the people and the gods traveled among the three worlds as they wished, like you said. I guess through those conduits you described. Thali was peaceful and beautiful and things were plentiful here. It wasn't a crime to be a magic user and we weren't called demons then. But then something happened. The gods blamed the Homeworlders for some terrible feats of magic and punished all of us by locking the doors to Chenoweth and the Homeworld. The storms came, and earthquakes, and our healers slowly lost their talents. So now, for our sins, it is only when we die that we are permitted to visit the Garden on Chenoweth and the gods who live there and wait for us."

"And so the Descendants are people who still have the talent for using… magic?"

"People like me. Like you. Dazai, the elder god, commanded all of us to be destroyed. No one but the gods is allowed to use magic. And so we are hunted and murdered by their emissaries. Their work is nearly done; there are fewer of us born with each generation." She sighed and paused before continuing, her eyes bright with unspilled tears. "Some say that we are no longer human. We're an abomination in the eyes of the gods and will not be welcome on Chenoweth."

"Yet you don't try to avoid the magic you find."

"Avoid it? Could you avoid it? Can you avoid breathing?"

Galen smiled thinly. "No, I don't suppose so."

"And so we live with this… this sin. We know what we do can cost us our lives on Thali at the hands of men, and it will cost us our afterlife in the Garden of the Gods. Yet we are unable to stop, like drunks who crave the next cup of wine. But we're not evil. We hurt no one." She considered for a moment. "Well, I suppose some of us engage in petty thievery and the occasional swindle. That's hardly evil."

He returned her grin. Aletha was again struck by the warmth of his eyes and his smile. Yet even on this moon, where struggles and warfare among clans was commonplace, he and his kind were the worst enemy imaginable. Were these people not supposed to look like monsters, like some evil spirit unleashed by their equally evil magic? Was it possible that he and his twin were as ordinary as anyone else here that shared her gifts?

"All this talk of gods and Chenoweth has me feeling very dramatic." She slouched back in her chair with a careless shrug. "You've caught me in a weak moment, Homeworlder. Displeasing the gods bothers me less than being feared by my own people. Who can tell what truly happens when we die? While we pray for redemption, we have our doubts. While we elude the emissary, we question their authority. Maybe the Garden is waiting for us and maybe it isn't. We'll find that out soon enough." She waved a hand in Chor's direction. "You and your brother, however, are real. You intrigue me. Why do you think I belong over there? You didn't travel all this way just to rescue a god-cursed Descendant."

He smiled. "We did. Your gifts, your talents, are much stronger than you think. You need a skilled mentor to show you what is possible for you."

"Ah," she said dryly. "And so you've come all this distance to be such a mentor?"

"I'm just a messenger." He jerked his chin toward the bay where dozens of sailboats would be bustling among the islands, tides permitting. "Although it rises from the ground, imagine that chi'ro is like the wind. Sometimes it's stronger than at other times, and sometimes it's more consistently found in some places than others. If you have a sail you can use this wind as a source of power. Some people have a better sail than others, or perhaps they are better sailors. No amount of wind can help you if you don't know how to harness it. Chi'ro is like that, and you, Aletha, have a very good sail that you don't know how to use. You have far more talent than most people on the Homeworld. That is why we were sent to fetch you. The Homeworld needs your help now."

"Oh?"

He listened for a moment, assuring himself that no one loitered in the hall, perhaps with an ear to their door. "There is a war coming. The... gods of Chenoweth are returning, this time to the Homeworld. You said, before they left here, they ordered the magic users destroyed, through their emissaries. We fear the same will happen on the Homeworld. They are powerful and we need your gifts to help us against them. Without you, we won't be able to withstand their forces."

She stared at him, wordless. After a time she got up and paced across the room. She stopped to gaze out over the harbor for a moment and then left the window to look down at Chor's sleeping face. Pleasant lips, she thought idly before realizing that her mind kept slipping from the subject at hand as if it were too large to grapple. "If the gods choose to return now, to punish your people again for your deeds, who am I to stand in their way?"

Galen was momentarily speechless. "Those gods want you dead, too," he said at last. "Would you take their side?"

She turned back to him. "Would you have me prove I'm a demon by defying them? How do I know your side must win this war?"

"Because you are one of us."

She froze.

"You were stolen from us when you were only a child. You don't belong here. We've been sent by... your family to return you to them."

Aletha turned her face toward the hazy planet in the sky. Everyone who lived on Thali had at one point gazed at the colorful orb, thinking about the people who had caused their exile, and wondered what life on the Homeworld would be. She knew that her ancestors, the Old Ones, had come from another world a thousand years ago or more. They had settled on the beautiful Homeworld and then set out to explore her moons as well. The thought that she might actually belong down there filled her with both longing and unease. "I was a foundling," she said finally. "Or so I was told. No one ever mentioned the Homeworld. But my people are not the sort who steal children."

"I can't pretend to understand it," he said. "But you know you're different, don't you?"

She nodded slowly, her eyes still on the planet. "Are they like me?"

"Adepts tend to run in families," he said. "They want you back, and they need your help."

She rubbed her face with both hands. "This is all so much. Too much. I have to think about this."

"Think about it?" he exclaimed. "Think about what? You're hunted here, despised even. People want you dead. I'm offering to take you where you have a family. A wealthy one! Freedom to use as much magic as you want. Safety. You belong with us. You know you have to leave this place."

"I know," she sighed, feeling fatigued again. What he told her was so enormous and so wonderfully strange that it just didn't seem possible. And yet it felt right. This man felt right. She sensed no ill will toward her, although clearly he was not as self-assured as he tried to appear. Something worried him. "Your offer seems a lot more appealing than some schemes I've come up with. How would we get there? Through one of those conduit things?"

"Yes. There is a place north of here, in the mountains, where I'll have enough chi'ro to create a conduit. The launch is a sort of crystal among the rocks there. They're very old and very rare. We should leave as soon as you're well enough to travel."

"What is it like on the Homeworld? Is it better than this moon?"

He looked around the crude room. "I'd say. It is comfortable and peaceful, most of the time. It rains less."

"No one is afraid of demons?"

"Almost everyone is a demon!" He laughed. "You will never again have to hide your talents."

"What about the giants?" she asked.

"What about the giants?" he repeated. His smile faded when he said that.

"It is said that there was a race of giants on the Homeworld. Some of them were exiled up here, too, when Chenoweth locked us away. Many of them were killed or driven away. We are told the giants will return some day and destroy us. Is this true? Are there giants on the Homeworld?"

He regarded her wordlessly, a slight frown deepening a groove between his eyes. It seemed as though he would answer but then something stopped his words

Seeing his hesitation, she smiled and busied herself with gathering some things for a trip to the bathhouse. "How ridiculous that must sound! We are full of legends and fanciful tales on this moon. We've spent so much time wondering about the Homeworld that we imagine the most bizarre stories of what's happened in the past. You'll no doubt hear more of them. Tales do grow with the telling."

Galen looked over to his twin, still appearing to ponder something. Finally, he shrugged. "Few people on the Homeworld are taller than we are. Yes, tales grow with the telling."

THREE

Not having heard from the Homeworld since arriving on the moon, Galen and Chor were in no real hurry to return to the launch site in the mountains. Aletha needed a few more days to recover from her ordeal and so one of the twins stayed with her while the other nosed around Phrar, the first large town they had encountered on this moon.

Phrar was a town completely immersed in the business of fishing and shipbuilding, using methods invented even before humans had arrived on the Homeworld. Loud, untidy, perpetually soggy and rodent infested, the harbor area formed the heart of the town where life and livelihood were inextricably tied to the sea. The stink of the fish processing shops was as much a part of this quarter as the biting fumes of hot pitch wafting from the shipyards. Above the waterfront, a crescent of hills followed the contour of the bay, sheltering a scattering of suburbs less crowded, less raw and, to Galen, far less interesting.

Following the entire western seaboard of this continent, thousands of small islands filled the sea, some separated by no more than a few feet of shallow water. A confusing network of bridges and stilted walkways connected groups of inhabited islands with each other or the mainland, some barely wide enough for one person to pass, others elaborated with cart tracks and tollgates.

The low tides revealed these islands to be quite extraordinary. Instead of revealing themselves as connected high points of some submerged ocean shelf, the islands rose into the air on pinnacles, suddenly inaccessible but for those connected to others by bridges or rope ladders. From higher points in the hills above Phrar, one could see patterns in the arrangements of the islands, showing the directions of the deep fissures that had some eons ago split the islands from the main landmass. Like an old ice floe breaking up, the mainland was crumbling apart along its edges.

On the other side of this chain of islands was the Great Strait, a body of open water and the continent's main sea-lane. Remembering observations from the Homeworld, Galen knew that nothing but a string of barrier islands protected the lane and coast from an endless, tempestuous ocean covering more than half of the moon's surface.

Not once since arriving on Thali had he sensed anyone working with chi'ro, if only covertly. Descendants were difficult to perceive on this moon; even Aletha's gifts were barely discernible. Either they had found the means to hide their talents or they were so afraid of them that the potential of using chi'ro to make their lives easier was left unexplored. Clearly, any reminders of once powerful adepts had been suppressed into superstition and fairy tale and their descendants hunted close to extinction. Galen wondered why this would be so, although he suspected fear and jealousy at the root of the Angry God legend.

He was able to use the rare resource when he found it, careful to use it for nothing more spectacular than to improve locks and dry rain-soaked clothing. He was increasingly aware that he, not having been born on this chi'ro-starved moon, was incomplete without it. He felt weakened and hungry and often had to go in search of a riser, no matter how insubstantial. How the original settlers must have suffered as they tried to adjust to this new place! It was beyond him to understand why they would have chosen to settle here at all.

* * *

"When I was very small, Minh told me that I came here from Chenoweth," Aletha told the twins. "I think she was trying to make me feel better for being so different. She called me her Gift From The Gods. She'd be surprised to hear that I really came from the planet!"

They were on the porch of one of the many waterfront inns, sharing a leisurely mid-day meal. The twins were becoming used to the eating arrangements here, which at times included sharing the communal supper platter with complete strangers. More importantly, they were overcoming their squeamishness about some of the ingredients. Just now the otherwise well-prepared rice and vegetables had included not only pieces of broiled water fowl but also something with tentacles that appeared to be moving, a generous heap of bitter sea weed, and things looking suspiciously like eyeballs. Galen hoped they had been fish eggs of some sort; at least those he'd gotten used to by now. None of this seemed peculiar to Aletha, who ate with evident enjoyment. Chor had finished and now reclined in a hammock from where he gazed silently beyond the streams of water curtaining the frond-covered porch.

Galen hitched a hip onto the porch railing. "Why did you leave her? Where is she now?"

Aletha pointed seaward. "Back there, in the outer islands to the West. The ones on the other side of the Great Strait. You can't see them from here. She is a Descendant but she prefers to hide. Among the people of the forest she can use her gifts and no one really thinks anything odd about it. She sent me to the mainland to learn things. There isn't much to do out there. Phrar is much more interesting." She waited while a servant brought another jug of ale and moved out of earshot again. "Even having to sneak around the emissaries is worth the trouble when there are so many things to see here. I've even been inland a few times. There's nothing east of the mountains but a few rivers. Other than that, just fields for farming. Rice paddies. Couple of towns. I got dizzy with all that open land around."

"You might have to get used to that. There's a lot of farmland on the Homeworld." He reached for the jug to refill their cups. "You need grains to make ale like this. But if all goes well we can find some jungle for you, I'm sure." He swiveled to look into the direction of Chor's gaze, his attention caught by something among the islands not far offshore.

The tide was out and the islands rose to the height of ten men above the water on a column of rock pockmarked by small caves and outcroppings. Some people were busily lowering a complicated network of ropes over the side of the escarpment. A few of them began to rappel down, carrying with them baskets and sacks. "What are they doing?"

"Hunting," she said, squinting into the distance. "You have good eyes. When the tide goes out lots of sea creatures get stranded in the rocks. Shellfish, shrimp, eels, brae, things like that. Seagrass, sponges, and roe, too. They only have to haul it up in their baskets."

"Seems like a good way to make a living."

"Dangerous work. When the tide moves out everything goes with it. Even you couldn't beat the currents."

He nodded. On his trip south to Phrar he had seen how rapidly the tide moved away from the continent, rushing away through the rising islands like water let out of a basin. Anything in its path was sucked along and, in narrower channels, the rushing flood turned into churning whitewater raging along sharp-edged rocks not yet eroded by currents or waves. Whirlpools were commonplace and the undertow deceptive. Without a doubt, anyone falling from their ropes at low tide would be lost to the ceaseless motion of Thali's oceans.

He had also seen this same motion used for navigation. Small, flat-bottomed boats were floated into the outgoing tide, to be sucked through the maze of towering chasms and into the calmer strait beyond. These boats had steady keels and shallow rudders, and all sides were thickly padded against the inevitable collision with exposed rock. Their captains were skilled pilots of unwavering courage, hired by those who had more wealth than time on their hands. For the most part, the low tides were waited out and ocean traffic was scheduled for calmer waters, plied by caravans of wooden vessels.

"Idea!" Aletha suddenly announced. She poked Galen's knee for emphasis, startling him. "You said we had to travel toward the mountains in the north. Why don't we go by sea? It's much faster than riding along the coast."

Galen hesitated while his eyes returned to the jagged rocks and the people who challenged them. "It'll be safer by land, don't you think?"

"The road north is steep in places and unless you want to hire a company of guards we'll always have to look out for bandits. On the water you can see them coming. I grew up in boats. I can handle any sea."

"We don't have a boat."

"I have a friend who sells them. He'll give us a good price. Perhaps he'll even lend me one, as long as we leave it where he can get it back. He's got a house up there." She gestured east toward Topside, the section of Phrar rising above the sprawling downtown on a ridge of hills. Elevated above the floods and built of solid stone, the mansions housed the town's elite of merchants and administrators. "He's wealthy and doesn't mind sharing with us wharf rats. We'll just need a small boat, anyway, because we'd go through the North Islands, rather than go the long way around in open water. It'll be fun!"

"I'm not convinced of that."

"Hey, Chor!" Aletha said to the dozing twin. "What do _you_ think?"

Chor turned his head. After a moment he gestured toward his brother. "What he said."

"Don't you two ever disagree?"

Galen grinned. "No, we don't," he said. "All right, we'll go your way."

"You'll like it out there. We'll travel through the islands and then sail up along the Great Strait, just out of sight from the open water. There's always a lot of traffic along that way and it's not likely that we'll run into pirates. We'll be able to leave just as soon as I've gotten a few things together. We'll need to get provisions and a tent and—" She cocked her head and scrutinized the twins with narrowed eyes. "Hmm, this won't do."

"What won't?"

She pointed at Chor. "Do you dress like that on the Homeworld?" He was reclining comfortably, long legs encased in well-worn leather and solid boots, a dagger lashed to his thigh. A lightly armored leather vest gaped to reveal a pullover shirt likely designed to display his torso to good advantage. She turned to examine Galen who was outfitted in similar fashion.

The twins scrutinized each other. "No," Galen said. "We got these things from some people in the mountains. Cold up there."

"Mercenaries, from the looks of it. Well, we'll have to get you some proper traveling gear. Things that can stand getting a little wet." Snatching up her broad rain hat, she was out of her chair and halfway to the street before he was able to express his opinion about being damp. "Come on, let's get some gear together! We'll go see my friend. He'll look after us."

"Aletha..." he called after her.

She came back into the shelter of the veranda, curious about his thoughtful expression.

"It might be wise if you didn't tell people where we are going, or why."

"Oh," she said, startled. "I hadn't even thought of what to tell people. I'll have to tell them something."

"Your friends know you live in fear of the emissaries. Tell them you're going to hide away for a while, after what happened to you with the slaver. Perhaps you hired us as guards. I don't think it's a good idea to tell people about the trouble between the Homeworld and Chenoweth or your part in it. Chenoweth is their paradise. Don't take it away from them."

"You are very kind, Galen," she said softly. He had placed his hand on the porch railing and she covered it with her own. "And you are right – we'll tell them nothing. Maybe I will return some day when I understand it all better."

Galen returned her gaze, but then had to drop his eyes. He pulled his hand away, loathing his deception. He doubted that Aletha would ever be allowed to return to Thali. "Let's go see your friend," he said curtly.

"Come, it isn't far." She hurried ahead into the soggy street. In deference to the twins' peculiar aversion to being rained upon, she chose paths that offered awnings and covered sidewalks to keep pedestrians dry, their quality and availability increasing as they made their way uphill toward the wealthier part of town.

"I want to stop here for something," she said when they had reached about halfway along the incline toward Topside. "We can wait until the rain lets up a bit."

"As if that's likely," Galen scoffed. "What is this place?" He followed her through a rusted metal gate into a small courtyard. The house to which it belonged seemed long abandoned and Aletha passed it by to hurry across the weedy expanse of cracked flagstone and ancient rubble. There were signs of squatters: an old fire pit, a broken crock, a few discarded rags. The damp air smelled of decay and the blooms of some vine that had gone rampant in here to cover most of the crumbling stone wall that surrounded the yard. Aletha found a break in the wall and slipped out of sight.

When Galen and Chor followed her the smell of earth closed around them as though they had stepped into a tomb and they felt an instant longing for the overcast sky they had left behind. With the encouragement of a vague source of light ahead of them, the twins managed to squeeze through the short tunnel that had swallowed Aletha. When they were able to stand upright again, they found that the tunnel had widened into a long cave extending into some smaller alcoves to the left and right. The floor and walls were smooth stone and, although the frequent comings and goings of people had worn paths into the dust, there was no hint of permanent occupation.

From somewhere a faint draft kept the air moving and Galen hoped for a second exit – claustrophobia began to nag him when he thought how easily they could be trapped in this tunnel both by earthquakes and a posse of emissaries. In the dark recess of one of the alcoves a group of people was gathered in a circle, drawn together in murmured conversation. One of them looked up and waved, but neither he nor Aletha chose to exchange further pleasantries.

"This is one of our sanctuaries," Aletha explained. "For me and my fellow demons," she added with a grin. "Don't be using your magic in here or you'll give us away. There'll be questions you don't want to answer."

Interested, Galen cast about himself, searching through the space, feeling its moods, tasting its ambient chi'ro, and softly touching the people at the far side of the chamber. At his cautious prodding, one of them shrugged his shoulders as if to loosen a knotted muscle. Another looked up and around the room as if a sound in the distance had drawn her attention. Galen was well trained in covert investigation and none of them felt themselves scanned and measured. No true adepts, he concluded. Minor talents, all of them; their gifts would be unremarkable on the Homeworld.

"Galen? Chor?"

Galen turned. "Huh?"

Aletha was holding some dry rags out to him. "I said I'll be just a moment. See if you can dry off a bit." She gave another towel to Chor. "You know, you'd be less bothered by the rain if you cut your hair short. Most men here do."

Chor stared at her, the cloth raised halfway to his head. "Are you mad?" he said before catching her mischievous grin. Rolling his eyes, he turned away to shake out his hair. "I'd rather run naked through town square," he mumbled.

Aletha considered the prospect. "Well..."

"What are we doing here, anyway?" Galen interrupted her musings.

"Huh? Oh. We have a long journey ahead of us. I'll feel better about leaving this place if I can take a little while to pray to the Goddess."

"Pray? Now?"

She grinned. "It's good insurance. All sailors stop at the harbor temple before heading out. It seems sensible to do the same, even if our patron is an unlawful one."

"What do you mean?" Curious, he followed her across the open central space to the far wall of the chamber. There were some cushions and mats strewn on the floor but he saw no type of altar or whatever else people here used for their worship. Aletha bent to pick up a long rod, which on its end had a small bucket and a long, thin rope. After filling the bucket with water from a nearby urn, she raised the pole over her head. Then, deftly handling the rod and rope, she tipped the bucket to let a trickle of water spill over the rock face before them.

Galen and Chor gasped in unison and took a step backward, away from the wall. The water had darkened the stone to reveal thin lines etched onto its surface. The lines glinted faintly in the light of the torches, some running together to form a pattern, others revealing words. The main theme that emerged was a tall likeness, towering high above those who came to worship in this cave, of a woman sheathed in long flowing robes and a cascade of white hair.

"Is something wrong?" Aletha asked.

Galen continued to take in the inexplicable drawing, deaf to Aletha's question. The woman on the wall was delicate and well formed with wide-set eyes in a narrow face. Her full lips were curved in a benevolent smile and her hand was raised in a blessing. He recognized the tilt of her head, the set of her shoulders, even the way she had of standing with one foot slightly askew. Although depicted in the rich robes of royalty she never wore, in all ways this was the La'il, ruler of the Home Planet, rising high over his head to mock him with flat silver eyes that seemed to follow his every move. Galen reached out to touch the glittering veins embedded in the rock, but stopped his hand before he made contact. "La'il" he whispered.

"You know of her?"

He ran a hand over his face and into his hair. "I do. What is she to you?"

Aletha shrugged. "La'il is La'il. Her altars and shrines are everywhere here, hidden from the emissaries. She opposed the other gods when they exiled Thali. There were thunderous battles and because of her intervention the other gods finally left Thali before they succeeded in destroying all the mortal magic users. She became our goddess, the patron of the Descendants left behind here. In the end she went away, too, and now we pray to her to lead us to Chenoweth. We pray in secret, of course, because to openly appeal to the La'il would bring the emissary upon us."

Galen shook his head in disbelief, his lips stretched into a shape neither grin nor grimace. Was it possible that the La'il was over three hundred years old? Had she actually been a part of some terrible upheaval that resulted in the severing of the conduits? He looked up at the glistening wall, strangely amused by La'il's evolution into a goddess. He wondered if she would be pleased to hear about this and whether it would appeal to her already considerable vanity. When it occurred to him that she might be aware of her status on this moon his grim smile faded.

"Do you worship the La'il, too?" Aletha wanted to know.

"In a way."

"You're not so different from us, then, Homeworlder." She pointed over her shoulder. "There are some stories about her written on that wall." Galen watched her settle comfortably on the ground, her arms wrapped around drawn-up knees. She sank into a serene silence, her half-closed eyes on the deity.

Rubbing his hair with the rags she had given him, Galen withdrew to put some distance between himself and the etching. When La'il had sent them on this journey to find and return Aletha, why had she not mentioned her part in Thali's history? Obviously, she had been here and had enough impact on these people to be revered for something. Then again, thought Galen, she rarely explained herself to anyone, certainly not to her servants.

Wandering about the chamber, taking care not to disturb the people gathered here, he came upon more drawings on the wall, visible without the offering of water. He peered closely at the murals, barely making out a mix of words and pictograms etched into the stone. They were of some mythical significance, something about the afterlife and the doorway to heaven. A crude drawing showed the solar system with the Homeworld and her two moons exaggerated in relation to the sun. Bemused and with some difficulty, he read that Chenoweth, the larger of the moons, was considered home of the gods to which all pious folk should aspire. He followed the writings along the wall, at times rubbing at the soot to discover their meanings.

He came to a symbol that could only represent La'il. She stood with arms outstretched, powerful, rising above those who bowed to her. Galen's gaze moved toward the far wall, where his leader's likeness was beginning to fade back into the drying rock. "What are you doing here?" he pondered.

* * *

"Letha, my Aletha!"

A slim, blond-haired man hurried across the vaulted entrance hall of the mansion, both arms stretched out in greeting. He embraced her and swung her off her feet to twirl her about. "Where have you been? I've been mad with fear for you. Yala came by but she would tell me absolutely nothing useful! We heard about Jora and Owl and I've been so worried—" he halted abruptly when he saw Galen and

Chor in the doorway to his home. "Uh, hello."

Aletha freed herself from his embrace. "I'm sorry, Delann. It was thoughtless of me not to send another message. I've been ill. This is Chor and Galen. They helped me escape. What have you heard?"

Delann glanced nervously around the hall and then motioned them to follow into an adjoining room without taking time for the ritual of offering dry clothing to his guests. He continued to hold both of her hands in his as they sat on a low, armless couch. Chor remained standing by the door; Galen flung himself into a nearby chair.

This house was a welcome change from the dilapidated buildings along the waterfront. Expensive, with furniture elaborately carved from the dark, fine-grained wood of the jungle, the well-maintained estate bespoke the owner's standing in the community. Woven and dyed grass mats covered stone floors worn to a rich gloss over many years, and above them high ceilings and open archways helped to channel the humid breeze. Expertly carved sailing ships and stone sculpture were displayed before tapestries telling of past legends and heroes. Like many of the oldest houses here in Phrar, the doorways of this building were strangely oversized, harking back to a time when its occupants had been taller.

One entire wall of this large sitting room was open to the gardens. The well-worn flagstones, friezes and blunt sculpture seemed as if they'd always been here and always would be. Water dripping from the fluted roof tiles outside struck a trough of rounded stones, plants, and metal objects designed to create a tranquil display of moving water and soothing sounds. The moss on stone and columns and even the green patina on copper edgings seemed to grow in patterns most pleasing to the eye. Twin statues in the shape of some mythical beast flanked the terrace, one of them currently a perch for a large yellow lizard. Unmoving, it surveyed the mist-veiled garden, like everything else here unaware of the passage of time.

Although he had seen a sword rack in the hallway, there were no visible weapons in this room and when Galen cast his thoughts about the rambling building he found no unseen guards either. Three people in the kitchen near the front door, two more out back, someone was sleeping upstairs. There was nothing unsettling here; the house and its inhabitants were at peace. Aletha's friend was the exception.

Delann's voice was a nervous whisper when he spoke. "I heard only that Owl and Jora were found dead in Shep's warehouse. They said Owl and Shep attacked some intruders and Jora got in the middle of it. Shep got away. His boys are safe, too. When I heard you and Parran had been taken I feared the worst. We all feared sooner or later you'd be betrayed, or you'd betray yourself. This is all so sad. I wasn't able to attend, but I heard that they sent Owl and Jora on their way on the same pyre, like they would have wanted."

Aletha sighed. "I saw them kill Owl but after that don't remember much. They were emissaries, I'm sure of that. I don't know how I ended with the slaver. Any word about Parran?"

"Taken to the enclave for purging."

She closed her eyes.

"What does that mean?"

Aletha shifted on the bench to answer Galen's question. "It means he's dead or soon will be. Usually, when a Descendant is captured, he or she is sent to Anhkar, near the delta, where they are kept by the emissaries. Enslaved, although the emissaries say they are there to take instruction and discover the true meaning of Dazai's decree and so give up their magic-using ways. Most of the people who are sent away aren't even Descendants. Parran is a friend who was with me that day in the warehouse. I was teaching him how to help Owl with his bad back. Parran has some talent, as you call it, and he'll not be allowed to live." Her lower lip twitched and she bit down on it. "They... they may question him about me. About the others. We've all heard stories about that. After they... I mean when they..."

Galen raised his hand to spare her the recital of ghastly details. "Do you know where they keep him? Perhaps there is a way to get to him."

"You can't!" Delann said at once. "Don't even consider it. They'll purge the whole quarter."

"All right, just a thought." Galen nodded to Althea who looked as shocked by his suggestion as Delann had. "We have to leave here. Soon."

She turned back to their host. "We need a boat."

"Where are you going?"

She dropped her eyes. "Down the coast a bit. Then inland."

Delann made as if to protest but then nodded. "That's probably best. I'll get you passage on one of the ships. I've got a frigate going south in a few days."

She shook her head. "We can't wait that long. If I'm found out, you're found out. I'm hoping to get out tomorrow. I want something small. A dinghy will do. We'll stay in the tributaries and then head east to Tandalay."

"Not much there," he said doubtfully. "Although you'll be less conspicuous," he added, meaning the dark-skinned twins.

"It'll do. Can you help us?"

"Of course I can help you! But stay here tonight," he looked up to include the twins in his request. "We'll have dinner, some friends, music. Who knows when we'll see you again. What do you say?"

Aletha turned to Galen.

He held his hands up in acceptance. "From the looks of this place I'd say your cooks are probably a little more accomplished than those at the inn."

Preparations were made, messengers sent, and the new guests shown to comfortable quarters. Although Delann's home was spacious, Galen and Chor elected to share a room. The upper story was as opulent as the main floor, but these private rooms were enclosed to protect the rich fabrics, wooden floors and collections of books and maps from

Thali's humidity. Aletha took advantage of a well-appointed bathhouse and then accompanied Galen, Chor and Delann to some of the stores that her friend supplied with trade goods.

There, Delann allowed them to choose clothes and other supplies for their journey. Aletha assembled camping gear, bedding, tarps, some fishing tackle and a few extra weapons, expertly appraising the merchandise to sort the practical from the frivolous. The current traveling fashion seemed to consist of voluminous trousers, tight at the ankle, and loosely woven blouses held at the waist by a wide sash wrapped several times about the body. This was then covered either by simple tunic or an open vest reaching to the knees. Women dressed the same, in more elaborately decorated fabrics. Although most comfortable in sandals or barefoot, Aletha added boots and warmer items for the last leg of their journey, which would take them into higher elevations. Delann's servants were sent to take their new gear to a ship waiting at the docks. A store of food would be purchased at the wharf when they were ready to sail.

Galen tried to pay for their choices but Delann refused at once.

"I am trying to ease my conscience," he said to Galen, but his eyes were on Aletha across the room. She was trying to persuade Chor to try on a broad straw rain hat without much success. "I should be taking her away rather than let her rely on strangers. I mean no offense to you, of course. She won't take money from me. Let me give you these things to make up for my weaknesses."

"Weaknesses?" Galen said.

Delann smiled ruefully and shrugged. "I am a coward. It's that simple. I've loved Aletha since she arrived in Phrar. I don't even know if she knows this. But she is dangerous. There are those who fear her for her strangeness and those who hate her for her gifts. I have much to lose if I took a stand by her side. May the Gods forgive me, these soulless, meaningless *things* I amass by the day mean more to me than this woman or the happiness we could have."

"You risk all of it by your hospitality. Her friends lost their lives when they tried to protect her and the same can happen to you. You call that cowardice?"

Delann observed Aletha with great fondness. "She is so very special. More than we'll ever know, I'm sure. She deserves a friend who's not afraid."

"Of her?" Galen said quietly.

Delann held his gaze. "Of her," he said at last.

* * *

The guests arrived as the sun disappeared behind the bulk of the Homeworld. With them came musicians, acrobats and storytellers. Soon more than a hundred people were scattered throughout the ground floor rooms and the gardens of Delann's home, brightly chatting and gossiping, tasting the exotic foods arranged on heavily laden tables, and trying to catch a glimpse of the rarely-seen Aletha and the remarkable set of twins accompanying her. But Galen and Chor had disappeared.

"Aletha!" Delann found her in the crowd. He was in high spirits; already several bowls of wine had gone to work on him. He looked dashing in a colorful tunic reaching to his bare feet and she smiled at him with great fondness. "What a wonderful get-together! Find your friends. I told some people they traded near the mountains and they want news from there."

Aletha began to look around, stopping often to chat with Delann's guests, many of whom she knew. All had wondered what happened after the tragedy in the warehouse although only few suspected that she was, indeed, a Descendant. Yala had been instructed to create gossip about the slaver, an easily accepted story. Both Owl and Aletha would fetch handsome prices on any market. Aletha avoided conversation about the matter, deftly turning aside some of the more direct questions that greeted her in one room after another on her quest to find Galen and Chor. When she searched for them upstairs, the twins' bedroom was empty. The overheated kitchen was a lively confusion of harried household staff and a few guests intent on lending a hand but the twins were not among them. She quizzed the stable boy and then checked the rain-soaked gardens before finally entering the mansion's bathhouse.

The steam-filled rooms were silent except for the drip of water on tile. The fire under the main bathing basin was well banked, the water inside clear. Playful, somewhat suggestive murals decorated the walls, and the stone benches were well stocked with linens, dishes of soaps, lotions and herbs as well as wine and platters of food. No doubt some of Delann's guests were expected to find their way out here before the night's carousing was done.

Passing under some stone arches that mimicked the grand entrance to Phrar Thali's council hall, she found the twins in the dressing room. One lounged on a bench, his eyes closed, a large sheet wrapped around his waist. The other stood nearby, his hands in his hair. As usual, they did not speak, apparently content to share a comfortable silence.

Although she was motionless, both twins abruptly turned to look at her.

Aletha blushed. "I didn't mean to disturb you. I'm sorry."

"We don't have these bathhouses on the Homeworld," he said and sat up to put his feet on the floor. "I think I'll build one when we get home. I wonder if I can find tile work like this. It's very beautiful, don't you think?"

"Which one are you?"

His eyes shifted to study a competently rendered mural of some nudes engaged in activities other than bathing. "Galen," he replied. "You could make an effort to tell us apart."

"It's easier when you've got clothes on." The comment was meant as a joke but she felt silly for having said it. She found it difficult not to stare at the long-limbed, muscled body displayed in front of her but looking at the decorated walls instead did nothing to ease her embarrassment. The honey shade of his skin was not confined to areas he normally exposed to the elements and she found herself wondering if it felt as supple as it looked. His broad chest was hairless and she saw a long, badly healed scar twist across his left side. "That must have been some accident," she blurted.

He moved his arm to look at the scar but did not comment.

"Maybe I could tell you apart if you two always wore something special to tell who's who."

"Maybe we could tattoo our names on our foreheads."

She frowned. "You make no effort to make it easier for people to tell you apart. You wore that earlier today," she pointed at Chor's copper belt buckle. "No wonder people get confused."

"Well, it doesn't really matter who's who, does it?" Galen said.

"Of course it matters!"

He came to his feet, seeming to unfold himself endlessly until he towered over her. "Why?"

She backed away a little, feeling herself blush again. He seemed possessed by some odd mood, preoccupied with something that had nothing to do with grooming. His fingers were tapping nervously against his thigh as he spoke to her with a sharpness she had not heard him use before. Chor, in contrast, seemed more withdrawn than usual, eyes distant, head tipped as if he was straining to hear the fragments of music drifting through the open doors from the main house. As so often, the conversation around him failed to capture his interest. "Anyway," she said, flustered. "Delann wondered where you were. He wanted you to join us."

"I'll be along in a while. I don't like crowds much."

It sounded like a dismissal. "What about you, Chor? Are you coming?"

"In a while," Chor said pointedly, apparently aware after all. "Those are your friends, Aletha. Say your good-byes. We'll be along." He lobbed a leather wristband toward his brother. Galen seemed to know this and reached up to catch it without glancing in Chor's direction. Aletha turned and fled.

The evening's agenda proceeded from the informal dinner to the entertainment, which included many fanciful stories and some lively music from the other side of the continent that few here had heard before. Aletha enjoyed the talk and laughter around her even though she was well aware of surreptitious glances as people observed her for evidence of aberrant behavior. She was distracted by the twins, who had eventually joined the party. They were the targets of admiring glances from the female and not a few of the male guests and many sought to talk with one or the other. In spite of Galen's dislike for crowds, the twins seemed amiable and were quick to smile at the ladies.

"What's bothering you, Blossom?" Delann found her in the main commons room and came to sit on the arm of her chair. He lifted her hand to kiss her palm. "You haven't spoken to me all evening. What can possibly be more fascinating than me?"

"The twins."

"I'm wounded!" He looked across the room. One of the brothers was speaking to Delann's captain, the other sat nearby, silently listening to the chatter of a woman whose fluttering hands seemed to worry him.

She grinned. "Sorry, I didn't mean that the way it sounded. I think there is something strange about them. I don't think Galen treats Chor very well."

"Why do you say that?"

"Look there. I'll bet that's Galen talking to Ferd. He always does all the talking. Chor just shuts up and agrees with everything. Galen never talks to Chor, either. Not once."

"They must have something to say to each other."

"No. Never. Not a word. I think maybe they can, you know, talk with their minds."

Delann squirmed uncomfortably, glancing around the

room. No one had heard her. He chuckled nervously. "You don't believe people can do that, do you?"

"We've all heard of it. Don't tell me you haven't. I think they're so close to each other that they don't even have to talk any more. They just know what the other is thinking. Earlier, I saw Chor toss something at Galen and Galen caught it without even looking."

"I think you're making something out of nothing!" Delann scoffed. "Maybe the other one is just a little simple, or maybe he just doesn't like to talk. If anything, it sounds to me like maybe those two are spending a little too much time together, if you follow."

Aletha snickered. "Don't be crude, Delann. You should have seen it. If I had thrown it at you like that, it would have hit you. Galen just reached up and caught it like he knew it was coming at him."

Delann threw his hands in the air. "So you want to travel around with these two? I'm not all that happy about you going off alone with them in the first place. I still think you ought to hire on a few more guards. Even if these two are trustworthy, as you seem to think, it's hardly proper for you to be alone with them out there. Let me hire you a maid to take along with you."

"I don't need a chaperone!"

"Sorry!" he said quickly, his hands raised in a placating gesture. "I'm just worried. You're a danger with your dagger but it's not going to help you much if these two brutes don't turn out to be as polite as they seem. If you have any doubts, maybe you should straighten some things out with them before you find yourself at their mercy out there."

"I think I'll do that." Before Delann could say another word, she had crossed the room to stand behind Chor.

He was sitting on the steps leading to a raised dining area, his arms folded on his knees, apparently trapped in a one-sided conversation with one of the dancers Delann had hired. Although the revelry in the room had begun to reach the first stages of immoderation for which Delann's parties were famous, neither Chor nor Galen had taken up cups. Aletha waited silently as the woman chattered at Chor, who replied only with an occasional nod or some other gesture to show that he was attending. By now, Althea knew enough of Chor's ways to be amused by anyone, no matter how flirtatious, attempting to draw him into a conversation. But today Chor wasn't just disinterested. His half-closed eyes were focused on nothing and, although his body was arranged in a casual slouch, she saw that it was tensed, as if ready for flight. A pulse beat rapidly at his throat and his teeth were gripping his lower lip. She leaned forward to peer into his face.

"Are you sure you're well enough to travel tomorrow?" a low voice said behind her.

Aletha drew back, startled by Galen's question. "What? Oh, yes. Sure, I am." Galen, too, seemed to be anxious about something. The twins had not shaken the odd mood that had possessed them earlier. She turned back to Chor, who was also looking at her now. Something troubled them. "Is there something wrong?"

"Wrong? No. Why do you ask?"

She shrugged. "He looked ill just now."

"Ill?" He looked at his brother. "Are you ill, Chor?"

Chor came to his feet, undoubtedly to the dismay of the woman by his side. "Right as this never-ending rain. I'm tired." He turned and left without another word.

* * *

Aletha lay wide-awake in her bed, listening to the night. For once the incessant patter of rain falling on the lush vegetation outside the open window was unable to lull her to sleep. Water gurgled through a spout to strike some well-placed instrument in the garden as a gentle counterpoint to the rain. Occasionally, the breeze brushed through a distant wind chime to add an ephemeral refrain. The alien conversations of nocturnal animals completed the arrangement as they vied for food, or mates, or space.

Aletha slipped from her blankets and walked to the window, intending to close it against the night noises. But the damp air greeting her at the window felt wonderfully refreshing, cooling her body without chilling her. Delighted, she leaned out to breathe deeply of the night air, wondering if she had drunk too much wine tonight.

The party had wound to a close long after the twins had left the festivities. Aletha, too, had retired while there were still people here enjoying themselves. Gradually, the great house had quieted as the guests either left or were shown to private rooms, there to sleep or to continue more private merrymaking. But instead of falling asleep then, Aletha was kept awake by nagging thoughts about Galen and Chor.

She realized that, although they had undoubtedly saved her life and had treated her with nothing but polite deference, she was no longer sure that this peculiar course of events was truly the path she ought to take. She knew so little about them and what she did know only confused her. Was she really prepared to travel alone with two men who were complete strangers to her?

Her life these past few years among the wharves and alleys of Phrar Thali had taught her something about the unsavory side of human existence. Which of those sometimes painful lessons had prepared her to leave this moon, her home, for a place of which she knew so little? By the twins' account, she was going to a world preparing for war, not the sort of local skirmish so common here but an all-or-nothing confrontation between the Homeworlders and the gods of Chenoweth. Yet here she was, ready to leave everything she knew and follow these strangers to wherever they may lead her. Why?

Their story was intriguing. The idea that there was a place where she would go unpunished for using her strange talents, where she would be encouraged to hone them and use them to help people, was almost too wonderful to imagine.

She could not deny the far more basic appeal that was pushing her to accept their offer. Galen, especially, made no effort to disguise his interest and feeling those soft eyes on her had begun to touch her in some interesting ways. Was she thinking clearly?

Aletha looked forlornly over the verdant vegetation of the garden. This was her home, and none of the wonders of the Homeworld, nor any obligations to some long-lost family, would change that. But the temptation the twins offered was overpowering. To remain on Thali moon would mean denying her gifts and any hope of testing their limits. Here she would always be a swindler and thief, skulking about in the slums and spending her days in eluding the emissaries. Aletha smiled sorrowfully, finding herself once more firmly on solid ground, now surely able to sleep. Her decision was made.

She leaned out to close the shutter when something in the gardens below caught her attention. Two figures moved along the vine-covered walkway connecting the main building with the bathhouse. When the door opened, light from inside outlined their easily recognized silhouettes in stark relief. What would the twins be doing in the bathhouse in the middle of the night? Was Chor ill, after all?

She considered only briefly and not very carefully. She had questions for them and perhaps Delann's advice that she should work out her suspicions before leaving with the twins was well-founded. Perhaps it was time to really talk with Galen. Resolutely, she slipped out of her room and into the hall.

* * *

"Galen," the sweet voice purred. "My love, how very kind of you to notice my call at last. I've been tugging on your sleeve for hours."

Galen tried to avoid the woman's eyes, balling his fists to remain calm. The vision swam in front of his face and he was forced to look upon the La'il. She was a slight woman, clothed in rich, clinging fabric and a mass of white hair, her beauty the cold elegance of marble. Nothing visible hinted at her immense presence, in complete control of all power on the Homeworld. Her mind probed into his like a dark tentacle. "I noticed," he said, offering the words grudgingly. "I couldn't leave. What do you want?"

"I've missed you," she smiled. She lifted her hand to caress him and, in spite of the thousands of miles that separated them, he felt the silken fabric of her sleeve brush his cheek and neck. Her image hovered close to him and he strained back, helpless in her power. Her heady scent enveloped him and her heat blasted him like a furnace.

He tried an indifferent shrug. "You sent me here. You'll have to live without me."

The vision swam backward and he dared to breathe, taking deep gulps of the humid air to clear his lungs of her intoxicating scent. He could hear the rustle of her robes and perhaps even the whisper of skin as one leg brushed the other. Her white hair billowed like seaweed in a gentle current.

"I'll bring you back," she promised. "Soon. I see you have found my dear, dear sister."

"Wasn't easy! There is something strange in the way she's learned to manage her talent. I think they all try to hide it – makes them hard to find in a crowd. Aletha is practically invisible to me unless I scan very deeply and there just isn't enough chi'ro here to do that. But when she's handling chi, or even just walks into a riser, she lights up like a torch! She is the one you're looking for."

"Does she trust you?"

"I think so," he said, glad that she seemed to be in an amicable mood. He began to relax and the pounding of his heart subsided. "This is a strange place. Few risers and the ones I can find are weak and don't regenerate very quickly. No wonder they've lost their talents. I don't know how they learned to manage without chi'ro. I'm losing strength by the day, it seems."

The La'il frowned. "What else?"

"Not a bad place, if you like fish. These are good people,

for the most part, and the moon is very beautiful. But some odd bit of de-evolution's happened here. These are farmers and fishermen, mostly, and some hunters in the forests. Everything here revolves around the water, the miserable weather, tides, seafaring, pirates. No fossil fuels in use, no significant machinery or industry. Schools are rudimentary and doctors are little more than lucky guessers. Those with any common sense seek out people like Aletha to get healed. Slavery is part of the economy as much as clan warfare and barter commerce. And religion and fortune telling! They shun anyone with any real talent, even hunt and murder them. It seems most of the time they just round up anyone who appears peculiar. Adepts are called Descendants here. She's in danger, like you suspected. When I found her she was being held captive, overdosed on chibane. They use the stuff to subdue the Descendants they capture, to keep them from casting some evil spell on them or something."

"Can you tell if it damaged her?"

"She seems fine. Did you know that they blame us for what happened with Chenoweth? The primes that were here at the time got turned into gods. They believe that Chenoweth is heaven and Dazai is alive and up there, too! For some very strange reason, you are lumped in with the gods. Tell me, Holy One, how long have you been around?"

"Farmers and fishermen!" she scoffed. Galen tried to prod her, nudging her mentally into giving something away. None of his findings seemed to surprise her. She appeared oblivious to his intrusion. "Gods, indeed! Barbarians! It's time you started to make your way to the launch in the mountains. I should be able to bring you home soon."

"We'll be there. You didn't answer me, Great One. Have you visited here since the gates closed or are you really that ancient?" He tried to look into her mind, carefully probing through her defenses like someone trying to dislodge a nest of hornets. But he had misread her mood. With no more than a mental shrug, she slammed him out of her mind, sending Chor reeling to the floor and leaving Galen in a great deal of pain. "Don't even try, Galen!" she snapped. With another thought she flung him across the room where he crashed painfully into a basin and slashed his shoulder on a broken tile. "Remember your place!"

Groaning, Galen tried to gain his feet. His head ached. He groped for Chor who was lying motionless on the ground. "Can't you leave him out of this?"

"He's all right," La'il said. "It's time for you to return to the mountains."

"We're leaving in a day or two," Galen said, angry now. He pulled himself up, his shoulder on fire, blood soaking his blouse. Now that she had displayed her temper by hurting his body, his fear had given way to anger, as usual. His rage reached across the thousands of miles between them and she smiled when she felt it enter her like a draught of strong liquor. He cursed himself for giving in so easily. Again. "We're going by boat. Apparently faster that way."

"Does she know who she is?"

"I told her why she's needed on the Homeworld. She knows nothing about you." Galen shrugged out of his shirt and used it to wipe the blood from his shoulder. The tile had cut nearly to the bone. "Except of course the part about you being the favorite goddess up here, champion of the downtrodden. She has no idea about the extent of her abilities. She's discovered some tricks along the way on her own. The good townspeople fear her and avoid her, unless it's to have their palms and tea leaves read. She's got some talent as a healer. No one's publicly accused her of being a witch. Yet. She has never been taught to use her talents properly."

"I'll take care of that. It is best that she does not discover her true abilities until she is home. Tell her nothing more. Much safer that way. We cannot risk any accidents while you're so isolated."

"She's got to know sooner or later. What they fear most here, besides the wrath of Chenoweth, are giants. There are some pretty terrible legends about them, from what I've seen so far. It's going to be hard for her when she gets to the Homeworld and finds out about us. I can't keep lying to her."

She sighed as if indulging the whim of a child. "You don't have to lie. Just don't volunteer anything. She is one of us. She will be, again. This won't matter once she's here. Don't jeopardize her willingness to come here with scary stories. Just get her here and let us worry about how she'll adjust."

"Will you let her return here if she doesn't?"

"Just bring her home."

"She likes it here, she has friends in this place. She would not be happy if you didn't allow her—"

"That is not your concern, Galen!"

He shrugged. "I like her. I am concerned."

The vision swam nearer, hovering before him. "I suggest you do *not* like her. Once she is here you won't see her again. It will not matter to you." He felt her hands touch his bare chest and tried to turn away.

"Stop that."

"Bring her to me," she whispered. Her lips brushed his ear. "She is in danger on Thali. She will always be in danger there. You know that Chenoweth is also trying to find her. If they can't find a way to use her against us, they will destroy her. And if you stand in their way they will kill you, too." She gestured at Chor. "They'll kill both of you, or one. It would be the same, wouldn't it? Chor is everything to you, isn't he?"

"Don't talk like that," Galen said, feeling her cool hands on his feverish skin and unable to stop her. "We'll be safe once we leave this town."

She laughed. "You won't be safe until you have returned. To me." She seemed to be all around him now, writhing in the air, her robe revealing glimpses of smooth skin as she turned. "Just don't return without her."

Galen felt a familiar haze of fury settle over him, not brought about by his loathing for her, but by her skillful tampering of his brain. "No," he gasped. "Not now. Not here. Leave me alone." He looked into her lovely face, hating her.

With a flash of her jewel eyes she reminded him of a night, or ten nights, they had spent together. He closed his eyes against the memory, recalling the mindless hate and rage she had woken in him then.

He shook his head, slowly. "No," he breathed, watching the vision drift before him. Something within him clamored to turn away, to refuse her intrusion, flee from this place if necessary, but he pushed that voice aside to reach for the woman, eager to relive her past tortures. His fingers grasped her robe even as she began to fade from his thoughts. Her laughter receded into the distance despite the hand that he closed around her neck.

"Now is hardly the time," she grinned but he saw fear in her eyes. Fear?

Even locked within his boundless hatred for her, the creature that owned him, he was surprised that she would let him overpower her so effortlessly. She, who fed on his fury like others thrived on love, easily matched him in physical strength. The power of her mind would never allow him to triumph over her if she did not wish it.

"Too easy!" he snarled. "Are you bored down there without me?"

The La'il laughed. "You forget," she said dryly, "that this all in your head." The mental blow she dealt him shocked him out of his insane mood like water thrown onto fire. She disappeared, leaving him dazed but aware of his hand still gripping Aletha's throat.

Galen released her at once, unable to bite back a coarse expletive. When he moved away he saw that her clothes were torn.

Aletha leaped away from him and backed toward the bathhouse doorway. She turned to run and stopped only when she collided painfully with Chor standing in her way. She recoiled from him, too aware that a scream from within this secluded building would not be heard at the main house.

"You should not have come in here."

"He hurt me!"

Chor nodded. "You're in no danger now."

She glanced around him to the door, ready for flight.

He sighed impatiently. "Use the talents you have, Aletha! Feel me." He raised his arms as if actually expecting her to touch him. "You know you have nothing to fear here." He gestured at her torn night robe. "Cover yourself." He moved to his brother, apparently sure that she wasn't about to run screaming into the night. He helped Galen to a low stone bench and examined the deep cut inflicted by the broken tile, dabbing at it with a towel. He did this wordlessly, without emotion. "Let me explain," he said finally.

"You? Why you? You were lying on the floor. I saw you. I thought maybe he hurt you, too. How do you know what happened?" Aletha looked from one to the other. "I was right! You know what he's thinking, don't you? You two can talk with your minds. That's why you don't speak to each other. You don't have to."

"No, we don't have to."

"You could have told me!"

"I thought it was obvious." Chor fell silent, his attention on stanching the blood still pouring from Galen's wound, and left his twin to defend himself.

Galen raised his head, looking very tired. "I am sorry about what happened here," he said. "I didn't mean to hurt you. I... I was dreaming, a vision, whatever. There is someone I hate very much. You disturbed that vision. I did not know it was you."

"That's it?" she demanded. "That's all?"

He nodded.

"And perhaps next time you take a nap you'll take a knife to my throat?"

A brief flash of anger crossed his face. "I did not ask you to follow me here."

"You knew this vision would visit you. That's why you were acting so strange tonight. That's why you left the house and came here. Who is this woman you hate so much?"

Galen looked up, startled. "What woman?"

"I heard her laugh. I think. Maybe it was in my head. Who is she?"

"No one important. It doesn't matter."

"I will not go anywhere with you as long as you lie to me. Explain this or go back to the Homeworld without me."

"You won't like my answer."

"Tell me who that was!"

Galen looked at his twin, taking a while to consider his words. When Aletha shifted impatiently, about to repeat her question, he replied. "The La'il."

Aletha stared from one to the other. She tried a confused smile, certain that she had heard wrong. "What?"

He nodded, already regretting his reply, voiced for no other reason than to spite the La'il.

"What are you saying? La'il? The Goddess? Our Goddess?"

"Your Goddess."

Slowly, Aletha let herself slide down along a wall until she sat on the floor, her arms wound tightly around her knees. "I don't think I understand. You are visited by the Great Mentor, the One who defied Chenoweth? Why? Why is she sending you visions?"

"More like projections."

She frowned, grappling with what this man was trying to tell her.

"She is on the Homeworld, Aletha. She sent me here to find you."

"She… what…" Angrily, Aletha raised her voice. "She speaks to you? What does she tell you? Why do you hate her?"

"Aletha, you will soon learn and see things that will be strange to you. You have to accept that some of the things you've always taken for granted are nothing like they should be."

"Tell me about the La'il!"

He sighed. Having begun now, he saw no way of

extricating himself from where this was heading. "She is not a goddess. Not the way you think of gods, anyway. I don't know how or why your people here know of her. True, she rules the Homeworld by the power of her mind. She has made many magnificent things possible there. She can..." he faltered when he realized that he was likely well on his way to describing what would pass as a god on this moon. "I mean she's not the only one who can do these things. She's a Descendant like you and me. She just does it better."

Aletha's eyes narrowed. "Perhaps you are gods, too."

He shrugged tiredly. "To you maybe we are. But we are not all-powerful. Not even the La'il is. She can't rule this moon. Nor can she reach the colony on Chenoweth. Not now. To ourselves, we are just ordinary people."

"And Chenoweth?"

"People. Humans. Mortals like you and me. Separated from the Homeworld just as Thali was three hundred years ago. They are Descendants like your people, only far more powerful."

"Are you telling me that we have no gods here?" Aletha said angrily. "Chenoweth is a place of warmongers and the La'il is just an ordinary woman? The gods we pray to are just... people? People like you? It is all for nothing?"

"No!" Galen said. "Don't say that. You need your gods. I am only telling you that the La'il is not one of them. She is just an adept with a talent so great that she can do the most incredible things with—"

"And so she *is* a goddess!" Aletha exclaimed. "That is what gods do, after all, isn't it? They make the impossible happen?" She glared at him, despising him for revealing the unknowable.

Galen closed his eyes, suspecting that he had bungled this assignment in a rather spectacular way. "All right, Aletha, maybe she is. I'm sorry if I upset you. I didn't think you believed in all that, anyway. You were joking about your priestesses just yesterday. You pray because everyone else does. You called these people superstitious and simple-minded. You live in fear of their priests."

"Well, I don't believe, not really," she said. "I just don't want to be proven right!"

"I would have thought you'd be pleased."

"Pleased? About what? That there are no gods? That we're only here because the Old Ones, my own people, left Thali to fend for itself? That there is no purpose in our being here and when we die we don't even get to see Chenoweth?" Aletha struggled against her tears. "You tell me our goddess is just a woman, from what I've seen not a very kind one. And you expect me to be pleased?"

Chor peeled the bloodstained rags from Galen's back and threw them into the fire beneath one of the tubs. Galen stood up and held his hand out to her. "I am sorry. I don't understand your ways. Come with me."

She wiped her face. "Where?"

"I'll show you my gods."

Aletha rose without relying on his offered hand and followed him and Chor out of the bathhouse. The twins stepped off the path to leave the beautifully tended formal garden and led the way through some shrubbery into the kitchen yard. It was darker here and Aletha's steps faltered when they continued past a small plot of vegetables into the orchard. Neither twin seemed to notice that she was less and less willing to follow them into this remote corner; either they did not care or they had a fair estimation of her curiosity. Finally, near the end of a row of fruit trees, one of them sat down on a stone bench while the other continued to move about, his arms slightly raised, his face tilted upward as though listening for something. At last he beckoned for her to join him.

"What are you doing?" she whispered.

He smiled. "Look over there."

She peered into the dark beyond his outstretched hand. "What?"

He hesitated, remembering the La'il's cautions, before he moved to stand behind Aletha. He reached around her waist to pull her against himself and placed his hand over her forehead. She gasped and strained against his loose embrace. "Relax," he said, his voice low and soothing. "I won't hurt you. I'll make you see."

"But—"

"Shhh," he whispered, close to her ear. "Don't speak. Don't think. Open your mind to me, look for my thoughts."

"You are reading my thoughts?"

"No, but I can feel what you feel. If you let me." She felt him shake his head. "No, don't think of me. Not *of* me." He said nothing more and they stood unmoving in the light drizzle until Aletha was able to turn her mind from the unsettling pressure of his body to whatever it was that he was trying to show her. At last, he raised his hand toward the orchard wall. "Look," he said. "Then see."

"Dazai's mercy!" she breathed. "What is that?"

Near the base of the garden wall something moved. She felt it more clearly than she saw it; a definite *something*, drifting up from the ground like a piece of fog that hovered momentarily, then dissipated into the night air. It had no color, no shape but it was strangely real, strangely familiar.

"*Chiaro*," he said, the word a gentle exhalation against her ear. "That is the magic you can feel sometimes. It is the fuel that lets you use the talent you were born with. The wind in your sail." He stepped away from her. "Watch."

She gaped in silent astonishment when he lifted a hand and the emanation drifted toward him to envelope him completely. He smiled. "This is the magic these people fear so much. It is nothing more than the power of this moon, as it is the power of the Homeworld and the power of Chenoweth. It is the power of the La'il. Some of us can learn to shape this chi'ro to suit our purpose. It is earth power, sun power, but it isn't magic and it isn't evil. We can't conjure something out of nothing. We can only affect what already exists, and then only if we have the skill and the chi'ro to do so. Look!" He pointed at his brother. Almost at once, the stone bench began to rise from the ground, carrying Chor with it until it was level with the treetops. Chor grinned and jumped off. When the bench descended again, he pushed it as easily as a boat in water to restore it to its former location. "We can shape chi'ro, move it, push it around with our thoughts. We can use it to transform things. And while we are exposed to it, it enhances our minds to sharpen our senses."

"But it must be magic," Aletha marveled. She raised her hands toward Galen, palms out. "I can feel it around you now, like you're wearing it!"

"Chi'ro is everywhere, all the time. It sustains us and all living things like the air we breathe. It exists in such small quantities, especially on this moon, that only a few of us can do anything useful with it, like keeping a door locked. We call that ambient chi'ro. But in places like these, random spots, the chi'ro is concentrated in much greater masses. We call these places risers. Look closely."

She bent toward the arm he held out and saw that whatever it was that surrounded him was keeping the rain from his skin as well. Then, with a twist of his hand a fragment of the substance danced over his fingers, suddenly glowing brightly to illuminate this corner of the garden. Aletha gasped and clapped her hands. "That is amazing!"

"It can be very powerful," he said. Chor bent to pick up a fallen branch and lobbed it into the air only an instant before Galen flicked his fingers to hurl the ball of light after it. The branch exploded in a shower of sparks before it reached the orchard wall. "These flares are really a waste of chi, since so much is used up to create light. It does the same damage without the sparks, but doesn't impress quite as much. This is how I got this scar." He placed a hand over the seared, twisted flesh at his side. "An argument with another adept."

Before she could react, he touched her arm and the chi'ro flowed over her like a warm breeze, softer than anything that had ever touched her skin. "It feels familiar," she whispered. "I've felt this before but I didn't know what it was."

"It isn't magic. You, too, can use this. And for more than

to keep the rain off! You are an adept, one who can shape this matter and put it to use." He turned halfway and gestured at the ragged tear on his shoulder. "Heal this," he said.

She raised a trembling hand and held it above the wound, as she sometimes did when using her talents to heal. Not knowing what he expected, she thought only of stopping the pain. She could feel something, some contact between her hand and his shoulder. She knew that the pain was gone, the nerves soothed and the healing begun as the flesh started to knit itself together again. "By the Gods, this seems easier now!"

"This is a gift from our planet, these moons," Galen said, his voice a low murmur. "These are our gods. Down on the Homeworld you will feel this almost everywhere." He closed his eyes and tilted his head back to savor the contact with this magic. "Feel it, Aletha! Why would you need gods in human form if this is the true power of these worlds? Of what purpose are your temples and shrines when none of the gods ever answer your prayers?" He turned to her and grasped her arms. "And this is nothing compared to what can be found on the Homeworld! You will be part of that, Aletha. You will learn how to use this element to suit your purpose."

His energy-infused presence suddenly seemed overwhelming and she pulled away from him. "So you say. I just hope my only purpose is not just to fight some war!"

FOUR

The nervous clip-clop of many feet hurrying along the vaulted passage echoed against ancient stone walls, repeating and amplifying until the space seemed filled with the sound, assaulting his eardrums with its discordance. The emissary resisted an urge to order everyone to remove their footwear and proceed in bare feet along the damp stone slabs toward the lobby of the priory. The ancient breezeway seemed to stretch on forever, one side open to the central gardens where several slaves toiled in the drizzle. He snarled at the sight of them, shoulders hunching ever tighter as if he were prepared to ram head-first into the first obstacle that dared present itself. Their acolytes and novices ought to be tending the gardens, not some hapless souls appropriated without pay, forced to work while the apprentices grew fat and lazy.

His subordinate emissaries huffed and panted behind him, trying to keep pace with their leader, mindful of the acid mood that had taken hold of him when he had arrived this morning. He had come unannounced with only two attendants and no guards, having ridden a day and a half from the delta with barely a moment of rest. Their mounts had been near collapse, the riders filthy and exhausted from the arduous journey. Tsingao had insisted on seeing the new captive immediately.

The entire enclave here in Phrar had been shrouded in silence since their chief emissary had learned that the woman was not safely confined in the cells below. No one had dared so much as whisper since the priest, white-faced and barely able to suppress his rage, had listened to the housemaster's stumbling report that the Descendant had disappeared in the night. When the bearer of these news began to babble about dark magic and witches who flew with the dawn star light, Tsingao had struck him across the face and marched out of the room. After ordering a search for the magic user, he had retreated to his chambers and the enclave had sunk into a dismal mood, only the constant drip of water daring to infringe upon the silence. Those without sufficient excuse to leave the compound anxiously waited for their master to emerge, the punishment for their neglect decided upon and ready to execute.

Then, by some strange fortune, a witness had arrived. Someone who could offer some explanation, perhaps deliver enough useful information to satisfy the chief emissary to the point of leaving Phrar, hopefully for a very long time. A delegation of emissaries had hurried to Tsingao's private rooms to inform him of the arrival of the witness and then raced back with him, having little time for anything but the furtive exchange of bewildered glances. Their leader was not known for public displays of enthusiasm; the escaped Descendant was either another obsession for an obsessed man or a matter far more significant than they had imagined.

The group came to an untidy halt in the vestibule of the enclave's public area, walking up each other's heels to avoid colliding with their leader. Tsingao frowned at them, as if seeing them for the first time. "Bring him into this room." Without another word, he stalked through an intricately carved door and into the small sanctum beyond.

Once inside and alone, Tsingao strove to calm himself, pacing slowly across the room and back again, straightening his impeccable blue robe and running a hand through his closely cropped black hair. Murmuring some prayers under gradually calming breath, he finally stilled himself and stood gazing out of the arched window by the time the door opened.

A novice emissary entered and behind him came another man, this one dressed in ill-used trousers and blouse covered by leather armor. His weapons had been confiscated but there was no mistaking the look of a mercenary about him. Not a particular successful one, judging by the quality of his clothing and the scars on the visible parts of his body. Tsingao's instant distaste for the man did not appear on his face; few things ever did. He nudged the window to allow the fresh garden air into the room.

"You requested a meeting," the chief emissary said, dispensing with niceties. The acolyte withdrew without having raised his head to look at his leader.

The soldier nodded absently, his eyes taking in the rich décor of the room, likely unaccustomed to seeing such splendor. The carvings and woven straw tapestries nearly succeeded in relieving the gloominess of the stone walls but there was no mistaking the dire warnings of the allegorical frescoes above the prayer benches. A single small shrub grew in a pot along one of the walls, somehow imbuing the austere room with life and color. He smiled at a lively display of crystals hanging in the window and pointed at it, about to comment. Then he seemed to remember where he was and dropped his hand again. He bowed awkwardly. "Sire, yes, sire."

The emissary lowered himself onto a wooden bench but did not offer a seat to the visitor. "You have it," he said, keeping his impatience well hidden. Feet flat on the flagstones, hands splayed loosely on his thighs, spine perfectly straight, he waited.

The visitor licked his lips, unnerved by Tsingao's equanimity. The emissary regarded him with black almond-shaped eyes that seemed to be gazing through him as if the wall behind the soldier held some revelation for him. The broad face was unmarred and even, as if painted. Neither its soft contours nor the full lips eased the mercenary's suspicion that something dangerous lurked behind that mask of indifference. It occurred to him that coming here today had been the gravest of errors. "When I heard you had come to Phrar I came at once," he said. "Them other ones here, they don't listen to folks like me but I know you'd be wanting to know what I seen. What happened."

"What did happen," Tsingao said.

The man took a step closer to Tsingao, realized this, and stepped back, again licking his lips nervously. "The demon that got away. We was hired to watch her. In some room in the north end. Ufer and I was to be watching her all the time, make sure she got her medicine and stay quiet. Then a few days on, boss took us to Ichi's Tavern, in behind near the creek. Some folks there looking for slaves, but he wasn't getting any offers he liked much. Till later, when someone else shows up. Dark man, Inlander maybe. He was interested but they didn't make no deal. But he came after us, with another one to help waylay us. Killed Ufer, killed the boss. I got knocked about some, but I lived to see the day. As you can see for yourself, sire." He chuckled uneasily.

Tsingao pondered this after first prevailing over his irritation that the Descendant's escape had become common knowledge. "Describe her."

The mercenary leered. "Small thing, black hair all curled up. Boss made her wear a little dress so he could sell her better. Delicate, but some good parts on her, if you understand me. Was going to have me a piece of that but boss put a stop to it. Was too drugged up to be much good, anyways." He paused his monologue when he noticed a look of disgust on the emissary's face. "She had a tattoo on her arm. Jungle folk, but she didn't look it."

"Did she at any time use magic in your presence?"

The man blinked. "Uh, no. Don't think so. I think she was getting to that but then the stranger showed. I didn't see nothing."

"Describe him."

"There was two of 'em. Twins. Big fellers, with long hair going gray. Quick with a knife."

"That wharf scum is thicker than a school of broadfins," Tsingao said, wondering what this peasant wanted. Nothing he had said so far was of much importance to the emissary. "No doubt some of her friends succeeded in rescuing her."

"Wasn't no harbor rabble," the mercenary said. "Costly gear on them both. Talking like no one around here. Not the sort you see moving about Phrar. But they weren't just foreigners." The witness paused for effect, clearly enjoying the drama of the moment. "Magic users, both of them."

"They were Descendants? How do you know?"

"Seen it! One of them put his hand on me, right here, see? And down I went, like a coin tossed to Hella's whirlpool. I woulda played dead, anyway, but I couldn't move a single limb 'till long after the watch found us lying there. The demons put some questions to the boss and I hear'im scream about Descendants before they killed him. Tore his throat right out with their bare claws! Then disappeared into the night with the witch."

"Hardly much evidence," Tsingao said, gripped by a surge of new hope and excitement. Two more true Descendants in Phrar! This was it, then, unfolding the way the Gods had described. He was so close now; surely this time she would not slip through his fingers. He returned his attention to the man before him. "How did the woman get to that room in the north end? Were you not paid to break in here and take her there?"

"No! I swear it! She was brought to us." He lowered his voice. "You see, Eminence, that's why I come here. Something else needs knowing. Something you want to hear for certain."

"Is that so."

The mercenary's eyes shifted about the room, flicking fretfully from the tapestry to the window and back to Tsingao. "I was wondering if the news I have isn't worth a bit of coin, sire. I'm not a wealthy man – surely a small reward for my trouble is in order..." He shuffled his feet and waited for the emissary to respond.

Tsingao's expression remained immobile, his black eyes resting on the mercenary with the same cold patience he had exhibited throughout the interview. "Surely," he said. "Continue, please."

The man nodded uncertainly, surprised by Tsingao's quick acquiescence. "Yes. Well, all right. There was another man. He was the one brung her to the boss and gave him the potion they use to keep the Descendants feeble."

Tsingao leaned forward. "Who was he?"

"One of your own!" the brute crowed. "Wasn't wearing no blue, but the woman put up a good fight for him, till we got her tied down. He lost his hat in all that and I saw his hair. His was marked like yours, the way you have of shaving the Chenoweth sign into it. He had that. Besides, don't no one act around common folk like the emissaries, pardon me for saying so. Boss gave him some crystal for the girl, and then he left."

The chief emissary was stunned. It was not unheard of for magic users to be traded like some prized talisman or performing act. But this was no common Descendant! He ground his teeth, enraged to have come so close to his quarry only to lose her to the greed of one of his own people! "Wait outside," he managed, scarcely above a whisper. The mercenary withdrew, walking backward until he bumped into the door, which opened only after some panicked fumbling to allow his escape.

Tsingao sat in silence without moving, without thinking. He watched a bud forming on a branch of the potted plant and listened to the snuffling sound made by some creature outside the window. In due course his chest rose and fell in an even rhythm, his shoulders dropped, his jaw unclenched. "Gynn," he said at last.

A latticed door to his left opened and a blue-robed man entered, his steps hesitant. Another emissary followed, no less cautiously.

Tsingao watched them approach. "You heard?"

Nods from both men. Another long silence.

At last: "Take that thug and make him point out the one who sold the girl to the trader. I want him before me before the day is out."

"Yes, Emissary."

"Kill the mercenary when you're sure you've got the right man. We don't need more talk about this spreading about."

"Yes, Emissary."

The chief emissary rose. "We must pray."

"Certainly, Emissary," Gynn said, gesturing to his companion to take a place at the prayer bench, surprised when Tsingao strode to the door. Exchanging a confused shrug, both emissaries hurried after their leader.

Tsingao moved purposefully through the lobby and back onto the covered walkway bordering the tended grounds of the enclave. Unmindful of rain and soaked groundcover, he left the passage and walked among grasses, herbs and shrubs, following no path but the one in his mind. The hems of all three priests' robes were damp to the knees before Tsingao stopped in a small grove. It was an ordinary tangle of brambles, a small corner of the grounds used for growing berries. A few blocks of stone and ancient carvings lay scattered about, perhaps the remnants of some sort of outbuilding, their original purpose long forgotten.

"Sire, it's nearly nightfall. Perhaps the sanctuary would be a better—"

"*This* sanctuary," Tsingao said, "is where we shall pray." He regarded the other two with obvious contempt. "You hide beyond stone walls, keeping your hides dry, hoping to hear the voices of Chenoweth. When have they last spoken to you?" He did not wait for a reply but turned away to close his eyes, his mind calling to his gods; deities whose presence seemed to seep from the ground to surround him with their grace and benevolence.

Shamed, his companions did likewise, sending forth an invitation to Chenoweth, offering their lives and services to their gods. Time passed in which their meditation deepened. Gynn was sublimely aware of all that surrounded him, no longer annoyed by his damp feet and chafing robe. He seemed to become part of this verdant corner of the gardens, of the ceaseless drip of water on glossy greenery, the rich smell of earth and vegetation alternately perfumed and spicy, and the very humidity that lay upon his skin, his hair, his clothes. A strange peace enveloped him, somehow making him part of this grove, and he wondered why he did not spend all of his time here, just standing, just listening. He glanced at his fellow emissaries to see that they, too, reveled in their trance, eyes half closed, immersed in the moment. Tsingao spoke.

"I hear you, Chenoweth," he said. "Thali moon listens."

Gynn was intensely aware of Tsingao, uncomfortably close, almost as if he were touching the emissary. Although as firmly rooted in this garden as if they themselves were plants living within it, all of them seemed transported into some other place and he could see what Tsingao saw and what Tsingao saw was Chenoweth. He sighed in wonder and exaltation. What use were their precisely recited prayers, sacrifices and rituals, when they only needed to stand knee-deep in brambles and damp clover to feel the presence of their gods?

Dimly, almost imperceptibly, something swam into focus somewhere between his mind and what his eyes would let him see. It was a male shape, rotund, aged, clothed in loosely flowing trousers and knee-length cloak of some insubstantial material. Enthralled, Gynn stood in slack-jawed wonder, striving to understand the vision hovering before them. Had this corner of the grounds not offered such absolute reassurance, he might well have fled. Some thoughts reached him, not in the form of words, nor images, but simply as ideas forming in his mind as if they were his own. The apparition's attention was only on Tsingao, a question placed before them.

The god's displeasure over the woman's disappearance

was palpable. The image blurred and faded and they saw him turn away as if conferring with someone nearby. A long time passed during which a thousand questions formed in Gynn's mind, revised a thousand times, and then discarded. Tsingao, motionless beside him, did not offer any answers, nor was Gynn convinced that he wanted them. His heart was beating too fast, the blood pounded too loudly in his ears. The thought that he might faint came to him, pushed aside by his need to savor this experience.

The god came back into focus. He seemed to know that two others had joined the Descendant and that they would try to keep her from the emissaries. Chenoweth sent an image of them entering some sort of door in the sky. There was a dire warning, imploring them not to let this happen. None here missed the utter loathing harbored by the god for the Homeworld and its inhabitants, conveyed with such emotion that Gynn again felt lightheaded. The final part of the revelation was of a more concrete nature. It showed the hills above the town.

The vision faded, the nebulous image of the deity dissolved, its wordless contact severed. Gynn was once again aware of the lush vegetation surrounding him and was prepared to remain standing here forever, lost in contemplation. But he felt a hand on his wrist, tugging him along, and he reluctantly followed, stepping carefully, slow to allow himself to emerge from the depths of his meditation. He became aware of a cooler breeze, brighter light, more solid ground beneath his feet. His eyes focused on Tsingao.

"Our search continues," the leader said softly, perhaps as affected by this encounter as his subordinates were. "The Gods show us the way."

Gynn turned to look back into the mist-obscured grove. What had happened there? He had walked through that bramble many times and had never felt the odd sensation creeping up through the ground. It reminded him of why he had become an emissary in the first place: that strange sense of being called to *something* distant, of connectedness to this moon, of purpose beyond his understanding. Tsingao had been right. The raptures that had fascinated him in his youth were not to be found within the walls of the enclave. How could he ever have lost sight of this? The peace he had found here was not to be duplicated inside the stone sanctuary with his scrolls and books, the sensation of wellness was not brought about with potions and liquors. The appearance of the god here in this garden almost distracted from the mysteries he yearned to explore here. "I… well, this… I mean…" he frowned, trying to formulate his thoughts into words.

Tsingao seemed disinterested in Gynn's rediscovery. "We have our answers," he proclaimed. "That mercenary spoke true. Take his description of those men, those strangers, and comb the city. They can't be hard to spot. Start with the mansions on the hill, as Chenoweth advised. Use care. I'm certain they are powerful. Mobilize everyone."

"We've already requested assistance," Gynn said. "When we realized that she escaped, messages were sent out in all directions. Emissaries from as far away as Solyet are arriving daily to help us find her." *What did Chenoweth mean?* he wanted to ask. What is the meaning of that passage in the sky? Why were they not allowed to enter it? "I need to—"

Tsingao shook his head. "You won't find her. Find the twins. Find them and you've found that woman. They must be killed before they can carry out their plans. Chenoweth has said so."

Gynn frowned. Had Tsingao seen something in their vision that he did not? He knew of Tsingao's quest for this elusive magic user; a woman whose powers had grown over the years but who remained invisible to even the most observant emissary. Some had even doubted her existence until one of their men had stumbled upon her in a derelict warehouse. And now even Chenoweth seemed to agree that her capture was of the utmost importance. Gynn didn't care. Purging the witch would mean an end to their leader's obsessive search and perhaps a chance to relax their guard for a while. Perhaps if Tsingao found his demons and took them away, life in the enclave would return to its placid routines and he, Gynn, would have a chance to examine the mystery of this grove. Still, he felt an odd sense of gratitude toward his leader. "This vision... Chenoweth... It is true what they say. The Gods speak to you."

Tsingao's scornful eyes bored into him. "Chenoweth does not speak to you?" He looked at the other, silently waiting emissary. "Do none of you pray? Do none of you meditate? How, then, do you manage to capture any magic users at all?"

"We pray for wisdom and guidance. The Descendants here in Phrar are discovered in the act of using their evil magic, or are brought before us by those who have witnessed it. Their confessions condemn them."

"But Chenoweth does not?"

Gynn paled, his mouth suddenly dry. He took a step backward without realizing he had done so. "Forgive my inadequacies. Although my life belongs to the Gods, Chenoweth does not favor me. I must admit that today's vision has been my first; I've never been privileged to stand before the Gods. Before this I believed the claim that you, for all your successes in purging the demons from this world, are able to track them as if by smell or sound."

"Are you suggesting that some magic guides me?"

Gynn gulped for air, cursing himself for letting today's miracle loosen his foolish tongue. The chief emissary's zeal was well-known, his hatred for all magic users equally common knowledge. What had possessed him, Gynn, to speak aloud of matters that were never discussed above a whisper, and then only among the closest of associates who denied the rumors as quickly as they passed them along. He regarded his leader warily, knowing that the tranquil demeanor could erupt into unbridled rage just as quickly as it could lash out with soft-spoken cruelty that cut more deeply than the dagger at his belt. "Certainly not, sire. Only my poor way of expressing my awe at what you have shown us here today."

Tsingao placed a hand lightly on Gynn's shoulder. The older man had to fight an impulse to pull away. "You must continue to pray for guidance from Chenoweth," the chief emissary instructed gently. "You administer Phrar; this town must rely on you to rid them of demons and those who consort with them. Come to this place, meditate, and open your thoughts to Chenoweth. Perhaps they will answer, as they have done today. But understand that the Gods are secretive and will test your faith and your willingness to obey their laws. We, the emissaries of Chenoweth on Thali, have done our work well – rarely do the Gods find the need to intervene. Do not expect them to point out every Descendant hidden in this town. Continue your efforts to root out the magic users through diligence and careful investigation, as you have in the past." He raised a finger as if to make sure that Gynn was paying attention. "Those methods secured that female demon, did they not? By the time the Gods had told me of her presence here, she was already captured. And she will be re-captured, in good time. Only this time the Gods are part of the chase!"

Gynn nodded eagerly, a new resolve replacing his doubts and his revulsion for their leader. He had witnessed the man's abilities for himself; Tsingao's favor among the gods was indisputable. "We shall redouble our efforts, sire," he said, meaning it. "Have you any instructions?"

"Yes, it's time to get to work," Tsingao turned back to the priory. "The Gods are watching and judging! Start with this enclave. Dismiss the slaves. Sell them, I don't care. Put the boys back to work – they are learning nothing from their books. Send them on pilgrimages to some remote areas to search for demons instead of drinking and whoring their days away. Get rid of any woman here who is not priestess, family, or servant. Perhaps if you spend less time in bed you'll pay more attention to your work."

"Yes, Emissary," Gynn said.

"They may try to leave Phrar by ship," Tsingao's thoughts

returned to the fugitive Descendants. He fixed his eyes on the fine mansions of distant Topside as though he could spy them from here. "But they can't get out before high tide tomorrow. You yourself are to visit that gluttonous fop that leads the town council by first light. I want orders for the harbormaster to close the docks, rescind all traveling papers. No one is to leave the bay."

"Yes, Emissary."

"Are there any magic users confined here now?"

"One. Taken when we found the woman. He's restrained."

Tsingao nodded. "Purge him in the morning. At the harbor temple. Let it serve as warning to those who shelter demons."

"He was to be sent south, sire," Gynn objected.

Tsingao slowly turned to face his subordinate, his hooded eyes not even on Gynn's. The face seemed a lifeless mask, not belonging to any man, but some hideous monster made all the more terrifying because of its flat, ordinary features. Gynn leaped back with a squeal before catching himself, and quickly disguised his fright with a hurried bow. "I'll have it done, sire."

FIVE

Galen rose early on the next morning, even before the bulk of the Homeworld began to encroach upon the sky. No one else was awake yet; those of Delann's guests who had spent the night were still sleeping off the evening's excesses and the house was quiet. Feeling restless, he decided to walk to the harbor to continue his exploration of Phrar. He stopped for a quick bite in the kitchen and then headed toward the wharves.

There the day had begun even earlier. Many of the boats had already returned with the first catch and the fish traders were busy hawking their wares or loading them onto carts for transport to elsewhere. The streets were wider here, near the harbor, allowing cargo to be transferred from wharf to warehouse on lumbering, wheel-mounted platforms. On market days this arrangement left plenty of room for sales tables and stalls, roving merchants, animal pens, traveling exhibits, and the antics of entertainers. People were everywhere, buying and selling, strolling, thieving or preparing for journeys to other parts of the moon. Galen walked slowly, enjoying the bustle of the market, his senses alert to the riot of color and noise and the smells drifting on the ocean breeze.

When he found a cloth merchant he handed over a few

triangular coins in exchange for a broad scarf. Observing the fashions of some other men in the crowd, he wrapped it loosely about his head and neck to cover his hair and leave his features in shadow.

Obscured now, he continued along the boisterous confusion of these streets, choosing his direction at random. Although the market was lined with enticing displays of merchandise, most people here seemed to gather to meet others, trade gossip, or produce a jumbled cacophony of noise, apparently music.

"I have me a thought that the breakfast you're wanting is exactly what I've got on the cooker," a raised voice drew his attention when he threaded his way past some stalls specializing in foodstuffs. The smell of things roasting and baking and marinating in spicy sauces seemed to have pointed his feet into this direction. He turned to see a woman standing beside a brazier from which a variety of foods were offered for sale. An infant in a brightly colored sling was asleep on her back and a small girl clung to her skirts, wide eyes on the stranger looming over them.

Galen tugged his hood away from his face and winked down at the child. "From the smell of things I'd say you're thinking right." There was something interesting bubbling on the coals but it wasn't clear if the concave, slowly charring pod that contained it was to be eaten as well or merely served as a cooking utensil. "What's that?" he pointed at some charred lumps of meat beside the pods.

"Tongue."

He looked up. "Whose tongue?" He bypassed a selection of roasted insects and took a skewer of tender meat, choosing one bearing the least resemblance to a sea creature. She handed him a bowl of yellow rice to which she added a ladle of sauce. Galen sighed with pleasure. "This is wonderful," he said and picked up another skewer.

The woman smiled. "Try these. Fresh baked an hour past."

He accepted a flat sort of biscuit. "You're not from here,"

he said to the woman, idly looking over the merchandise displayed on her cart. Besides her delicious ready-made morsels, she also sold fruit, vegetables, and dried meats. Herbs and various other items that he could not name were hung from the rafters of her stall. He studied a bulbous, purple bit of produce, wondering if it was fruit or vegetable. Or quite possibly sentient.

"Eastwards," she confirmed. "How came you to guess it?"

Even his limited experience with Thali's people and geography had allowed him to easily detect her dialect, delivered with an amusing twang. The bright weave of her clothing and a ruddy complexion also hinted at some inland origin. He pointed at one of the baskets. It contained several round balls of cheese; some wrapped in cloth, others in wax. "No one milks the fish around here," he said.

She laughed, a sound as pleasant as her accent. "From the deer of the Chaliss'ya foothills. Our own, and very fine. Will you take some away with you?" She reached for the basket when her gaze moved beyond him to the street. Stepping back, she lowered her head and reached for her daughter as if to shield her from something.

Galen turned to see what had startled the vendor. Four men walked toward them, one of them leading a saddled charger. They were dressed in somber clothing dyed blue, emblazoned with intricate, mysterious designs. Two wore hoods but the others displayed a bold pattern shaved into their closely cropped hair. They were engaged in conversation and paid little attention to the crowd around them, acknowledging neither the people who met them with great deference, as this vendor had, or those who turned away with barely concealed disdain. As they passed Galen, the man leading the animal raised his head to look at him, his eyes stabbing out at the Homeworlder from the depths of his hood. Meeting the hostile stare with a perplexed frown, Galen wondered why he suddenly felt noted and marked.

It was not until the group had rounded a corner that

Galen noticed that the lively clamor of the market had been subdued during their passing and now recovered with fervor defiant in its volume. Baffled, he turned to the woman. "Priests?" he guessed.

"Emissary," she said and described some arcane symbol in the air with one hand. "Many of them in town these days. I even heard tell this morning that the Chief himself has come to Phrar. I had not noticed their number when last I came by, this month past. I say you were not to his liking."

"I'd have to agree." Galen handed her a payment for his second breakfast. "Why do you think there are so many of them here?"

Before she had time to reply, someone came running at the cart at full tilt, barely stopping in time to avoid a collision with the brazier. Galen raised his arm, envisioning the runner, the brazier, and a load of hot coals descending upon the woman and her children. But the newcomer stopped in time, although not quite soon enough to avoid frightening everyone present. The food-seller frowned but said nothing. Her quick glance at Galen was a warning and so he swallowed the reprimand to which he was about to give voice.

"Give us a three-count," the young man, little more than a boy, said breathlessly. He scurried around Galen to help himself to some goods at the far end of the stall. He was barefoot and wore a long blue robe although, Galen noted, there was no priestly emblem shaved into his unruly yellow locks. "Is this all you have?" he exclaimed, rooting through her bins. "Stupid woman! I can't be running from shop to shop, taking all day for this."

Galen scowled and turned to tower over the lout, a cheap yet effective use of his intimidating physique to remind the rude and obnoxious of their manners. When the boy turned back to the vendor, still complaining about the trouble she was causing him, he found himself nose to chest with the stranger. He leaped back with a squawk and dropped his purchases.

The woman stepped quickly around Galen and bent to gather the small lumps into a pouch, her movements nervous. Galen also bent to reach for one of the dropped bits of vegetation but stopped his hand before he could touch it. He withdrew his arm and straightened again, wiping his fingers on his vest as if he had actually handled the stuff. The woman threw him a puzzled look but the youth had other things on his mind. Tossing a payment at the vendor, he ran off again, uphill.

Galen watched the woman dart back behind her brazier, her eyes averted. "You sell poisons?" he asked, astounded. The mushroom she had sold to the youth was not even permitted to grow on the Homeworld. Those who traded in chibane risked the harshest of punishments.

She glanced at him for only an instant before looking away again. She was trembling now. "Poison only to some," she replied with a furtive glance along the street. Galen hoped that she wasn't looking for a guard to raise an alarm.

He pointed in the direction where the boy had run without taking his eyes from the vendor. "What will he do with it?"

She shrugged. "I suppose it's needed at the temple today." She jerked her chin uphill, away from the harbor. She appeared to want to say something further, but then pressed her lips together and lowered her head. Her coy cheerfulness of a few moments ago had disappeared, replaced by distrust and fear.

"I am not a monster," he said sharply, irked by her demeanor and further annoyed when she shrank back. His eyes dropped to the frightened little girl hiding in the folds of the woman's dress. Suddenly ashamed by his reaction he drew back, shaking his head. "I'm sorry," he said. "This is all very strange. Forgive me."

Receiving no response, he sighed and turned away, toward the direction those emissaries and the youth had taken. The vendor startled him by placing a hand on his arm.

"Chenoweth has reasons for the things that are, I'm

certain," she said, barely lifting her eyes to look into his face when he turned back to her. "But the way some wield God-granted powers is beyond the grasping for the likes of me, or mine. Think not that our dread of the emissary is matched by our scorn for the Descendants, for the priests are more deserving of it."

Galen briefly put his hand on hers before she released his arm. Wordlessly, he tugged his cowl over his face and turned away to follow the emissaries uphill.

Something began to seem askew, somehow, as he felt the familiar pull of chi'ro beckon him from a distance. Expecting a riser nearby, he followed his instincts into a wide street leading north along the shore. The contact with yesterday's riser after his ordeal with the La'il had restored him appreciably and he suspected that, instead of thriving on the ambient chi'ro that suffused all things on the Homeworld, here he needed direct, physical contact with a riser to sustain him properly. Perhaps Thali's dreary weather was the cause of the risers' lack of real power. It seemed wise to take advantage of even the most insignificant source.

Although he had left the market he was still surrounded by people, all heading in this same direction. Curious, he watched them enter a stone edifice on a rise overlooking the harbor. It was a massive building with a domed roof; by the size of it he judged it several hundred years old, patched and rebuilt when needed, with smaller doors set into the oversize entrance. This structure seemed to be one of the temples Aletha had described and he let his curiosity lead him inside.

The vast chamber was smoky and dark in unpleasant contrast to the lively morning he had left outside. Walls of huge blocks and rows of square columns disappeared into vague shadows below the ceiling. Murals and tapestries decorated these walls, but the stories they told seemed to depict maritime heroics rather than any sort of recognizable spiritual theme. Worshippers dressed in somber clothing stood in small groups or, for lack of furnishings, sat on small rugs, their eyes on the rituals taking place on a raised dais at the far end of the hall. Not understanding the meanings of the droning chants rising to the soot-stained ceiling, Galen meandered through the throng, pretending to be a worshipper in search of a better vantage point.

He watched robed priestesses walk about on a raised platform where they poured liquids and gestured in some sacred manner while chanting and singing. One of them took a candle from a niche in the wall and, holding it aloft, descended a few steps onto the floor of the hall. The crowd parted respectfully, allowing her and the other priestesses to pass to the middle of the room where the women formed a circle around a shallow pit. Galen peered over their heads to see the makings of a small fire there. The priestess with the taper bowed and touched the flame to the wood. The fire came alive at once, burning brightly and evenly as if the wood had been treated with some combustible oil. The assembled crowd sighed and bowed, and then most began to drift away, their rituals complete for another day.

Galen stayed by the fire. There was something strangely familiar here. He crouched to have a closer look, squinting against the flames. Although the encircling hearth of stones and tiles was blackened and cracked, the ground beneath the burning wood looked like a black, fractured crystal, its gleaming surface unmarred by heat and smoke. This was a launch! He suddenly had no doubt that here was one of the gateways, sealed now like the others, its power only symbolized by fire. Unusable, but still venerated as a link to the gods.

Smiling, Galen looked up as if to share his discovery with someone. But of course no one here would either remember or admit to know about magic conduits. This building, clearly very ancient, had surely been one of the original transport stations to the Homeworld or perhaps Chenoweth. His people hadn't erected churches in nearly a millennium and certainly would not have expended the effort to build one for this new settlement on Thali moon. These stone walls were meant as shelter for people who waited for friends to arrive, perhaps, or maybe there was some sort of immigration procedure to help new arrivals as they stepped through the conduit. Almost all of the launches on the Homeworld showed evidence of having been enclosed at some point. Of course it would have been prudent to protect the gateways so that nothing was accidentally swept into the open conduit.

Galen backed away from the pit when he saw some of the priestesses observe him quizzically from their stage. Loitering by the dead launch for a while longer, he probed it in search of the riser he had felt earlier. But there was nothing there now. Unlike on the Homeworld, there was no abundance of chi'ro nearby to power up the launch. Had it even been a riser he felt earlier?

He turned to leave, intending to find some private place to contact the La'il. If she could activate this crystal it would be a simple matter to sneak into the temple when fewer people were about and step through the aperture with Aletha. Instead of making the long journey back to the mountain, they would be home in mere moments.

A small commotion demanded his attention. The people who had remained here were excited about something happening in the back of the hall, perhaps something out of the ordinary. A low, thrumming sound vibrated through the air now as some unseen acolyte strummed a drumharp to the accompaniment of low murmurs from the crowd. Galen studied their faces and saw a peculiar mixture of dread and curiosity, as if something unpleasant was about to happen. The sort of unpleasantness that always seemed to invite onlookers and thrill seekers.

He followed their gaze to see a group of people enter the hall. A dozen men or more, dressed in long robes dyed in shades of blue, approached the center of the temple, struggling with someone held in their midst. Galen frowned when he realized that this was some sort of prisoner, obviously brought here against his will. His clothes were torn and dirty and he bled from several wounds. Galen was accustomed to dealing with criminals who violently resisted arrest, but he wondered why they would bring someone to justice inside a place of worship.

The captive was led to the defunct launch, where he was made to stand at its edge. His hands were bound and he wore a wide metal collar attached to a long pole. It was this pole that allowed his captors to control him from a safe distance. The man stood trembling, staring into the fire still burning on the seal as though it was a bottomless pit into which he was about to be cast. Then he looked up and his eyes found Galen, standing on the opposite side of this altar.

Galen groaned. This was an adept! Captured by the emissaries, he was about to meet his fate as these men prepared to follow the decree set out by their deities centuries ago. It had not been a riser he had felt earlier, but this man's desperate attempts to find enough chi'ro to save himself from the zealots.

His thoughts reached out to the doomed adept as he tried to find some way to help him escape from this nightmare. He recalled Yala's warnings that, however unlikely, these emissaries were able to perceive chi'ro surges. If this were true, at this close range, surrounded by both emissaries and a crowd hungry for a spectacle, he would not escape detection and capture. The man was indifferent to Galen's guarded mental nudge although there was undoubtedly some talent there that perceived it. Galen recalled the hurried purchase of chibane in the market and realized that, unless he was able to send a tremendous amount of chi'ro to the captive, nothing would help him escape his stupor.

Helplessly, he watched one of the emissaries move toward the man, his fists raised to the ceiling, each holding a long, thin blade. After a brief incantation he crossed his arms in front of the adept's throat and, cutting deep, uncrossed them again in a swift, savage motion. He quickly stepped aside to let his victim pitch into the fire, sending a whirlwind of sparks to the smoke-shrouded ceiling.

Galen staggered backward, wanting only to be away from

here. Turning to the entrance, he bumped into the person behind him, nearly flinging him to the ground.

"Careful, friend," the man said, making a point of straightening his clothes. His robes were blue.

Galen realized now that there were emissaries everywhere, scattered among the onlookers or gathered in small groups, intent on the sacrifice. Some of them had taken notice of his odd behavior and he felt their suspicion and curiosity reach out to him. Was the hooded man in the back the same that had stared at him in the market? Several of the priests began to drift closer; someone pointed at him and whispered something to another.

"Yago, by the Gods!" someone suddenly hissed. "Have you seen enough?"

Galen turned to see a young emissary, his cowl thrown back to reveal Chenoweth's sigil shaved into his hair, hurry toward them. His eyes were on the man whom Galen had tackled and his expression was one of annoyance and impatience. "It's time to go! The others are waiting and here you are, watching them fry demons. If we don't get to the bridge we'll end up having to walk all the way to Topside. And Dazai help us if Tsingao finds the witch and doesn't have enough people to capture her."

Upon hearing the chief emissary's name the man named Yago turned away from Galen without sparing him another thought. "How many people has he got searching the place?" he asked, hurrying after his colleague, long robes billowing in the haste of their departure.

* * *

Aletha heard the front door of Delann's home slam and then voices in the hall.

"Aletha!" one of the twins shouted up the broad staircase. "Quick!"

She hurried to the landing outside her room and looked down. "What's happened?" She was alarmed by the grim expression on his face. "Where's… your brother?"

"He'll meet us at the harbor, at Delann's warehouse. Get your things. We're leaving this place. Now." Chor loped up the stairs to help her collect their belongings. They hastily gathered clothing and the twins' weapons before he rushed her downstairs again, past the bewildered maid.

"The town is infested with emissaries," he explained at last, standing by the front entrance open just wide enough to allow him to peer outside. "Galen had a close call in town. Chenoweth priests are everywhere and some are being sent up here to search Topside." Chor fastened a long dagger to his belt. "Who is this chief emissary? Delann is almost beside himself."

"Gods!" she breathed, her face bloodless. Somehow her legs seem to have lost the ability to hold her upright. "Tsingao? He's here? In Phrar?" She held her bundle tightly in her arms as if to hide behind it. "If he's come to Phrar then he's got reason to be. They say he can uncover any Descendant, no matter how well they're hidden. Chenoweth commands him and he follows only the dictates of the gods. And he won't just execute them like criminals! His sacrifices are celebrations to Chenoweth; sometimes he waits until they've captured a whole group of them. There are such dreadful stories..."

Chor grasped her arm, almost painfully. "Stop this, Aletha," he said. "Tales grow with the telling, you said so yourself. Remembering them won't help us get out of here." He glanced at the door. "There is no one out there now. You'll have to lead us down to the wharves without using the main roads. Can you do this?"

She looked back into the safe, comfortable interior of the house before taking a deep, not quite steady, breath. Then she exhaled forcefully and gritted her teeth. "Try to keep up, Homeworlder."

Once outside, they slipped through the side gate of Delann's estate and scrambled through a maze of rear gardens, service roads and bridle paths until those turned into the cobbled alleys of the lower quarters. Twice, they sensed the presence of several men rushing toward them, forcing them to hide breathlessly until the mob moved by. At last, the sound of gulls and the unmistakable smell of seaside offal, hot tar, and fish in various states of existence announced that they had reached the harbor. Aletha led them past several warehouses until they arrived at their destination.

Her young friend, Yala, loitered by the entrance, posted there by Delann as lookout. They hurried through a side door to the end of a long corridor. Delann's office was furnished with the same dark wood and artwork that graced his home, along with a profusion of books and charts and the tools of his trade. Sunlight slanting through opaque glass cast a mellow gleam over the room. They found Delann and Galen there, bent over some maps.

"You don't think we can hide somewhere until this calms down a bit?" Galen was saying when they entered.

"And risk more of her friends?" Delann replied tersely. He looked up. "There you are. I was beginning to worry."

Galen watched him embrace Aletha. "Delann is going to take us through the islands in one of his ships tonight, at high tide," he explained. He tossed another of the rough-spun headscarves to Chor. "We'll go on alone from there. I suppose they had to catch up with you sooner or later."

"*She* was doing quite well," Delann said, not looking at the twins. "They're after *you*. Two dark men, from the north, who are spreading evil magic throughout the quarter."

Galen cursed. "I'm sorry, Delann."

"Don't worry about me, wizard," Delann said, a bitter note in his voice. "Although you could have told me what you were. I can deal with the emissaries – some of them are well supplied from my stores."

Galen sighed, sad to hear the scorn in the merchant's words. "Is the way south to the river still open?"

"That wouldn't get you very north, would it?" Delann's gesture invited them to study his maps. "I know you're not going inland. Nothing there but more emissaries. I suggest we run you across the strait and drop you with the dinghy on this side of the outer islands. Aletha knows every corner of shoreline there. The lagoons are crawling with small vessels this time of year and they can't all be stopped and searched. You should be able to reach Riva Sound before dark. Safe after that; I can't imagine they'll bother chasing Descendants all the way out there. You can then thread your way through the islands northwards and come back to the mainland by crossing the open water right here." He stabbed a pointed measuring tool at a narrow channel between some islands and the continent. "Follow the shoreline back south to Harlyn, a nice enough town where you can disappear for a while. We'll see about laying a false trail south, as if you fled upriver to Marandha. I'll send a message when things calm down here."

Aletha peered at the map and then looked up at Galen. "Before you say anything, yes, it looks shorter taking the coast road but it'll be safer on the water. Trust us with that." She turned to Delann. "I hope someday I can repay you for all you're doing for me. It means so much to me."

He lifted his hand to brush the back of his fingers over her pale cheek. His gaze hardened when he turned it upon Galen. "Just get her someplace where she can live in peace. It's the only payment I need."

"Del, someone here to have a word," Yala's voice came from the dimly lit corridor outside the office. "Important, he says."

"I'll meet him outside." Delann called to her and left, closing the door behind him.

"Are you all right?" Galen said to Aletha. She stood pale and silent, arms wrapped tightly about herself. "Worried about the priests?"

She nodded and bent over the scattered maps, careful to avoid his eyes. "This is getting complicated. I know those islands but it's a long way away. I'm afraid that…" she hesitated, unable to explain her fears. "I'm afraid," she said simply.

"You're probably thinking you'd be safer if you'd just

stayed hidden. Do you regret leaving this town? This moon?"

"No," she whispered.

"Of me?" he said sharply. "Of us? You are afraid of us? Because of last night?"

"No!" she turned from the maps. "I'm afraid for Delann, for his people, for you. This is all so much trouble, so much grief. I've known for a while now it was time to leave this place and I should have been long gone. I'm a danger to you all." She lifted a hand to touch his chest. "But I'm glad I don't have to do this alone."

He looked down at her hand and then raised his eyes to search her face. She did not have to be a magic user to see the concern not only showing in his face but something she would have felt even if the room had been in complete darkness. He put his hand over hers. "You are not alone," he said softly.

"Well, that's a plan gone down the river!" Both Galen and Aletha flinched when Delann burst into the room, his exclamation sounding as aggravated as his expression looked. He waved a piece of paper at Chor but paused when he saw Aletha's unhappy face. "What's wrong, other than what I'm about to tell you?"

Galen stepped away from her. "She doesn't want you to get into trouble over her."

Delann sighed loudly and wagged a finger at Aletha. "And you think you have some magic that can stop me? Huh? Can we get to serious matters now, please?"

Aletha had to smile. "What's happened?"

"They're locking down the harbor! Damn emissaries. Once the harbormaster gets his orders, no one leaves the bay. By the time we can move out on the tide those orders will be in his hand."

Galen cursed under his breath. "What if we tried to get out now?"

Delann looked at him as though he had suggested flying to Chenoweth. "The tide is about to turn, wizard. It's going out! No way will we get through the islands now." Delann began to pace about the room, rubbing his hands through his short yellow hair until it bore a startling resemblance to Yala's.

"How about traveling inland? We'd have to get over those mountains but there must be a way to turn north from there."

Aletha nodded. "There is, but they're at war there. They've been brawling since winter. I'm not sure we want to get caught up in that. They'll conscript anyone and I don't intend to fight someone else's battles. We might be safe in a caravan. What do you think, Delann? Can you spare some of your people?"

"You'll be stopped for certain. No, you'll go by ship. Now, like he suggested. But we'll run south through the kelp flats for a few leagues and heave to in Ayrlie. Pick up some hides from my warehouse or something. As long as we're not searched we'll be fine. I pay people to make sure I don't get searched. Once the tide is up we'll get through the islands and into the strait. Let's go."

* * *

The distance from Delann's warehouse to his ship was a matter of minutes along a narrow alley and out onto the pier. Yala leading the way, they hurried past freighters and galleys, skirting stacks of cargo and passenger queues, meeting no trouble until Delann abruptly halted and shoved Aletha behind a passage broker's booth.

"Emissaries. On the wharf!" He gestured for the others to join them behind the stall. He looked up at the towering twins. Although their burnooses hid their easily-recognized features, they only served to make the imposing figures more menacing. "This would be a lot simpler if you weren't so obviously strangers here!"

"I'll learn their purpose," Yala said and darted away from them, toward a tall ship waiting a few hundred paces away, before anyone thought to object. They watched from their hiding place as the girl made a nuisance of herself, badgering the seamen with questions and worrying the emissaries with thoughts of pick pocketing.

Galen studied the pier. Several freighters, a sow-bellied ferry, and a dashing cutter or two were tied to the wharf where there was steady traffic from dock to deck as cargo and passengers were loaded. Although the waterfront was bustling with activity, none of it seemed unduly hurried, as might be the case if the impending order to close the harbor were common knowledge. "Which one is yours?"

"The brig with the yellow foresail," Delann replied with some pride. "The *Ruane*. Should be ready to sail. Your boat's already been hoisted up."

"Fine ship," Galen said appreciatively. Although he knew little about sail ships he could see that this one was built for speed as well as long distance hauls. The small single-mast dinghy they were to use later in the day had been hoisted into a cradle at the stern, not an unusual accessory for any ship too large to enter the shallow lagoons to take on fresh water, passengers or cargo. "What's that gear on the ship beside her?"

Delann looked at the massive frigate Galen had pointed out. "Weaponry," he explained. "Those racks along the side can hurl a dozen spears a great distance. The catapults there are for tossing burning tar at enemy sails. The shields are for the crossbow marksmen." He saw that Aletha had gone pale. "That ship is not for us, Aletha. That arsenal is defensive and the ship's for transporting troops and supplies. The emissaries aren't known to hunt Descendants with ships of war." He pointed out two almost identical single-mast cutters on the next pier, also equipped with shields and catapults. "Those worry us. Smaller, faster, and they can get into the straits between the islands. As likely belonging to the coastwatch as to fly a pirate's banner once out of sight."

"What is she doing?" Aletha interrupted.

The others scanned the wharf for Yala and soon spotted her near the clutch of emissaries. She had crouched down as if inspecting something on the ground. Now and again she poked at it with a stick.

"Having a listen, I'll guess," Delann grinned. "Don't worry so; she knows to keep out of their way." He turned to the twins. "Yala's mother was taken away by the emissaries. I don't think she remembers much of that, but not a day goes by where she doesn't visit some grief upon at least one of them."

"And someday it'll get her killed," Aletha scowled.

"Her mother was a Descendant?" Galen asked.

Delann glanced at Aletha before shaking his head. "No. Just pretty. One of the emissaries wanted to take her as mistress, but she was a freewoman and of course had the right to refuse him. He offered her wealth and when that didn't change her mind her husband was set upon by some thugs. They broke his knees. He was left unable to work but instead of taking up the emissary's offer she complained to the magistrate. She was denounced as a demon Descendant. She wasn't purged for some time. Until then she worked in the emissaries' enclave near the delta. Many of the female Descendants end up there for a while."

"Stop it," Aletha hissed angrily.

Delann put his hand on her arm in silent apology but continued anyway. "All but the *real* Descendants. The true magic users can only be drugged for so long and emissaries fear them more than they fear the wrath of the gods. If you are discovered you won't be locked up for long."

"How do they prove their case?"

"They don't," Aletha snapped. "The gods speak to them and show them the way. And sometimes they are even right."

Galen frowned. "How often?"

"Enough for us to believe there is some truth to it," she said. "Of course, most of them use their blue robes to lord over the people with more power than is wielded even by town council. No one opposes them. In anything. Yala's mother is not the first to discover that."

"Here she comes," Delann said, ending the conversation.

Yala now ambled back to them, detouring to balance across a precarious conveyor rail with careless grace, like all children of her age assured of her own invincibility.

"Those four of 'em is all," she reported upon her return. "No more to be seen. Marlo said none been asking questions or paying much mind to the *Ruane*. But they're watching. Except I don't think they're watching any particular ship."

"Well, that is good to hear," Delann said. He peered around the stall to survey the busy dock. "I wonder how long they'll be hanging around."

"There'll be more of them," Yala said. "Ship coming in from Tandalay before the tide. More emissaries and some soldiers. They're looking for someone." She grinned up at the twins. "Big Inlander killed an emissary this morning. Right in the enclave itself! Came upon him at prayer and gave his brains a stir until they turned to soup. There was a guardsman nearby and the demon's icy breath froze his soul. They'll not stop till they've found the magic user and cut his throat."

Delann and Aletha gasped in unison.

"An emissary?"

"You didn't!"

Galen scowled at the urchin. "Of course I didn't. Nor could I. Brain stirring? Ice breath? Must we send a child to listen to stories like that?"

Yala giggled. "I just tell what goes in these ears. I know you didn't harm no emissary. Been following you since you left Del's house this morning. For a warrior you're not paying much mind to what's about you, Mister."

Delann squeezed the back of Yala's neck and gave her a gentle shake. "Don't frighten us like that," he said before turning back to the others. "Looks like waiting isn't an option. Now how do we get you on board?"

Galen studied the waterfront and the characters populating it. Both twins removed their expensive vests, boots and belts and tied them into a bundle that they handed to Delann. "We'll join those loaders." Galen nodded toward a line of deckhands carrying bales and boxes onto a waiting ship. "Do you often bring women aboard, Delann?"

Delann frowned. "What? Uh, sometimes," he said with a sidelong glance at Aletha.

"Ladies?"

"Not always," the merchant grinned, now guessing Galen's plan. "Take off your vest, Aletha."

"What for?" she said but shrugged out of her knee-length overvest.

"What have you got on under there?" Galen gestured at her shirt.

She frowned. "Nothing you should be wondering about—" she faltered when she realized their intent. Sighing dramatically, she unlaced the front of her blouse to improve the view and then knotted up its hem to leave her midriff bare. Finally, she tugged the waistband of her baggy trousers to below her navel. "How's this?"

Galen appraised her for longer than was absolutely necessary, aware of Delann's discomfort. "Nice. How much per throw, wench?"

Delann rolled his eyes. "Let's get going already."

Aletha hugged Yala and gave her messages to take to their friends, explaining and apologizing for her unexpected departure. Before things could threaten to turn tearful, she clasped Delann's arm. "Care to show a lady around your ship, esquire?" She batted her lashes at him.

Together, they strolled along the wharf, brightly chatting and giggling, his high color as easily a sign of his libertine intentions as it might have been of his state of anxiety. Aletha was not the only woman hanging on a sailor's arm on this pier, where soldiers and dockworkers also had their pick of companions for hire. Apparently oblivious to the loitering priests on the wharf, the couple promenaded past them to the gangway, where Delann stopped to chat with one of the crewmen. Aletha threw him a flirtatious wink before going aboard, simpering coyly when several sailors rushed to help her step down onto the deck. Delann climbed to the forecastle to speak to his captain.

Soon, they saw one of the twins amble toward them among a group of porters, a bale of cloth balanced on his shoulder to hide his face. Not long later, the other twin followed, bent low over the cart he was pushing. Once both of them were aboard, Delann gave the order to put out to sea and head southward.

Galen found his assumptions about the ship's seaworthiness to be correct: she ran easily before a strong wind from the north and seemed to fly along the coast despite the receding tide already nipping at her heels. He was accustomed to much faster modes of transport on the Homeworld, where chi'ro allowed them to power aircraft and passenger vehicles of all description, but there was something strangely exhilarating about this ship. Standing near the bowsprit, he felt as though he were riding some strange mythical beast, somehow brought to life by the power of the wind that he perceived as keenly as any surge of chi'ro. The ship seemed alive, her sails straining against the confines of the rigging, banners snapping exuberantly in the wind. With regret he gave up the fantasy when the *Ruane* slowed to struggle against the tide, soon limping south along the coast as if dragging some immense weight behind her. Someone reminded him of the mundane by calling him to share a midday meal.

He found his companions on the quarterdeck with a few of the off-duty sailors, out of the way of the crew. Someone had brought food and wine but neither twin was particularly hungry.

"Not seasick, are you?" Aletha inquired, grinning mischievously.

Chor grimaced into the shared vat of boiled noodles and greasy fish. "I will be if I eat that," he said. "Someone's following us." He answered Aletha's unspoken question with a curt nod. Emissaries.

Indeed, not long later the lookout reported a ship in pursuit. The approaching cutter appeared to be on a straight course toward them, still too distant to identify by build or banner.

None of the sailors seemed inclined to question why another vessel would pursue them. Galen suspected that Delann's cargo was not always part of the legal transactions of Phrar, evidenced by a tight-lipped crew and their efficient departure from the harbor. He had seen panniers of messenger birds doted upon by their handler and noticed that some of the crew had little to do but walk about well-armed. Was Delann a smuggler? A pirate, perhaps? It was an oddly intriguing theory; perhaps there were some interesting ways of making a living on this moon, after all. He was amused to realize that, in spite of his pretense of prosperous gentility, Delann was as much of a felon as any of the harbor rabble.

The crew, however, did not know that the contraband on board was three Descendants and not whatever ill-gotten treasures might be concealed in the holds below. Galen looked south along the shore. "More coming. From over there."

Delann vented a series of ripe curses. "That's coming from Ayrlie." He went to the quarterdeck rail and ordered his men to arms. The mood of the crew changed at once. Barefooted sailors leaped from the shrouds to the deck or came from the holds below, swords were brandished and crossbows readied. Delann used a crystal spyglass to scan the shore. "They've dispatched more cutters. That's a lot of trouble over a bunch of Descendants. Are you sure you didn't kill that priest?"

Aletha gripped his arm. "There'll be soldiers aboard those ships and that's bad enough," she whispered urgently. "But in another moment your crew will see the blue robes. Will they stand against emissaries?"

Delann paled. "Emissaries? On those ships?" He looked over his men preparing for battle. Many of them had sailed on his ships for years and had had to defend his payload against pirates, thieves and even the greed of customs officials on numerous occasions. The lot of them were god-fearing men but ashore were more often found in the alehouses of the wharves than in the temples. None of them were likely to regard an emissary with any fondness. "Perhaps they would," he said. "But I'm not sure that I can."

"Go through the islands," Galen said. "Before we have to find out."

"Have you lost your mind? This is a brigantine, not some flatfooted gorge raft. We'll be chopped to kindling!" Delann gestured at the islands rising into the air as the sea level dropped with the receding tide. Black, glistening rock beckoned them with treacherous edges.

Galen gripped Delann's arms. He jerked his chin toward Aletha. "We are Descendants," he reminded him. "Demons the likes of which you have never seen. I saw them kill a Descendant this morning, probably Aletha's friend you were talking about yesterday. Whoever this Tsingao is, he's not going to let us go. If you want to get out of this, order your ship into the islands and take your hands off the rudder!"

All realized that a stunned silence had fallen and the startled crew, weapons uneasily at the ready, had gathered around Galen and Delann. Time froze in this silence until, finally, Delann waved them away and pulled out of Galen's grasp. "On your head, wizard," he said and turned to his captain. "Change course for Tamtam. To the strait."

"Sire? The devil tide is in the channels!" Astonishment mixed with grumbled objections until angry shouts rose from the sailors. The *Ruane* would surely be tossed through the chasms of the islands like an umbrella in a hurricane.

"Fire!" the lookout suddenly cried. "They're readying fire slings! Gods, what brought this upon us?" The cutter that followed was close enough for everyone aboard to see the torches lit, ready to ignite missiles to hurl at *Ruane*'s sails.

Delann shoved Aletha toward the shelter of the forecastle. "Get down!" he yelled at the twins.

"Watch out!" Aletha screamed as a fireball tore past his head and exploded in a shower of spark and flame on the deck. Galen whirled about to see more missiles speed toward them, lobbed with astonishing range and accuracy. Another missed the mainsail and landed on forecastle, splashing burning threads of whatever it was made of onto Aletha and the crew that cowered there.

Chor leaped to the railing and focused on the ship closest to the *Ruane*. He saw the blue-robed passengers among the crew, mostly standing agape at the railing, perhaps no more familiar with sea battles than he was. He raised his hands and a wall of water rose from the surface of the bay as if a giant had drawn a curtain between the two ships. The wall crashed over the pursuing ship, drenching the incendiary weapons, attacking the sails to throw them askew and tangle their rigging. Galen, beside him, drew a smaller waterspout from the tide, raised it over their heads, and then let it crash onto *Ruane*'s tarred deck to extinguish the flames.

The men aboard the *Ruane* were as astonished as those on the other ship. "Descendant!" someone shouted, pointing at the twins. "Magic!"

"The very same that will get us through the islands," Delann snapped. "To your posts! Strike the sails." He threw a worried look in Aletha's direction before jogging up the ladder to his bewildered captain. His men scattered, avoiding the twins and Aletha, to follow his orders.

Slowly, the *Ruane* came about and tacked toward the island channels. Those whose hands were not busy with easing the ship into the rapidly more powerful current stared in wonder as the looming cliffs approached, seeming impossibly high now, the water at their feet black and ominous.

"They're coming after us!" Aletha cried. Two of the coastguard cutters were in pursuit.

Galen took her hand and pulled her to the front of the ship. "Don't let go," he said. Chor took her other hand.

She nodded, gaping at the cliffs towering over them. She saw trees and buildings up there and clusters of people who gawked in disbelief, waving their arms to warn the ships entering the narrow channels with some of their sails still up. "May the gods find us all," she whispered.

Galen also had a few prayers but his dealt mainly with cursing the La'il's name. He watched the serrated rock faces close in on the ship, fringed with churning foam thrown up against boulders jutting into the channel. The walls loomed so tall now that the sun was blocked out and they hurtled onward in shadow. Aletha rocked on her feet when a wave broke over the side of the ship and drenched her to the skin. Galen moved his hand to grip her wrist and felt her do the same before half-turning to shout over his shoulder. "Release the rudder!" The helmsman stared at him in disbelief, no more able to release the wheel than he would have been able to leap voluntarily overboard at this moment. Cursing, Galen waved his free hand toward the man to throw him onto a stack of coiled rope. He remained there, resigned to his fate. None of the crew were moving now, able to do nothing more than watch the craggy cliffs rush past or stare at the demons in wonder.

Galen and Chor, with Aletha between them, raised their free hands toward the walls of the chasm. *Ruane* bucked under their feet, her keel unable to handle currents like these and all of them felt her thrash angrily in the rushing water. The twins struggled to create a cushion of chi'ro between the foundering ship and the rock. Not a difficult task as he had planned it, but repelling the enemy ship had badly drained the twins' resources. "Can you feel it," he gasped. "Can you touch that?"

"Touch what? Galen, I can't…"

"The riser. Feel it, Aletha. Like you did yesterday!"

"I feel it!" she shouted. "From over there somewhere!"

He did not hear. Using her talents to augment their own, the twins drew upon the riser to keep the ship in mid-channel, careening dangerously through the narrows. "Delann!" Galen shouted. "Where the hell are we going?"

Delann scrambled across the pitching deck to where three Descendants stood. "Starboard!" he yelled, no longer doubting the twins' ability to steer this vessel. "See those flags at the top of the cliffs? Follow the yellow ones. That way leads to the Great Strait." He raced to the railing to look back the way they had come. One of the cutters, smaller and more agile than the *Ruane*, followed closely, too closely, the second one farther behind. Blue-robed men could be seen aboard those ships, clinging to the rigging in terror. Delann nearly toppled overboard when the *Ruane* lurched sharply to turn into another channel. Barnacle-encrusted rock whipped past his face within reach of his hand. Frozen, he watched the emissary ship miss the turn and smash heavily into the rocks, crumpling like a child's paper boat.

The adepts at the bow were oblivious to anything but the rocks rushing past. They seemed nailed to the deck, swaying with the pitch of the ship as though part of it, looking for the markers that would lead them out of the labyrinthine channels. The next turn was a tight one and a wave towered up beside the *Ruane* to crash onto the deck. Chor stumbled against Aletha and lost his grip on her hand when she slipped. Quickly, the twins scooped her up and fumbled for some ropes swinging loose from the yardarm. All three of them now huddled there, arms tightly linked, the twins' attention once more on the walls of the gorge. Wedged between them and trembling, Aletha buried her face against someone's chest, not wanting to see, waiting for the ugly sound of splintering timber.

Again and again, *Ruane* switched channels, somehow remaining upright, somehow keeping her distance from the walls of the chasm and the boulders strewn about the bottom. The crew, having conquered the worst of their fears, dared to breathe again and looked around in amazement, pointing at the rocks jutting into the channel and even whooping victoriously when they passed without crashing into them. The second of the emissary ships no longer pursued them; no one here assumed it to be still in one piece.

Finally, after uncounted turns, the *Ruane* passed through a narrow portal and abruptly found herself in open water, still tugged along by the ebb, but out of danger. Bright daylight greeted their entrance into the Great Strait and everyone aboard except for the Descendants turned in wonder to watch the islands loom behind them. A raucous cheer rose into the air as the men yelled themselves hoarse, free of the terror that had possessed them during the headlong rush through the chasms.

Galen, Chor and Aletha drew apart, slowly, dazed, fighting to remain on their feet. But none of them had the strength to stand and, one by one, collapsed slowly onto the deck, clutching one another for support.

* * *

Aletha came around first, finding herself still on the deck, sprawled across one of the twins. Or parts of both of them. The ship was once again under full sail and a makeshift canopy had been erected over the unconscious Descendants to shade them from the sun as they recovered. A warm breeze tugged at this shelter, drying their clothes and cheerily snapping the canvas as if to wake them. Seabirds cawed relentlessly overhead and she felt someone's heartbeat through the quilted vest under her cheek. She felt drowsy and insubstantial but also strangely comfortable - remaining like this seemed a pleasant way to spend an afternoon. She blinked tiredly at the banners flying above the ship, aware of Delann anxiously waiting nearby. The twins began to stir and one of them reached around her waist to rearrange her gently as he sat up, as if finding her draped over himself was a daily occurrence. It took some time before all of them were sitting upright, owlishly blinking about themselves. Delann passed around cups of water.

One of the twins, Galen perhaps, rose to his feet like a man in the grip of a massive hangover. "Where are we?"

"Halfway across the strait." Delann glanced at Aletha but then had to look away.

She ran her fingers through her tangled curls, feeling tired and disheveled. "I'm sorry we got you into this, Delann."

He shrugged. "Into what? Pirates approached us and we got sucked into the current when we tried to flee. It happens. We'll reach the South Islands in a few hours. I'll send *Ruane* from there on a trade mission while I get a passage on another ship home. No one will know I was gone. We'll be all right. I doubt any of these men will want to say much about what they've seen here today. Not while there are dead emissaries washing up in the islands."

"Those aren't your fault, Delann!"

He shrugged again. Fault in this matter was irrelevant. While defying the emissary in anything was an unpardonable crime, injuring one meant the forfeit of his life and also the forfeit of his eventual place on Chenoweth. He was stunned to not only find himself in these troubles but to have dragged his men into his damnation, as well. For a dizzying instant he considered rallying his crew to rise up against the Descendants and deliver them to the emissaries who surely still followed and so redeem himself in the eyes of the law and his gods. He looked into Aletha's worried face and remained silent.

"Is anyone hurt?" Galen asked.

"Some burns. They're being seen to below."

He nodded. "I can help with that." But when he turned to the hatch leading to the crew quarters, one of the silent sailors that loitered nearby moved to bar his way.

"Don't," Aletha said quietly. She glanced at the other twin. "Leave them alone."

He frowned but then shrugged in resignation.

Aletha embraced Delann awkwardly, distressed when he flinched at her touch. "Please don't be angry, Delann. I didn't know they'd be so persistent in coming after us."

"You must be worth the trouble. And them," he added, meaning the twins. "What kind of dem... Descendants are you? How did you do this? What magic is this? I don't understand this at all."

She was saddened by the resentment coloring his tone. He'd always known that she was a Descendant and accepted it like some eccentricity politely kept private. But now, aided by the demons that accompanied her, she had displayed her cursed origins in a way that left no doubt that she was the reason that emissaries existed on this moon. They were no longer peers; she had now truly left Phrar behind and stepped into the world belonging to Galen and Chor.

Troubled by this, she turned to the twins who were watching them in silence. She wanted to talk to them about the strange sensation she had felt while the magic, this chi'ro, cursed through her during their flight through the islands. They had been joined, somehow, as if they had become one being, its only ambition to shape the chi'ro into a tangible force to hold their ship on course. And why had their efforts exhausted them so? Once clear of the deadly currents, she had felt as if every bit of strength had been sapped from her body. She started to say something, but one of the twins shook his head in a minute gesture and moved to pull Delann to his feet.

"Drop us off as soon as you can, as planned," he said to Delann. "If what happened back there is an example of what's to come we'll be pursued as soon as they can get through the islands. Besides, I think your crew is ready to throw us overboard."

Delann nodded. "They'll not want magic users aboard. We will reach the edge of the outer islands by midafternoon. Aletha knows the way from there."

The *Ruane* completed her journey across the open water without encountering other battleships. Once hidden from view in one of the numerous inlets, the nervous crew moved quickly to lower the dinghy to the water, glad to be rid of their dangerous cargo. The new craft was a small one, without much room to move about but large enough for their gear, Aletha, and the long-limbed twins. They would have to make camp on dry land rather than sleep in the boat. The twins applied their powerful bodies to rowing their vessel away from the tall ship into the open water where Aletha was able to set the sail. The breeze carried them into the shallow straits between the islands and it was not long before even the tips of *Ruane*'s sails had vanished.

"Gods, I miss him already," Aletha said. Her and Delann's good-byes had been tearful and prolonged but Galen suspected that it wasn't just this one friend to whom she referred. Although there had been many of her acquaintances at Delann's home last night, some of her dearest friends were not the sort that frequented the mansions above the harbor and she had not said farewell to any of them.

"You'll see them again," Galen said automatically.

"Will I?" she replied flatly. She sat on a small bench, her hand on the rudder, curls whipping about her face as she looked forlornly back across the strait.

"I'm sorry, Aletha. You could have used a little more time to get ready to leave."

She turned to look at him but her eyes were filled with tears and he doubted that she saw anything at all. When he leaned forward to touch her cheek the tears spilled over his fingers but she remained composed, silent. Slowly, she put her hand over his, holding it for a moment before pulling it away. "I'll never be like them again, will I?"

He hesitated before shaking his head.

"Will I be like you?"

This time he held his pause longer. "That is up to you," he said finally, thinking of the La'il. "You can be whatever you want."

"A goddess?" she said, without any intonation he was able to interpret.

"Aletha, I—"

She lifted her hand to wave away his reply. "Perhaps you are gods; perhaps I am one, too. Those are just words now, aren't they? Last night, after we went back to the house, I stayed up for a while. I cried. I grieved, I guess, for the gods I knew. The ones that are gone now. For me, anyway. I can't go with you unless I believe what you say. I choose to believe." She looked at her hands. "I've already changed, somehow. Believing changed me. Touching the magic changed me. I suspect I'll keep changing." She looked up and bent from the waist to lean closer to Galen. "But I won't change who I am. I saw what your... La'il did to you. I will be an adept but I will not be a goddess. Not like that."

He drew back from the intensity of her expression. How much of the La'il had she seen last night? "I know you're nothing like that," he said.

She turned to scan the shoreline and adjusted the tiller. He saw her take a deep breath and let it out again. "Of course," she said, her voice steady. "We needn't worry about this now. Here we are, mighty gods of Thali, floating about in a little tub in the middle of nowhere, running away from the emissaries. Hardly dignified. Are you sure we shouldn't be rushing to meet the La'il on thunderous clouds or on the back of a saber whale or something?"

Galen chuckled. "Appropriate but unfortunately impossible. How about you teach me how to sail this tub, Captain?"

She cocked her head. "You don't seem the sailor types."

Over the next few hours Aletha's usual high spirits returned. She was a skillful mariner and seemed to enjoy their trip as she showed them how to direct the boat by moving the sails to take advantage of the light breeze. She chatted about her past seafaring experiences and they talked about many things of little importance.

Galen noticed that she avoided further talk of gods and magic and what might be in store for her. He, too, steered clear of the subject; perhaps it was for the best. They would soon be away from here and then the La'il would initiate Aletha into her rightful place on the Homeworld. She would learn the ways of the adept and discover the extent of her abilities using safe, tightly controlled techniques. Everyone whose latent talent surfaced during adolescence had to endure years of adjustment and rigorous training before mastering their abilities, fitting into his or her place within the society of adepts that steered the Homeworld. Aletha was already well past the age where training began and, he was certain now, had a gift surpassed only by that of the La'il, making La'il her only possible choice for mentor. The thought of La'il taking anyone under her wing filled Galen with a strange sort of unease.

By late afternoon they were completely surrounded by hundreds of islands. It seemed impossible to determine where one ended and another began or how one could find a course through the ever-present sandbanks, weed-choked narrows and keel-scraping submerged rocks. Yet Aletha never faltered in choosing their direction, apparently steering by sense of smell or some internal compass possessed only by the island dwellers. As Delann had promised, the waters out here were busy with traffic from across the strait, mostly fishing boats dragging for crustaceans and spear fishers stalking the shallows. They discovered that in their haste to leave Phrar no food and water had yet been put on board although the rest of their gear had already been stowed. They would have to find a trading post or seafaring merchant before long.

"Now I suppose I'll have to teach you how to fish, too, Homeworlder," she teased him. Not particularly worried about their shortages and confident that the twins were able to manage the boat across the stretch of open water ahead of them, Aletha curled up among their packs and parcels and promptly fell asleep. Galen watched her for a while, not for the first time affected by the frailty so deceptively harboring a powerful mind. How had she survived so far? He imagined her at the mercy of the emissaries, teetering helplessly at the edge of the sacrificial bowl, and shuddered. Maybe it was possible to begin teaching her to use her gifts to protect herself. To hell with La'il's cautions!

They sailed past ever more remote island groups where fewer and fewer boats and ships crossed their wake until there was only the occasional trade junket in the distance, journeying in floating caravans to foil pirates. A blue-plumed bird rose from a shoreline tree and swooped toward their boat to caw noisily at the intruders. It was not any sort of bird they had seen before. Although it had the stilt-like legs of a wading bird, its feet ended in fierce talons more appropriate for a raptor. Feeling somewhat surreal, Galen shooed it away when it tried to perch on the bow of the boat. He checked the fishing line, needing to keep his mind on undemanding tasks and find a way to turn this strange trip to Thali into some sort of vacation, where at the end he and Chor could simply return home and pick up where they left off. But like that annoying bird, unbidden thoughts continued to swoop into his mind, distracting him and vying for his attention. The ugly scene in Phrar's temple continued to haunt him.

Galen's eyes fell on his twin who was also dozing the afternoon away, less worried about the sun's rays than Aletha, who had taken great care to shade herself. Galen looked at the long daggers on Chor's belt, the powerful arms and strong hands that had on many occasion brought a miscreant to order, coerced a confession, killed in battle. He remembered the people who died when he and Chor had freed Aletha from her captives. He felt no remorse over their deaths, certain that their deeds, this one and past crimes, had earned them their fate. But now he thought about the emissaries, the zeal in which they approached their task, no doubt firmly rooted in unshakable faith. Were they any less qualified to assume the role of executioner than he was?

Chor opened his eyes to study his hands, unable to sleep under Galen's scrutiny. He looked back at his twin, like Galen seeing little more than a well-made weapon wielded by the La'il to control her enemies. A carefully designed specimen, whose show of brawn was often enough to extract compliance among the commoners, and whose talent as adept allowed him to control more esteemed adversaries. The emissaries followed the orders of some long-gone masters. The twins obeyed the mandate of the La'il. All of them obedient, without question. He shook his head, as if to clear his confused thoughts.

"You know," a gentle voice intruded. "This is the first time I've seen you two talk with each other."

Both men turned their heads, startled. "What?"

Aletha stretched her limbs, yawning. "The way you were looking at each other just now. So intense! I could almost hear your thoughts flying through the air!" She looked over the side of the boat, reading the shape of the shoreline. "Although I don't suppose it was a very pleasant conversation. I've not seen you looking quite so downcast. Is something wrong?"

Galen shook his head. "Nothing really. Wondering how those emissaries knew we were on Delann's ship."

"Someone probably saw us pull out of the harbor and sent message birds to Ayrlie to warn them. Then again, you two are such tall drinks of water that they probably saw you from a distance. When they catch you they'll nail a lamp to your heads and post you by the harbor entrance as nicely matching beacons."

Galen grinned and felt his bleak mood evaporate in her bright presence. How simple things seem when she smiled at them, he thought, and how easily it chased the demons from his thoughts. He resolved to delay his unproductive soul searching until his return to the Homeworld. Meanwhile, he was on vacation!

SIX

"This is a perfect place to spend the night," Aletha declared when she nudged their small boat deftly along a rickety dock that had appeared in the middle of a small bay. Having navigated by sight until it was almost too dark to make out more than a suggestion of shoreline, she was pleased to find this cove as she had last seen it. At first glance this unremarkable anchorage consisted of a cluster of boats tied up along a dock raised above the water. But there were no permanent buildings here, no warehouses, residences or even supply depots. In fact, the shore was an undisturbed stretch of seaweed-strewn beach some distance from the boats which huddled like some strange island in the cove.

They pulled up to a long concourse permanently connecting several large, ramshackle ships. A collection of smaller vessels of various size, quality and purpose filled in the berths between the behemoths. Some torches had been fixed to the catwalk, illuminating the comings and goings of crews and passengers from all shores of this moon. Someone stopped to catch Aletha's line and tied their boat to a ring bolted to the dock. She scrambled up a questionable ladder and waited impatiently for the twins to follow.

"What is this place?" Galen asked after the twins had made their way onto the concourse.

"Riva Sound," she said, grinning. "A waystation. Our sort of waystation."

Curious, the twins followed her along the pier, amazed to find an entire trading post on water. Some of the boats here seemed to be permanently in residence, perhaps not even seaworthy, looking more like houses than ships. Other vessels were obviously in transit, like themselves on their way to somewhere else. They passed a few private crafts, then one with clothing, foodstuffs and weapons for sale. Next to it was some sort of celebration in progress; Aletha was amused by a very drunk man at the bow of his sailboat, feet dangling, singing some raucous shanty at the top of his lungs. They continued past an inn, a tavern, another shop or two, and a few more private boats. Even out here the cleanliness so valued by Thali's people was for sale on a barge offering steaming tubs of water.

Everywhere torches burned, music played, voices, shouts and laughter drifted over the still water of the cove. People passed them along the walkway on their way from one boat to another but no one here seemed to take much notice of the twins. This place was not one where questions were often asked or freely answered. Remote and well guarded, protected from pirates by their number, travelers here were likely the sort to prefer this arrangement over the confines of a harbor town. No doubt one would not have to look very hard to find smugglers, thieves, fugitives and even a number of Descendants among the shops and hostelries.

"I think I like this place," Galen said, slowing his steps to look down onto the deck of a barge where several dancers were displaying their talents. A circle of women gyrated to the spirited sound of drum and flute, their scant costumes flashing with sequins in the light of the torches. He smiled when one of them raised her arms to him without halting her dance, most of her chest bared for his inspection.

Aletha prodded him onward and then took a step back to tug on Chor's sleeve. "Let's go! I'm hungry."

"What is that?" Galen said behind her, sounding startled.

"What?" Aletha turned and looked up at whatever he had spotted in the sky. "Chenoweth, of course."

"I know it's Chenoweth. What's that thing *on* Chenoweth?"

"The Garden," she said with some reverence. "Have you not seen it before?"

"Garden? You mean your Garden of the Gods?" Galen said, thunderstruck. Several massive, uneven shapes were visible among the frozen wastelands and dead mountain ranges that comprised most of the moon's surface. Their edges were distinct, as if he were looking up at verdant islands of green in a sea of rock and ice. Deep blue jewels lay among the greenery, suggesting that, after all, surface water existed on Chenoweth. A grim smile formed on his lips. For centuries, his people had observed the distant moon and had seen only hostile wasteland. Arrogantly, they imagined the exiles huddled on Chenoweth in misery, awaiting the opportunity to reclaim the Homeworld. But with all the chi'ro available on that moon it would not have been a complex undertaking to create a comfortable living space. And, prudently, they had done so out of sight of the Homeworld's prying eyes.

"Isn't it magical?" Aletha said, flinging her arms up as if to embrace the distant orb. "It's so very rare to get a clear view of it. Once the rainy season starts you won't see it at all."

"Rainy season?"

"It's a good omen to see the Garden. Be sure to conduct yourself well in case the gods are watching!"

Galen saw a number of other people with hands raised skyward. Many stood in silence, some mumbled prayers under their breath. Even the cheerful bawdiness of the dancers had changed to a sinuous waving of arms at the heavens with only a soft flute to accompany their salutation. "This explains much. I couldn't understand why you people were so keen on going there someday. I've always thought of Chenoweth as a cold and unfriendly place."

"We think of it as warm and gentle and peaceful. And look! Not a storm cloud to be seen! Is that not the sort of place where you would expect to find gods?"

They walked back the way they had come to board a hulking craft refitted and renovated so many times that it no longer even resembled a boat. Once aboard, they picked their way through boisterous companies of revelers lounging on the deck, ignoring comments, invitations and the occasional groping hand as they passed. Having had their fill of fresh air for the day they went inside where, although smoky from the fish oil lamps, it was warm and, Galen was glad to see, relatively clean. Whatever was cooking in the back of the tavern reminded them that they had not eaten since the noon hour. They chose a quiet table some distance from other visitors where Galen and Chor sank to the floor cross-legged while Aletha kneeled on her cushion, able to sit that way for hours without both of her legs turning utterly numb.

A servant came to their table with a bowl of water, some clean rags, and a jug of ale. She was a little flustered by the men, astonished by the resemblance and taken by their charms, which Aletha turned to her advantage by securing two bedrooms for the night at an excellent price. She thought to herself that the maid would no doubt find it odd that the twins shared one room while she had the other when it occurred to her that she found that odd, as well. She had never met siblings so content in each other's company.

"I have an idea," she said after their dinner had arrived. They dug into their shared bowl of rice, vegetables, and various types of meat and seafood with great enthusiasm. There was also a whole grilled fish, its stuffing of shredded pepperweed and mushrooms exuding a mouthwatering aroma. "You might as well agree to it now, because I won't take 'no' for an answer."

"Is that so?" Galen said, most of his attention on the fish.

She nodded confidently, licking her fingers. She used the water basin and rags to clean her hands before withdrawing Delann's map from her sash. She spread it out on the table, using the heels of her hands to smooth out some wrinkles. "We're about here. Depending on the wind, we'll make our way through here and, hopefully, we'll end up over there."

The twins peered at the map. "And…?" Galen said.

"See this little inlet there? It's called Alarit Dunn. Where I grew up."

"Uh huh."

"I want to visit there on our way through the islands. It's barely out of our way." She looked up at them, a hopeful expression on her face. "Please? That is my family. I haven't seen them in over two years."

"Hmm, I don't know. We have to get to the mountains. We're already taking much longer than we should to get back home." Galen pulled something that still had excessively slimy scales on it from their stew and placed it on her side of the platter.

"Just a day or two. Please?" She reached across the table to shake his arm.

He considered, remembering the sadness with which she had left that miserable seaside slum behind. Given the slow orbit of the Homeworld and her moons, two years was a long time. Surely the La'il could wait a few more days. "I think we can manage that. Yes. Why not?"

She smiled happily. "Thanks, Galen, that's sweet."

"So how did you know I'm Galen? You're getting better at telling us apart."

"Not really." She pointed at Chor. "He just doesn't talk very much. And he always looks like he's in a daydream or something."

Chor only smiled.

Galen looked at the map again. "Are you sure you can find your way through there? Looks messy," he added, meaning the hand-drawn cartography.

"Yes, I know the way. In my sleep! I grew up around here. We took many trips through these islands. I've been in this bay before." She returned her attention to the food before them, changing the subject, as she often did, in what seemed to be mid-thought. "Tell me more about the Homeworld. Does it look like this place?"

He thought about this. "Mostly, compared to the other planets circling our sun. I guess the open conduits allowed so many life forms to travel back and forth that the planet and this moon evolved the same." Catching the quizzical look on her face, he backtracked. "Chenoweth is too cold to have much life... Hmm, well, except for your Garden it is. But Thali is a lot like the Homeworld. You have many of the same, or at least similar, plants and animals. I can breathe this air and drink the water. Long ago there were more connections between these places. I can imagine something as simple as the seeds for these vegetables drifting through the conduits to find their way up here. Of course, many things were brought here by the people arriving from the Homeworld."

"But you don't much care for some of our things." She peeled and ate the scaled thing while the twins watched in disgusted fascination.

"Well, things have probably changed over time since the launch sites were sealed. And we don't have nearly as much water on the Homeworld as you do here. There are things living in your oceans I can't even begin to imagine. The eel-thing the other day frightened me."

She laughed. "Your boots are made from the skin of it. What else is different? Tell me about your people."

"Our people are... taller and our skin is darker because we get more sun than you do. My people like the sun. I miss it. We live well and want for nothing." His eyes traveled around the room, taking in the assortment of unkempt patrons that frequented here. "Sickness isn't common and injuries are easily healed. We live a very long time."

"How long?"

"The average is about a hundred and fifty or so." His thoughts strayed to the La'il and her possibly long history in this place. "Adepts live longer."

"You do live well! How old are you two?"

"Sixty-two."

Aletha gaped at him in astonishment. "The truth now!"

"It's the truth," he grinned. "Although, by your reckoning, we're probably not much older than you are."

"But for your gray hair," she amended.

He inclined his head in acknowledgement. "Not an uncommon trait among us."

"Is it true that La'il's hair is pure silver?"

The easy smile faded from his lips. "It is white," he said after a moment.

She pointed heavenward. "Tell me more about her."

"What do you want to know?" he asked, looking into his mug of ale.

"What do you want to tell me?" When he did not answer, she rapped her knuckles on the table to get his attention. "I know you do. Tell me why you hate her."

"Because she wants me to."

Aletha frowned, puzzled. "She wants you to hate her? Why?"

He shrugged. "She enjoys it. The more I hate her, the angrier I get, the happier she is. I don't know why. It's a game to her."

"Do you enjoy that?"

"No! Of course not."

"Then why do you play this game?"

"I have no choice." He paused, searching for words. "She can touch my mind and change the way I feel. I try to stop her but I can't get away. The more I try to fight it, the easier it is for her. She makes me angry and then I feel such hate, Aletha; it's like nothing I'd ever feel, if it weren't for her. It isn't me at all!" He reflected on this before shaking his head. "No, it is me. I feel these things, and I react to those things. I want to do the things she makes me do. I've even tried to kill her." He closed his eyes against the memory, knowing that it was unwise to tell Aletha these things. "Stupid idea. I could never touch her if she didn't want me to. Her mind makes her much stronger than me - I've got scars to remind me of that. But I try, anyway."

Aletha nodded, thinking of the previous night. "That's an evil thing to do to someone," she said.

"You shouldn't think of her as evil," Galen said, reminding himself of who she was and regretting some of the things he had told her. It would be better for Aletha if she met the La'il without prejudices instilled by his loathing for their leader. "Her rule is competent and we live in peace now, most of the time. Her mind makes these things possible. I know you will like it there." He paused briefly and then shrugged. "I'm only a diversion for her, a plaything."

"But you've made love to her," Aletha guessed.

He laughed without humor. "No, I've never done that. I've raped her. Or she's raped me. It's the same either way."

"How can you get free of her?"

"I can't! She can get to me even here." He pointed at his injured shoulder. "She can't touch me here, on this moon, but she can make me think she can. It wasn't she who threw me across the room, it was me. She made me do it!"

"Sounds to me like you're less of a plaything than someone she needs to lord over. Maybe she needs to feel powerful."

"She has all the power she wants. No one dares to oppose her. There is nothing she can't have. Or just take if she wants it."

Aletha propped her elbow on the table and rested her cheek in her hand. "Sounds to me like she can't have *you*. Not without taking it."

Galen drained his cup and reached for more. It seemed impossible to convey to Aletha to what depths the La'il twisted his emotions. Perfectly aware of his own actions and physically aware of his own body, when his hands were upon the goddess, handling her in ways that would badly injure another human, he no longer fought back. He wanted blood and he wanted pain and it mattered not whose it was.

He looked up again to find Aletha still watching him expectantly. "Better not touch that," he said finally.

"I wish I could help you," she said. "It must be terrible to be so controlled by someone. To be made to do such horrible things without meaning to."

Galen leaned back when some travelers lurched noisily past their table, glad for the interruption. "I do mean to," he said when they were alone again. "Once I've let her get inside my head, I believe anything she wants me to see."

"So she can't hurt you if you don't let her in? Why do you let her in at all?"

"Because I work for her. All prime adepts do. That is why we exist. But most of them cannot communicate with her the way I do. It's the main reason I was sent up here instead of someone else."

"It seems so, well, magical. She is so very far away. How can she do these things?"

"I don't know for sure," Galen said. "Somehow, the La'il knows how to find something unique to each person and use it to find them and to touch them with her thoughts. It's a rare gift. Communicating like that is not a common talent among my people. Other than the La'il, there are only a handful of adepts on the Homeworld able to do this and I am one of them. Not very well, really, but each generation improves. It's wonderful, but hardly magic."

She nodded and turned her attention to carefully folding her map again. "I think I've pried enough. But you frightened me yesterday. Should I lock my door in case she comes back?"

He peered at her closely and after some time decided that she was joking. Hopefully. "Aletha, if anything happened to you the La'il would come up here herself to roast me over a slow fire."

She grinned back at him. "Listen," she said, changing the subject once again. "While we're traveling around like this, why don't you teach me some of the things you can do with this, this magic you showed me? Like the way I was able to fix your shoulder."

"There isn't much to work with here."

"Maybe you'll find some along the way. Please?"

He had already decided to help her develop her talents, if for no other reason than to keep herself safe from the emissaries. Besides, it would be a sure way to displease the La'il. "Sure," he smiled. "Why not?"

"This is so exciting! What sort of thing will I learn? Like calling up a waterspout like you did?"

He nodded. "We'll take it slow. I don't want any accidents."

"Accidents!"

"You saw that missile, that fireball, in the garden yesterday. Things like that can get away from you. You can underestimate how much chi you need or end up applying too much. I know of no novice who hasn't collected a fair share of pain while learning how to handle chi'ro. Your mentor's job is to see to it that there aren't any bystanders also getting into some of that pain."

"You got some pain?" She snickered. "Other than that nasty slice there?" She gestured at his side.

"Hey, that is an honest battle scar. But, yes, my training was no easier than anyone's, or what yours will be like. I remember one year I fell out of the sky twice!"

"You can fly?" she gasped.

"Well, let's call it floating. You can learn that, too. But not on this rock."

"I can't wait!"

"You have to know it takes a long time to learn how to do anything more than just push things around. Just *wanting* something to happen works sometimes, like when you want to heal someone. But imagine how much better you could heal someone if you knew exactly how they were hurt and exactly where to apply chi'ro. You have to know *how* you want something to happen, and what you must do to accomplish that. These things aren't easily explained, or mastered."

"Like how you steered the ship today. I was terrified."

"Well, actually, that wasn't very difficult and didn't even

take much chi. It's a boat on water; it moves easily. We only had to make sure there was always some distance between it and the rocks. If the water in the channels had been shallower we would have crashed. But even with the little chi'ro it takes to do this, it took all three of us to get us through. There just isn't enough of it on this moon. And as you saw, it knocked us off our feet."

"I meant to ask about that. I was exhausted."

"Remember how you felt when we were steering the ship? When we pulled in the riser?" Galen watched her nod; that much chi'ro channeling through her body, whipped into palpable energy by the two adepts, would have been a matchless sensation. "It's easy to feel invincible when you're sucking up so much chi. You can lose track of the riser itself and when it's used up there is only the ambient chi'ro. That's gone in moments and you can end up draining yourself before you even notice that there isn't any more to work with. We call it *going over*. It's like bleeding bits of yourself to continue doing whatever it is you were doing. It's dangerous and we receive much training to handle shortages like that. But today we couldn't just stop before we got clear of the islands and so we ended up going over. Happened to us a few times already on this moon. On the Homeworld this would have been easier."

"It wouldn't have made us so tired?"

He smiled. "We wouldn't even have noticed. We wouldn't have to pull in the riser. In fact, we wouldn't even have to steer the ship." He reached for her hand to grip it tightly in making his point. "Aletha, on the Homeworld you could have picked up the *Ruane* and flown it across the islands. You could have sunk all four of those emissary ships with a thought. You could have reversed the direction of the tide itself!"

She looked from him to Chor, her eyes wide in astonishment. "You can do that?"

Chor shook his head. "You can."

She stared at nothing for a long time while the twins

watched her immobile face, wondering if she was beginning to understand the enormity of what lay before her. Galen did not for a moment doubt his estimate of her abilities. During those harrowing minutes in the island channels he had felt the power of her mind as clearly as he saw her face. The talent was there, sleeping and untrained, never tested with any fuel but the pitiful shreds of chi'ro produced by Thali moon. The only time he had stood in the brilliance of a mind such as this was when he was tethered to the La'il.

He was surprised when Aletha suddenly laughed. "Wouldn't it be funny if that dreadful Tsingao could see that? He gets so incensed when someone whistles up a sleep-song, imagine what he'd do if he saw a ship flying through the air!"

He joined her laughter and even Chor fell in. None of them were aware of the two men at a nearby table, hunched over bowls of wine. They continued to strain for bits of conversation from the three travelers but talk had turned from magic to a list of gifts the woman wanted to purchase in the morning to take to Alarit Dunn. When a musician arrived to fill the cabin with the gentle sounds of a stringed instrument, the men left to hurry to a boat moored not far away. Under the large moon lighting their way in shades of gray and silver, they slipped away and headed for the strait.

SEVEN

The next morning dawned through a blanket of mist, promising rain later in the day. After purchasing some supplies and gifts for Aletha's people, she and the twins headed onward with the tide, hoping to cover many miles of shoreline before rain-whipped waves would make it impossible to sail the boat any farther. Aletha knew of a sheltered cove where some caves worn into the seaside cliffs would let them stay dry during the coming night. On the following day, she promised, they would reach the small village she had once called home.

The day on the water was anything but monotonous. Aletha had many stories about her life in Phrar Thali and the people she had encountered. In turn, Galen told her about the wonders of the Homeworld made possible by the powerful force emanating from the ground, useful to those who had the talent to recognize it. He began to coach her to recognize the power she had found in Delann's garden and try to locate it nearby. He was surprised at how easily she came to pinpoint the directions of distant risers, accurately describing even the size of the emanation. Past noon, they detected a source close by and, with Galen's help, Aletha was able to draw it near. Once captured by Galen's mind, she tried to shape it into a simple gust of wind to propel the boat, delighted when the small craft accelerated. Galen was pleased with her efforts and a little awed by the talent that so effortlessly absorbed this new knowledge. Her tentative experiments grew bolder with each success and he had to guide her progress on only a few occasions.

The ominous clouds had not yet overtaken them when they reached the shelter of a small inlet. They unloaded what they needed and left their craft to beach itself with the receding tide. Galen had detected a curiously strong riser in the distance and so they set out to find it once their camp was made in the cave she had promised. He hoped it was powerful enough to show Aletha more interesting things to do with it. A few hours' walk after two days at sea seemed an enticing prospect, even if their hike took them through dense, humid forest. She was completely at home here now and delighted in showing the twins how to orient themselves in the dense underbrush, avoid poisonous growth, and recognize the bewildering confusion of animals that thrived in these parts.

"Look, lobefruit!" Aletha sprinted ahead of the twins toward a stand of squat, green-stemmed trees. Galen looked up, thinking that one tree here looked much like the next, to see clusters of green-orange fruit weighing down the branches. "I think they might be ripe. I'll get us some." Aletha climbed into the tree, apparently not encumbered by the laws of physics. Galen smiled as he watched her reach her prize, stepping closer to catch a few choice specimen – or her, if necessary. "The seeds are the best part," she called down to him.

He handed some of the fruit to Chor. "We have something like this on the Homeworld, too. Not as large." He took a bite. "Or as sweet!"

She leaned forward to stretch out on her branch and studied the twins with a thoughtful expression. "What did you do on the Homeworld?"

"What do you mean?"

"Do people work on the Homeworld? What do you do

with your day? Here we have fisherfolk and builders and traders. What sort of things do you do on the Homeworld?"

He furrowed his brow. "We're gods, remember? We just lounge about all day and do godly things." Still unsure of her sense of humor in this matter, he was glad when she laughed out loud. "We do all of those things there, too. Most people work at something. Not quite as much fishing," he added dryly.

"You're an adept. Adepts work?"

He nodded. "You need adepts to wield chi'ro and so we are builders or weather makers or healers or we transport things around the planet, each according to their degree of aptitude."

"And you?"

He thought for a moment. "Hmm, I wanted to be a… a healer and I studied for a few years after I was ranked as prime adept. But then La'il needed me for other things and I became a, hmm, a guard I guess, a hired soldier, like those you have here. I hunt people who harm others, or the way we live. As does Chor."

"Oh, like a watchman."

He thought about the drunken hoodlums hired by the townspeople of Phrar to discourage others from acting like even worse thugs. "Not exactly. We work mainly for the La'il and her ministers. You can probably imagine that there are ways to misuse chi'ro. We try to prevent that."

"You said your world is perfect."

"Did I say that? I think I said we live well and want for nothing. For some people it's not enough. We have our share of law breakers."

"What do you do to them?"

"Do we have to talk about that?" he said, feeling rather peculiar about standing in the middle of a forest and talking up a tree. "Come down from there before you break something."

"You do something to their minds, don't you?"

"That's rather harsh." He looked to his twin, trying to

determine the direction of her inquisition. "Well, if we have to. If there is no other way. Sometimes we use chi'ro to… to control them."

"Are you a good adept?"

"Well, as things like that are measured, I suppose so."

She continued to gaze at him as if observing a particularly interesting insect. "But you've killed people also."

"Why do you say that?" he asked, a little annoyed by her questions.

"You killed that trader in Phrar. And his men. They weren't the first you've killed. You knew how."

"The work we do means we make enemies along the way. There isn't always chi'ro about when you need it. Certainly not up here! And so, yes, I've had to learn how to do my work without it. You were dying. Should I have waited and bought you fairly the next day?"

"You didn't have to kill them."

"They might have sent people after us." Her exploration into his line of work was a little too reminiscent of the one to which he had subjected himself only yesterday.

"They did anyway, alive or not. You were angry. Because of how they treated me. Because that man hit me. You don't show it, but you're angry all the time. La'il knows this."

"Ridiculous."

"Chor's not angry. That's why she doesn't bother with him, I think."

Galen glanced at his twin. After some silent exchange Chor laughed and started to walk onward, shaking his head as he went.

Aletha dangled from her branch and then dropped to the spongy ground. "Do you have a family?" she inquired blithely as they continued their walk through the forest.

"Yes," Galen said. "I was born near the mountains. That's far from where I spend most of my time. But I visit as often as I can. We do, I mean." He gestured at Chor.

"I meant do you have your own families? Wives? Children?"

He shook his head. "Perhaps I will, when I'm older. We live so long now that we choose our time carefully. La'il has seen to it that we don't have many children. She foresees a time when we might run out of room for everybody."

"How could that be?" Aletha marveled. "The Homeworld is so huge!"

"These things can happen, Aletha," he said. "It happened before and it's why our ancestors left Earth." He shrugged. "And so the La'il has slowed the rate at which we multiply. It seems to be for the best."

Aletha looked from Chor to Galen, incredulous. "Um, so you don't... I mean... uh..." Involuntarily, her eyes moved down along his body, causing a deep blush to color her cheeks.

Galen laughed. "Yes, we do."

"Then how did she do it?"

"She made a law," he said. "People need permission to reproduce. Not everyone is happy with that, but for the most part it works. Or were you expecting some magic at work here?"

"Hmm, yes."

He considered for a moment and then decided to dodge the subject of contraception. "And you'd be right," he said.

"Here on Thali people have many children. Not all of them live, of course, but there are enough to keep a family growing."

"We don't have families like you do. My people form clans and raise the children as part of that group. So when they have permission to have another one, they choose the parents carefully, usually at least one adept. Everyone wants their child to be born with some talent."

Aletha stopped walking, her hand halted halfway to lifting a branch out of her way. "You are joking with me now," she accused.

"I'm not. People look to the adepts to provide their offspring with some advantages. Because of that each new generation produces more adepts and also more powerful ones. I've done that a few times, myself."

"You've done what?"

"Passed on my genes. We're prime adepts. This sort of genetic material is in demand. And if we manage to breed some talent into someone's kid our worth as adepts increases."

She frowned. "So you sell your children."

"What? No, of course not. Why do you say that?"

"Well, if you give away your children and receive some favor or wealth or status for it, then it's like you're selling them, isn't it?"

He gestured for her to keep walking, once again made uncomfortable by her explorations into his life. "No, that just the way it is on the Homeworld. Those are not my children. They belong to whoever raises them. I just... helped to cause them to be, that's all. We weren't raised by our birthmother, either."

"Your mother gave you away?" she exclaimed. "It's not just the men who do this?"

"Some women do. But she didn't. We were supposed to be part of her clan. But there was an accident and she died. Something happened to our father, too, but I'm not too clear what that was or who he was, even. We were raised by another clan. A farming place. I loved it there. La'il took us away to the schools when our talents emerged."

Aletha's eyes shifted to Chor some distance ahead of them, as usual seeming content in his silence. He moved steadily through the underbrush, like Galen showing no sign of tiring as he leaped over obstacles with easy grace or effortlessly moved deadfall out of their way. "You were... made to be like that? To look like that? To be adepts?"

Galen nodded, embarrassed by her scrutiny. "Both of our parents were prime adepts. And their parents. Some of our children are, too."

"It would seem to me things like that ought to be left for the gods to decide. Breeding people like farm animals! What a world! But I suppose it must amuse you to bed so many women."

He shook his head, biting back a grin. "That isn't always appropriate."

"Then how do you do it?"

Galen pondered her question, wondering how he would explain such matters to someone likely ignorant of the finer points of human anatomy and certainly the more scientific applications of chi'ro. "Magic," he said at length. "And it doesn't happen as often as you seem to think. A lot of rules of selection have to be followed or blood lines would get pretty tangled. We have people who do nothing but keep accounts of who is related to whom. They help find suitable sires when one is needed."

"This sounds awful! Don't you want to keep any of your… your offspring?"

"Sure, some day."

"If La'il lets you," she amended.

He shrugged. "I qualify within our law. I'm too busy for that sort of thing, though. We're away too often right now."

"Hunting renegade magic users for the La'il?"

"Well, yes. But I wish you wouldn't put it like that. You make me sound like an emissary."

She kept her eyes on her feet, picking her way through the dense growth as cautiously as she was choosing her next words. "I didn't mean you couldn't lawfully have a family. I meant La'il won't let you, anyway. Let you have wives I mean, or whatever they're called on the Homeworld."

Galen threw his half-eaten fruit into the thicket, stung by her comment. Would she? Would the La'il ever grant him the freedom to pursue any significant bond with another woman? Would anyone want to enter a union with someone utterly enslaved to the cruel whims of the Homeworld's supreme ruler? He thought of the women who had passed through his life and his bed over the years. He remembered few faces and even fewer names. It wasn't something that had ever really mattered to him. "I've never thought about it," he said truthfully but he felt the ever-present chains that tied him to the La'il as if Aletha's words had tightened them a little more.

Mindful of the morose expression on his face, Aletha did not press onward with her questions. "We've reached the edge of this forest," she said. "I can smell the sea." Indeed, they soon broke from the trees into a meadow of shrubs and tall grasses where a fresh breeze greeted them. The ground now rose toward a steep ridge of stone and they began to climb, sometimes needing their hands to help in the ascent. Breathlessly, Aletha looked around to get her bearings. "I've never been this far inland."

Galen studied the smooth, bare rock rising before them. The slabs of stone they were traversing were volcanic. The twisted surface here seemed pliable, like masses of thick dough left here to harden for eternity. Black sand filled crevasses and gathered in between the larger rocks, crunched beneath their boots, and made the stone surface slippery. Scrubby vegetation clung wherever a little soil had accumulated. "I have not seen any volcanoes," he said, mostly to himself, looking around. Indeed, he saw thick, gray plumes of smoke and dust rise into the air in the distance.

"What are those?" Aletha asked.

"Volcanoes? A mountain with a hole at the top that spews fire and smoke and ashes into the air. You can see it for many days' travel in all directions. These formations here are caused by them."

"Nothing like that here. We call these fire chasms."

"Fire chasm?"

She nodded. "Deep fissures in the ground that contain molten rock. Do you have those on the Homeworld? Some people here call them lava crocks because it's as though someone was cooking stones."

"These must be very new, then. Have you always had so many earthquakes?"

She shrugged. "You know our stories. They say this place changed after the gods left us here. The quakes are worse in the north. The really strong ones only come along every few years. They make big waves, too. The waves are worse than the quakes. I think we fear that more than anything."

"I would, too. Can you feel the riser?"

She nodded. "Yes, it's over there. You know, I've sensed this in the past but I didn't know what it was. It used to scare me. Since you showed this to me in Delann's garden I can feel it more strongly. It's like, oh I don't know, like a breeze blowing past me, through me, somehow." She found something of interest on the distant horizon and shaded her eyes with her hand. "*Into* me. It… it fills me up, I feel…" She glanced at him. "Kind of sated. I'm blushing, right?"

"It can have some interesting effects." He grinned. "What you feel is the power of the risers moving toward you, into you, so you can use their energy. Like what happened on the ship. Your talents are then a hundred times stronger than usual, aren't they? Without knowing it, you've already taught yourself to use this to some purpose. Imagine if you had limitless amounts of this. Imagine what you could do if you had a teacher!"

"You can teach me," she said, a stubborn edge creeping into her voice.

He shook his head. "I can teach you how to light a fire, but I cannot teach you to direct the weather, or how to move tremendous payloads through the air, or to send people between planets. Once you know how you could even prevent earthquakes! But for these things you don't just need an ocean of chi'ro, you will also need a proper mentor."

"Like the La'il," she said. "Who isn't very nice."

"She'll be nice to you," he promised. "Look, we're almost there."

They had reached the flat, windswept summit of the hill that afforded a dizzying view of the coast. Fingers of densely forested land jutted into the island-strewn water below them and, distantly, the northern mountains beckoned. A sharp breeze buffeted them to herald the oncoming storm, tugging at their clothes and hair. They stood on a crest of rock stretching for a distance to the north where it disappeared into the jungle. Before them, just a short walk away, the ground had cracked as if by lighting, emitting a dull red glow. Plumes of slate-colored smoke were quickly carried off by the breeze toward the Great Strait to the east. The volcanic fissure was spectacular enough, but it also contained a riser that vented into the air, unaffected by heat and gases.

"Don't go too close. The air there is poison."

Galen nodded and raised his arms toward the riser to draw it closer. Soon, it washed over them to refresh them after their long walk. He closed his eyes and gave himself up to the soothing influx of chi'ro with a smile and a sigh.

Seeing him so engrossed, Aletha was able to study his face. A few fine lines radiated from his eyes, their creases lighter than his sun-browned skin. Besides the silver strands in his hair, she now also saw a few gray hairs peppering his unshaven cheek. Apparently the people on the Homeworld did not age more slowly in all ways, she thought idly, and let her eyes drift down along his body before she remembered that Chor was standing nearby. He cocked his head as if wondering why she was scrutinizing his brother so closely. Something seemed to amuse him. "You two need a shave," she said.

Galen roused himself from his encounter with the riser. "It takes the keen intuition of an adept to make such an astute discovery," he said sarcastically, grinning at her before turning back to the fledgling volcano. "There is something odd here." His senses probed the source of the emanation, somewhere in the depth of the gas-choked fissure. What he felt there seemed familiar, albeit in a rather inconvenient location. "I think this might be a launch."

"A what?"

"One of the access places I told you about. With enough chi flowing into it, a conduit is formed that can reach through space to the Homeworld or to the other moon. You can step through this like a doorway."

She peered doubtfully into the depths of the fire chasm. "Looks dangerous."

"Well, this one is peculiar. Usually the launch sites look like big slabs of crystal. Or they do now, anyway. Something must have happened here to rip open this fissure."

"How do these things work? The ones that do work, I mean."

"We think they were formed by enormous amounts of chi'ro concentrated in a small area. Originally, these apertures, these crystals, were connected by conduits to random points on the planet and the moons, fed by their risers from both sides. They were so stable that it didn't even take much chi to keep them open. By stepping onto them you were able to travel from one place to another almost instantly. We learned from that and some of us can form a short conduit from one place to another on the Homeworld. But to get from the Homeworld to the moons you need one of the crystals to amplify the riser's power."

"And I'm not supposed to call that magic?"

He chuckled. "Whatever it is, it doesn't work anymore. The Chenowans sealed the launch sites up. Now it's a few hundred years later and La'il has figured out how to open them again. I saw her take an incredible amount of chi'ro to shape a conduit on the crystal. This opened the seal just long enough for us to get through. We'll have to do that when we get to the launch in the mountains."

"We are? How?"

"I don't know. She will show us. Show you, I mean. Chor and I don't have the ability to open the seal. She thinks you do."

"Me? Why can't she make another conduit to come and get us?"

"Not enough chi. It takes a whole lot of it to open a conduit for even just a moment. And then it's just a sort of one-way door. You would need an adept on both sides to anchor the conduit properly, to keep it open and stable. Or a constant source of chi'ro. And that just doesn't exist on Thali." He realized that she was regarding him with a mixture of puzzlement and annoyance. "What?"

"How did you think you were going to get home again if I hadn't turned out what you thought I'd be?"

"What do you mean?"

"What if I hadn't wanted to come? What if you hadn't found me? What if the emissaries had killed me before you got to Phrar? Was she just going to leave you up here?"

"Well, yes."

"And you agreed to that?"

"Hadn't occurred to us to disagree. It isn't healthy to refuse the La'il when she has her mind set on something." He shrugged. "There is a lot at stake here. This is what we do. This is what we were bred to do."

"To give up your life for your ruler?" she exclaimed. "For her?"

"No, for my Homeworld. But I don't intend to exile ourselves up here. We'll get through the seal."

She glanced back at the poisonous fume rising from the fissure. "Please tell me that one is a bit cooler than this thing."

"Actually, it's very cold in there. Come, let's have some fun while we're here." He sat on a boulder and tipped his head toward the riser. "Draw this chi into yourself and then pick up that rock and move it over there."

"I've moved things around before," she said. "Sort of. But the rock is too heavy."

"Yes, it's heavy," he said. "But not for you. Touch it with your thoughts, understand what it's made of, how much it weighs and then apply enough chi'ro to move it. Never use more than you need. Try sliding it."

She gripped her lip with her teeth, concentrating on the stone, and pushed outward. "Ah, I can feel it, it's moving!"

"Use your hands if you need something to focus with. Or a stick, even."

"Will that make me look like a novice?"

"Yeah. But it also lets people know what you're about to do, or who is doing what. It's a polite thing to do."

"Well, I am a novice. I have no pride." She lifted her

arms toward the stone, pleased when something seemed to nudge it a little further out of place.

He shook his head. "With this you couldn't find work in a stone quarry! You can do better."

"I happen to think this is going very well!"

"Let go, Aletha. No one can see us here; no one forbids what you're doing. There are no emissaries here to stop you. You are not even close to using the talents you have. Pick up that rock and throw it into the volcano."

"What? How?"

"Just do it! Pick it up!"

She looked back at the rock and projected outward, thinking only about its shape and weight, and laughed out loud when it scraped along the ground, caught on something, and then tumbled away, bouncing end over end until it dropped off the side of the hill. "That's it!" she cried. "I got it. I understand what you mean! Oh, this is so exciting!"

"That it is. Now do it again." For the next hour Galen directed her through simple exercises, moving rocks around the hillside with increasingly more precise targets, velocity, or elevation. She delighted in each success, especially pleased when she nearly matched Galen's accuracy in a game of aiming pebbles into the cauldron of lava.

It was a while before they tired of the sport and she looked for greater challenges. "Show me how to make fire." Aletha peered over the edge of the plateau and let her thoughts reach into a tangled heap of deadfall near the foot of the incline. "Let's burn that thing. Uh, wait, it's stuck on something."

Chor strolled over to where she stood to observe her progress. "That's a whole tree. Are you planning a bonfire?" he inquired, looking into the ravine. He bent to gather a handful of moss from among the rocks. "This will do, you know."

She ignored him, captivated by the task of untangling the branches. Wielding chi'ro as a blunt force was no longer a secret to her. Using it for more complex manipulations seemed a far more intricate mind game. He watched silently, his amusement as palpable as if he were taunting her with words. At last, with a muttered oath, she hauled at the tangle with great force and simply snapped the main branch. Unfortunately, it snapped too far and swept toward them, bark and leaves scattering in the wind, and slammed into Aletha and Chor to fling them both to the ground. He slid down the hill and Aletha tumbled after him, erasing blouse and skin from her elbow. She cried out when their rough descent finally bounced them over a sharp outcropping and they were momentarily airborne. There was a peculiar shift in the air or light around them and she realized that Chor was projecting chi'ro outward in a desperate attempt to break their fall. They struck the ground hard, cushioned from more serious impact much like he and Galen had cushioned the ship in the island channels, bounced, and lay still.

Chor coughed and, with a groan, raised himself up on his hands and knees. "Are you all right?" He flung aside some of the forest debris that had tumbled down the hill with them. Worried, he bent over her to look into her dazed face. "Hold still."

Not inclined to do much else at this moment, Aletha watched his hand hover over her body, moving slowly as he scanned for injuries. He, too, was still gasping for breath and she thought it very strange, indeed, for him to be exploring her body in this state, even if he was not actually touching her. It was barely perceptible but what little she felt was vaguely pleasant, like some gentle warmth passing through her skin. "That tickles! Can I learn how to do this?"

He nodded, his attention on her abraded elbow. "You're fine," he said, moving his hand in one final pass over her. "Some scrapes and—" His eyes widened when Aletha gasped in surprise. "Sorry," he said quickly and withdrew his hand. As if suddenly aware of the strange intimacy of this encounter, he moved away from her.

Aletha exhaled sharply. "Can I learn that, too?" she said, grinning when she saw his face flush. She looked uphill.

"We're all right, Galen," she shouted in the direction where they had last seen his twin before peering more closely at Chor. "Um, are you all right? Nothing broken?"

They regained their feet, brushing dust and debris from their clothing. "Perhaps this is enough exercise for today," he said, picking some thorns out of his palm.

"I'm sorry this happened. I got impatient with that stupid tree. I didn't think it would break like that!"

"We're lucky there was a riser nearby. Without it we would have been in trouble. You're learning things much faster than expected. Don't get ahead of yourself. This moon isn't a good place for this training and we're not suitable teachers for you. Some things will have to wait."

"I'll be more careful, I promise!" she exclaimed. "Don't stop now! This is so exciting. I think I'd die if I couldn't learn more. Please don't give up on me."

He stepped out of the way when his twin dropped from the ledge above. "I guess we don't really have a choice," Galen said. "I can't imagine what you'd get up to if you were left to your own devices with this."

* * *

By the time they returned to their camp it had begun to drizzle and soon a steady rain fell, creating a curtain of water across the mouth of the cave. Only the light of a few candles illuminated their shelter, leaving most of it in the dark. "I had no idea that so much is possible with this magic of yours," Aletha said. "It's almost like I've waited my whole life to find out what I really am. I can't wait to get to the Homeworld. It must be wonderful where there is so much more to work with."

"It can be." Galen leaned back to let Chor move past him into one of the cave's side passages where he had laid his bedroll. "But not everyone has as much talent as you do. Some people have none at all, like here on Thali. Your worth on the Homeworld depends on how adept you are. What you are able to do with your gift suggests the kind of work you do, your wealth, your privileges. And although there is much more chi'ro on the Homeworld than here, even adepts like us can't simply do what we want with it. Most of it is needed as fuel for things like heat, or power for trains. I spend much of my time tracking down people who take more than their share. Battles have been fought over how chi'ro is shared."

"What will you teach me next?"

He considered. "There is a war coming. I don't know how La'il will use your skills, but you will need to know how to protect yourself. You will be a target. I think you need to learn some, well, battle skills. If you can heal people, you can also harm them."

"I don't like the way that sounds."

"We'll hunt something down tomorrow. You can kill quickly and painlessly. There are many ways—"

"Absolutely not!" she exclaimed, appalled. "You want me to murder some innocent animal just so I can learn how to murder people? Are you mad?"

"No, I'm tired of eating fish. If you can kill a squid then you can kill a reef crane. Preferably one with nice plump legs with lots of meat on it."

She grimaced. "Well, it just seems wrong. In the end, you want me to kill people. I don't think I can do that." She shook her head, looking more resolute by the moment. "I won't do that."

He smiled, thinking of the La'il. What would she make of this adept? Possibly the greatest weapon that ever existed and one that refused to be aimed at the enemy. What would it take to change Aletha's mind? "Then don't. There are other ways you can help, I'm sure. What else would you like to learn about?"

"That thing you do with your heads," she said at once.

"What thing?"

"The way you talk to Chor. Or the way you talk with the La'il. Is that hard? Do you need a lot of chi?"

"Not really. Usually. I'm sure the La'il is using quite a bit of energy to reach me all the way up here. It's a long way for a thought to travel."

"I'd like to try!"

He frowned. "I don't know..."

"Please? I just want to see if I can reach you. Just for a moment." She shook his arm. "Please? Please?"

He laughed, touched by her enthusiasm. He was reminded of his own discovery of his talents, and the wonder and apprehension that accompanied each stage of his training. He, too, had wanted to test his limits well before his mentors had thought him ready for his ambitions. "All right! Just don't look where you shouldn't."

"I promise," she said earnestly. "But you've got to help me."

"If you think it's that easy," he said, amused. "Good luck." He leaned comfortably against the cave wall. "Okay, go ahead. Just don't expect this to work. You're too green for this."

"What do I do?"

"Let's start with a touch. Eventually you won't need that with people you know well, or those you touched before." He raised his hand and waited until she grasped a few of his fingers. "Focus your thoughts on me, like you did in Delann's garden. Just try to hear me. Hear what I'm thinking. Or, better yet, try to send a thought to me. Or an image."

She nodded and narrowed her eyes. "Okay, here I go. Tell me what I'm thinking."

Galen waited, indulging her whim, expecting nothing. But then, as clearly as if they were standing outside in bright daylight, he saw an image of their boat, coming unbidden to mind. "The boat!" he said, surprised at how easily she had reached him. "You were thinking of our boat."

"It works! I can do this! Let me try again."

He closed his eyes, waiting for her next thought, when his mind was suddenly filled with imagery, none of it the product of his own thoughts, in a wild jumble of color and shape. "Slow down," he said, wincing. "It's too much. I can't make any of it out."

She tried to hold her exuberance in check and let her mind float freely to linger over each image. He saw an impression of Delann and one of a woman whom he now knew to be Minh, her foster mother. He grinned when Aletha conjured an image of herself, captured from his own memory. It hadn't been her face he was studying at the time. Then he saw himself or Chor and wondered if she really saw them like that. "Very flattering," he murmured, opening one eye to look at her. "Is that me or Chor?"

He felt her look for his mental link with Chor. "Leave him out of this," he said quickly and pulled his hand out of her grip. "He's not agreed to this."

"Images, sensations, no words, though," she said. "I wanted to talk with you in your head, like you two do."

"We were bred for that, don't forget. Your talents came together all by themselves. You're trying to hear with your ears. Images are words, too, like those writings in your temples. La'il doesn't talk in my head, either. She makes me think I can see and hear what she's trying to show me. In the end, it's the same thing as really seeing her, isn't it?"

"I'm going to try something else now," she said. "Hold still."

He felt her mind probe into his, carefully, slowly, giving him enough time to shut off from her those things better not shared, her touch far gentler than the La'il's. He knew that she wanted to find out how the La'il was able to rearrange his synapses to change his moods to her purposes. He hoped that she wasn't about to goad him into some unpleasant outburst. He thought that it would be wise to stop these experiments now.

But the sensation he felt was one of absolute peace and contentment. He smiled broadly when he felt a surge of wellbeing and he seemed to be floating, aware of her somewhere nearby, completely free of any worry, fear or memory that had ever plagued his mind. "Hmm, nice," he murmured. "Don't stop. Happy. Content. Warm." He opened his eyes to gaze out of the cave into the night beyond. He turned his head to look at her eager, excited face. Her dark eyes seemed to look directly into his thoughts. "Love, I think, but no desire."

She leaned forward and put her hand on his chest. A low moan escaped him when every nerve reacted to her touch. There was no more imagery now, only a single sensation flaring through his body and filling him with the most basic of needs. He fought it, knowing it to be false, instilled in him by her mind and touch.

"Don't do this." He raised his hands as if to push her away, shook his head in denial even as he gripped her arms, drawing her close to kiss her, his mind filled with her need as well as his own. She responded in kind and they shed a minimum of clothing before he entered her, his powerful body exhausting her own as he reacted to the passion she had deliberately unleashed in his mind. Galen remained aware of Aletha, but the release he sought was physical and had nothing to do with the woman in his arms. It was not long before, shuddering, he collapsed beside her.

Many moments passed before his heart resumed a more dignified rhythm and he was able to breathe normally again. Turning his head, he saw Aletha curled up beside him, her arms covering her face. He closed his eyes, disturbed by his savage reaction to her botched experiment.

"That one got away from us. Do you understand now why you need a proper mentor?" He leaned over her to move her arms out of the way and realized that she was crying. He sighed. It would be easy now to blame her for this transgression, put it aside like some inevitable accident of her training, and continue on their way to deliver her to the Homeworld. Easy, uncomplicated, and far less likely to infuriate the La'il. And absolutely impossible.

He brushed a tear from her cheek. "Did you think I needed convincing? Let's make this right." He kissed her softly; demanded nothing until her lips parted under his and he felt her touch his face. Her breath quickened when he began to unlace her blouse to bare her body before him. When his hand moved over her, delighting in every curve, she bit back a moan, knowing that his twin slept nearby. His lips followed his hands as they made their way along her body, taking their time, tasting, feeling until they knew all of it. His patience broken at last; he lifted her over himself to fit their bodies together as they seemed meant to fit, watching her face as they began to move languidly without the mindless fervor of their earlier encounter.

"Open your thoughts to me," he whispered, reaching for her.

Both of them gasped when he entered her mind as pleasurably as he had entered her body, each suddenly able to feel what the other did. Together they explored this new sensation, as foreign to him as to her, and let it fuel the rising passion brought about by their physical contact until they reached a crest of ecstasy neither had attained before. Their minds remained as passionately entwined as their bodies and it was a long time before, sated, they fell into a deep, exhausted sleep.

* * *

Aletha awoke to find herself alone in the cave. She huddled in her blankets, not entirely sure if the night before had not been a dream. Or should have been. She had woken in the pre-dawn to find herself cradled in Galen's arms, cushioned by his strong body. She had remained awake for a long time, listening to his even breathing, letting it calm her and put her worry and confusion aside to find a few more hours of sleep.

Slipping into her blouse, she wondered about this new talent she was discovering and if using it taxed the mind and body - she had noticed neither Galen nor Chor rising and leaving the cave. But she felt wonderful, strong, and as though her perceptions had been heightened and made more powerful. She knew that the clouds were breaking up although much of this coast was swathed in fog that wouldn't lift for a few more hours. She could tell that this cave used to belong to a pack of wet-woods cats that had moved on two seasons ago. She also knew that one of the twins was now approaching.

Damp daylight greeted her when she crawled out and sat in the opening of the cave, tousled and slow to wake. Her perch overlooked a gentle decline toward the cove on one side and the edge of a forest to the other. She could almost feel the sun reaching through the clouds up here but drifting patches of fog obscured both the boat and the trees.

One of the twins appeared below, carrying an armful of firewood. His steps faltered when he saw her but he approached their campsite without changing his blank expression.

"Galen?" she said, already knowing the answer.

He looked up at her call and shook his head. His hair was still wet from his morning swim but he was dressed and ready to continue their journey.

"Where's Galen?"

"In the creek," he said.

She watched in fascination as he touched some dry tinder to a stack of kindling and, after a moment of concentration, carefully blew on it. Small flames leaped up and soon reached for the larger pieces of wood.

She came down to the fire and crouched nearby, drawing her bare legs under her blouse. "Uh, Chor," she began. "About yesterday..."

"What about it?" He handed her some fruit.

"Did Galen tell you what happened?"

He nodded, suspiciously examining a piece of dried fish that even Aletha found less than appetizing. Shrugging, he flipped it into a small pot of rice and water. "Are you all right?"

"Me? Of course I'm all right. Why?"

Chor's lip twitched in what might have been a fleeting grin. "He was out of his mind and you're a bit on the frail side."

She gasped, feeling a furious blush coloring her cheeks.

Had Chor been awake during her and Galen's rather voracious lovemaking? "Frail? Me? I happen to be just the right size for this moon, you behemoth! He could keep the details private, in my opinion. What else did he tell you?"

"He's upset."

"Upset?" she said, astounded. "Why is he upset?"

Chor looked toward the trees as if to see his brother walking among them. "Maybe you should ask him."

"I'm asking you!"

He took a moment to balance the pot over the fire and then sat back on a rock, his arms folded on his knees. "It was not his decision, you gave him no time."

"He's thought about it," Aletha said, knowing that Chor was right. "I saw it in his mind. He wanted me. I only let him know it was all right."

"There are other ways to do that." Chor began to unwrap a parcel of tea leaves. "*She* uses him like a toy, at her whim. She can make him feel things and do things and make him believe that he wants those things, too. You did exactly the same thing. Not only that, but it got away from you. And most definitely away from Galen." He held up his hands to stop her protest. "Yes, not on purpose and no one got hurt. We can help you become anything you want, Aletha, but don't make him the playground for another goddess."

Aletha scrubbed her face with her hands. "I've made a mess of it, haven't I? At least I think I know why the La'il does what she does. She gets power from it. Real power. When I was doing those things to Galen's head, I felt strong. Powerful. Much more than when I was playing with the risers. It's like he's a mirror that amplifies everything I send to him many times over. I think the La'il uses him to make herself stronger. I don't think she does this just because she wants to hurt him."

"I've wondered about that," Chor said, sounding interested. "If she just wanted to injure him she could easily do worse. She could just make him *think* he was in pain and he would be. But she doesn't. She wants him angry. Are you saying you were able to *feed* on Galen's mind?"

"As good a word as any. But not on his mind. On the way he felt. His emotion at the moment. The better he felt, the more power I received from him. It must be even stronger when it's a bad feeling or she wouldn't do it, would she?"

He shook his head, pondering her theory. "I have no idea."

"Well, he's got something she finds useful. I'd bet she'd be fiercely furious if she couldn't get a rise out of him. Maybe he should try to be nice to her. See what that does."

"She'd tear his lungs out and have them for breakfast."

She grinned. "I think I'll go for a swim and then figure out how to apologize to Galen."

Chor offered a rare smile, now looking exactly like his twin. "You just did."

She stood up. "I think you two should stop discussing me when I can't hear you!"

She left him for the small stand of trees where a stream passed near their camp. The cold water did much to clear her head. She thought about the previous night and smiled when she recalled Galen's passion. Then she blushed when she found herself wondering if Chor was equally skilled.

Still bemused after her bath, Aletha wandered through the woods in search of Galen. She felt his presence farther along the stream and found him seated under a tree, watching the fog dance across the small meadow. He wore only his leather trousers and she slowed her steps to admire the broad, smooth chest, remembering the feel of his body as if he were touching her even now. His wet hair curled glossily to meet wide shoulders marred by the wound he had sustained in Delann's bathhouse. But for his scars he and Chor were identical; why was it only Galen's eyes that caused her breath to catch, only his smile that she felt down to her knees? Surely he had known how his presence had affected her – what good could come of hiding it? She sighed and approached him.

"You're right to be angry with me," she said, crouching beside him. "I'm sorry. I guess you know Chor already shouted at me."

He said nothing.

"But I was so excited about this... this talent I have. I wanted to try it on something big. Something more important than just showing you pictures. I got carried away. I'll never do it again, I promise. I am not like... her. I didn't mean to touch you like that. But then I couldn't stop..."

He shifted his attention from the riverbank to her. "I should have been able to stop you," he said. "If I really thought it was so wrong, I should have been able to."

"Chor said—"

"I know what Chor said. I was angry, but only with myself. I'm tired of being manipulated. So why can't I stop it? I can only blame myself for what happened last night. I could not stop! You have a great talent, Aletha, but you are a novice, you know nothing. And yet you got past me as easily as La'il."

She started to say something, perhaps something kind and reassuring to chase away the tired hopelessness she saw in his face, but his words had stung. Had the previous night meant nothing to him? "Maybe I got past because you wanted me to. Have you thought of that?"

"Of course I wanted you to." He ran his hands through his hair and looked up into the trees for answers. "But I can't tell if it was me doing the wanting."

Aletha winced, knowing that another wrong word from either of them would lead to disaster, yet unable to stop. "How can you say this? I would never have done that if I thought you didn't want it. How dare you suggest otherwise?"

He blinked, startled. "That's not what I wanted to—"

"Oh, stop it, you're confusing me!" Angry now, Aletha came to her feet. "I promise to take more care and not touch you in the future. That way you can be sure who's put what thoughts in your head." She turned away but had barely taken a step when his hand closed around her wrist.

"Don't say that," he said, looking up at her with a crooked grin.

"Say what?"

He tugged on her arm until she sat back down. "About not touching me."

"But you said—"

"Forget what I said. I was out of my mind only the first time. I'm not now. And I'm finished with the pouting." He wrapped his hand around the back of her neck to pull her closer. "I've wanted you since the day I almost bought you." When their lips met she did not need to touch his thoughts to feel the craving that so closely matched her own. Almost effortlessly, their minds joined as their bodies did, fixed only on this encounter, neither attempting to look beyond what the other offered. Together, they found the means to shut off all other intrusions into their space, pulling a mental barrier like a blanket over themselves. Time slipped away as they made love, then rested in the soft grass by the bank, drowsily talking of nothing only to come together again, mentally, physically, or both at once.

It was nearly noon, the morning fog long since chased away by the sun's attempts to break through the clouds, before they ambled back to the camp. Aletha could still perceive Galen's content state of mind, happy to note an unmistakable, uncomplicated fondness for her that he did not bother to hide. He raised an eyebrow, sensing her scrutiny.

"You like me!" she blurted.

"I noticed."

"I'm sorry. I shouldn't pry."

He shrugged. "I'm used to it."

"You don't have to be, you know. You can keep her away."

"Not if we want to get back home. We can't reopen the launch without her getting into my head to show us how that's done."

"I don't mean keeping her away when you need her for something. I mean keeping her away when you don't want her there." She reached up to stroke away the vertical line that had appeared between his brows. "I think I can help you," she said. "I know it can be done; it's just a matter of finding the right place. Like the way you showed me how to recognize chi'ro. I know I can do this!"

"Keeping her out isn't all that difficult, as long as I'm paying attention. She's hard to notice sometimes. It's when she's already in my head that things go horribly wrong. That is when I need a way to get loose."

"Then we'll start with that. With you fighting me. It'll be easier, I'm sure, but if she's not there to make you... do things while you're fighting, you'll be able to concentrate better on what you have to do to get free."

"Concentrate? With you in my head?" He bent to kiss her before resuming their walk back to camp. "Well, no harm in trying but we can't let her know you're doing this. Don't forget that she will be your teacher on the Homeworld. I'm sure she's not very happy with us right now, anyway."

They soon reached the cove near the foot of the cliff that had sheltered them during the previous night. They would have to leave now or spend another night, waiting for the appropriate tides to clear their way through the islands.

Aletha hesitated. "Uh, about Chor..."

"What about Chor?"

She blushed. "Well, I mean, does he have to know everything that goes on? I'd be so embarrassed."

"Chor doesn't care," he said.

"Are you sure?"

He observed his twin coming out of the cave with their camping gear. "I'm sure," he said.

EIGHT

It was not a good day for doing business at the reservoir. The usually barely-felt vibrations from below were uncommonly strong, to the point where the floor itself seemed to move. The air around the squat tower shimmered and swirled as if an unfathomable heat was rising from the ground. People in the employ of the La'il hurried from chore to chore, careful to draw no attention upon themselves. In a mood like this, their leader was, at best, unpredictable.

The La'il was in her private rooms, pacing now and again to keep herself from exploding. She knew that her current mood was agitating the stockpile of chi'ro concentrated in the silos below into a disturbing force perceptible by even the most obtuse mind for miles. Chi'ro was a perfectly innocuous matter, incapable of affecting anything it encountered until a human mind shaped it into something purposeful. But the aggravated state of her mind today incited the chi'ro to the point of affecting the other people around her, causing concern and unwanted inquiries.

La'il forced herself into calmness. Gradually, the vibrations subsided and the essence again flowed at a measured pace to and from the reservoir, to be of use to those who needed it to do their work. She could almost hear the sigh of relief throughout the tower – in the personal space afforded to some, in the places of business, and in the processors below.

The La'il passed through the doorway onto the open-sided overlook that, along with her own rooms, took up much of the top floor of the reservoir tower. Except for gentle breezes, no weather was ever allowed to sweep through this belvedere and so she spent much of her time here, including many nights during which she stared up at Chenoweth's unhurried orbit and devised her plans for the future. Her bare feet made no sound on the finely detailed blue and silver tiles when she moved past her raised couch to the stone balustrade.

She leaned over it to observe the thin streams of chi'ro arcing through the air and into the caverns below, drawn there by her adepts. Without her steady control over its ebb and flow, the precious resource would be squandered by anyone for any scheme, a waste of the very essence that gave life to the Homeworld and protected it from the elements.

Although less generously appointed, there were towers like this wherever nodes of chi'ro converged and made the construction of a reservoir practical. In other places, single risers were used to produce electricity to be dispensed to all parts of the Homeworld, needing no adepts to transport it there. Even small emanations were carefully managed under heavy guard, leaving only some in the most far-flung areas of the Homeworld to those who could help themselves. No riser on this planet could be claimed as private property.

Assured that her barely-controlled temper was no longer interrupting the routine flow of chi'ro into the reservoir, the La'il returned to her worktable to stare at sheaves of petitions that had piled up there since only yesterday. She sat down to read about a proposal for not only chi'ro but also two adepts to direct it in an attempt to lift an ice floe from the southern pole to a drought-stricken region on this continent. That one would more likely find approval than the request to change the course of a major river because it did not fit the schemes of the city planners.

She glared at the demands for more and more chi'ro for more and more outlandish projects. Well, there was no more of it. While the supply of chi'ro was steady, it was transient and limited and once used had to be replenished over time. And so its distribution must be efficiently managed, a feat made possible only through the unequalled power of her mind.

Eventually, she knew, there would be more people with more needs attempting to share the Homeworld's finite supply of chi'ro. Within a few hundred years there would only be enough to supply the healers and the power plants, perhaps continue some system of communication. And then? Would chaos take over as the major adepts of the day laid claim to individual nodes, each single riser? Would they become what Thali had become: a lawless mob of idol worshippers, eking out a living as best as they could on an inhospitable planet?

For now her laws controlled the wealth; any blatant waste of the resource was penalized. She knew these laws to be harsh, even unfair, and her system of justice more concerned with curbing dissent than resolving conflict. Opposition to her methods had come and gone over the years, suppressed through quick retribution for real or supposed threats to her sovereignty. Uprisings had taken place and battles had been fought during which people died and enemies were made. There was never any mercy for those who opposed her, but anyone choosing to live in peace was rewarded with the comforts and sustenance that made life on the Homeworld pleasant. Her vision assured that no one suffered from any lack or malady - a worthwhile objective that left little room for dissidents and revolutionaries.

The greatest threat she faced was not open warfare. A wave of a hand by her or a number of her prime adepts could scatter an advancing force like a foot brought down upon an anthill. But she herself had been the target of assassination, both physical and political, plotted by unseen enemies who delivered poison or intrigue even to her private chambers. Her bodyguard surrounded her at all times and watchers like Galen roamed the planet to search out the plotters and schemers and terrorists.

The La'il's gaze moved through the room's open windows to search for Chenoweth in the sky. And now this! After centuries of peace, that rabble of colonists was stirring from their self-imposed exile. The stalemate that had begun with the severing of the conduits was in danger now and she could feel their attempts to break through the barriers between the moons. Stupid of Dazai to die without passing on the secret of the seals to his people! How fortunate for the Homeworld that La'il had uncovered that secret before Chenoweth did, allowing her to get through the launch, if only for an instant, to send the twins to Thali. She knew Chenoweth had also tried to create a conduit in an effort to seize Aletha. They were still prying and pounding on the frozen seal and perhaps it was just a matter of time before they succeeded. They must not succeed! With the girl in Chenoweth's control, La'il's dreams for her planet would come to an end.

An angry hiss escaped her lips. The girl! La'il wanted to reach out at the smaller disk hanging in the sky and throttle Galen, Chor and the girl all at once. How dare he!

The adept left her table to pace to the enameled door to the hallway, aware of her renewed agitation once more affecting the chi'ro. She halted her hand on its way to the latch and walked back to her desk. She should have sent someone else to retrieve the girl. But only her strong mental link with Galen made their quest possible. Few among her adepts had this connection with her and only this connection would enable her to bring them back again. And until now, no one else had had such a connection with Galen.

She had felt Aletha's touch on Galen's mind all the way from Thali, waking her in the middle of the night. She had suspected a great talent asleep within Aletha, waiting for someone to awake and train it, but nothing had prepared her for a mind as powerful as her own. With proper guidance, the possibilities were infinite! The La'il had been pleased to discover this, content with the knowledge that Aletha's great talent would soon be within her grasp to manage and control, the way she managed and controlled all life on the Homeworld, which flourished under her tyrannical but ultimately beneficial leadership. She had been amused by Galen's helpless reaction to Aletha's clumsy seduction.

This morning, however, was another matter. She had reached Galen in time to discover his entirely unwelcome feelings toward Aletha. Not only did he seem to harbor some absurd affection toward her, but had also begun to question his role in La'il's plans for the girl. Did he actually mean to keep her? When Aletha had come to him again they discovered the means, somehow, to erect a mental barrier to keep anyone from looking into his thoughts.

La'il touched her flawless face and then ran her fingers lightly along her body, its perfection maintained throughout the centuries by an immense amount of chi'ro. It didn't take great insight for her to understand that she, who ruled everything and every person on this planet, had allowed herself to be taken by some insane, uncontrollable jealousy.

Temporarily, she could make Galen do and feel anything she wished but never, not even on those few occasions long ago when he had come to her bed willingly, had he particularly cared for the La'il. It had never really mattered to her – she craved and cultivated his darker emotions. But now she understood that he was perfectly capable of caring, of tender thoughts and of wanting those feelings returned, freely and openly. And all of it he squandered on that girl!

She rushed back to the door and, this time, flung it wide. The hall outside, like her sumptuous rooms, was a vaulted, stone-pillared excess of tiles and carvings, improved upon by hundreds of years of artistry since the reservoir tower was first built. Here, too, the walls were practically non-existent, allowing light and air to flow through the uppermost story of the building.

La'il stepped into the breezeway to see a cluster of adepts

loiter at the far end. Some of them had been in her service long enough to know that being readily available when she was in a mood like today's was preferable to being hard to find. "Get me Rangii!" she shouted at them, satisfied when they jumped to attention.

Rangii rose from his perch on the banister and moved toward her in that smoothly gliding step that irritated her on the best of days. His floor-length vest was casually unfastened to reveal his snug shirt and tights and that annoyed her even more. The stately robe was something favored by the elder adepts and he wore it like a dressing gown, knowing it emphasized his height and elegance. Not surprisingly, he was shadowed by Caelan, his companion since the boy had come of age and joined the tower staff.

Arriving at her door, Rangii touched the back of his fingers to his brow but she had already turned away, disinterested in his salutation. "What do you know about Vankrug and his people?"

Rangii followed her into her rooms and took a chair beside her worktable, something only the most exalted of prime adepts dared without invitation. Caelan, more aware of his place in her estimations, remained by the door. "Small rebel faction near Morningside," Rangii said, trying to guess her mood. Perhaps seating himself had been a poor choice; his leader had remained standing, her stiff posture clearly revealing her tension, even if the whipped-up chi'ro flying about the place hadn't given that fact away. "Too much time on their hands. Thinks he ought to get access to the riser that's popped up in the middle of his pasture. Minor annoyance."

"Well, this minor annoyance has just gotten himself two more primes." The La'il gestured at some messages on her table. "Shai is one, not sure about the other."

"Shai doesn't surprise me. She's been making noise about Vankrug's faction for a while. She's a little soft for the brawny types. She'll come home when she tires of him."

"I want her home now. I need you to fly out there and—

" La'il's eyes snapped to Caelan waiting patiently nearby. He returned her gaze fearlessly for a moment, an inviting smile playing over full lips before he lowered his head. She surveyed the youth, aware that Rangii had noticed her interest and let the moment spin out until his apprehension became something she could taste and feel. He came to his feet but did not quite dare to stand between Caelan and the La'il.

"Wait for me in there," she said softly to Caelan and nodded toward her private chamber. Her couch was clearly visible through the open door. She struggled to keep a smirk from her face when Rangii's indignation threatened to explode into what would surely be a regrettable incident. She was disappointed when he brought himself under control before deciding to open his mouth.

Caelan's secret smile reappeared as he moved to the exit, slowing his steps when he passed Rangii. "Can he come, too?" he said, his soft eyes on his companion.

"Rangii is busy," she replied. She watched him leave the room, turning at the door to close it gently, his last lingering glance for his leader. La'il turned her attention to Rangii who stood silently fuming in the middle of the room. Deciding to tighten the screws a little more, she gestured toward her bedroom door. "He's beautiful, isn't he?" She briefly closed her eyes when she felt anger mingle with the resentment exuding from the adept. His thoughts were tainted with selfish insecurities – not nearly as satisfying as the pure, unchecked fury she was able to wake within Galen. "And so very talented. Like his father." Pretending not to notice his mood, she walked briskly around her table to seat herself. She did not invite him to take his chair again. "How many people are with Vankrug?"

Rangii blinked. "What? Oh, him." He folded his arms in a futile effort to regain his composure. "I have no idea. His clan isn't big, but he practically runs the town. Owns a lot of land."

"I want them gone. Go there yourself and take them

out."

"Gone? What do you mean?"

"Gone! Make an example of them! I don't intend to build a fortress around that riser and I will not have my adepts turned against me. I want Vankrug and his posse dead and his lunatic followers scattered. Accuse him of growing chibane. Confiscate his farms, but leave his tenants alone."

"Vankrug is Chor's assignment," he said, taken aback. Up until now, the dissidents had done nothing more unlawful than rally around a few angry speeches and refuse to pay their levies. Certainly, Shai would not be there if chibane was grown or stored anywhere near the place. "He's got some of his people in there. I don't know who they are and I wouldn't be able to get them out. Can't this wait? Vankrug isn't doing any harm right now."

"Two more adepts betraying me is a lot of harm! Chor isn't here and the situation requires a resolution. I can't wait until they get back here. I'm giving it to you."

"He'll kill me," Rangii whined. "Galen and I don't get along so well. Can't you send someone else? I don't think I have the stomach for—"

"Get out of my sight!" La'il hissed, barely loud enough to be heard. "And bring Shai to me when you're done. Alive, if you can manage that." She watched him stumble from the room, his cultivated poise no longer in evidence. A placid smile touched her lips. Galen would be furious over Rangii's interference. It had taken them months to get close to that faction in a bid to settle things peacefully. Now it was gone. She could make anything gone. It was wise to remind Galen of that.

NINE

When the fugitives on Thali moon finally arrived at Alarit Dunn, they were more than a day later than intended, having missed the turn of the tide once or twice, perhaps not entirely by accident. Aletha directed the twins to steer their craft through a bewildering maze of increasingly swampy bays, inlets and rivers until they were not so much rowing as punting the craft through shallow, silty lagoons. The canopy of trees above them closed in along with swarms of stinging insects. Rubbing their exposed skin with the juice of some large, freshly-crushed flower turned it an interesting shade of yellow, but also kept the stinging insects at bay.

At last, having left most of their gear in the boat, the three travelers marched single-file along an overgrown path toward what Aletha assured them was Minh's village and the home of her youth. Chor grumbled under his breath, used to the perpetual damp of a rainforest even less than the perpetual damp of the coast. Patches of mist filtered what little light reached down from the treetops and he felt uncomfortably crowded by the jungle that hid the many eyes he felt upon them.

"Here we are!" Aletha announced brightly. They had come to the edge of a small lake where canoes and rafts were tied to long banks of steps hewn into the shoreline rocks.

Some distance from the lake, the forest once again formed a dense, seemingly impenetrable barrier. At its edge, nestled among the outermost of the colossal trees, a village perched on a framework of stilts, some of the buildings connected by short walkways and bridges much like those connecting the pinnacle islands along Phrar's coast. A few of the small dwellings were wrapped right around the trunks of large trees and some of them were even slung one above another or hung from massive branches like they belonged to some monstrous birds living in these wilds. More bridges connected these nests to form aerial walkways among the treetops. To Galen's surprise and considerable relief, the buildings seemed snug and neatly maintained, built of wood and tightly woven grasses. The floor of the village was carpeted with a springy layer of chipped wood through which water drained quickly to provide a dry surface. Because of remarks overhead in town, he had half-expected to find a tribe of savages eking out a dismal living in the depths of the jungle. But this place looked to be no more primitive than what they had left behind at Phrar's waterfront.

Livestock and small children did whatever livestock and small children did on the ground below the houses, and noisily at that. Seeing the new arrivals, the children forgot their games and raced toward them, their joyful noises muted only a little when they neared the towering pair of twins flanking Aletha. The commotion brought out some of the adult villagers who came to greet them with broad smiles, happy to see Aletha and unreserved in their welcome.

The children stayed below when Aletha and the twins made their way up a ramp to the level of the stilt houses. Most of those were single-room dwellings of woven mats and wide fronds lashed together. Water dripped from leaf-covered roofs but the interiors, open to view through sheltered doorways, looked dry and inviting. They continued along the catwalk until Aletha stopped in front of a large communal area. Bowing slightly, she entered, beckoning

Galen and Chor to follow.

"Aletha!" she was greeted by one of the men, who smiled wide and gap-toothed in greeting. "Have you come to be my bride, at last?"

Aletha laughed. "Of course!" she said and embraced the man fondly. "But mostly I've come to see Minh."

The man's expression changed to one of regret. "She and her brood are out gathering her remedies Aletha," he said. "We don't expect her for a few more days. She'll be back for the harvest feast."

Galen sighed. While he was more and more reluctant to return to the launch site that would take them home, a stay in this village did not appeal one bit. Although he felt no hostility from any of these people, here, in the close silence of the forest, their every move seemed watched and scrutinized. Even now he felt curious eyes stare at him from doorways and dense vegetation. How far more enticing a prospect, he thought, to travel onward alone, with only his silent, unobtrusive twin to disturb their newfound need for privacy. Aletha pinched his arm affectionately, perhaps guessing his thoughts.

"Well, then we will wait," she said. "Do you have room for us?"

Their welcome in this village seemed assured. The man led them to a nearby hut, his disappointment obvious when he saw that Aletha would not be sleeping there alone. It was a one-room affair – not one of the interesting-looking tree houses but one in a row of smaller buildings along the raised walkway. It contained little more than a large sleeping platform covered with brightly colored blankets, a few shelves and storage containers, and a central brazier venting through a hole in the roof. A clever turret above this opening kept the constant drip from the treetops from entering the hut. As in other parts on the moon, people here tended to crouch or kneel when at rest and instead of chairs there was a scattering of padded mats. Chor was shown to a similar cottage next to this one.

While Galen inspected their new quarters, Aletha rummaged through a large basket to find something suitable among the dry clothing kept on hand for visitors. "Here, put this on."

After watching her discard her traveling clothes in favor of a colorful wrap, Galen shook out the bundle she had handed to him. "I can't wear this," he said. He held up the sarong she had given him. "Not that I mind wearing a skirt, but I rather not walk about bare-chested."

"Why not?" she asked, puzzled. "Oh, you mean your scar? Does it bother you when people see it?"

He nodded with some reluctance. "I'm shy, truly."

"Is that a new thing with you?" She handed him another piece of clothing made of a deep blue material. "We do have shirts here, too, you know. But with all this rain it's just easier to get your bare skin wet than wear damp clothes all the time."

"I think I've figured out the trick of keeping my clothes dry on this sponge you call a moon."

She grinned and ran her fingernails lightly across his bare chest. "Yeah, but I like you better undressed."

* * *

Several days passed during which they did nothing except spend pleasant hours in the company of the villagers, explore the surrounding forest, or make love. Aletha was completely at ease here, a creature of the forest like the others, in her element of water and damp earth. The twins got used to the constant presence of her people, an easygoing lot with a great love of poetry and music. They did not subsist merely on what the forest had to offer but exported well-made carvings and musical instruments, some of which Galen even recognized from their short stay in Phrar. He learned that these people lived out here by choice, having migrated from the seaside towns set up by the first colonists on Thali. With the emergence of the emissary sect, they had simply left the coast to try a simpler existence in the wilderness of the barrier islands. His careful mental explorations revealed a number of Descendants among the villagers, many of them more gifted than the people of Phrar.

Even here small risers vented from the overgrown ground, albeit weak ones. Galen continued to train Aletha, showing her increasingly difficult feats, knowing that the pupil would soon outpace the teacher. He tried again to persuade her to learn to use chi'ro as a percussive force, useful in combat to strike out at an enemy, or as a source of fuel to create fiery explosions in battle. She refused stubbornly, too appalled to even consider using her talents to crush internal organs or shock a mind into irreparable damage. She seemed more excited by her discovery of how to keep the leeches and stinging insects away without even needing to draw upon a riser.

Resigned, Galen shifted her training to medicine and began teaching her how to use her gifts to hasten the healing process of almost any ailment. Chor contributed to her studies by helpfully stepping on a poisonous insect, enduring without complaint when Galen drew out his discomfort to make sure that Aletha understood the injury before attempting to treat it.

They also continued to explore their ability to join their minds, not only to perceive the other's moods and sensations, but also increasingly able to communicate without words, even if not as easily as he was able to speak to the La'il. Predictably, their experiments often led to less scholarly explorations of their bodies, but Galen realized that he valued their cerebral couplings as much as their physical ones. He had known other prime adepts, both mentally and otherwise, but none had Aletha's powerful, yet utterly uncomplicated gifts.

Daily, Aletha goaded him into a mental battle in which he was forced to expel her from his thoughts or suffer an unending stream of unpleasantries ranging from an onslaught of nauseating images to cloying poetry. It was easier to keep her out of his thoughts than to force her out and these exercises often left him shaken and exhausted and unwilling to continue. Gradually he became more adept at controlling the degrees of intrusion permitted and the amount of chi'ro required to accomplish this.

For his part, Chor refused to join their games. Unflappable and thick-skinned, he was less prone to La'il's assaults and rarely allowed her to enter his thoughts. Although Aletha worried, Galen did not press him to change his mind.

* * *

"It's a harvest day mask!" Aletha exclaimed. "Isn't it beautiful?"

Four days after their arrival at the village, Galen and Aletha had strolled down to the lake to investigate the preparations for a celebration that was to take place at the shore a few days from now. One of the colossal *harith* trees had fallen during a recent storm and everyone capable of such work had been busy cutting its dense, black wood and hauling it over a great distance back to the village. The islanders did not cut living wood and occasions like these supplied them with raw material for their trade to last for years. Even the twins had been recruited to help store the timbers and rounds in shelters every bit as protected from the damp as their own living quarters.

The day's heavy labor done, several craftsmen had gathered around a wheezing, smoky fire near the water steps, intent on their carvings, occasionally joining in the soft, rhythmic humming that often accompanied their work. One of them had held up a mask he was crafting for their inspection.

Galen and Aletha dropped into the sand near the group to admire the fine workmanship. "These masks are made of the *harith* wood," Aletha explained. "It's part of the celebration. Look how carefully these shells are embedded."

Galen had to agree that this piece, carved only with a straight blade, was evidence of remarkable skill. He turned it over in his hand and as he did so noticed dirt under his fingernails. Some beaded leather thong was wrapped several times around his wrist, looking like it had always been there. His hands and feet were cut, chafed and bruised from exploring this forest barefoot and using his hands to help with chores instead of relying on chi'ro. He let his gaze move over the small group on the beach. Already, he recognized some of these people on sight, knew their names, and understood their habits. Tuarin had brought his flute and its plaintive song now joined the craftsmen's baritones to send a melancholy mood over the lagoon. How peculiar, he thought, that he would follow these villagers' ways so easily. Squatting barely dressed on a damp beach, skin and hair perpetually wet, eating raw fish; only yesterday Chor had climbed a tree to reach some tender shoots whose sap was considered a delicacy. Were they taking this vacation just a bit too far? He no longer bothered to comb out and tie his hair and instead let it hang unbound in curling strands over his shoulders. On the Homeworld most of his friends would think it strange to see his hair out of place or some stain on his clothes. His combat-ready body was the result of carefully calculated physical training and precise mental disciplines. Here it was exercised by hikes and rowing and climbing. He grinned down at his sand-encrusted feet, shaking his head.

"What?" Aletha smiled.

He ran his fingers through his hair. "Nothing. Feeling good. I used to love shaping wood as a boy. We don't have such fine timber, though." He leaned back to nudge one of the artisans to ask for a piece of the material, a half-finished carving discarded because of some flaw. Taking Aletha's hand, he rose to walk a little further along the beach where they sat down again. "Watch."

His hands turned the smooth wood to explore its shape and texture. He began to rub it, following its natural shape, applying gentle pressure here and there as if to test its resilience.

"What are you doing?"

"Shh," he said. "Pay attention."

She leaned forward to see his long fingers stroke the wood, pressing it a little more now, and gasped in astonishment when the wood began to change, subtly at first, but soon taking on a new shape. His hands seem to compress the wood like a potter would shape a measure of clay. Before her eyes, the piece took on the contour of a crane they had seen this morning among the reeds. "That is amazing!" she marveled, watching the slender legs form without splintering the wood.

He looked up briefly before returning his attention to his handiwork. "Look closely."

She did, her eyes on his thumb as it stroked the wood, making only minor changes to the smooth surface. Mesmerized, she followed the movements of his hands. "Uh," she grunted, unable to manage more than that. She could feel his mental touch and now she was the piece of wood in his hands, feeling the gentle motion of his fingers not with her skin but with her mind. Her breath quickened and she gripped her lower lip with her teeth, intent on the pleasure he gave. He applied a little more pressure, watching her taut face as she responded to the rhythmic friction. A small whimper escaped her when he lifted the wood to his lips.

"By the gods, are you without common sense today?" a harsh voice suddenly intruded.

Galen looked up just as someone snatched the sculpture from his hands. It was one of the elders, his name was Lyros or Laros or something like that, who had come upon their somewhat intimate pastime. Something was most definitely worrying the old man although Galen suspected that it had little to do with their mental fondling. The elder examined the bent wood, his dismay clear. "Just look at this! Look what you've done to the grain! Have you any idea of the danger you can bring down upon us all if this were to find its way back to the city?" He waved it at Galen, who flinched, both puzzled and amused. "This wood grows in few places and you mark it as clearly as though the word Descendant were engraved upon it! Have you no sense?" He stalked away and thrust the sculpture into the fire made by the carvers, nearly dislodging a pot of tea balanced above it.

"He's in a bad state," Aletha marveled, still befuddled by the moment they had just shared. Galen bit back a chuckle and nodded in solemn agreement.

The elder returned to them, still ranting. "Have a care, son, or you'll bring the emissary down upon us for certain!" He seemed less worried about a demon in their midst than any evidence of the fact lying about.

Inexplicably, Galen felt a great liking for the irate man who, for all his indignation, seemed to count the strangers as part of his village-clan, which included the privilege of reprimand when called for. It had been a long time since Galen had been so casually included – as a prime adept he stood forever apart and above those who might otherwise be peers. And here he was, yelled at by a skinny old man for misbehaving. A bubble of laughter welled up inside him, barely suppressed. No wonder he felt this strange sense of kinship here – to these villagers, as Aletha's companion, he simply belonged.

"If you have nothing more to pass the time than to bend wood into peculiar shapes, perhaps the both of you can help with the preparations for the evening meal. More hands are needed there." Grumbling, the elder turned away before remembering the reason he had come to the beach. "But first you ought to go to Minh's lodge. She has just now returned."

"Minh!" Aletha exclaimed and sprang to her feet. Barely waiting for Galen to follow, she sprinted back toward the village.

Galen caught up with her, Chor at his side, just as Aletha arrived at Minh's cottage. He saw a woman there, younger than he had expected, surrounded by a swarm of children. They scattered when Aletha flung herself into her mentor's arms, crying joyful tears over seeing her again. Galen watched from a polite distance while the woman fussed over her foundling, admiring her hair or some minor change of her figure, only to embrace her again. Some of the children also clamored to be the first to greet Aletha.

A considerable amount of time passed before Minh discovered the twins nearby. She froze, staring first at Galen, then Chor, for an interminable moment. His smile of greeting wavered under her intense scrutiny.

Aletha was startled by the suspicion on the seer's face. "Minh, this is Galen and Chor. They've brought me to see you."

Minh's eyes moved slowly to Aletha. "You have much to tell me, it seems."

Aletha nodded brightly. "I do, love, so very much."

Galen raised his hands and smiled good-naturedly. "I see you have a lot to catch up to. We'll bow out of the women-talk, if you don't mind. We'll be down there, scraping fish or pounding seaweed or something. I think we're having silt worms tonight." Catching a peck on the cheek from Aletha he turned and walked back the way they had come, Chor close behind him.

Minh watched them go, and then turned to Aletha. "The day has come, then," she said finally.

Aletha frowned. "What day? What do you know about this?"

Minh's eyes traveled upward to the sky, although neither Chenoweth nor the Homeworld could be seen this time of day even if the dense forest had allowed a clear view. "I only know you're destined to leave Thali, dear. But I cannot see where you're going."

"They say I belong to the Homeworld."

"So you may. But is that where you want to go?" Minh's pale green eyes gazed beyond Aletha, to the place where the twins had turned a corner. "Those men share the power of the Old Ones. I feel it. They have taught you. You know about the magic."

Aletha nodded. "They call it chi'ro. Why have you never told me?"

Minh smiled sadly. "I am only a wet-woods seer who reads the weather and predicts the harvests. What can I teach you? Would I tell you about such wonder only to have you frustrated by your inability to use it? Draw attention to yourself by failed attempts at magic?" She shook her head. "I've sheltered you for as long as I could. They have found you now. And so you must go." She ran her hands through the younger woman's unruly curls, her smile wistful. "Now, let me put my things away while you tell me all about your years in the city!"

* * *

Galen cursed under his breath when he felt the La'il like a tap on his shoulder. It was late, but Aletha was still with her mentor at the other side of the village. Gritting his teeth, he lifted aside the barriers he had placed against the La'il within his mind and promised himself to remain composed.

"You are too kind," she sent sarcastically, floating into view. She was dressed in a tight-fitting suit and her hair was wound securely around her head. Combat-ready, Galen thought. Her expression did not disguise her opinion of his current appearance. Chor, lounging nearby, returned her frown with a bland smile. "Gone native, I see."

Galen shrugged.

"Why are you not on your way north? I am expecting you. All of the Homeworld is expecting you."

"Why the rush?"

The La'il's eyes narrowed. "Why the rush? While you are playing in the forest, Chenoweth is preparing to launch their conduits and conquer the Homeworld! How dare you put your own interests before all of us here?"

"She and I—"

"You and she are nothing! Chenoweth has almost succeeded in opening the seals. You have to get her out of there now or all will be lost. Leave for the mountain tomorrow. If you miss another orbital alignment it'll take me twice as much chi to reach you."

"I had no idea things were going that badly. We had to detour because those emissaries were after us. Barely made it out of Phrar."

"Emissaries? You mean those priests?"

"Hundreds of them, but I'm not sure I'd call them priests. They're a zealous bunch. Nothing to do with ministering to the faithful." He told her about the unsettling incident at the harbor temple.

"Fanatics!" La'il spat. "Another reason for you to pry yourself loose from your new playmates and come home."

"I will," he promised. "But why do we have to use the launch in the mountains? There is a crystal right in Phrar Thali." He sent her a mental image of the temple. "You could have brought us back days ago."

"Interesting. I thought the other sites were all under water by now." She probed carefully. "Well, no risers anywhere near there. No wonder it's not detectable from here. It's useless to us. The launch in the mountains is the only one that will do."

He stretched out on the comfortable sleeping mats covering most of the hut's floor. "Fortunate for me. You know, I'm rather enjoying this vacation. Boating, hiking, plenty of sleep and fresh air. Not to mention the dazzling quality of naked-time." Galen felt a mean satisfaction when La'il briefly turned away, hiding from him any reaction she might have displayed at this barb.

"Yes, I saw your little romp in that cave. It was entertaining. You're a talented—" She interrupted herself. "You two aren't still playing head games, are you?"

A distant smile played over his lips when he recalled some of the moments he had shared with Aletha. He did not display those to the La'il, knowing that his new skill for hiding things infuriated her beyond endurance. "Can't help it. I swear I didn't show her, but she can whip up a chi spike that would make even you blush. Last night, when I was about to—"

"You are playing with fire, Galen! How dare you risk

yourself. What if she damages you? You don't have enough chi to get out of trouble."

"We don't have enough chi to get *into* trouble," he replied, but her words worried him. Aletha now accomplished with ease tasks that even on the Homeworld required a high level adept. Knowing that she would soon have nearly unlimited resources to use as she wished, he tried to curb her excitement and instill upon her the need to move cautiously, to understand a thing absolutely before subjecting it to the power of her mind. But already he felt her impatience with his vigilance, aware of her growing confidence in her abilities and her desire to forge ahead. The La'il was right; a disastrous mishap on Aletha's part would be beyond his skill to remedy.

"I can handle it," he said finally, wondering what she would say if she knew how far their head games went beyond the bedroom. "I'm not showing her anything harmful. She's not even interested. She could be a great healer or mentor but she will never play your war games. I don't know how you'll get her to oppose Chenoweth."

"Leave that to me." She tilted her head and observed him thoughtfully. "You know, there is something I meant to tell you earlier, but you know how busy I am."

"Tell me what?"

Her form hovered in front of him, her size nearly true to his. She touched his chest to send an icy jolt through his body. When she floated closer to him he felt her breath against his ear. It was cold. "Your time is running out. Yours and Chor's. The longer you're up there, the less likely I'll be able to restore you. I don't suggest you take a liking to Thali. That moon has ways of changing people, physically, like it changed all of them over the past thousand years. If you change, either of you, or both, I won't be able to help you."

"You knew this and you said nothing?"

"You were only to be gone a few days. Leave for the launch tomorrow." A cruel smile touched her lips. "You have no choice, Galen. In this or anything else. You never did."

"Don't be so sure!" he snapped.

"You've tried to defy me before, and failed," she said. "I can get to you no matter where you are."

"Getting harder, though, isn't it?" he said. "I can beat you, La'il."

She laughed. "You're not even close to that." Her hand stabbed out to grip his throat. Remembering Aletha's theory that La'il was perhaps benefiting from the rage she was able to provoke in him, Galen fought against his instincts and remained motionless, his eyes on her. Unbelievably, her arm met with no resistance and her incorporeal hand passed through his neck.

Galen looked down at her pale arm and a slow grin formed on his face. "I will beat you, Goddess. In time."

She withdrew her hand, astonished by what had just taken place, and decided to change her tactics. "If these tricks amuse you, so be it. Did I mention the problem with Aletha?"

"What problem?"

"I didn't want to mention this before, but it might not be possible for me to restore her to the size she was meant to be. She's been on Thali for a very long time." She arranged her fine features into a tragic, wide-eyed expression. "I've consulted with the primes day and night! There just won't be anything to work with! Failure on our part could cost her life." She sighed and gestured as if to pat his shoulder in commiseration. "So that means, of course, once you've returned home and I've restored your body to what it was, you will be a giant to her. Obviously, you cannot continue your... dalliance with her."

"Dalliance!" He swung his arm to push her away. His hand met with nothing yet the gesture was not lost on the La'il. "You knew this would happen when she gets home! What will become of her?"

"Of her?" La'il snapped. "She will save your world, Galen. She'll be short but she'll have saved almost ten million people!"

"Then let her return here when you're done with her. At least here she fits in."

La'il sighed. "Must you be melodramatic? Do you really think she'd be willing to give up the things I will show her just because she can't reach the light switch? For what? Avoiding the local imbeciles bent on exorcising devils? Have you completely lost your mind?" She peered at him more closely. "You know, I believe you have. You are in love with the girl!"

"Don't be absurd."

Her silver eyes flashed at him, her laughter a tinkling of bells. "I've warned you, Galen. Don't get involved. The last thing I need is your broken heart to mend."

He snarled at her, knowing that she was right. He had begun to imagine ways of staying with Aletha once back on the Homeworld, from vaguely seeing himself sharing whatever golden cage the La'il was preparing for her, to considering an escape to some distant part of the planet. Wishful thinking, he understood now, easily dreamed up and impossible to realize. Not because he would be restored to his former size, but because the La'il would make certain he would never see Aletha again. "Some day, La'il..."

"Some day I hope you come to your senses! Don't you understand what lies ahead of her? She will have anything and anyone she wants. You're just another adept among many. Do you really think once I've shown her all that is possible for her she will bother with someone like you?" La'il reconsidered. "Well, perhaps she might. You're an appealing diversion when properly motivated."

"I doubt your perversions interest her. She is nothing like you."

"She is exactly like me! My sister, remember?" La'il laughed. "Consider this for a moment: Why do you give a damn about what happens to Aletha? You've only known her a few days and you're infatuated. There are a hundred pretty women here ready to share your bed, some of them also powerful adepts. Has it ever occurred to you that Aletha is making you feel the way you do? On purpose?"

"What do you mean?"

"She's been in your head. You know exactly what I mean. Since when do you care who's in your bed, as long as it's female and decently adept? How do you know you really feel the way you do about Aletha? Maybe she put those thoughts there. She's playing with you. You're no stranger to having your synapses scrambled. Does this not feel familiar?"

"Nonsense. I'd know the difference," he said but an edge of doubt lined his words. Would he know the difference? When the La'il rode him, the false emotions instilled by her powerful mind seemed completely his own. At those times some vile monster seemed to be in control of his actions, oblivious that it was not part of his true nature. It never felt wrong at the time. Was he equally oblivious now to Aletha's influence? "Why would she do that?"

The La'il shrugged. "She's done it. In that cave, remember? Maybe she likes it; I know I do."

Galen glared at her, considering the possibility with rising unease. He was drawn to Aletha. Incredibly so. Certainly, when their minds touched, there was no place he'd rather be, nothing he'd rather be doing than to be with her at that moment. She seemed to belong in his thoughts and he felt incomplete when they were separated. La'il was perhaps right to question his inefficiency in carrying out his mission on Thali. Every minute wasted on this journey meant another minute spent with Aletha, far away from their obligations on the Homeworld. "You're lying," he snapped, furious at her for putting these doubts in his mind. "She would not do this."

"You have no idea what she's capable of." La'il hovered close to him, her words a sibilant whisper in his thoughts. "How does it feel to be inside her mind, letting her touch you like that? How can it be real?"

He closed his eyes but that did not remove his tormentor from his sight.

La'il smiled when she touched him and her hands met his body, firm and unyielding – corporeal once again. "It isn't real because she put it there."

He pushed her hands away and came to his feet.

"Do I have to tell you that this adorable new weakness you have for the girl is giving me another weapon against you? You're making this too easy. Tell me, do you ever get tired of being played like a puppet?"

"You are going too far!"

She closed her eyes, perceiving his anger, drawing it into herself like a surge of chi'ro. "Yes, I am."

He felt her reach for him, probe into his mind, entice his rage to let it flow from him to her as if along a strong, throbbing pulse of energy. He tried to look away but she seemed to be everywhere, too close to him, too easily touched. Emotions that did not belong to him flashed through his brain and the battle for his mind commenced once again. Although adept, he was a soldier and trained like one and so their struggle was one of physical imagery. He saw himself throwing her to the floor of the cabin to wrap his hands around her slender throat, her body trapped beneath his, helpless. But here, as in reality, her strength equalled his, fuelled by the power of her planet, and she was able to throw him off and spring to her feet. His only thought, his mind's only solution, was to kill her and with that free himself of her dominance. Even through the rage robbing him of all rational thought he understood that his fury only increased her power, tightening her control over him. But it was too late to stop now.

"Still think you can beat me?" La'il taunted. "You need this. Admit it."

He pushed her into a corner of the hut, both of them utterly unaware of the thousands of miles separating them. When he pinned her against the wall with his body, her hand on his chest curled into a claw and her nails dug deeply into his skin. She was unprepared when he recoiled to hurl her across the cabin to his waiting twin. Chor twisted her arms behind her, forcing from her a yelp of surprise and, Galen hoped, pain.

"Didn't count on that, did you?" Chor rasped.

La'il strained away from him. "This makes no difference," she hissed at Galen, pleased to see the blood-filled crescents left by her nails. "Just remember that you brought him into this, I didn't."

Chor shoved her at his twin. "We'll all remember. Let's make this a night to remember." Galen wondered if the cold, unthinking malice on his twin's face was also written on his own.

Suddenly, unbidden, Aletha came into his mind as if he had called her and she had replied in startled surprise. Her image was like a cool breeze wafting into an unbearably stifling room and he clung to it, trusting her to pull him into the light and air that she seemed to be made of. It took no more than this shift of attention to break free from the La'il. Her piercing wail of protest drove into his brain when he withdrew to lock her out with one brutal blow from his mind to hers.

He counted many pounding beats of his heart before he dared to open his eyes. Cold sweat covered his heaving chest and his limbs thrummed from some great exertion although he had not moved a muscle during this encounter. He was in darkness, the glowing vision of the La'il dissipated, replaced by a foggy sense of vertigo making it hard to remember where he was, or who, or why.

He became aware of light footsteps hurrying along the walkway outside. A moment later, Aletha came into the hut, carrying a torch. He watched her enter, her face obscured by flickering shadows and thick curls. His lip twitched in a fleeting snarl. Why had she interrupted them, he thought resentfully, his fists digging into the sleeping mat beneath him. Why did she have to interfere?

"Galen?" She placed the torch onto the hut's brazier and crouched beside him, worried. "I felt you, like you were in pain, all the way to Minh's lodge." She drew back with a startled yelp when she felt anger radiate from him like heat. "Hey! What's this about?"

"La'il came by." He sat up slowly, with effort.

She leaned forward and moved her face up along his chest and into the curve of his neck, hovering closely as if searching for some scent. "Anger, hate, fading now." She closed her eyes, her breath touching his skin. "Must have been terrible, earlier. It's powerful, like something I can touch. I think I can..." After a moment she shuddered and shook her head. "Sorry, but you taste awful. How can she like this? Personally, I prefer you in a happy frame of mind."

"I bet you do."

She took in a breath, about to say something, but then cut off her retort. "Yeah, I do," she said instead. She touched his shoulder, feeling the tense muscles beneath his skin. "Besides, your neck gets all veiny when you're mad. Looks painful."

He exhaled forcefully, the spell broken. "I'm sorry. Don't know why I said that." He shook his head to clear away the memory of what had just happened here. "She's worse in my head than she is in person."

She moved over to where Chor sprawled semi-conscious on the floor. He groaned when she helped him sit up. Concerned, she stroked the tousled hair from his face and then turned back to Galen. "Are you okay now? You're shaking. Does she have to keep at you like that?"

He looked down at himself and saw no bloody indentations where La'il had clawed him. All that remained were some small red spots, quickly fading from view. "I'm beginning to see a way to throw her off. Once I got a hold of you I was able to shut her out. I'm getting there. I think I hurt her. She's furious. Unfortunately, an angry La'il is worse than a bored one."

"What did she want?"

"She is getting impatient. She wants us home. You didn't tell Minh about her, did you?"

Aletha shook her head. "No, I wouldn't even know how

to begin." She looked over to his twin. "You okay now, Chor?"

"Fine," he replied. "We have to travel on. If you're done here let's continue north." He came unsteadily to his feet and ducked through the door to find sleep in his own room.

"Why is she in such a hurry?" Aletha said to Galen. "Is this war about to begin? Why are you two in such a rush to get back there if she is so cruel to you?"

"Chor and I can't stay here. There is something that affects humans here. She told me if we stay here too long we might not ever go back."

She swung a leg over his and sat on his lap. "We'll leave in the morning." She kissed him while her hands sought to soothe his taut muscles. "When all of this is over, we have to get you free of that La'il. Both of you. Try to relax now."

He drew her close and returned her kiss, far less gently. Aletha responded readily but he knew he was holding her too tight, touching her too roughly. Thoughts of the La'il crept into his mind and he shuddered when he thought about where his mental battle with her had been leading. She had brought him down easily this time. Dismayed, he realized that his hand in Aletha's hair had tightened into a fist and, worse, that she was gathering a little ambient chi'ro to meet the demands of his too-tense body. With prodigious effort, he pulled away from her. "Not like this," he gasped. "Not you."

"It'll be all right. Let me help you." She reached for him but he caught her hands in his and kissed them before leaving their bed.

"I'm going down to the lagoon for a swim. Chor's on fire, too," he added with a lopsided grin. "It's… distracting. Don't wait up."

TEN

It was barely dawn when Galen awoke to the sound of the children outside as he had every morning since they had arrived at the village. He blinked into a beam of bright sunlight filtering down between the trees and into the dim comfort of their hut, yesterday's episode with the La'il fading from his mind like the nightmare it had been. He stretched lazily, feeling content, and turned toward Aletha curled up beside him. He leaned over her and buried his face in her disheveled hair, breathing of her scent. By his calculation it would take at least three days to reach the mountains, perhaps another to find the gate. Four more days of this loving and lighthearted woman who was destined to become as powerful as the La'il, perhaps learn cruelty and selfish vanity along with the knowledge to control everything that existed on the Homeworld. Four more days before she learned that her future did not include him. Would it matter to her? Now it did, perhaps, on their carefree journey through Thali's beautiful wilderness, but the La'il was right: Once Aletha discovered the true extent of her abilities, the prospect of losing his company would not bother her for long.

"Why are you growling in my ear?" Aletha mumbled sleepily.

He smiled and pulled back to look into her face. "I was purring." He nuzzled her neck and let his hand journey along her body.

"What is making you purr?"

"Probably your hand there is making me purr," he replied, stifling a moan.

She moved her hand again. "That hand?"

"Yeah, that one." His lips touched her breast. "How would you like to learn another new and interesting use for chi'ro?"

Aletha smiled and waited expectantly for his demonstration. He groaned loudly when a polite scratching noise near the door announced a visitor.

"Pardon me, please," a woman's voice intoned outside when no one answered her signal. "But Minh has asked to see the brothers immediately, please."

Aletha tried to sit up. "They'll be there at once!"

"Can't it wait?" Galen asked her navel.

She pulled the blanket away from him and gave him a little shove. "Come, get up. Wake Chor. If Minh wants to see you then you go to her. That's the way it is here."

"And I suppose you get to sleep another hour." After tossing his hair into some semblance of order, he tied a blue kilt around his waist and shrugged into a shirt.

Aletha blinked into the daylight entering the lodge when the mat covering the doorway was taken away. "Hey, you," she shouted at Chor. "I'm not dressed."

He smirked and propped his forearms against the top frame of the door, using his bulk to block most of the entrance and the view of anyone who might be passing by outside. His hair curled freely to his bare shoulders and the long, green sarong contrasted nicely with the deep tan of his skin. Aletha wondered if any of the women of this village had made their way past his own door yet.

Galen crouched beside her pallet. "I'll be back soon. Stay exactly where you are. Don't move."

"Hmm, don't know if I can wait."

He regarded her sternly. "Keep your hands outside the blankets until I get back. I'll take care of things then." He swooped down to kiss her before turning to leave.

Aletha giggles followed him as he ducked out of the hut.

But suddenly her laughter died in her throat. Her mouth went dry and the edges of her vision narrowed as if she were about to faint. Wide-eyed, she stared at the space that Chor had just occupied, the memory of him standing there etched in her mind. A low whimper passed her lips, threatening to evolve into something louder.

When Galen had just now stepped out of the lodge, his brother had turned aside, his arm still resting on the lintel of the door. Clearly, she had seen the broad, painful-looking scar twist across the man's ribs.

Jolted into action, Aletha scrambled to the opening of the hut to peer outside. Chor and Galen were at the bottom of the ramp, talking to one of the villagers. As she watched, the twin in the green sarong accepted a length of string from his brother and reached up to tie his hair back. The angry scar at his side was now clearly visible from above. Amazed, Aletha realized that the other man down there, the man who had just shared her bed, was none other than the taciturn, absent-minded Chor.

* * *

Galen and Chor ducked into Minh's hut, uncertain of the protocol involved when speaking to one of the village's leaders. They glanced about the simple room, seeing the many implements and accessories belonging to a healer but no obvious signs of power or religious significance. Like many of the cabins, the walls were made of loosely connected panels, lightweight and easily replaced if damaged in storms or earthquakes. Clean, woven mats covered the floor and something steamed gently on the brazier, exuding a soothing aroma.

Galen turned when someone entered from the rear room of the cottage. "Oh, hello," the man said, not particularly surprised to see the twins here. He carried a toddler on his hip and moved past the twins to rummage through some containers on a shelf. "Get comfortable," he said, gesturing toward the floor. "Minh's along in a bit or so."

The twins, forced to stoop in the low-ceilinged room, knelt gratefully on two mats set out for them. Another child padded into the room, stopping to stare critically first at Chor and then at Galen. Thoughtfully, she pulled a finger out of her mouth and reached up to poke Chor's eye.

"Tsu-Tsu," the man said cheerfully. "Don't be bothering them." He scooped the child into his free arm and moved to the door where he nearly collided with the healer. "We're out of tea," he said, maneuvering around her. "I'll send Geb to fetch some." He looked beyond her. "Now, everyone outside. Give your mother some quiet."

It was a while before the chatter in the back of the room subsided and the twins were left alone with the woman. The healer squatted beside the brazier in that oddly comfortable-looking way common to those who lived without furniture. Her arms were wrapped around her knees as she busied herself with some parcels on the floor, balanced perfectly on splayed feet. Her yellow hair was cropped very short except for a surprising fringe of ringlets around the hairline.

Minh remained silent and they followed suit, willing to observe whatever customs they encountered. This woman was no adept, yet Galen perceived a wisdom that by far outshone any he had found on this moon. Likely, she would be counted among the Descendants in towns like Phrar. He felt her presence, faintly, although the chi'ro she surrounded herself with was likely not enough to really matter. Here she was simply a healer and sage, perhaps using her small talent to bolster empathy and intuition to useful levels.

"I know who you are," she said suddenly, without preamble, startling them. "Or what you are. What Aletha didn't tell me speaks louder than what she revealed. Which of you speaks for you?"

"I do," Galen said after a long moment, regarding her

warily. "How did you—"

"You are of the giants," she said, settling herself onto a cushion. She fussed with the edges of her wrap, intent on arranging them neatly. "Somehow sent here by the Old Ones to bring her to the Homeworld."

Hesitantly, Galen nodded.

"And do you know why?"

Galen began to speak, but then suddenly realized no explanation could give this woman the answer to her question. While nebulous, undefined doubts had nagged him since he first learned of his mission to return Aletha to the Homeworld, the fundamental cause of it all had seemed clear: Aletha's ultimate role was to help protect the Homeworld from invasion by Chenoweth. Looking at Minh, he now knew that something eluded him. The seer did not have some peculiar gift for making him suddenly realize some formerly unknown fact, but something about her compelled him to tell her the whole truth. Unfortunately, this then made him realize that he simply did not *know* the whole truth. Perhaps at some point it hadn't mattered – questioning the La'il's motives was dangerous at the best of times and his job was usually far less troublesome if he stayed out of her politics. But this was no longer just a job. There was so much more to be known beyond the simple explanations with which he had been dispatched on this quest. Things that went far beyond anything he had imagined. His head spun with this knowledge, although he had no idea how he knew. He looked at Chor to see his confusion mirrored on his twin's face. At last he shook his head. "Tell me," he managed.

"I don't know much, but I will tell you what happened, how Aletha came to be here. She believes herself to be a foundling, and I suppose in some way that is true. I found her, but only after a long search. She was already three years old by that time. How did you two find her?"

"What you call magic is rare on this moon. We are able to perceive it at a distance, especially when it's disturbed. Aletha has a way of causing great disturbances of it, even when she's not aware of it."

"That is what guided me to her, but it took a long time. I lost my way many times, misled by curious apparitions seeking to lead me astray. But I found her. I purchased her from her parents who by then were so frightened that they were willing to hand her over."

"Her parents?" Galen asked, less surprised by Aletha's legal status as a slave than the news that she was of no relation to the La'il.

Minh nodded. "They would have given her to me, but I insisted on payment to cut all ties cleanly. She would have brought terrible trouble to her family if she had been found out. Don't think too badly of them; they did not part with the child easily. But they believed I would provide a safe haven for her, which was beyond them. The sound of her mother's weeping haunted me for a long time."

"What made you search for her?"

"We try to find all the new Descendants before the emissaries do," Minh said. "Sometimes, mercifully, their talents are so weak that they escape notice entirely. Others have a gift so strong that we must strive to suppress it, guard it until they have learned to use it only with great caution. Aletha has such a gift and was already wielding it as a toddler, to the peril of all those around her. I decided long ago to keep the extent of her abilities hidden from her, for her own safety. Then I taught her how to hide it from others, too. Even those with the gift find it impossible to detect the one within her."

"Such a waste." Galen shook his head. "No one on the Homeworld lives in such fear. Our Descendants use their gifts to benefit others. That is our law. Surely something like that is possible here also. Why hunt them for their talents?"

Minh reached into the folds of the gown pooling around her legs and withdrew a small bundle tied with a beaded leather thong. Placing it carefully in front of her, she unrolled a long, narrow strip of leather. It was worn thin by many years of handling, as supple as any woven cloth. She straightened it out on the floor. Galen bent to view the tightly arranged writings on the vellum.

"What is it?" he said. "This would take me a long while to decipher."

"This is one of the original transcriptions of the words left to us by the Old Ones, before they left this world. It describes their commandments as they gave them to their emissaries, not as those fools on the mainland would like to interpret them."

"Can you translate this for me?"

"That would take a long time. But I will tell you what it says." She pointed a finger at a section of minute script. "Thali moon, this world, was once like the Homeworld. People were able to live in peace, there was no sickness, and they were able to create a good life out of the abundance of this moon. No earthquakes, few storms, gentle tides. What a wonderful place this must have been!" Minh smiled happily as she contemplated. "Then changes came," she continued. "The people changed. Each generation brought people of smaller size. Those born here were so different that they were unable to return to the Homeworld. Nor did they want to. Thali had become their home." Minh traced her fingers over the writings, as if reading them for the first time. Galen waited silently, imagining this moon as she had described it. He thought of its beautiful landscape, long days, plentiful food sources, and an abundance of water - all of this without the storms and earthquakes now a part of life here. No wonder no one had worried about returning home again.

Minh's words nagged him, confirming some things La'il had said only yesterday. "Why were they unable to return to the Homeworld?"

"They sickened. Maybe because everything was the wrong size. Maybe the air just didn't fit into their lungs quite right again. For whatever reason, moving between the Homeworld and either moon was something you either did for a short visit, or forever."

Galen's eyes returned to her scroll. "Go on," he said.

"Well, then the great upheaval took place," Minh said.

"Upheaval?"

"Storms, fire, earthquakes," she pointed at a series of characters. "It turned to panic and some of our people were forced to enter tunnels leading to the other worlds. Magic users, mainly, and most of the giants here at the time. Some of them escaped and were left behind. Then the doors to the Homeworld were sealed. These were not gods who did these things, but a mortal man named Dazai and his followers. They retreated to Chenoweth and closed the doorway behind them."

Galen nodded, his brow furrowed. "Your document confirms our own account of this history. But ours makes no mention of adepts being forced to leave Thali. Why was the Homeworld blamed for all of this? Why are the giants feared? Dazai was a giant, wasn't he?"

Minh's thin fingers meandered over her archive, sorting through information that Galen was certain she knew word by word. "Yes, but the giants they left behind were blamed for his displeasure. They were just some poor magic users, visitors from the Homeworld who were abandoned here. We needed someone to blame, I'm sure. For their size, they weren't difficult to point out. They were murdered, and some driven away. We now have stories of giants still living in caves in the mountains, their bodies covered in fur because of the cold. Some think they will return some day to avenge their ancestors. Or the giants will come up here from the Homeworld for the same reason. You see, once abandoned, we were free to create our own history. Aided, no doubt, by the emissaries left here by Chenoweth."

"So the emissaries really were appointed by Chenoweth?"

She nodded. "By Dazai. Before they left, he gave us a commandment. No one, he said, was to use magic on this moon ever again. I suppose they feared that we would learn how to reopen the gates to the Homeworld. The emissaries were to enforce their decree."

"And turned it into a religion."

"Yes. That was about three hundred years ago. Since then many adepts were killed and unable to pass their talents on to new generations. And those born with it had no teachers to show them how to use it. Now there are few of us left, a miserable handful of Descendants who know about the magic even if our powers are limited. We hide, or we disguise our talents."

Galen stared at the ancient writings before him. "Does this talk about the La'il?"

"As Dazai's enemy. Bitter enemies. I could try to read the spaces between these characters and tell you that she killed Amaya, Dazai's companion. Then she took his sons and hid them on the Homeworld when the doors closed. What do you know of her?"

He hesitated. "I'm more and more convinced some things exist that should not be made known on this moon. Your people and mine are no longer even of the same race. We see the same thing but we have different truths for it."

The seer bent to furl her parchment again, her movements carefully deferential. "You have much to tell me, young man, but I no longer want to hear. This scroll has become a heavy burden to me and I don't wish to add to it. Few copies of this exist. There are truths in here that would change how people perceive Chenoweth. And the Homeworld. But there are facts that justify the emissaries' actions. We cannot risk what would happen to this if the emissaries had the chance to interpret it for the people. And so it remains hidden."

Galen watched her put the parcel away. "Are there not enough of you, people who know what you know, that can counter the emissaries' lies? I saw carvings of Dazai in the headman's lodge. Your own people here pray to Chenoweth. Even Aletha, even now, won't let go of her gods. How can you stand to let them live in ignorance? There must be a way to stand up to the power of the emissaries."

Minh cocked her head to study him for a long moment,

her brow furrowed. "Do you have gods?"

"Me? No, not really."

"Your people, I meant. The Old Ones."

Galen thought about the confusion of histories belonging to the people who had come here from Earth. "We have many. Sometimes it seems that each of our clans has their own set of deities. There are some very strange ones among them! It's an interesting study, if you care about things like that."

"And your people obey the commandments of their deities?"

He shrugged. "Only if they don't interfere with the laws of the Homeworld. Our laws are not given to us by any gods. They are decided upon by our rulers, to serve all."

"Good laws?"

He grinned, understanding her point. "Not according to some."

"We have no rulers here, son. No one to make laws for us except for our gods." She waved a hand at the scroll. "Of course, it's the priests who interpret for our gods. We have many good laws and our lives are made easier because of them. We have a tale that the goddess Aysel was turned into a seal by another deity. And so Dazai decreed that no one may hunt for food or profit the sacred crested seals that roam the southern coasts. How fortunate for us that he gave us this law, because those seals thrive on the poisonous leeches infesting the seaweed plantations. Our harvesters can dive there freely, knowing the seals are there to guard them, waiting for the leeches that seek human blood. We need those seals. And so I say: what difference does it make if our laws came from Chenoweth or if they were decided upon in the chambers of the Grand Priestess? The emissaries are simply a part of this land as much as those poison leeches. I know even some of our clergy view with distaste their besotted hunt for even the most circumspect of magic users. Of course they would not say so for fear of the emissaries' accusations. We could not rise up against the emissaries; we could not tell the truth about Chenoweth without endangering everything that keeps us safe here. We have no one as capable of maintaining order as our priesthood and the promise of the Garden. You don't like some of the laws you must obey. Do you rise up against your leaders? Surely not. Because they make things work, be that for better or not. Who am I to try to change our world for the sake of a few Descendants?"

"Yet you harbor some of them here," Galen said, tipping his chin toward the rear room of the cottage. "Those aren't all your children, are they?"

"My compensation for keeping this ugly secret!" She winked at him. "Sometimes changing a little piece of what you don't like is enough, don't you think? By sheltering Descendants here, I am opposing the emissaries very, very quietly." She chuckled. "Aletha is my own little rebellion."

"She was safe out here, with you. Why did you send her to Phrar?"

"To learn, Homeworlder. What could I possibly teach her here, other than to keep her great gifts a secret? This is her family, but she doesn't belong here any more than you do. Her abilities are far beyond anything any of us have encountered here. You know this is so or you would not be here. Her talents are even noticed on the Homeworld, after three hundred years of silence. Her destiny won't be found here in the islands. Maybe you are part of it, who can say?"

"She is so very important to us. My people believe Aletha's gifts will help us defend ourselves against… an enemy's advances."

"Your enemy," Minh said. "Is that also her enemy?"

He sighed. "I don't know any more. But if we fail to take her home our people will suffer. My choices are few."

"And what is her choice?"

Galen smiled sadly and rose to his feet, stooping under the low roof. Minh reached up to grasp his hand before he could turn away.

"Will she be happy there, Galen?"

He hesitated, unable to meet her eyes. "She will be well. She'll have power and influence and the means to do great things to help many people. I think that will make her happy."

* * *

Brooding over what Minh had told him, he returned to their cabin, needing to talk to Aletha about these things. But when the twins arrived there she was not inside. None of the villagers seemed to have seen her this morning. They walked down to the lake where she might be bathing. No one had seen her there, either. They combed the village and even walked a short way along some of the paths weaving through the forest. Nothing. At last Galen concentrated on a weak riser nearby, drawing its essence into himself. He cast out his mind, searching for any sign of her, any fleeting thought or emotion he would recognize as hers. Cursing her knack for remaining invisible, he returned to the village. The morning was drawing toward noon, but she had not appeared at the communal eating place by the time the twins joined the others there.

Galen barely took part of the large platters of steamed noodles, vegetables, and thick slices of the venison that abounded in this forest. The chatter of the people around him seemed very far away as his thoughts kept returning to what he had learned from both Minh and La'il over these past two days. Each passing minute of their fruitless search for Aletha this morning had seemed to double his need to talk to her about these things, as if the longer he waited, the greater the likelihood of something terrible about to happen.

She needed to know. She had a right to make her choice before he delivered her to the La'il. The danger presented by Chenoweth was no longer Aletha's concern; she owed allegiance to no one. Galen did not doubt that Aletha would consent to go to the planet, if for no other reason than to realize her potential as adept. But the lies had to stop. He was as much a part of the deception as the La'il had been, willingly or not. Galen glanced at his twin who hunched silent and brooding nearby. She would have to know the truth about Chor, too.

"Galen!" someone called from below the walkway when they returned to their cottage in hopes of finding Aletha there. "Chor, whoever."

Galen peered down to see Minh running toward him, waving something. He let himself drop onto the soggy ground below. "I can't find Aletha," he greeted her.

"She's gone," Minh gasped, out of breath. She thrust a parchment at him, closely inscribed with neat script. It was easier to read than the hieroglyphics more common on this moon.

Dearest Minh, Galen read. *I hope to be far away by the time you receive this. I won't remain here for even a moment longer. Galen cares nothing for me, nor my future. I only now discovered that the brothers have been sharing me like a toy for these past days. The pain I feel is boundless and I do not wish to face them again. I believe that my destiny can only be found on the Homeworld and I believe I can live my life freely there, without fear. And so I will continue north to find the way there on my own. Surely, the Gods will protect me and guide me. Be well, my love, if They will it, I shall see you again.*

"Damn," Galen whispered, his face bloodless.

"You're a fool!" Minh glared at him and he actually found himself recoiling from the anger she exuded. "Now she's out there on her own, upset, fleeing into who knows what dangers. There are pirates out there!"

"We'll find her," Galen said, barely able to find the words. "I'll make her understand."

"And how would you find her?" Minh scoffed. "No doubt she's taken your boat and we have nothing here for open water but traveling canoes, far too slow in a race with her sails. There is no way out of here for you but on foot, the long way, if you can find a guide to take you that far. It can take weeks to the nearest port."

Galen nodded slowly. "We'll fly," he said at last.

ELEVEN

As inspection tours went, this one was hardly out of the ordinary. The facility, like most of the newer ones, was reliably efficient, reliably productive and reliably uninteresting – in fact, it was a model of reliability. There were a distressing number of substandard processing plants further down on Yobar's list requiring his attention far more urgently than this one. Equipment failure, labor troubles, management incompetence and chi'ro shortages awaited him at those locations, but none of their problems were easily solved in the presence of the La'il. He had carefully maneuvered their agenda so that the trouble-free facilities were the first to be visited, leaving the headaches for a day when La'il was occupied with other things.

Briefly, Yobar reflected on the many times that he, as her closest advisor and, in some ways, mentor had maneuvered things, people and events around La'il to make sure that heads didn't roll. Lately, it seemed to have been his main function.

He followed the facility manager along a glass-enclosed ramp, their footfalls and voices muted by the padded floor and ceiling. The walkway served as an observation platform high above a vast chamber where dozens of adepts and novices barely kept their minds on their work, knowing that the La'il was among them.

Yobar stopped and waited for the others to catch up, wishing that this tour, little more than a state visit for the benefit of La'il's energy ministers, was already safely concluded. The flowing robes and long white hair worn by most of the entourage gave the procession the look of marble columns somehow brought to life, now gliding soundlessly along the incline, their diminutive sovereign in their midst. La'il, garbed elegantly in deep blue, presented a mask of polite interest to the eager administrators who, believing their power plant to be the cause of her foul mood, were anxious to find ways to please her. Knowing the facility to be flawless, Yobar hoped that someone wouldn't say something stupid out of utter desperation.

He bent over some charts while a staff member called La'il's attention to the new adepts who had come to work in this place. She nodded absently, overlooking the small islands of couches on which the new recruits reclined, some with mentors at their side. These were adepts of average talent, employed to propel huge turbines by drawing a steady stream of chi'ro into the building. The electricity produced here served most of B'wan Ghor, the oldest of the planet's cities. It was tedious work requiring unflagging concentration, a combination almost impossible to sustain for very long. On the other side of the glass walkway was an area set aside for recreation where the adepts rested while others took their place to keep the machinery humming.

La'il's presence nearly brought the rotors to a standstill as everyone's attention shifted to their leader. They had been warned of her visit and the mentors were alert to the novices' inevitable break of concentration, but even the seasoned adepts faltered when she walked through the overhead passage. A light began to flash, informing them of the flagging voltage.

Yobar shot her a worried glance, hoping that this inefficiency would not rouse her already volatile temper. She had not shared whatever had happened between her and

Galen yesterday but he suspected that she had taken a few unexpected lumps this time. Now she was moody and irritable and not in the least bit interested in magnets and copper coils. He recalled a recent visit to a similar plant, where some of the young adepts had stopped their work to create a magnificent lightshow in blue and yellow sparks finished with a glittering, bawdy message written in mid-air, pledging their services to her. She had been amused by this and passed their playful display with a gentle wave of her hand, her smile likely felt by each of them for a very long time. Today, Yobar suspected, such antics were likely to get someone killed for wasting chi'ro.

He handed the chart back to the plant manager and gestured for the group to keep moving, anxious to complete the tour. Perhaps La'il could be persuaded to let him continue to the next one alone; events like these bored her even when in the best of moods. He took his place beside her, hoping to hurry everyone along a bit.

La'il reached up and hooked her hand around his forearm. He bent to peer into her face, realizing that she was barely able to maintain her outward calm. Something agitated her, every adept in this building likely felt it, but this went far beyond her usual acid temper. The discordance she projected was not another mood but her tremendous effort to prevent some turmoil from affecting the volume of chi'ro flowing through this building. She looked up at him, an urgent plea in her eyes.

"I think," he said to the entourage in general, "that we have seen enough here. Lichet will complete the tour; I'll accompany the La'il back to the tower." Without waiting for the speeches of farewell prepared by the station's directors, he swept her forward to the end of the glass tunnel.

"We are to meet with the engineer," one of the two aides that followed reminded them, whispering urgently.

Yobar rushed his leader through a door into a deserted lounge, his mind already shaping a measure of chi'ro into a conduit. La'il's grip on his arm was becoming painful. "Stay here with the others, Tyla. No one is to follow." Barely waiting for the vortex to settle, he and the La'il disappeared into it.

* * *

"What has got you into such a state!" Yobar exclaimed, helping her to her couch as soon as they had touched down in her private suite. "You almost blew that entire plant to pieces."

The La'il growled at him. "Don't make such a fuss. I had to get out of there, that's all." She rubbed her temples. "It's the damn twins!"

"The twins?" he said, baffled. "Are they trying to contact you? What can they possibly be doing to affect you here?"

"I have no idea, but Galen's head is practically on backwards. I looked in on them during that interminable speech we had to endure and whatever chi spike he's cooked up just about fried my frontal lobe. They're still in that village. Can't tell what he's doing, though, but he's got Chor helping him, too."

Yobar sighed in exasperation and sat down beside her. "Is that why we left the processor in such a hurry? So you can check up on Galen? La'il, I was truly worried!"

"I'll be fine once I know what's going on."

"Thali is on the other side of the planet now. You can't do—"

"Help me, then," she snapped, her tone prohibiting any further objections. She reclined on the couch and placed her head on his lap. Resigned, Yobar put his hand on her forehead to join the power of his mind to hers, preparing to reach for the distant moon. He raised an eyebrow in surprise when they were able to hone in on the twins almost at once. La'il, too, made a startled sound when she understood what was happening.

"This is no ordinary spike," Yobar said, perceiving the impossibly large amount of chi'ro that the twins were drawing around themselves. "He's gathering power. He must be raiding the entire moon."

La'il sent a mental question to Galen who barely acknowledged her presence. His concentration focused on every riser, every last emanation within his reach, drawing it to him, building up the meager resource of Thali into a bubble of chi'ro over the village. She prodded him and received an irritable reply but then, grudgingly, Galen conveyed to her what had happened. La'il cursed. "I warned him not to get involved with her. Now look what they've done!"

"He's making a conduit?" Yobar said. "Will it be enough to transport them to her?"

"It better be, or we're lost. Unfortunately, he's probably as visible to Chenoweth right now as he is to us. Whatever he's planning, he better do it quickly." She lay in quiet thought for a moment, idly twisting a strand of hair around her finger. Her eyes travelled to Yobar's worried face when an idea struck. "Maybe there is another way."

She touched Galen's thoughts and found him fully immersed in his impossible task, too busy to even notice the intrusion. Aware of Yobar's growing disapproval, she delved into Galen's thoughts, posing questions that he was not even aware of answering, and looked to see what he had seen. In that way, she began to form a vision of what had gone before and the people he had encountered on this moon. Some time passed before she had the information she needed and, with a satisfied smirk, broke her contact with Galen.

"What are you up to, La'il?" Yobar said guardedly when she sat up.

La'il slid from the couch and unfastened her formal, intricately embroidered suit on the way to the adjoining dressing room. Yobar barely caught the rich fabric when she let it fall to the floor. Her exquisite body nude now, she walked to a wardrobe and flung it wide, considering her options. "I'm going to get some insurance, Yo," she said. "I will have that girl and I won't let Galen's blundering loveplay jeopardize everything. What do you suppose goddesses wear on Thali these days?"

* * *

Delann stood in the kitchen of his mansion high above the city of Phrar, careful to keep out of the way of his staff as he sipped a bowl of soup. The cook and his helper were busy preparing for a dinner party and their constant banter with the two maids did not abate for even a moment when their master joined them. He enjoyed his lunch in the noisy comfort of the large kitchen, smiling along with the servants but not joining in their repartee. Compared to this merry gathering, the rest of the house seemed empty and unused.

There had been a few days after his return from the islands when he had been ill with apprehension and guilt, worried about Aletha, furious at the twins, and angry with himself. He had felt duped into defying the laws of their gods, jeopardizing not only himself but also his crew. But how could he have known that there had been priests aboard those ships? The emissaries of Phrar were a lazy lot and rarely bothered to pursue a fleeing Descendant. When necessary, mercenaries were hired to hunt them down and deliver them to the enclave's prison. But for the most part, as long as the demons weren't plying their evil magic in this town, few of the priests cared to wonder what became of them. To find an emissary taking part in the chase was unheard of.

There had been a report about a small fleet of passenger ships wrecked in the channels, but the only thing noteworthy about the accident was the number of emissaries on board. Some gossip was traded among the townspeople for a day or so and then the incident was forgotten. Disasters at sea were commonplace and discussing them only underscored the peril of their lives. Fanciful tales of remote land wars and the monsters of the northern mountains were the stuff of far more interesting entertainment, made all the more comfortable for the distance separating legend from unwanted evidence. And so the rumors stopped, the emissaries summoned from nearby towns had begun to leave Phrar, and the nagging feeling of dread that rode on Delann's hunched shoulders as he went about his days faded away.

Now, as things returned to their usual routines, he busied himself with yet another of his frequent get-togethers, which brought his many acquaintances and business partners to this house for a few lively hours. But it was becoming more and more difficult to fill the hours between parties; those long hours where he worked at his desk or met with traders and merchants. His dealings up and down the coast required his presence here in Phrar and his captains and agents plied his trade, legal or not, on the seas of Thali in his stead. It had been a while since he'd felt the adrenaline that his adventure with the Descendants' escape had pumped through his aristocratic veins. He wondered why he was bored and he wondered if he was lonely.

Not that these past few days had been devoid of company! It just hadn't been the sort of company he normally enjoyed in his home. Only one day after he had returned to Phrar, a somber group of men had knocked on his gate with the arrogance of absolute authority. They had crowded into the hall, their heavy cloaks and boots dripping onto his polished tiles, ignoring his invitation to shed their rain-soaked gear. They simply hovered in a tight knot, like a hulking, ominous monster staring at him with many accusing eyes. Their blank faces seemed so very similar, nearly indistinguishably anonymous beneath the identically shaved patterns on their pates. Delann had been unable to tear his gaze away from the design – two broad bands from forehead to nape and a diagonal line across it. It was a symbol representing Chenoweth.

The emissaries had questioned him, there in the hall, within earshot of his household staff. They had not been discourteous but their menacing tone and stance never parted from the interview. He had sold a boat and supplies to a fugitive group of Descendants, they said. Two foreigners and a local vagrant. Where were they going? Had he had any other contact with them? Whom else did they visit here?

Delann nearly invited disaster by starting to deny his involvement. But surely dozens of people had seen the twins at his home. While Aletha was a notably pretty woman, it was the foreign twins who would certainly be remembered. Praying to all of his gods for assistance, Delann had launched himself into a hysterical tirade. "Descendants? Aiii Dazai! I was told they were visitors from the north, on a trade mission around the continent! Oh, for shame! Right here in my very home! Guests at my table! What tales they had of distant lands and, I must say, some rather interesting opportunities! Did you know that we could sell our brackwater clams up there for three times more than here? But Descendants! Oh, they blinded us all to that! I had no idea. I must have been bewitched! You must set after them immediately."

He carried on for some while longer in a self-righteous froth until his unwelcome visitors began to edge their way to the exit. He gave them detailed and entirely fictional descriptions of the boat and its destination and offered to send his staff to the temples in the morning to pray for an expeditious capture of the fugitives.

After the emissaries had made their escape, Delann barely managed to slam the door behind them and stagger into the kitchen. There he dropped heavily onto the crate of firewood, all strength having left him. One of the maids quickly revived him with a strong draught of liquor, her giggles echoed loudly by the cooks who were nearly hysterical with laughter. The stable boy looked up from his dinner to inquire whether there would be extra wages for having to attend services at the temple.

Delann grinned to himself at this memory, warmed by the steadfastness of his servants. Perhaps it was time to look for some gifts or some other favor to reward their loyalty. He handed his bowl to the maid when something nearby, some voice, called for his attention. "What did you say?"

"Me?" she said, startled. "I said nothing."

"No? I thought I heard…." Frowning, Delann left the kitchen for the hall, his head cocked as if to hear a sound too faint to be recognized.

"What is it?"

"I thought I heard someone call." Delann moved slowly to the door leading into the gardens. "Must be the rain." But it wasn't the rain. Something had touched him. Touched his mind and called to him, asking him, commanding him to leave the house and walk into the garden. He obeyed, both fascinated and strangely unable to resist, and found himself nearing the estate's bathhouse. "Dazai!" he whispered. A strange light shone through its windows, red in many shades, splashing over damp tiles and playing across the murals. Not particularly bright, it had been undetectable from the house. But he could see it now; a dull glow shifting as something moved within. Delann put his hand out to open the already unlatched door, unable and unwilling to stop himself.

"By the Gods…" he whispered.

She floated serenely in mid-air, swathed in rich silver fabric and reddish clouds of mist. The most beautiful, awe-inspiring creature he had ever seen and likely ever would. He stared in wonder, taking in the luminous features of her demurely lowered face, the white hair in a thick braid over her shoulder, the small hands folded in front of her.

She raised silver eyes to look upon him and he felt his heart burst in his chest. "La'il…" he breathed and fell to his knees.

It was She, he knew, although no images of Her existed other than a few crude carvings in the secret shrines. To the Descendants, she was Mother Goddess, the Exalted Deity of the Two Moons, The Lady of the Homeworld, Champion and Defender of Thali. He felt a helpless sob rise in his throat, just as he wondered why she would choose him, his bathhouse, to make an appearance.

"Rise, Delann," she said, her voice the sound of a distant songbird at dawn. Delann came to his feet, swooning.

The La'il regarded him silently for a long while, observing

his soft, awe-struck face and the way he stood, arms slightly raised in supplication, and wondered how to approach this. Finding her way back to this bathhouse, although hardly a suitable stage, had been easy. More difficult was the task of catching the attention of a non-adept whom she had never touched before and call him to her. Now, finally, the contact was made and the merchant stood before her, ready to serve. Unlike Galen, he could not even begin to imagine ways to keep her out of his head. If he even wanted to. "I am here because of Aletha," she said finally.

"Aletha?" Delann managed. "Why? What..."

Enjoying herself, the La'il allowed her face to change slowly from delicately angelic into something sterner, more befitting what they called the Mother Goddess here. "You sent her away, Delann!"

"I… what?" Delann stammered. "But..."

"She is among my favorite of mortals. You know how special she is, don't you?"

He nodded, still unable to speak.

"She was safe here with you, Delann. But you let her leave!"

He blinked. "She wanted to go. She said she had to! The emissary..."

La'il shook her head. "You sent her into great danger. She is in terrible trouble."

"No!"

"Those two men with her. Demons, both of them, who wish her harm. They have turned her against me, against her gods. They will try to keep her from me and they will use her for their evil purposes!"

"No, please, no!" he exclaimed. "I'll send for her at once."

"You will do more than that, mortal." La'il waved her hand dramatically and an image of Aletha appeared before him, her expression frightened and surprised. It was as the La'il remembered it from only a few nights ago in this very room, when Galen had mistaken Aletha for herself. The adept had to hide a pleased grin when she saw how well the vision blended into the background of the bathhouse, of course identical to the real incident.

"Aletha!" Delann's hands flew to his lips when he saw a large hand grip Aletha's neck. It was one of the twins, upon her at once, tearing at her clothes.

"This is where you have sent her, Delann! Instead of sheltering her here, where your influence protects her, you sent her into the wilds with these demons!"

She embellished the vision a little by convincing the trader that Galen had also struck the girl. Delann could not hold back the raw sound that tore from his throat as he fell to his knees again, his fists raised to shield his eyes from the ugly scene before him. Fascinated by his pain, the La'il observed him for a moment before deciding that he had had enough. The ugly vision disappeared and Delann was broken before her. She reflected briefly on what it had taken to break Galen to her will, if he had ever been completely broken. But Delann would serve, of that she was certain.

"What am I to do," he said, his voice without inflection.

"Stand up, face me, and listen," she said sternly.

He obeyed, his limbs trembling, possessed by a sudden thirst for mindless revenge.

"She has escaped them and is fleeing north toward the mountains. They will use their magic to find her if you don't find her first. Even now they are gathering their strength to strike out at her. You will command a great company of men and send them north. You will find her and deliver her to a place to which I shall guide you. Go well-armed. You may encounter Galen and Chor. They are sure to hunt her down."

"I will destroy them," he promised.

"I want them alive. And take care not to run afoul of the emissaries. They must not touch her! Let nothing keep you from your quest."

Delann nodded slowly, as if in a trance. It would not be difficult to assemble an army of fifty men, surely enough to contain the two demons. His brigantine had returned to the harbor, and a cutter was due to arrive this evening. If he started arrangements now, he could be outfitted and ready to sail by the tide.

"Dawn tomorrow," he said, as if to himself. "Two ships going north, a fleet of boats to comb the islands. They will not escape."

The vision of the La'il nodded, pleased. This merchant would hold together. His infatuation with Aletha and the images she had shown him assured his will to obey her, even if a visitation by the Great Goddess alone wasn't enough to convince him. She only hoped that in his fervor he did not take a knife to the twins.

* * *

La'il opened her eyes, taxed by the distance through which she had projected her image for the second time this day. Her body felt weak and in need of replenishing after her contact with the non-adept. While Galen's considerable talents made their mental exchanges almost effortless, maintaining her grip on Delann's mind had taken her to the edge of her abilities. Yobar supported her when she sat up, worried and frightened by what he had witnessed.

"I'm all right, Yobar," she murmured. "Or I will be." She concentrated on the great store of chi'ro below the building, drawing from it to refresh her depleted resources. While weakened like this she was prey to the intrusions from Chenoweth, which were making themselves felt more and more openly. Someone up there was watching her, feeling for her when her guard was down, making frequent forays to Thali dangerous.

"I am confident of your strength, La'il," he said. "And your ability to protect us all."

"But?" she said icily.

He practically squirmed before her. "These visits to Thali. The drain on our reserves is becoming alarming because of it. Feel it, La'il. Feel how depleted the stores are! It will be days before they are replenished. I've had to stop the construction of the northern dam because we don't have the resources. What if some disaster strikes while we are so wanting in chi'ro?"

"The next disaster to strike will be a conduit opening from Chenoweth to here, through which will come creatures who have done nothing for the past three hundred years but laze about and soak up limitless quantities of chi. And we won't be ready for them. Not until I have the girl. Once she is with us Chenoweth is powerless."

Yobar regarded her doubtfully. "You have much confidence in… your sister," he said.

"I do. Don't worry. That merchant and his people will keep her safe from Chenoweth's agents if the twins don't figure out a way to track her down. If she can stay ahead of the priests, she'll get to the launch."

"What of it? Even if she gets to the launch by herself, you still need the twins to open the seal."

La'il regarded him thoughtfully. "Do I?"

"Don't you?"

"All I ever needed was someone to help me contact her at the launch. If the twins can't manage that, then the smuggler will do, now that I have him. Through him, I will show her how to break through the seal and anchor a stable conduit between here and there."

"He is not one of us! He won't live through that."

"True, but I am not taking any more chances with Galen and Chor. Oh, this would be so much easier if I could just reach her myself!" She drummed her fist on her knee in exasperation. "She might as well not exist for all I can even perceive her mind. I can't even touch her through Galen! I wish I could just go up to Thali right now and take this job out of his hands. Did you feel him, Yobar? He's practically unconscious. I doubt he would even notice if I walked into that hut and slit Chor's throat."

"Losing Chor would kill him," Yobar warned.

"Maybe, but he's survived worse," she said, rising from

her couch. A distant expression stole over her features when she continued. "I've got grander plans for Galen. He might suffer for a while."

"You can't mean that. He's served you for a long time, La'il!"

She ground her teeth together, hissing her words. "They are useless to me now. He's learning how to shut me out. I no longer trust him. I no longer need him."

"Don't do this! You must bring them back!"

"There was never any purpose for them but this, Yobar."

"What purpose?"

"They were bred for this. Since the moment Dazai shut us out of Chenoweth, I've been working for the day when we will find the means to return to the moons. And for that I needed to send a new class of adept there." She touched her forehead. "Someone who can communicate with me from that distance. A mental adept."

"Is this why we're getting so many telepaths in this generation? You're breeding them for this?"

"Been breeding them for almost three hundred years, waiting for my chance. I thought I had a few more generations to go before I had someone who could do the job. I had intended to mate Galen or Rangii to Shai, which could well have given me what I wanted." She walked to the window and leaned out to look at the streams of chi'ro flowing to and from the tower. "Then Aletha came along and I knew I didn't have to wait any more," she said, smiling into the bright sunshine. "I had been trying to breed an adept who is both powerful as well as a telepath, but now all I needed was a telepath to let me communicate with her. Too bad I can't touch her or I wouldn't even need that!"

"And that's where the twins come in."

She nodded. "There are a few other adepts in this generation who might also do the job. Shai and Rangii, certainly, but Shai is untrustworthy and Rangii can't find his shoes without chi'ro to help him. That left Ciela and our beautifully matched set of twins."

"Ciela is capable. I'm surprised you let Galen leave here at all."

"It was a hard choice. But Thali is an ugly place and I'll not risk my dainty little Ciela up there. So I made sure the twins can work without chi'ro if they have to, they can ride and fight and get along in that waterlogged jungle. But the main reason I sent them instead of her was that little matter of their ancestry." She laughed to herself. "It's Dazai's blood in those veins, Yobar. Who better to bring Chenoweth to its knees than his own descendants? In finally triumphing over Chenoweth, I'll have my private revenge on Dazai himself."

Yobar made as if to rise from the couch but then remained seated. He didn't think his ancient legs would support him at this point. "Dazai's progeny? La'il, is that why you've singled Galen out for... for your games? Is that why you torment him?"

La'il gazed up at the pale disk hanging in the sky for so long that Yobar wondered if she would answer him at all. She her fingers along the pitted stone sill, lost in dreamy contemplation. "He thinks he's going mad, you know that?" she murmured. "He doesn't even know what he wants any more. Maybe, after all this time, he is finally starting to crumble. You think it's unfair of me to punish him for his sire's mistakes? Maybe it is. Probably it is! But every blow against him is a blow against Dazai." La'il trailed her fingertips lightly across her lips. "At first, I didn't just want to hurt him. I wanted to destroy his mind. But I found something else there: a powerful energy that I can draw from him as I wish. Properly provoked, he's like a living riser!" She chuckled at this comparison. "That little quirk is probably my fault."

"How so?"

She shrugged evasively. "I've been keeping an eye on Dazai's line since he left his boys here. I think I might have been around when certain people were busy being pregnant. You know how us women stick together at such times."

"You didn't!"

"Did. Just a little careful, hmm, zygote adjustment, I'll call it. So easy. The twins are almost pure, undiluted Dazai. And so, to me, Galen *is* Dazai. I guess you could say I brought him back from the dead. Isn't that wonderful? What's a few quirks in light of that?"

"We have laws—"

"I am the law, Yobar! And I change it as I need it to change."

"Just so you can have your revenge?"

"Well, yes. But it was a worthwhile experiment, in any case. This sort of… hmm, of genetic management is what's giving us the telepaths. Probably a little more useful than recreating Dazai." She snickered. "Didn't work out so well, anyway. I guess maybe I wanted Galen to grow into the sort of Dazai that could have been useful around here. But he just grew into every little weakness that I loathed in Dazai."

"Dazai? Weak? What weakness? Dazai was worshipped by adept and non-adept alike. His visions for the Homeworld are still with us."

"Because of me! Do you think the chi'ro distribution network would work for even an instant if I hadn't ensured safeguards? Our adepts are more powerful today than back then because I manage their breeding. I did this, Yobar! Dazai had only dreams and notions, without the resolve to carry them out."

Yes, Yobar thought, his troubled gaze on the excited, beautiful face from which her eyes flashed like diamonds. *Yes, you did all this. And those who stand in your way die. It's as simple as that. And that was not part of Dazai's dreams.* He wanted to shout this at her. He, perhaps the only one who could ever dare such a thing, felt a terrible need to just once, finally, tell her of his loathing and disgust for her ways, for the pain and torture she inflicted upon her subjects to keep her iron control of everything that moved on the Homeworld.

He took a breath and when she drew back, startled, he knew that something in his expression, perhaps, warned her of his intent. She regarded him expectantly and he realized that nothing he could say about Dazai or about her leadership would touch her. She would hear his words and allow him to live, because he was Yobar. But it would change things. He was her confidante and in some ways even her mentor, but he was not free to criticize, to censure or to judge. His unflagging support of her was what afforded him his position – without it he was just one underling among many, to be used but never to be trusted. He dropped his eyes, defeated without having begun the battle, and sighed. She knew who she was and what she was. Perhaps she even knew the real reason why she recreated Dazai.

"Galen is not Dazai, La'il. Dazai spent his life in study and discovery. Galen is too busy working for you to take that path. He's done things in your name that Dazai never would. He is not the same man."

Only the slightest twitch of an eyelid disturbed her features before she shrugged carelessly. "Can't waste all that brawn, can we?" she said. "But, sadly, he's ruined now that Aletha is showing him how to hide from me. A little mental trick I'm sure we don't want to encourage in the telepaths. He's practically off his leash. I have no more use for him."

"You mean to kill the twins, then?" He had never regarded Galen with any fondness and, if he dug deep into the hidden places of his old soul, he knew that the man's sordid involvement with the La'il filled him with a jealousy that made him feel profoundly unclean. He, Yobar, knew the La'il better than anyone and, in spite of the ruthless, remorseless ambition fuelling her actions, he cared for her deeply. To see her fail to win Galen's heart and then take him by force pained Yobar without measure. Yet, for all his resentment of Galen, he respected the adept's talents, strength, and loyalty that did not waver even when she turned him from a scholar into a warrior. Surely his service to the Homeworld did not earn him and his twin the sort of death that might satisfy the La'il.

She smiled. "Oh yes. It'll be sweet. Even sweeter will be to take Chor first and let Galen live through that. After I'm done with Aletha."

An anxious shiver crept upward from the base of Yobar's spine until it made the hair at his nape bristle uncomfortably. Was she about to confirm his suspicions? "La'il? What are you saying? You were going to bring her down here. She is to help you defend this place when they come."

La'il returned to her inspection of the bright day beyond the banister. "I don't need her down here. Chenoweth is made up of a scattering of wasteful degenerates that would be outlawed on the Homeworld. If they were really so unstoppable, they would be here by now. Any handful of prime adepts can defend this place against anyone. You, Lichet, Rangii, Fromm. But you see…" she hesitated, teasing him. Her hand reached out to some birds roosting below the sill. They ignored her. "I needed someone far more powerful for what I have in mind."

Yobar's throat worked convulsively as he tried to swallow his panic. "Powerful enough for what, La'il?"

She turned, her face alight with excitement. "To give me Chenoweth, of course. Think, old man! This is almost too simple: I just need to get to Thali myself. I need a stable conduit. And the only way to do that is either with a huge amount of chi over there, which just doesn't exist, or with the help of a very powerful adept able to anchor it. That would be our sweet little Aletha. That's it. Job's done, we can take it from there. When I get there I punch a hole into Chenoweth's seal and tap their chi like a barrel of wine."

"And then your next visit will be to Chenoweth itself."

"It will." La'il let a wisp of captured chi'ro swirl through the trailing blooms of a censer plant clinging to one of the pillars. A cloying fragrance invaded his senses and he thought he might choke. "The Homeworld will once again be joined to her moons and we'll be able to manage our resources properly. The way it's meant to be."

"You're taking much for granted," he fretted, fixed on the practical in order to avoid the horror of what she was proposing. "You can't be sure of her talents. And you don't know what awaits you on Chenoweth. What if this fails? Even just attempting this madness will be a terrible drain on our resources!"

"Only for a moment, Yobar. I've thought about this for three hundred years. I have *prepared* for this for three hundred years! I've explored their abilities on Chenoweth and none of them are as adept as I am. This won't be easy, but it won't fail." She smiled sweetly at her aide. "I don't suppose I'll need Aletha after this. One supreme goddess is plenty, don't you?"

He could stand it no longer. "But what of the people of Thali!"

She glanced at him, her mind busy with a dozen schemes. "Thali is doomed anyway," she said absently.

TWELVE

Minh walked slowly around the perimeter of the village, perhaps for the third time today. Just as she had done yesterday, after the twins had withdrawn into their hut. Her restlessness was not only the result of Aletha's sudden disappearance. Although it had been reckless to strike out on her own, Aletha was an able seafarer and, if necessary, could vanish into the forest. The source of Minh's unease was this strange magic taking place right here in the village. The tension she felt permeated the air as if some unfathomable weight was pressing down upon them all. Almost, she thought, like the hour before a terrible storm when the skies turned and those with any sense headed for shelter.

Galen and Chor remained in their cabin, leaving only at night to eat and refresh themselves, their eyes vacant, their movements stilted and tightly controlled, as if every last bit of their concentration was focused on some distant, unseen event. The villagers stayed out of their way and only Minh dared approach them. She knew that they were collecting the magic substance, calling it closer to fashion some device that would let them find Aletha. Some uncanny way of sending a stream of magic upon which they would launch themselves into the distance. Minh worried.

* * *

Galen gradually emerged from his self-induced trance as if waking from a long sleep. He tested the volume of chi'ro pooling over this village. It was nearly time; he had gathered as much of the precious resource as he could find. He would draw it into himself, and then send out a beacon to find Aletha, needing only the briefest response to pinpoint her location. Once certain of it, the twins would use the accumulated chi'ro to create a local conduit to launch themselves through empty space to reach Aletha in an instant. This form of travel was common among the adepts of the Homeworld to reach far-flung locations. But here on Thali their efforts would most likely land them on their heads in some remote corner of the jungle. Nevertheless, it was the only way to find Aletha. He did not doubt that she would respond - his mental touch would at least rouse her curiosity.

The twins had changed into their traveling clothes and now sat motionless on the floor of their cabin. Breathing evenly, they began to transform the chi'ro, a pleasant sensation that drew a smile from both of them. The essence flowed through the walls, floor and roof to enter their bodies, infusing them with physical and mental vigor they had not felt since leaving arriving on Thali. A sudden longing to return to the Homeworld, where this state was constant and natural, reminded them of the task at hand: find Aletha and then the launch. Flee this beautiful, hostile, chi'ro-starved world, with or without her consent. The moon's deficiency only underscored the potency of the essence and their utter dependence on it for their well-being.

Galen closed his eyes, preparing to reach out to Aletha. It would have been easier to do this had the villagers not decided to make this a day for making noise, quite possibly another of their frequent foot races or contests of strength. Galen frowned when the shouting broke through his concentration. Why did these women have to shriek so much?

"Galen!" Someone rudely tore aside the woven mat from the doorway of their lodge. "Wake up, Chor! Please!"

Galen strained to see Minh outside on the catwalk, her panic obvious. "What is it?" he said, maintaining his grip on the influx of chi'ro.

"Soldiers! Coming this way. They've murdered Dlen and Miru!" The seer squinted into the dim hut. "What... what's happened to you?"

Galen's mind grappled with its trance, ordered his body to move, reach for his weapons, even as he wondered why soldiers would invade the peace of the village. He lurched for the door, daggers in hand, aware that Minh drew back in alarm when she perceived their strange, altered condition. "Stay here," he snapped and leaped from the walkway to race to the edge of the village from where he could hear screams of terror, Chor only a few steps behind.

They were the cause of this, he suddenly understood. These had to be emissaries, here to rout Descendants and those who harbored them. What had led them here, so far into the barrier islands? He rounded an animal pen at the edge of the village to see dozens of armed men breaking through the edge of the trees, waving swords and daggers. One of them hacked at one of the villagers, someone Galen knew to be friend to Aletha.

He stormed forward, his mind focused on the uniformed men and the blue-robed ones that followed. One by one, they were lifted high into the air, only to be slammed to the ground or against the jungle trees. It was as if an invisible hand had reached down from the sky to destroy these intruders. The twins stopped and stood side by side in the middle of the clearing, their outstretched arms directing their gathered chi'ro at the invading army, tossing men aside left and right, killing some, maiming many. Using kinetic energies, he picked up one of the men and, turning him sideways, hurled him into a trio of soldiers coming into the clearing from the path. An attacker, about to skewer a terrified villager, suddenly plunged his dagger into his own chest. A surge of energy directed at a cluster of advancing soldiers turned all metal fittings and weapons red hot to sear skin and set clothing on fire. Spears, quarrels and an axe flung in the twins' direction were harmlessly turned aside. Five men circling from the left suddenly fell, clutching their chests as if to restart their damaged hearts.

Unnerved by all of this, some of the soldiers turned and fled the way they had come. Others had frozen in stunned surprise. Rumors of the Descendants' terrible power had always been a part of their lives and here, finally, was proof of the legends, come to life not in the shrines and secret enclaves of the cities, but in this remote community deep within the islands. The villagers, too, ran to hide or cowered in terror, alternately staring at the twins and looking skyward to witness the wrath of the gods.

Galen realized that they were spending the chi'ro that was to have brought them to Aletha, pouring it from their bodies to defend this village. He felt his power waning as the surge of chi'ro subsided and he knew that Chor was also expending more energy than he could afford. Perhaps they had enough strength to escape into the jungle. Galen raised his daggers and charged toward the soldiers barring the way into the forest. Some of them backed off in fright, others fell to his attack. He slashed savagely, more to frighten and injure than to kill, his only thought to get away from this place before these fanatics harmed more of Aletha's people.

Seeing their quarry nearly at the edge of the trees, one of the emissaries bravely stood in his way, a metal emblem clutched in his raised fist. "By the Gods of Chenoweth, you are—" He squealed in terror when the demon grasped the front of his tunic, his dagger raised.

Then Galen froze. Slowly, carefully, he lowered his knife arm and released the terrified priest whose legs refused to support him. Galen watched him crawl away, suddenly aware of the silence that had settled over the clearing. Barely daring to breathe, he turned, slowly, to face the soldiers behind him. He dropped his knives, his eyes on his twin who lay on the ground, his chest still heaving from the exertion of the battle, the tips of several swords at his throat.

* * *

"Wake up, Demon!" A booted foot crashed into his ribs, not quite hard enough to break them. Galen moaned and pulled back against the chain securing him to the ship's rail. Chor slumped beside him, barely conscious, his hair obscuring his bruised face. Someone kicked him, too, trying to rouse him. Galen glared at the soldiers, but said nothing.

They had been forced from the village at knifepoint, giving up their struggle only when another of Aletha's people was murdered to serve as example. Once the emissaries realized that the twins would not risk either each other or further casualties among the villagers, they had simply taken along a number of hostages, promising to kill one at any attempt the twins made to escape. After a futile search for Aletha among the lodges, a contingency of men had been left behind to search the area.

Galen was relieved when the hostages were left at the beach where longboats awaited them in the shallows. Surrounded by armed soldiers, they were rowed through the narrow inlet and finally out into the bay where a tall ship lay at anchor. Carefully, the twins began to cast about for any remnant of chi'ro remaining in the area. Nothing. There was not even enough of a riser within the range of his senses to tip this boat. He doubted that a desperate lunge over the side would prove to be much of an escape – the water here was shallow and perfectly clear.

They had been brought aboard the ship and tied to the railing on the quarterdeck. Only then had the soldiers fallen upon the twins, seeking retribution for their dead and injured comrades, stopping their assault only when both twins were beaten unconscious. Once in a while, as now, some of the soldiers came by to torment them further, emboldened by the discovery that these magic users didn't seem to be very magical any more.

It was now nearly dark and, although the ship had undoubtedly covered many leagues already, the twins were still not able to find enough chi'ro to restore themselves. A soldier bent over Chor and grasped a fistful of hair to tip his head back. Galen winced at the sight of Chor's cut lip and blackened eye. His shirt was in shreds and his arm was slashed from elbow to wrist. Chor glanced at him and Galen knew he didn't look much better than his twin. Seeing the hatefulness with which these men treated Descendants, Galen was glad that Aletha had left the village. The soldier shoved Chor aside and turned menacingly to Galen.

"Enough with this now, please," an impatient voice demanded their attention. The soldier turned to the emissary behind him, a sneer on his face. But whatever comment he had for the priest remained unsaid – one did not insult an emissary without dire consequence. Especially not this emissary.

The blue-robed man crouched beside Galen to peer into his face. "Stop torturing them," he instructed. "We need them alive." He placed a jar of water and a small bowl within Galen's reach. "Don't speak to them. They are dangerous, even now. Be about your business." Apparently expecting his commands to be followed, the emissary turned and went below deck without another word.

"You hear that?" Galen said, aching for the water beside him. "We're dangerous. Move along. Sharpen your weapons or march up and down for a while." He held his breath, waiting for another kick to the ribs. The soldier seemed ready to pounce, his huge fists clenched, but he held himself in check and finally withdrew. Galen breathed a sigh of relief. Although having nearly invited another beating, he now had a fair measure of the emissaries' authority over the soldiers. His next task would be to see where the crew's loyalties lay.

The twins remained unmolested for the next few hours. Occasionally a soldier strolled by with some hateful threat or a crewman passed nearby to take a look at the prisoners. Chor had passed out again, or perhaps he was sleeping, and

Galen tried to take his mind off his injuries by attempting to listen to conversations taking place in the cabins below. There were dozens of people in the lower holds, likely off-duty crew and soldiers. During his exploration his attention was drawn again and again to a small group of people, below deck and forward, that stood out among the rest. Galen sensed two strong presences and a few weaker ones among the bland manifestations of non-adepts. Were there other Descendants held captive on this ship? Was this merely an exercise in rounding up random Descendants for some large sacrificial celebration on their calendar? Perhaps this didn't have anything at all to do with Aletha or the Homeworlders.

A small sound interrupted his exercise and when he turned to discover its source his new hopes were dashed. He sat up, impatiently pulling on the chain around his wrists, and leaned back against the railing. Shaking his hair from his face, he growled into the dark, "Does your father know where you are?"

The shadowed figure came closer and soon revealed a familiar face and tangle of bright yellow curls. Looking even more ragged than when they had last seen her, Yala crouched beside Chor to study his injuries with some fascination. When she lifted a hand to poke at a particularly interesting bruise, Chor opened his eyes, startling the girl into a quick leap backward.

"Leave him be," Galen advised.

"They sure made him over, didn't they?" Yala said. "And look at you! I heard them tell about what you did back there. Wish I'd seen that. How come you don't throw some more magic at them?"

"None left," Galen said. "Why are you here?"

"Heard 'em talking down by the harbor, after you sailed off. The chief emissary set everyone after you. They were looking all through Phrar but he wasn't thinking you'd still be there. I got me hired aboard as soon as I heard tell that they were sailing after you. Wasn't hard, neither. Them emissaries always need someone fetching and carrying after them, and their women won't do for themselves. I don't mind. The food's not bad."

Galen tipped his head back. "Don't remind me. I'd eat squid tonsils right about now." Once again, he sent his thoughts to the nearby shores, looking for the energy he so desperately needed to heal his battered body. Still nothing there. It seemed as though they had used up every last puff of chi'ro venting anywhere for miles around. At another time he might have been impressed by his ability to fetch such small amounts from such great a distance. Whatever ambient chi'ro they could absorb would have to sustain them.

Yala picked up the bowl that the emissary had left. "There is some stew here."

Galen shook his head. "Chibane," he said.

"Eh?"

"Same stuff they gave to Aletha to make her sick. It does some strange things to your head. Heads like ours, anyway."

Yala grinned mischievously. "Wait here," she said and scurried away.

Galen almost laughed out loud but a sharp pain in his side turned it into an agonized cough. He rolled onto his side, waiting for the pain to subside, wondering where Aletha was spending the night, and if she was safe. Would she know to stay vigilant, alert to those who followed? Surely, she would have perceived the great surge of chi'ro amassing over the village and then dispersed with great force. Did she know what had happened? Galen hoped that she hadn't decided to turn back to the village, worried about her people, and fall into the hands of the soldiers that had been left behind there. A more frightening possibility was that she would try to apply her gifts to help the twins escape. Then again, he thought, she would likely enjoy administering a few kicks to his ribs, as well.

Yala's return was a welcome relief from his dark thoughts. The girl had brought water and a bowl of rice, along with half of a roasted bird. The twins ate quickly and then tossed the bones and empty bowl overboard, moving awkwardly with the heavy manacles around their wrists. Galen also dumped the poisoned food from the bowl that had been left earlier and poured out some of the tainted water.

"Better," Galen sighed when it was done. Chor, too, seemed more lucid now and sat up, his eyes on the sails above. "We're being watched. Don't get caught helping us."

Yala shrugged. "I'm just the cabin maid. No one pays any mind to me most times, anyway. I'll just be swatted for being where I'm not supposed to. Seems I'm all the time where I'm not supposed to! The soldiers bear watching though. Mean ones among them."

"Stay out of their way. Do you know anything about the others on board? Are there any other Descendants? Captives?"

"Um, no. Just emissaries and soldiers. No Descendants among the crew and their kin, they'd know that for certain. I been all over the ship, looking at things. No one hidden away. No one locked up but you."

Galen nodded. "I don't suppose you have any idea where we are."

"None, though I heard say we're making for the mainland in the morning."

"Back to Phrar?"

"I'm not thinking that. We're very north now." Yala looked from one twin to the other and finally dared to ask. "What's happened to Aletha? I heard emissaries tell she wasn't found."

Galen closed his eyes, craving sleep. Preferably tucked safely into the comfort of his own bed in his warm, clean, dry and well-appointed home down on the planet. "She's all right, I'm sure. She left before the attack came. We... hmm, we were separated and..." He sighed. "She got angry at us for something and left."

Yala's eyebrows shot upwards and she pursed her lips in a comical expression of surprise. "You irked her? How?"

"Never mind how. It's private."

Yala laughed. "You must have irked her truly, for her to run off and leave you out there. Needn't worry, though," she said confidently. "She's has a temper sometimes. Soon enough she'll be back and all is well again." She thought about that for a moment. "Well, usually she would be, but you being out this way is making that a chore. Think she can tell where you are?"

"Maybe, if she happened to be looking for me. Not sure what good that would do. There isn't any— someone's coming. Get lost."

Galen slouched tiredly, like Chor assuming a dazed expression when a group of men approached from the starboard side of the ship. Soldiers among them, but emissaries for the most part. A few crewmen were along, carrying lamps. The small crowd stopped several paces from where the twins were tied to the rail and one of the soldiers stepped forward to kick Chor's leg, although not with the force they had used earlier. "On your feet, wizard."

Galen pulled himself up, feeling every bone and muscle in his body as he did so. Chor tried to get up but collapsed again. One of the emissaries in the front of the group gestured impatiently, ordering him to remain on the deck. "Why were these men beaten?" the priest said sharply, his question directed at the captain of the guard.

"Killed nine of my men! More below, grievously injured! Broken, blinded, torn to pieces! Likely to lose two more before dawn. The lads had more than they could stand from these demons."

"Your lads," the emissary said pointedly, "are undisciplined. Did you think we came to admire the scenery?"

"This is not the first demon chase I've led," the Captain glowered. "None of them ever turned savage like these before."

"I did not promise an easy hunt." The emissary took a step toward Galen but carefully stayed outside the reach of his chain. A quick glance at the empty bowl on the deck assured him that the strangers' evil talents had been subdued. "I am chief emissary of Chenoweth, Tsingao," he told Galen. "By these witnesses to your abominable acts, you are accused of blasphemy in the eyes of our Gods, by defying the laws granted to us by the sovereign deities. Let all of us hear your reply: Are you a Descendant?"

Galen cocked his head as if in scrutiny of a particularly interesting piece of art. Like the others, the priest was dressed in blue, his robe cleaner and of better quality. His pale face was broad with full lips and flat black eyes that offered no insight into his current mood. He carried a strong presence that continued to blaze from his small, wiry frame even when Galen briefly turned his head to study some of the other emissaries. These were not the sort of common clerics that patrolled towns like Phrar in search of demons. There was more here than that.

Galen shrugged with an indifference he did not feel. "Of course I am."

A murmur ran through the assembly as people commented on the belligerence with which Galen was meeting this solemn court. At this point most would expect to hear emphatic denials or desperate pleas for mercy. This particular demon seemed fearless and unrepentant – no wonder the chief emissary himself had come to judge him.

Galen jerked a thumb at Chor. "He is, too." He gave Tsingao a friendly smile. "As are you." A collective gasp rose from the crowd. The chief emissary glanced quickly at the soldiers bracing his prisoner. Galen looked at one of the other emissaries standing nearby. "And that one," he gestured at the man. "Hmm, not you, although you wish you were." Galen was about to point out someone else when a soldier stepped forward and clubbed him. He toppled to his knees, dazed.

"Bring him below," Tsingao barked. "If he speaks again, if he so much as steps on your foot, throw the other one overboard."

His ears ringing from the blow he had received, Galen

was manhandled down the companionway and dragged along a dark passage into one of the ship's cabins. There he was shoved onto a narrow bench running along the wall and made to wait while some of the emissaries stood in whispered conversation by the door. A few of the soldiers stood guard over him, waiting for their orders. Galen moved back into the corner of the bench and raised one leg onto it, as much to ease the stabbing pain in his side as to appear unconcerned. He placed his bound wrists onto his drawn-up knee and studied the cabin. Escape was not among his options at the moment. The small window would never allow him to squeeze through and the single door into the hall was crowded with guards. This wooden bench and a low table with some uncomfortable-looking cushions placed around it were the room's only furnishings.

"You know," he said conversationally. "A bit of paint would go a long way to making this place a little more hospitable. Or maybe a nice rug."

The soldier closest to him sneered but said nothing. The emissaries at the door had turned as he spoke. The man called Tsingao came into the room, followed by two of his fellow priests. He motioned to the guards to leave and waited patiently until they had obeyed. The three emissaries arranged themselves on the far side of the table, not speaking, taking their time. Galen found it strange that they would seat themselves below their prisoner, surely an unusual interrogation technique. But there was something oddly effective in their approach. They knelt at a comfortable distance from each other, hands loosely clasped on their thighs, clean blue robes draping neatly into correct folds. The table before them, although of rough construction and without adornment, was scrubbed to a mellow gleam. A single overhead lamp cast a static pool of light onto its bare surface and left their victim in shadows. While they sat composed and patient, Galen slouched in his corner, dirty, bleeding and bedraggled, clearly a creature beneath their station. While he felt ill and agitated, they seemed perfectly at ease, exuding an air of tranquility. Galen smiled, appreciating the strategy. No doubt their finely honed air of self-assurance would unnerve most opponents. He, however, could feel their tension and uncertainty like smoke hanging in the room.

The emissary nearest the door turned and picked up a bottle made of the hazy substance that passed for glass on this moon. Placing it on the table, he said, "Water?"

"Chibane?" Galen replied.

"Certainly."

"Already had some, thank you."

The emissary shrugged and left the flask where it was.

Another long pause followed; no doubt he was expected to at least start fidgeting. Instead, he tipped his head back against the wall and closed his eyes, again feeling for any nearby source of chi'ro. There seemed to be some of it, but so distant that he could not even begin to get a grip on it. Its presence, however, gave him some hope. He peered through half-closed lids at the emissaries, who still had not moved. None of them seemed to have noticed his efforts to reach out to the riser.

Tsingao spoke at last. "Where is the woman?"

"What woman?"

"The one that was traveling with you. The witch."

"I don't know any witches."

Pause. It was beginning to irritate Galen. He resolved to make a note of this. He raised his hands to push the tangled hair from his face but then realized that it might be taken as a sign of nervousness. He bit back a comment he was about to make and decided to play along.

"You were seen with her at that floating pig sty near Riva Sound."

"Was I," Galen said flatly.

They seemed to wait for him to say more. Galen kept his eyes on the emissaries, offering nothing. They heard water sloshing in the bilges below and the massive timbers around them creak in response to a shift in the sails. Some voices were briefly raised in a distant cabin and then fell silent again. Galen saw one of Tsingao's eyes twitch but the man remained composed. At last the priest pointed at the emissary to his left. "You called this man a Descendant, earlier. Why?"

"I did not," Galen said. "I called you a Descendant, and him." He gestured at the man to Tsingao's right. "You know he is."

For the first time, the chief emissary's composure seemed to slip. "I know no such thing!"

"What is it that you know, then? Why is it that some of you can detect the presence of a Descendant, and others cannot? Your talent is limited; you can only perceive the strongest of us and even then only in the vaguest way. If it were any other way, all of the Descendants would have been wiped out by now. Something guides you, something allows you to sense our presence. And the only reason for this is because you are one of us."

"Blasphemy!" the emissary beside Tsingao hissed angrily.

His superior placed a calming hand on his arm. "This demon hardly warrants your anger, Torbyn." He turned back to Galen. "Yes, something guides us. Our Gods guide our steps to root out the magic-users and heretics who flaunt their evil ways, an abomination in the eyes of Chenoweth. We need no other guide and certainly not your sinful magic. Those who live in contravention of Their laws must be stopped."

"Murdered."

"They are demons. Chenoweth demands it."

"Why?"

"It is written." Tsingao reached into a pocket and withdrew a thin volume of bound pages carefully enclosed in a leather envelope. Taking his time, he paged through a few sheets of vellum and then placed the book onto the table in front of him. "'After the storms abated," he intoned, "the Gods of Chenoweth banished the magic-users to the Homeworld. They gathered a cadre of agents and entrusted them with the fate of Thali moon. None henceforth may draw forth from the ground the essences that belong to the Gods. To do so is death. Let the emissaries of Chenoweth guard this decree and pass their duty on to the generations that follow.'"

Galen whistled. "Well, that's pretty clear. What storms?"

"A great destruction caused by the wantonness of the magic users. They were punished." Tsingao touched the edges of the book as if caressing a much beloved companion. "The Gods retired to Chenoweth and peace came to Thali. You are a threat to that peace."

"We are trying to leave this place. If you let us go we'll be gone in a matter of days."

"Where would you go? Have you no more convincing lies than this?"

"We're magic users, remember? We have the means to return to the Homeworld where we belong. We can show you the place from which we have to leave. You can watch us disappear forever."

Tsingao allowed himself a thin, satisfied smile. Here was further proof that he was finally reaching his goal, that these were the demons whose quest to fly to the Homeworld must not succeed. "The Gods demand their sacrifice," he said. "The magic you have taken from this place must be returned." He placed a finger on the page in front of him. "'None henceforth may draw forth from the ground the essences that belong to the Gods'," he repeated. "You have taken this essence. You must return it."

"What? By bleeding it out? That isn't how this works!"

"These words are unequivocal," Tsingao said, carefully stowing the book away again. "You and your brother will subject yourself to the will of our Gods. And then we will find the other one." His gaze moved to the small window beyond Galen. "We have been searching for that woman for a long time. I've known of her existence for years. Only now she is becoming stronger by the day and, at last, I can follow her steps. It will not be long before her beacon shines as brightly as yours, Descendant."

"Even I have trouble finding her. But even so, you are a far more talented Descendant than your minions. We walked among them in Phrar for days before anyone noticed my beacon. Perhaps if you weren't so busy murdering your fellow Descendants you could recruit more talents like yourself."

The emissary called Torbyn could stand it no longer. "You will desist at once," he shouted, his hands gripping the edge of the table. "This is sacrilege!"

Galen ignored the outburst. "I'm intrigued by the weaponry of your ships, Emissary. How is it possible to defy wind, distance and gravity to pitch a fireball such great distances, I wonder?" His eyes remained on Tsingao's when he raised a hand and pointed at the flask on the table. "Prove me wrong, chief. Drink from that."

Tsingao's already immobile face took on a granite hue, turning the man into a sculpted study of inertia. He looked at the bottle and back at the demon before him, his controlled breathing barely noticeable, his shoulders apparently relaxed beneath his robe. Only Galen noticed the tautness around his eyes, the subtle change of color beneath his nails as he pressed his hands onto the table. He forced a careless tone into his voice. "To me this is little more than water. But no doubt you will turn it to poison as I drink, demon."

"Then this will be the proof," the priest at his side said. From a pocket he took a small, enameled box. He placed it ceremoniously onto the table before him and slid its lid aside. Within it lay a gnarled piece of mushroom the color of dried blood. "Only the Descendants among us will feel the effects of this," he proclaimed, reaching up to light a long wick on the lamp suspended above the table.

Galen sat up, his lifelong conditioning alerting him to the danger with almost superstitious apprehension. No adept regarded chibane with indifference and, although its effects where usually temporary, contact with it was considered practically life threatening. Burning even a small quantity of it in this closed room would incapacitate him for hours and would have lasting effects in the days to follow. He noticed both Tsingao and the third priest observing their companion with possibly more trepidation than he did. Would Tsingao subject himself to the poison simply to prove him wrong?

Torbyn blew on the wick in his hand and then bent to place it onto the chibane in the bowl. Something crackled in the dead silence of the room and a flame licked along the edge of the mushroom. Galen slowed his breath, preparing to conserve oxygen as long as he could, likely better trained in this than his captors. A thin, yellow thread of smoke curled up from the bowl. Fascinated by it, Galen nearly missed the quick exchange of glances between Tsingao and his other aide.

"Torbyn," Tsingao said. "We have no need to prove ourselves to this demon. Don't allow him to draw you into his schemes."

Torbyn looked up from his task, making no move to extinguish the incense. Although there was a moment when his eyes were unable to meet those of his master, eventually he stiffened his spine along with his resolve. "Like this demon, sire, I've had my doubts. Your ways confuse and frighten me. Forgive my inadequacy, but I require proof to continue to serve you."

Galen grinned, surprised by the audacity and completely unprepared when Tsingao's arm shot from his lap and smashed the heel of his hand below the priest's nose. Before the younger man's body had even reacted to the force of the blow, Tsingao's other hand lashed out to deliver another, this one lethal. Torbyn was thrown back against the wooden wall of the cabin. The other emissary rose and shattered the cabin window with a fist quickly wrapped in a fold of his robe.

Startled shouts rose on the other side of the door and then it was flung open to admit the guardsmen stationed outside. "Get out!" Tsingao snapped at them and strode to where his captive sat frozen in utter surprise. He lowered his face close to Galen's and hissed angrily, "Just because you and I share some of the same gifts and some of the same weaknesses, do not mistake me for one of your legion of demons. As long as the Gods are on our side, you and I have nothing in common. I will not have you turn my men against each other with your lies."

He went to the door. "He's murdered Torbyn. Take him away. Make landfall in the morning. We'll celebrate the dawn with a gift to Chenoweth. Two gifts."

And so the twins were reunited at the stern, where Galen found Chor feeling slightly better but shivering in the cold night air. Huddling close, they tapped the ambient chi'ro in an attempt to keep warm and ease some of the worst of their injuries. The promise of a distant riser was now closer but still outside their reach. A few miles more, perhaps, unless they changed course.

Near midnight, Galen's occasional probes into the dark finally brought some results. He sighed when he perceived the La'il, not sure if he was glad to see her or should add her among his misfortunes at this moment. Resigned, he lowered his defenses and let her image compose itself in his mind, this one neatly dressed in a plain white robe, white hair unbound and flowing over her back. She looked at once ethereal and girlish, the pallor of the display drawing attention to the opaque silver eyes that missed nothing. He sensed curiosity from her, then amusement when she understood his predicament. A derisive grin accompanied her thorough scrutiny of the twins' injuries.

"This is truly spectacular," she said. "First you lose the girl and then you get yourself captured by a bunch of primitives. I'm very disappointed. Living without chi'ro must be a hard lesson. I don't know how you can stand it." She shuddered in mock sympathy. "I recall just a few months ago when you took on that Morningside adept and his scum. Over forty violators fried and sent to Tower Hill and not a single civilian caught up in the fray. And you didn't even break a sweat. Is that nose broken?" She pointed a delicate finger at Chor.

"No," he growled. "You could do something to help."

She shrugged. "Even if I cared to, what can I do? On Thali I exist only in your head. Well, sort of. Are there no risers around there at all?"

"Not now." Galen relayed today's events without disguising his revulsion and guilt over the massacre that their presence in the village had brought about. Clearly, if the emissaries were capable of tracing Descendants then the twins themselves had led them there. The La'il, however, seemed amused that they had to squander all of the carefully hoarded chi'ro to defend the villagers. She laughed when he concluded by telling her about Tsingao's assault on his subordinate and his suspicion that, had he not dared the chief emissary to drink the chibane, the young priest would still be alive.

"Sometimes a little compassion would look good on you, La'il," Galen snapped. "The people in that village are Aletha's family, for pity's sake."

"A week ago you didn't even know they existed. Now listen to yourself!" The La'il snickered. "You know, you have one major flaw that continues to stand in your way. You are one of the more powerful adepts on the Homeworld; you even exceed the design of your generation. You should be working among my most senior ministers. You could be helping us shape this world into whatever we decide, but instead you are nothing more than a hired thug, a strong-arm content to roam about the planet in search of chi'ro infractions and terrorists! And even at that you are less than effective. And do you know why?" Her hand lashed out and he felt a sharp-nailed finger stab his chest. "You're soft, Galen! You will never be part of the machine that really drives the Homeworld because you don't have the stomach for it. You squander your talents on trivialities. The only way I can make sure they're not wasted is to take your strength by force and use it myself! With your spectacular reluctance to get the job done you'll soon have no better use than to be put out to stud."

He rolled his eyes. "That sounds like fun, too. Tell me, did you pretend Aletha was your sister only so she'd take your side over Chenoweth's?"

"Why else? These people are completely brainwashed by their obsession with Chenoweth. Clever of Dazai to play god and turn us into demons. I didn't think she'd turn against them just because we ask her nicely. But if I'd known you only had to take her to bed to gain her cooperation I would have suggested it to begin with. Cooperation for *our* side, Galen, or have you forgotten where you belong?"

"What side does she belong to?"

"None. She's as much a genetic accident as I am. Too bad we've lost the chance to breed you two. Or I suppose I should say: You three!" She laughed raucously, reminding him of his headache. "With adepts murdering themselves out of existence on Thali, it's a miracle that she even came into being. And, considering her annoying talent for remaining invisible, it's a wonder I found her at all. I watched for a long time until I saw a pattern in the way the chi flares followed her around. Once or twice I got close enough to find out what she was. Unfortunately, so did Chenoweth. She must reach that launch and the Homeworld before Chenoweth manages to get through! Pray she finds her way there without you!"

"Even if she does, how will you contact her, to bring her to the planet? You can't get into her head. You can't tell where she is right now any more than I can."

"I have my ways, Galen," she said, sounding disturbingly unconcerned. "Obviously, I can't rely on you to keep track of your charge."

Galen shivered and leaned back against a storage box bolted to the deck. Cold, hard drops of rain whipped across the bulwark, carried by a freshening breeze. "You know, I think you were right," he said.

"About what?"

"About Aletha doing things to my head." Although speaking to her, his eyes were on the middle distance and his thoughts even farther away. "I can't get her out of my mind. It's driving me crazy that she's angry with us. No, not angry. Right now I'd think angry would be better than what she must be feeling. Now that's she's gone, I feel like something big is missing. Funny thing is, I don't feel that in my head." He put his hands to the center of his chest. "It's here. It's like someone's ripped something out of me. I don't like it."

La'il regarded him suspiciously. Was he mocking her? She tried to delve deeper into his thoughts but he held her off, almost without effort, something he had not been able to do until now. Was he serious or merely toying with her to rouse her jealousy? His carefully guarded expression gave nothing away. "You're a bigger fool than I thought," she said.

He nodded, grinning through cracked and swollen lips. "Yeah, and that's a good thing, I think." He slowly raised his eyes. "I feel like I'm dying and Chor is dying and maybe tomorrow we'll have our throats cut because I volunteered to fly to the moon. But the thing that keeps going through my mind is how her hair tickles when I kiss the back of her neck or how her hands always feel cool and light when she touches me. I'm completely insane for that, La'il. Soft? Damn right I'm soft. Did she put this stuff in my head? I don't think so. But even if she did, so what? I liked it. At least I got to feel *something* besides the trash you put there. I would rather die than hurt her, even if she had the strength of ten of you, and this damn well means that I don't need you or your twisted ways. You can't touch me anymore. Not in any way that matters. Someday I will break your neck but I won't be doing it for me."

Her careless chuckle sounded forced in both of their minds. "I'd prove you wrong, but I doubt either one of you could get up to it right now." Looking through his eyes, she watched a small girl creep up beside Chor to throw a ragged blanket over him. "Isn't that adorable," she said sardonically. "Quite the army you're getting together up there."

Galen took a bowl of soup from Yala. "Aletha has some interesting friends. These people have a great loyalty for each other."

La'il laughed. "I agree completely!"

"What do you mean?"

She shook her head. "I'll leave you now. I'll try to make it for your execution or sacrifice or whatever these festivities are called. If I'm not too busy."

Galen shivered when he felt the La'il slip from his thoughts. Needing warmth, he sipped from his bowl. Fish soup, he discovered, but its watery, flavorless heat felt like a tonic. "Going to have to get out of here," he told the girl. "Bitch is up to something."

"Huh?"

Galen shook his head. "Don't be getting caught helping us."

"There is bad talk down below," Yala said. "Heard 'em talk about you and him."

"What are they saying?"

Yala hesitated. "The soldiers are mad at you 'cause of what you did in the village. Someone died, below, a while ago. They're all drinking guango and some are wanting to tie you up there, 'neath the crow's nest. By your hair, they said. Or your feet, others said. Or cut off your—"

"I think I get it."

"—tongues, so you can't be saying evil spells over them. But their captain put an end to the talk, on account of the emissaries. They need you whole for the gods, he told 'em. They're going to take you to shore in the morning. Going to purge you and then go find Aletha. The emissaries are going ashore, too. They brought their things, I'm sure." Yala's haunted expression hung like a pale apparition in the night, her eyes overbright in the light of a torch near the main hatchway. Her thin voice rose, trembling. "I seen what they do to people. I seen it!"

Galen reached out his hands to calm the frightened child, surprised when Yala responded by moving closer to him and even more surprised to find himself looping his arms around the child. Yala shivered, in fear or from the cold, but she did not cry. Galen comforted her as best as he could, wondering about the things that the girl had likely witnessed in her few years of living in the harbor slums. Considering the urchin's considerable flair for bravado and belligerence in the face of danger and poverty, it was easy to forget how young she was. Hers was not the sort of life children on the Homeworld enjoyed. Sighing, he gathered up the drowsing child and moved her over to curl up against Chor.

He had felt a riser in the distance, and another nearby. Stronger now and discernible without effort. Patiently, Galen drew it toward himself, using it to restore their energies, heal the worst of the damage inflicted by the soldiers, and build reserves against whatever the morning would bring. It was not nearly enough to fashion into any sort of weapon against their captors but it would serve to restore them. Gradually, he felt a renewed sense of vitality. The alarming swelling around Chor's eyes began to recede and his breathing became less labored. Galen's headache finally faded.

An hour passed before the riser was depleted. Just as he absorbed the last of the chi'ro, something else in the distance caught his attention. Another riser, perhaps. But there was a consciousness there, a faint expression of curiosity, exactly what he had been hoping to find. Fleeting, but it was she. Somewhere among the islands, Aletha had finally perceived his questing thoughts and responded, however briefly.

He tried to call to her, but her thoughts had already moved on, dismissing him. Was she ignoring him on purpose? Did she think he was following her with some evil intention because she had left him in the village? As much as her familiar touch had felt like a distant voice from home, he was glad that she had withdrawn. If he could now perceive her from a distance, how soon would other adepts, on this world or elsewhere, also tune into her presence?

THIRTEEN

Thudding vibrations on the wooden deck startled the twins awake only a short while after Galen had finally fallen asleep. Squinting into the night, they saw the light of several torches approach from the bow. Raised voices and angry shouts preceded whatever was coming their way. Chor sat up, grabbed Yala, and flipped her into the air and behind the bin that had sheltered them from the worst of the sea spray. She made a startled sound of protest but immediately fell silent when Chor hissed, gesturing for her to stay hidden.

The twins stood up, careful to feign a weakness they no longer felt. Neither was in the perfect state of health they had enjoyed before coming to this moon, but at least they had taken in a helpful amount of chi'ro. Without the power supplied by a riser they were no more likely to succeed against the emissaries' men as they had been this past morning, but perhaps there would be a chance at a leap over the railing. Galen promised himself that a number of these thugs would end up sacrificed before he and Chor lay on Chenoweth's altar.

Galen realized that they were confronted by what was little more than a mob. Bleary with drink, staggering and malevolent, the soldiers at the vanguard shambled to a halt. There was a confused pause when someone waited for someone else to begin whatever they had come to do. Finally some of the soldiers lurched toward the twins. The manacles around the twins' wrists were released and they were shoved forward into the circle of light and oily smoke produced by the torches. No doubt the mob's desire for revenge was held in check only by the presence of the emissaries among them.

Tsingao stepped from the crowd. He seemed harried and had somehow lost his cultivated expression of saintly tranquility. He glared at the inebriated mercenaries, daring them to stand in his way. The soldiers moved aside, allowing Tsingao to approach the twins.

"A change of plan," he said. "It has been decided not to wait until morning."

Galen gazed over the reeling, cursing soldiers crowding the deck and saw several of the ship's crew among them, including the captain and his mates. Small huddles of emissaries stood nearby, looking both frightened and disgusted by this turn of events. Their authority was absolute in the coastal towns but out here, in the remoteness of the islands, the conventions of civilization did not apply. Out here, on this hired ship, the emissaries were nearly as openly despised and feared as their captives. The mutiny had happened – not against the ship's commanders but against their employers.

"Hang 'em over the side and let the fishes have their fill!" one of the men roared.

"Keelhaul!"

"Get me my crossbow, it's time for practicing!"

"Stake 'em for the vultures!"

"No, wait, first let me have a turn with the pretty one!"

This last comment was met with a roar of raucous laughter at which the chief emissary turned and raised his arms. His outrage was clearly marked on his face although Galen sensed a growing desperation there that would soon rise to the surface. Grudgingly, the soldiers backed away and the shouts subsided.

Galen leaned down to the emissary to whisper in his ear.

"Maybe you should train your own army instead of hiring thugs. Let me know if you need help. I've got some experience with that."

Tsingao jerked away from Galen to put distance between them. "Stay away from me, demon." He addressed the soldiers, his voice thundering. "Stop your barbarous rants. You want these demons gone and we will make them gone. If you cannot wait until morning then let this thing be done right now. But we will follow the dictates of our Gods, not your boorish call for retribution. There will be no lynching!"

"No?" Galen said, desperate to gain more time. There was a definite presence of chi'ro in the distance now and he strained to touch it. "So is there going to be a torturous sacrifice instead? Can we pick the lynching?"

Tsingao froze for many beats of his heart during which he fought valiantly to retain control over himself even if he'd clearly lost it over his soldiers. His fellow emissaries glanced nervously about themselves, clearly uncomfortable among the rabble. None noticed when Chor, standing slightly behind his twin, began to reach for the new riser. It was faint, a barely-felt scent of chi'ro, and he had to concentrate all of his abilities to capture its essence.

"We will dispatch them correctly and then consign their bodies to the sea," Tsingao decided, his voice firm. "Bring those torches over here."

Someone stabbed a spear at Galen to force him to a spot Tsingao had pointed out. Chor was also shoved forward, stumbling when his focus was torn from the distant riser. One of the emissaries had brought a low table and now placed upon it a flat, lacquered box. Moving with ritualistic care, the emissary lifted the hinged lid to reveal a row of instruments, most of them with finely honed edges. Galen saw awls and sickle-shaped knives, amulets, phials, pincers and other instruments he preferred not to identify. Each tool gleamed spotlessly in the light of the torches. Tsingao bent over the box and selected a curved knife before turning to the twins.

All eyes followed the instrument when he raised his arms, about to give voice to the spoken part of his ritual, but then a commotion near the back of the group startled the crowd. Someone cursed and there was some jostling before two of the men brought forth a fiercely struggling cabin maid.

"Let me through, you pig's arse, or I'll know what!"

Tsingao lowered his hands. "What is this?"

"You're not to hurt them," Yala shouted. She tried to leap at the chief emissary. "They mean no harm to anyone! They done nothing!"

Tsingao crossed his arms over his chest. "Do you know this guttersnipe?" he said to Galen.

Galen cursed inwardly. "Do I look like a family man to you?"

"Take her away," Tsingao snapped.

Yala cursed and struggled as she was dragged off. Some of the men laughed when she managed to bite her captor's arm, forcing a pained yelp from her victim. The emissary scowled at the twins – the incident seemed to have removed whatever solemnity remained of this ritual. His eyes narrowed when he saw both Descendants looking into the direction the child had been taken, their concern evident. He raised a hand. "Bring the brat back here," he commanded. "Let her see what happens to those who befriend Descendants." A malevolent sneer touched his lips when he saw the boundless loathing for him and his kind on the twins' faces.

Yala was returned to the circle of onlookers, someone's hand clamped firmly over her mouth. Galen could feel the girl's fear as distinctly as he felt the oily smoke of the torches biting at his eyes. Reaching for Chor, he followed his twin's connection to the distant riser, preparing to draw upon its power to defend themselves. Still not enough! Yala's presence was a distraction.

Tsingao returned his attention to the sacrifice to be made to his gods. Surely, the offer of these two Descendants would please them, ensuring his safe return to the mainland

and away from these foul-mannered brutes. And, as always, the prospect of sacrificing these demons in the way he devised, their drawn-out agonies surely reaching even the most preoccupied of the gods, carried with it a strange excitement. His fellow emissaries preferred to dispatch captive demons quickly and cleanly at the end of the prescribed ceremonies. But surely the spoken incantations carried far more power when accompanied by the slowly dissipating life force wielded in such abundance by these creatures. He had seen their magic with his own eyes in the village as it leaped from these two, wielded with more force than he had ever witnessed. The protracted demise of the twins would surely please the gods as much as it would satisfy his own needs. He motioned to the soldiers. "Hold them."

The twins were grasped from behind, a burly soldier holding each arm and another laying a dagger at each twin's throat. Tsingao held up his bone-handled knife with both hands while murmuring his incantation. One of his emissaries moved forward to tear away what remained of the twins' shirts, baring their chests to the priest's knife. Galen heard Yala's scream, muffled by the hand held over her face.

"By the Gods!" a sudden exclamation rang out. "How can this be?" Some of the men withdrew while others surged forward for a closer look, fingers pointed, babbling in speculation.

Enraged by this new interruption, Tsingao pushed someone aside even as he tore the torch from his hand. He held it close to one twin and then the other, close enough to raise blisters on the skin of Galen's chest. "This is not possible!" he roared. When the demon grinned back at him and shrugged, Tsingao no longer felt the need for an elaborate sacrifice. Tearing an axe from the hand of a nearby crewman, he raised it in both fists over his head.

The twins tore away from their captors and thrust a burst of energy outward in all directions. Those standing nearest were thrown back to slam into the spectators behind them.

Some of the torches were extinguished or fell to the deck where they rolled among the feet of the panicked men. Galen projected toward Tsingao to hurl him aloft in a wide arc far out into the sea. Another emissary followed, and then some of the soldiers. The twins leaped to the side of the ship to scan for signs of the shore. A mercenary stabbed at them, slicing his weapon deep into Galen's hand, before he was tackled overboard, his neck broken by a sharp strike of Chor's fist. It was a long reach to the shore, but Galen thought they could make it if the current didn't drift them too far off course. Dimly, he recalled Aletha's yarns about sea monsters and deadly undertows.

"Yala!" he shouted back to the panicked mob after climbing onto the ship's starboard railing next to Chor. Why had the girl not followed? The mainsail had caught fire, as had some of the emissaries' robes, adding frenzied shrieks to the angry shouts of the men who dared not approach the twins. Galen ducked under a spear hurled in his direction. Then he saw that one of the emissaries had captured the child, realizing her value as hostage. Before he could rush back to free her, one of the soldiers, wielding a heavy cudgel, slammed into the twins. Instantly, both lost their footing and pitched into the black water.

It seemed an eternity before the twins fought their way back above the waves, disoriented in the dark. Someone flailed in the water nearby, screaming for help. Galen looked back to the ship and after some moments saw Yala topside, yelling something at him. The emissary was behind her with a firm grip on the girl's tunic, preventing her from leaping after Galen and Chor. Desperate, Galen looked about for some means to get back on board and found none. Both he and Chor had expended every bit of chi'ro and physical strength they had managed to recover over these past few hours, with perhaps just enough adrenaline remaining to help them reach the shore. He realized that he had to leave Yala behind, alone at the mercy of the emissaries' anger. The helpless rage he felt was stronger than any he had harbored against the priests up until now.

Suddenly something seemed to tug him into another direction. He felt a presence nearby, a very familiar sensation that could only be a surge of chi'ro. Tuning into the essence, the twins replied in astonished relief. A vortex of chi'ro rose up before them and Galen reached for it as if it were a rope tossed to a drowning man. They found themselves lifted up and backwards, bodies suddenly weightless as they spun through cold, empty space. I'm dead, Galen thought. I'm dead and it doesn't hurt, after all.

* * *

Then he landed and it did hurt. Chor landed on top of him and that hurt even more. They lay motionless, unable to breathe, unable to move.

"Galen?" he heard finally, through the ringing in his ears. "Chor?" He began to move various parts of his body, unsure of which belonged to him and which to Chor. His twin was also slow to recover, content to remain draped over Galen indefinitely. "Here," Galen managed.

Aletha made no move to help them as they extricated themselves, testing their limbs, checking for new injuries. Galen looked around and discovered a pleasant campsite, fire neatly banked for the night, her boat moored securely nearby. The ground was springy with a bed of evergreen needles and mosses, the tangy scent of brine berries mingled with the smoke of the fire. The night air carried a chill, hinting that she had reached the northern strait where cooler air flowed past the mountains to the island chain guarding Phrar's coast. She seemed to be in no immediate need of rescue or of protection by the nearly incapacitated twins.

"What was that all about?" Aletha exclaimed. "Were those emissaries? Just look at you!" The brothers, well rested and in good repair the last time she had seen them, where covered in torn rags and a mass of half-healed bruises and cuts. "You're freezing. Come to the fire," she said, dismayed to see them dragging themselves to its warmth, obviously fatigued beyond endurance. She added more wood to the fire and fanned the flames.

Galen raised his slashed hand over his head to slow the bleeding. "How did you find us?"

"I didn't mean to, believe me."

"Aletha, I—"

"I have no idea how I found you. I felt you a few hours ago, or I thought I did. But I've been trying to use less chi'ro – I think maybe the emissaries can feel it when I do. But just now there was something so… wrong. You seemed to be in pain, or very angry, I'm not sure. I tried to send you some chi'ro from that riser north of here. And then when I felt you grab it, I just reached out and pulled you through. It was so easy!"

Galen scanned the area and found the riser she had mentioned, now mostly depleted. "You created a conduit of sorts. A connection from one place to another where space doesn't exist. Some of us train many years to learn how to do this. Not everyone succeeds."

Aletha set that bit of information aside for later contemplation. "Why are you in such bad shape? You're completely gone over. What happened?" She placed her hand onto Chor's bruised face, apparently plucking energy from the ambient chi'ro as effortlessly as her lungs took in air. He closed his eyes as her ministrations began to take effect and the throbbing pain around his eye receded. She then took Galen's damaged hand, distressed to find his palm skewered. She closed her hands around it as if to shake it in greeting, unmindful of the blood that soaked her blouse. Minutes passed before she released it to wrap it in a length of cloth torn from Chor's shirt. "Is that a burn?" Steeling herself, she placed her hand over the blisters caused by Tsingao's torch and felt them burst. "I'm sorry!" she exclaimed when a loud groan escaped his clenched teeth. He grimaced, holding his breath against the pain, but placed his hand over hers until the damaged nerves calmed and his skin began its process of healing.

"So what happened to you?" She upended a water skin to wash the gore from her hands.

"Emissaries. They came to the village after you left. With mercenaries. I was in a cloud of chi and didn't feel them coming. They attacked and I killed some of them. Some of your people were hurt—"

"Minh! What about Minh?"

"I didn't see her after it started. She wasn't among the injured."

She jumped up. "I have to get back there!"

Chor caught her arm. "They were there because we were, that much is clear. The best thing you can do for your people is to stay away from them."

She shook him off. "Don't touch me." She stepped around the fire and stood staring into the night, fuming silently. "You saved my life, Homeworlders," she said finally. "And now I've saved you. We are even. Clearly, we're in danger and it's safer if we travel together but I don't even want to talk to you until we reach that damn launch."

"Would you please listen..." Galen began.

She wrapped her arms around herself. "To what? More lies? Haven't I had enough?"

"No more lies," he said. "You've had enough."

She took a shuddering breath and slowly came about to face them. "Then you won't deny that I've... been with both of you?"

Both twins shook their heads.

"How often?"

"I don't know."

All color drained from her face but her expression remained frozen. "I believe it would be possible for me to kill both of you and it wouldn't take much effort."

Galen remembered the sudden flight over what had surely been many miles when her conduit had carried them with only a meager riser to fuel it. "You could," he said finally. "But maybe you could hear what I have to tell you, first."

Seething, she wanted to refuse his explanation, but then her need to know, to put more of these odd pieces into place, overwhelmed her and she nodded. She sat on her bedroll but with her tightly crossed arms and angry jut of chin looked far from restful. "Talk, then."

Galen exhaled sharply. Would this day never end? "Well..." He scratched his head, unsure of where to begin. "Aletha," he said, taking a deep breath. "Chor and I... well..."

Aletha drummed her fingers on her arm.

"All right," he took another breath. "Chor and I not twins. We're not even brothers."

"What..." Aletha looked from one to the other. "Of course you are."

He shook his head. "I am he and he is me. There is no difference. My name is Galen Chor and there is only one of us here. He can no more act on his own accord—"

"—than I could," Chor finished, the distant expression on his face gone. "You see two of us here, but there is only one mind, one will."

Aletha shook her head, slowly. "No," she whispered. "That is not possible."

"Do you really think even twins can look as alike as we do? Sound as alike? Do you really think you wouldn't be able to tell the difference between two people, no matter how closely related, when you make love to them?" Both men moved up on their knees, their movements eerily identical, and lifted the hem of their tattered blouses.

"By the Gods..." she murmured, as baffled as the men aboard the emissary ship had been when she saw the long, badly-healed scar twisting along both twins' ribcages. No conceivable coincidence would ever produce two scars so completely identical. She watched them replace their shirts, again each movement the same.

"It's easier for me if I don't have to move both bodies separately," they said, speaking as one. "Having two bodies is like hammering a nail with one hand and writing a letter with the other. You ought to—"

"Stop it!" she shouted. "Stop talking like that!"

The twins fell silent.

"Stop it," she repeated, near tears. "Make him go back to sleep, like he always is. Don't both look at me like that!"

Galen nodded and Chor stood up to walk away from the camp, toward the boat where he busied himself with their packs. "I'm sorry, Aletha," Galen said. "I shouldn't have done that."

Unable to look at either of them, Aletha lowered her head onto her folded arms. "Why didn't you tell me?"

"Because it didn't matter. I was sent here to fetch you, nothing more. You are equal only to the La'il and I had no expectation this would mean anything to you once we return to the Homeworld."

Aletha was silent for a long while before she lifted her head from her arms. "Is that what you think?" she said, her voice tightly controlled as if to keep it from trembling. "That this doesn't mean anything to me? Did it mean nothing to you? Did it mean so little that you would lie to me, play with me?"

"Things weren't supposed to go this way. There just hasn't been a good moment to tell you the truth. First I was ordered to tell you nothing, for your own good. We had no idea how you would get on with all this. You've got gods and giants and monsters in the seas. You are going to a better place; I was just trying to get you there the easiest way I know how. You might never even have known that Chor and I are one person. But then things changed. Things got complicated. I've been trying to figure out a way to tell you the truth since we got to the village. I thought we had time and I was worried how you'd feel about this. I wish it hadn't happened like this."

She lifted her head. "So do I! Complicated, indeed! How did any of this give you the freedom to..." She gestured toward Chor.

He scratched his chin. "Well, it's like this: Does it matter if I touch you with my right hand or my left? Or look at you with my right eye or my left? Hardly. It's no different with Chor. He's just another part of my body, completely interchangeable. I don't even know if I'm Galen or Chor right now."

Aletha crossed the space between them to crouch before him, taking some time to examine his face very closely. He was not prepared when she raised a fist and punched his shoulder, forcing a groan from him when the still tender wound there flared painfully. "Galen," she informed him and moved back to her side of the fire. "Galen got that in Delann's bathhouse."

He held his breath until the pain stopped. "I suppose I deserved that," he exhaled finally. "All right, I'm the one you thought of as Galen. But it doesn't make any difference who you think we are. In my mind I've always been just one person. It just seemed easier to pretend whatever was convenient. That's why I didn't try to make us look different. I've only been in this state a few weeks. I can barely prevent us from moving in complete synchronicity. And so one of us is always more or less immobile or doing mindless things requiring no concentration. If I didn't have to think for two separate bodies I don't think we would have been captured in the village. I just wasn't able to defend both of us. Both of me. Whatever. Eventually, it seemed to be a personality, as though Chor was the quiet one, or like he didn't care or was even only half-bright. But whether he was me or I was him when I was with you, I have no idea. It didn't matter; it was both me. There is no one else here." Galen paused his fumbling explanation to study her expression. Dammit, how was she taking this? "You've got to believe that I meant you no harm. I thought you loathed the giants, that it would complicate matters. I don't know what apocalyptic legend has been shaped around the giants but I've heard enough about them to worry that it would change things."

She frowned. "Giants? What are you talking about?"

He bit his lip. "Uh, well…"

She raised a hand and pointed a finger directly at his face.

"This is the moment you stop lying to me, Homeworlder."

He lowered his head to run both hands through his hair and then fussed needlessly with the bandage around his palm. "I've never been very good at lying," he said ruefully. "My greatest flaw, La'il thinks."

Aletha grimaced, unimpressed by his admission.

"I guess I justified it because the way I am now is not important. Once home, Chor will be gone, I will be just me again and it'll make no difference to anyone what I was on this moon."

"What are you talking about? What will happen to Chor?"

"I was made like this so we could come here to find you. In my true form, I would never blend in with your people here." He studied his blank-faced twin for a moment. "I am one of the giants you people fear so much."

"Giants?" she said. "You? That legend is true?"

He nodded. "The giants were not some monstrous creatures in your past. Everyone on the Homeworld is a giant compared to you. Your people here were giants once, too. This moon changed you over the years, many hundreds of years, and made you smaller. The same happened on Chenoweth. We, on the Homeworld, remained the same."

"You mean," she said after pondering his words for a while, "that in order for you to be made smaller, the La'il had to cut you in half?"

He nodded again, surprised when she chuckled tiredly, shaking her head. "I see," he said, experimenting with a thin smile, "that maybe you don't fear giants quite as much as I thought."

"Why should I? You've destroyed one myth after another these past few weeks. You took away everything I've ever thought to be true and replaced it with lies. How can I possibly know what is real now? What am I to believe?"

"I don't know. I have also been misled. Lied to. Used by the La'il in more ways than one. I know that now."

"That isn't making me feel any better!"

Chor had returned to the fire with a pail of water and

some things he had found in their baggage. Both men started to peel off their sodden clothing, shivering in the cool night air while they rinsed the blood from their wounds. Aletha turned away, unwilling to allow herself to be affected by this casual intimacy, the sight of his battered body, or the fact that it was displayed twice before her.

"I am sorry; you can believe that," he said. "I'm sorry about all of this. I know it's upsetting."

"Upsetting? It's outrageous!"

Dressed in dry clothing now, Chor once again returned to his absent daydreams, staring off into the night. Galen held his hands out to the fire, wishing that he, too, could get some sleep. Several days' worth of sleep, in fact. He knew he sounded irritable when he spoke. "Outrageous would have been if Chor had accepted some of the offers he got from the women in your village. You wanted him to. You teased him about it. That would have been me, Aletha."

"How noble of you to decline!" She glared at him, torn between wanting to hurt him for his deception and the sudden need to come to him, let him fold his strong body around her, and let this darkness pass over them. Doing either of these things might ward off the disturbing truth hovering around their camp like the shadows thrown up by the fire. She turned her eyes skyward as if searching for meaning among the clouds. "There's more, isn't there?"

"What do you mean?"

"She," Aletha pointed up. "When she puts you back together, you will once again be a giant, won't you? Legends tell of people more than twice our size. You're practically there already! How much larger will you be when we get home?"

He only nodded.

"And me?"

"You are not one of the giants. I know that now."

Her eyes traveled to Chor, then back to Galen. "What will happen to me? You are taking me to a place where people don't even look like me. Why would anyone think I'd be happy there? I'm going to help you fight some stupid war against people I didn't even know existed and then what?"

"I swear to you, I believed the La'il would somehow change your shape as well. It just never occurred to me to wonder how she'd do this. I don't often see limits to her abilities."

"Is it possible that I, too, have another half on the Homeworld Perhaps I can be restored, as well!"

"No," he sighed. "I don't think that's likely. Before you left the village, I had a long conversation with Minh. You are not of the Homeworld. You were born here, and your parents were, too. Your talents are the result of some genetic coincidence making you the balance of power between the Homeworld and Chenoweth. You have no family on the Homeworld. We've both been deceived about that. After I found this out I was coming to tell you everything, but you had left."

Aletha shook her head, her movement barely perceptible. "No," she said. "That can't be! I'm a weapon? That's all? I have no other purpose?"

"Of course you do! You can do many things on the Homeworld, once Chenoweth has been dealt with. Think of all the things you've already learned here, with very little chi. With proper training you—"

"No!" she exclaimed. "Enough!" She began to say something, then didn't, began to move, then didn't. He thought she would cry, but then she didn't. The things she had learned in this hour had stunned her so completely that he almost wished that she would cry. Or shout at him. Anything but this.

"Aletha," he said finally. "I can't ask you to return with me. This isn't your fight any more."

Her eyes were on Chor's immobile face. "You can't return without me because you can't open the seal. And even if you could, La'il would kill you for failing to bring me down there."

"She'd come up with something worse than that."

"I can't stay here," she said dully. "Hunted by emissaries, am I to hide in these forests forever? Endanger my friends? My family?" She shook her head. "My only choice is to go your way. To the Homeworld. To fight your damn battles. I will be alone there, unique because of my mind and because of my body. But at least I'll be alive, isn't that so? No future disembowelment on the emissaries' sacrificial stone, no living in caves in fear of discovery. Just endless amounts of chi'ro to play with. Isn't that so?" She raised her voice. "Isn't that so!"

"You won't be alone."

"I won't be what I want to be," she said. "While you go back to the La'il's bed."

"That is going too far! What the hell do you want to be?"

"What I thought I was going to be," she snapped back. "Free to live among my own people. People like you. *With* you." Her voice broke on the last words.

Galen stared into the fire for a long, silent while. He shivered, feeling hungry and tired and utterly exhausted. His arm throbbed all the way from his lacerated hand to his shoulder and he felt the sting of every one of Chor's injuries. "I wanted that, too," he said at length. "And I believed in it."

* * *

The following morning roused Galen and Aletha with a blast of cold air from across the channel; neither was at first sure why they were not huddled under the same blankets for warmth and comfort. Grudgingly, they became aware of the past few days, of the night before, of Chor to remind them that not all was well, and an awkward silence hovered over the camp. Galen found the rest of his gear in the boat, glad that she hadn't dropped his parcels overboard after she left the village. He began to feel like himself again after a bath in a nearby freshwater stream and more help from Aletha with their injuries. All three travelers moved with exaggerated care, exchanging polite words as they took down the campsite and prepared a late breakfast. Then even the meaningless small talk failed as they hunched around a small fire, gripping their cups of tea as though a winter storm raged about them.

"I wish you'd stop staring at me like that," he said finally, trying to take the edge off his words with a crooked smile.

She stopped looking at his twin and directed her gaze at him. "I think I'll keep calling you Chor and Galen," she said.

He shrugged.

"I can see it now, you know. I just didn't think to look before. I can tell when you have to stop and think about what the other is doing, or when you get confused about who is moving where. It takes only a moment, but I can see it. You usually face the same direction, even if you're not looking at the same thing. You move quickly only if the other is holding still."

"It's not easy being two," he admitted.

"Is this why you're always so close together? So you can keep track of both of you?"

"We can't be very far apart, although I haven't tried to see exactly how far. He gets harder to control at a distance and then I have to switch my focus to him and leave this body idle. If both of me have to do something more complicated at the same time, I have to switch my attention back and forth very quickly."

"Can you feel the other? Like if you're in pain or hungry?"

"Yes, in the way it registers in my mind. When you hit me last night, both of us flinched. When Chor was bitten by that bug, I felt the bite, but not the poison."

A slow, joyless smile formed on her lips. "I suppose you feel the other's pleasure, too."

He nodded into his tea.

She shivered. "This is too strange."

"Probably another reason I didn't tell you," he said moodily, using Chor to talk while Galen got up to walk to the edge of the small outcropping on which their camp was made. "I thought you might find it creepy."

"Yes, I do," she allowed, letting another uncomfortable silence settle between them before she spoke again. "So how did she do it? Turn you into two bodies? How can such a thing be possible?"

"There are a lot of things possible on the Homeworld. You will see. Things you believe to be solid just aren't. They can be moved, and changed, and turned into something else. If you have enough chi and enough talent. As long as you understand something, its smallest parts, you can change it." He turned his hands up to look at them. "And we have thousands of years of knowledge to draw on. In this world, we can take half of a body to make another. But we cannot give it life."

"But you were able to join your mind to your twin and pretend he was alive. Like you join with me or La'il, in your thoughts. Except there is no one home over there. Just a soulless brain. That is creepy." She gestured to his twin who was looking across the strait to the mainland shore, his hands clasped behind his back. The northern mountain range loomed there without the preamble of foothills, rising straight from the water into the clouds. "What do you see? Is anyone following?"

"Not close enough to notice," Chor said. Galen's eyes saw a few small skiffs trawling along a spit in the distance and a single freighter had just entered the channel. "Doesn't Delann's ship have a yellow sail?"

"Many ships have them. It's a better cloth, but expensive. Although I guess one of his traders could be up here."

He dismissed the merchant ship from his mind. "That mountain there... the one that looks like a big piece has fallen off." She looked past his shoulder to see Galen point across the channel. "It is almost completely flat on one side."

"I see it."

"The launch is up there. About halfway up, where things start looking rocky. Not a difficult climb."

"When will we get there?'

He measured the distance across the strait and into the

deep fjord leading to the foot of the mountain. "If we leave now, by nightfall, perhaps. If the weather holds."

"Do you think they'll catch us?"

"Tsingao wants us dead. I don't think there is any other thought in his head. He won't stop. We'll have to get to the launch before he catches up. We used a lot of chi last night to get us healed up. Enough to be noticeable from a distance. Whether they can sense us now or Chenoweth is showing them the way, they know where we are. I'd rather not get into crossbow range."

"We've probably been leading them with that all along. Across the strait. To the village. Gods, we did nothing *but* play with chi'ro there!"

He winked. "You do glow brightly, Goddess. And your chi spike could wake a dead man."

Feeling a blush warm her cheeks, she grinned back at him and was, for a fleeting moment, transported back to only a few days ago when Chor was Chor and Galen was Galen and she thought she knew the difference. Her smile faded. Now Galen was Chor. If she looked closely. At this moment the man standing by the water was named Galen only because of the ragged bandage on his hand. Yesterday she would have assumed him to be Chor for no other reason than his silence. "I suppose I won't be able to tell you apart until we get to the planet," she said. "Even if you never again trade places with Galen, I would never be sure who I was talking to. Because you can't be sure. Or you don't care to. Or you don't remember to."

"I do care to," he said. He leaned forward and withdrew the slim dagger that she kept tucked in her boot. Taking a handful of his hair, he set the blade to it. "We don't have to look alike."

She gripped his wrist. "Don't do that. It doesn't matter anymore, does it? You're not Chor anymore, and he's not Galen. I don't know what you are, or who you are and I can't live like this, even if I think I understand how things happened the way they did. On the Homeworld you'll be someone else again and I'll still be me. All of this will be over."

Chor turned the knife with its handle toward her. A random beam of sunlight slid along its blade when he handed it back. For all its deadly purpose, her words had cut deeper than this dagger ever could. "Is it really so important how tall I am compared to you?"

"I don't care about how gigantic you'll be! You lied to me. You kept things from me. You like to think this won't mean anything to me once we're on the Homeworld. That makes everything so much easier, doesn't it? You think I'll turn into some sort of La'il monster. Someone who hates and whom you'll hate. And you are going to let it happen to me because that's your damn job, but you might as well enjoy the game until we get there."

"Stop this, Aletha," he said tonelessly. "I know you're angry and that's my fault. But you don't really want this."

"What I want isn't any part of this, remember? Don't tell me what I feel."

"I know what you feel," he reminded her and sighed when she retreated behind a mental barrier that, he knew, would be impenetrable.

"Too bad you don't understand it, too." She returned the knife to her boot and stood up. "Keep your hair, be whoever you want to be, it doesn't matter anymore. Besides, Galen's hand will never be pretty again. I'll tell you apart by that, if I need to. Let's be on our way. La'il is waiting."

FOURTEEN

"You're going to break something if you keep this pace up."

"Come on, will you? Hurry!" Aletha was practically bounding up the steep incline ahead of the twins, apparently untroubled by the loose boulders and shifting mounds of rubble under her feet.

"I don't think we need to rush quite this much." The twins stepped more carefully over the precarious ground, their eyes scanning the valley below for signs of pursuit. Earlier, they had seen the emissaries' cutter make landfall in the same bay where they had left their little sailboat. Tsingao and his people seemed to have survived the mutiny aboard their ship and brought their men under control. It was impossible to tell how many followed now. Although Galen was sure that their pursuers were still far behind, the presence of a significant riser nearby had begun to obscure the weak evidence of adepts other than themselves on the mountainside.

He, too, felt like racing toward the tantalizing riser near the launch site. He had not appreciated its magnitude when he had arrived on this moon only a few weeks ago; vents like these were not uncommon on the Homeworld. But here he had gradually done with less and less of the substance until he, like Aletha, was drawn to it as if to an oasis in a desert. Up here he seemed to be able to inhale it along with the cold mountain air, letting it fill not only his lungs but also his entire body. Instead of growing more tired as their long climb progressed, he grew stronger with each step until his recent injuries seemed as insignificant as if he had imagined them. In fact, the renewed vigor flowing through his bodies was beginning to assert itself in some rather uncomfortable ways and he did his best to keep his attention on his feet during their ascent. But his eyes consistently strayed back to Aletha moving ahead of him, likely drawn there because she had worn tight-fitting breeches instead of her usual voluminous trousers. The smooth muscles of her legs flexed effortlessly and, he thought, far too enticingly. Her sleeveless shirt was equally tormenting. The warmer clothes she would need later today were in a parcel slung across her back.

She waited on a narrow plateau until he had heaved both of his bodies onto the ledge. "We're close now," she said, breathing deeply of the thin air. The insufficient material of her blouse stretched taut across her breasts. "This is very exciting."

Silently agreeing with her, he turned his attention to the valley below. Most of it was shrouded in fog and it was surely raining now where they had left the boat this morning. "Let's rest a while up on that ridge. I don't think we'll make the launch before nightfall, after all."

"Can't we go on in the dark? We could use some chi'ro to light the way."

"Could, and be seen and felt for miles."

They scrambled over sharp-edged rocks toward the wall he had pointed out, slowed by the need to help each other over larger boulders and slopes of unstable scree. Galen muttered under his breath when he had to lift her over his head to where his twin waited atop the overhang, closing his eyes when she put a knee on his shoulder. Was she doing this on purpose? Surely, she could feel the effect she had on him – likely any adept on this moon felt it! Only a few days ago, the merest suggestion, the briefest sidelong glance from either of them would have them clawing out of their clothes and here, on the bare rocks, they would have—

Chor lost his footing and threw himself backward in a bid to keep her from falling, using the momentum to heave her over the ledge. Aletha whooped excitedly as she was flung through the air and grunted when she slammed into Chor on the ground. Galen might have been amused that his poor twin always seemed to bear the brunt of his lack of concentration except that he felt the pain of any scrape either body sustained, for whatever reason. This time Chor had knocked his shoulder on a rock and suffered a well-placed knee in the pit of his stomach when Aletha fell on him. Galen waited until she had rolled away from his twin before he switched his mental focus to Chor.

"This isn't funny," he said, flexing his shoulder.

"Yes, it is." Aletha reclined on the moss beside him, laughing at his discomfort. He was sure that she knew they were not talking about the same thing.

Shaking his head, he watched Galen gain the top of the cliff and move beyond them, toward a small stand of trees growing wherever a few handspans of thin soil allowed roots to find purchase. When he looked back down at Aletha he found her observing him curiously. She reached up to touch a loose strand of his hair and then nudged his chin to turn his head. "How could I ever have thought you were two people?" she marveled, spotting a small freckle near his brow, of course identical to one on Galen's face. Their eyes held for uncounted moments where neither dared to use their abilities to pry into the other's thoughts, knowing the barriers were in place and unwilling to be the first to lower them.

He forgot to breathe when she tugged on his hair, pulling him down until his lips touched hers. He kissed her as though this was the first kiss they shared, wanting to kiss her forever. It was a gentle, unhurried encounter until he placed his hand lightly onto her waist. She caught his hand and pushed him away. Shaking her head in answer to his baffled frown, she came to her feet. "Let's keep moving... Chor," she said resolutely, her lips forming a thin line to keep her voice from trembling.

He sighed and picked himself up to follow her to where his twin waited. Aletha dropped her backpack and searched through it to find some hard biscuits and strips of dried meat. There was little else left of their supply of food and the likelihood of finding anything edible up here without hunting for it seemed remote. She offered a water skin to one of the twins who refused it moodily. Night fell upon them like a cold, dank shadow and they huddled some distance apart without speaking.

Chilled by both the evening breeze and Galen's aloofness, Aletha dug through her pack for warmer clothing. Neither twin so much as glanced at her, nor did either go to any lengths to look away. She frowned, feeling sorry for her reaction to Chor's kiss, knowing it was unreasonable to continue to think of them as brothers. Yet, although he seemed set on ignoring her indefinitely, she felt neither anger nor frustration from him now. There was nothing at all and the chill she felt was made worse because of it.

"Galen," she said finally, aware of an unpleasant, pleading tone in her voice. "It's so cold here. Can we tap into that riser to get warm?" She leaned closer to one of the twins. "Galen? Are you all right? Galen?"

He was scarcely aware that she had spoken. His mind seemed to keep drifting off, as if beckoned from a great distance. Unbidden thoughts entered his conscience and he started suddenly, a strangled sound on his lips.

"Is it La'il?" Aletha said, worried.

He shook his head in a slow, half-finished gesture. "I don't think so." He squinted into the night as if this would sharpen his senses. There was something calling to him. Someone, but not the La'il. Curious, he turned toward the beacon, letting his mind drift until he knew he was touching the Homeworld. He thought he felt Aletha's hand on his arm, shaking it, but that seemed unimportant compared to the anguish in the voice reaching out to him. At last, a more coherent thought came through. It was an exclamation of distress so very faint that he could not understand its meaning.

"Help me," he said urgently and gripped Aletha's hand with both of his. When he felt her support, the nebulous contact from the Homeworld began to come into focus. He saw a familiar room, possibly somewhere in La'il's tower, judging by the elegant carvings on the plastered walls. Someone was in trouble. "I'm here," Galen whispered. The image before him moved and he knew he was seeing out of someone else's eyes. Not as accomplished a vision as the La'il was able to project, but clever nonetheless. The room shifted and suddenly he saw the image of La'il's closest advisor stare back at him from the depths of a mirror.

"Yobar!" Galen whispered. "What's going on?"

The older man blinked nervously. His eyes darted around the room, jarring the projection, and he seemed to be trembling. He was disheveled and pale and Galen was reminded of the adept's advanced age, something Yobar rarely allowed to show. Yobar's focus on their tenuous contact wavered and the vision threatened to dissolve from one moment to the next. Galen felt that something terrible had happened. Or was still happening.

"Bad news from Chenoweth?" he guessed. "Have they broken through?"

Yobar shook his head. "Do not go to the launch."

Galen frowned. "What? Why not? Where is La'il?"

Hesitantly, Yobar turned his head. The field of vision changed and Galen saw the La'il nearby, reclining on her couch. The room tilted when Yobar walked toward her. With the cold silver eyes closed, her luminous face was a gentle portrait of heart-wrenching loveliness. Her head was turned to the side and one arm draped to the floor. "She's asleep. I… I was able to… to reach her. I don't know if she knows what I'm doing."

"What exactly are you doing? How did you find me?"

A hysterical giggle escaped the adept. "I'm in her head! I was able to touch her once she was asleep. And then I found the link to you."

"Yobar, talk to me! What's made you do this? If she finds out you won't last longer than it takes her to tear your face off. Have you lost your mind?"

"Perhaps, but I won't stand by and watch this any longer." Yobar returned to the mirror. He squared his shoulders and the vision became sharper as he made a visible effort to pull himself together. "You must not go to the launch."

"Why not?"

"Because she will take control of the conduit as soon as it's stable and then head straight for Chenoweth. If she does that, all is lost."

"How? Why?"

"She will drain Chenoweth of its chi'ro resources. As she did with Thali. Thali is all but lost because of her. It is only a matter of time before that moon is utterly uninhabitable. Without a good chi balance, it's just too small to support that much water. Who knows what could happen to the lunar orbit itself! And the same will happen to Chenoweth. It is so dependent on chi that it may lose its atmosphere entirely. They are not our enemies, Galen!"

"Unbelievable," Galen muttered, awed.

"Believe it! The reason Dazai sealed the launches was to stop her raids on Thali. He hoped the moon would eventually be able to restore its resources and return to its natural state, if they left it alone for a while. They removed as many adepts as they could and then locked themselves up so she would not attack Chenoweth, as well."

Galen sighed. "And they forbade Thali the use of chi'ro for any purpose so nothing would be wasted. And in doing so they started a three-hundred year persecution of adepts!"

"Perhaps. I don't know." Yobar's projected thoughts grew more urgent. "She's waking. Don't go near the seal,

Chor!"

"Why would she do this? Not even she would risk so much."

"She cares only about this planet. The people on the moons mean nothing to her. Dazai found that out when he tried to stop her. You, more than anyone, know that the only thing that pleases her is the control she has over others. Over anything. Don't give it to her."

Galen felt a familiar presence intrude upon their conversation. It was befuddled and vague, but definitely part of the La'il. "You can stop her, Yobar," Galen whispered urgently, desperate to gain a few more moments. "Now. While she's out."

"No! Don't ask this of me! I could never—"

"Yobar!" Galen shouted. He barely ducked out of the way when the La'il suddenly realized what had happened as she slept. Her fury reached through the cold emptiness of space and slammed into his brain with the force of a sledgehammer. He moaned when he perceived Yobar's last coherent thought and watched helplessly as the adept's brilliant mind was destroyed by a brutal blow from the La'il. Horrified, his thoughts fumbled for Aletha and, perceiving her startled response, broke his contact with the Homeworld.

"Galen?" he heard Aletha's voice. "Galen, can you hear me?"

He opened his eyes, feeling a deep ache settle in his skull. Had this really happened? "Gods," he exhaled.

Aletha peered into his ashen face. "Are you all right? You're shaking! Who is this Yobar you were shouting about? What happened?"

Galen spoke haltingly, trying to make sense of what he had been told as he explained it to her. The flash of terror that he had seen in Yobar's mind kept returning, distracting him from the terrible facts they now needed to consider. Aletha listened to his account without interruption, shuddering when he described La'il's revenge on her trusted aide.

"Could this be a trick?" she said when he had finished.

He shook his head. "No, he's dead. I'm sure of it. I saw… I felt him die." His haunted gaze moved over the distant islands and to the horizon beyond. "I can't believe this. She left the original colonists to fend for themselves up here, knowing that this moon would die because of her."

"Why didn't she bring them back home? There couldn't have been very many of them at the time."

"I think there was some problem with that. Minh has some history about your people changing over time. They had become too different from us, and not just in size. Reintegrating them all again would have been a massive undertaking. It would probably take a great deal of chi to do that. A worthwhile expense for someone like you, but not a bunch of non-adept settlers." He paused, his brow furrowed. "Or maybe you weren't meant to come home!"

"Why do you say that?"

He closed his eyes, accepting the realization with a groan. "Why did I ever think that the La'il would be willing to share her planet with someone like you? It's possible that you are as powerful as she is. Or will be. She would never tolerate a rival! Have I been asleep all this time? She has no need for you on the Homeworld! No one is coming to start a war. She wants Chenoweth itself. And you're going to get her there."

"How would I do that?"

"La'il can't open Chenoweth's seal from the Homeworld. It's just too far away. She obviously thinks that it can be opened from here. And once open, she'll only have to reach out her hand to draw down as much chi as she wants. But she can't come up here on her own. That would be like sitting in the cart you're trying to push uphill. She needs you up here, the only person powerful enough to do this without chi. Or at least without needing a lot of it."

She stared at him wide-eyed, waiting for him to continue, perhaps with some admission that his revelation had been an evil little joke. But there was nothing more, his eyes told her. "We can't go to the launch, Galen!"

He had come to the same conclusion. He scanned the mountainside for the presence of others. Nothing much moved on these hills. The emissaries approached from the west where they had surely confiscated their boat. There were some people to the south, none of them Descendants. "I think there is a village or town in that direction. Can you feel them? We'll try to get there by first light, outfit ourselves a bit better and then move on. Inland maybe. Away from this launch."

"And then what?" she said in a small voice. "We hide on this moon forever? Wait until she sends someone else after me? I'll keep running and hiding from her as well as the emissaries forever. And you! She can find you wherever you are and so you might as well sit on your dagger now. Don't you don't want to go home?"

He considered several replies to that question of which most included the phrase *not without you*. Eventually he settled on another explanation. "A few days before I came here, I arrested someone for tapping into a riser to which he had no rights. He's done that many times before and this time I had to turn him in. There is no simple way to control a rogue adept. At least none that the La'il will bother with. He's likely dead now or perhaps his brain no longer works quite right. That's the same thing for an adept. Do you know what that makes me?"

Aletha winced. "You were obeying La'il's law."

"I am a damn emissary." He tipped his head back to look at the blackness above. There were no stars visible among the shreds of clouds hurrying overhead, and Chenoweth had not yet risen. The sky felt close enough to touch. "You know that. You even tried to tell me, on that day we found the volcano." He shook his head. "No, I can't go home. I won't. But you're right. I'm easily tracked here. She'll find me no matter where I am. Or Chenoweth will. You, however, are pretty much invisible as long as you stay away from chi'ro. You have to get away from me."

"That's not what I meant!"

"You are not safe with me!"

"I've never been safe. You can't leave me now. I need you!"

"Need who?" he said, more sharply than intended. "Me or him? You can't even bear to touch me now."

She started to yell something back at him, paused, suddenly exhaled sharply. Her small frame seemed to collapse in on itself and she slouched gloomily, avoiding his eyes.

He stood up. "Get your pack. Let's get off this mountain and find the town Delann suggested."

They turned their backs to the beckoning riser near the launch and headed vaguely southeast, away from the emissaries that followed. It was impossible to hurry; Chenoweth was now in the sky but once more the moon was hidden behind Thali's perpetual blanket of clouds. Slippery pebbles underfoot and treacherous gullies promised a turned ankle to anyone foolish enough to rush down the mountain. As in the forests of her island home, Aletha was sure-footed in the dark and moved with the noiseless confidence of the professional bandit. She scouted the path ahead of the twins to find her way unerringly among unseen obstacles.

They hiked at a careful pace in the dark, always downhill, stopping often to feel for their pursuers or to gauge the direction of the village Galen had detected in the distance. Definitely, a number of non-adepts were now not far ahead of them. But something about that group seemed out of place. Galen no longer thought they would come upon some peaceful farming community or roving herdsmen. There was nothing peaceful about them.

He was about to mention that to Aletha when she came to a halt in front of him. "River up ahead," she said.

They stepped out of the sheltering trees to the edge of a creek hurtling among sharp boulders on its way to the valley. It was not broad here yet but strong enough to force Galen to raise his voice over its thunder. "We'll follow it down into the valley. No doubt it'll take the most direct route."

She turned to go and he was unprepared when she suddenly leaped at Chor to push him back into the blackness of the woods. "People down there!"

They crept forward to peer around the shoreline rocks to look into the valley. It opened up below them in a broad expanse of grasslands through which the river meandered in lazy sweeps once freed from the mountain's steep inclines. At the foot of the hill, along a stretch of beach on the opposite shore, a number of fires were lit, visible for many miles. There were no houses or other permanent buildings, but a scattering of tents provided shelter to whoever had stopped here for the night. A worn, rutted trail followed the river, part of the road running along the coast and eventually leading to Phrar.

"What do you think that is?" Aletha asked. "They must be well guarded to camp so out in the open."

He touched a finger to his lips. Opening his mind and his senses he stood unmoving, barely breathing, both of his bodies focused on his surroundings. Aletha waited until he had gathered what he could. "About thirty of them. Men. Not talking much. Not resting well. Bored. Some are drunk. Some are pacing around." He inhaled the cool night air. "There are animals, but not a herd. Chargers, not many of them. An army of some sort? They're eating something I wouldn't mind a bite of." He opened his eyes. "Are there any wars going on up here?"

"Possibly. To the south this river is the border between two major clans."

He nodded, studying the terrain. Dense forest lined the opposite bank all the way to the valley, whereas this side was crowded with more of the ankle-breaking rocks and cliffs that too easily hid an approaching marksman. "We'll be seen against these rocks. Let's find a way across the river and make our way down through those trees. We'll take a closer look at the camp in the morning. Could be a caravan. With food to spare."

She led the way down the slope, no longer bothering to

move noiselessly along the riverbank. Always staying out of sight of the camp below, they continued for many tedious minutes before coming upon a narrow plateau. The river was broader here and moved around rocks and sandbanks with barely a ripple. "Doesn't look very deep here. We can hop over those boulders. Maybe just get our feet wet."

"Fine, let's cross. I'll leave him here while you and I go first. Might be better if I don't have to concentrate on two sets of feet."

Aletha moved ahead of Galen and stepped onto a flat rock just below the surface. Icy water sunk into her boots, bringing the instant realization that this river was likely fed by melting snow at higher elevations. She leaped onto the next rock and then, teetering a little moved to another. "This is so cold!" she sputtered. "I can't feel my feet."

Galen, close behind her, looked over his shoulder to where he had left his twin and cursed under his breath when he realized that he would have to do it all again when it was Chor's turn to cross. "Can we listen to Chor next time?"

"There are some bigger rocks here," she said through chattering teeth.

He watched her shift her weight onto one of them, desperate to get out of the water for just a moment. The boulder moved! Wheeling her arms for balance, she fell into the glacial water with a startled cry. Something large rose up, something with a glistening hump and shovel-sized flippers or fins or something utterly outside Galen's experience. He saw a snout and then something hit the side of Aletha's head and she went under.

He dove after her, feeling icy needles pierce his face and scalp. The frigid water closed like a vice around him. His body heat was instantly carried away by the frigid current, leaving him breathless and numb and as if assaulted by a hundred knives, every muscle turned to stone. Catching her arm, he heaved her up, relieved when she came to the surface, gasping and coughing.

When Galen started to lose his footing in the river's

current, Chor ran into the water, realizing too late that now both of his bodies were affected by the numbing cold. He turned his mind to the riser, hoping to draw it near, finding it too distant now to capture quickly. His concentration wavered when he felt Aletha's grip on Galen weaken and he threw himself forward to grasp her arm. At that moment she slipped from Galen's numb fingers and was swept away. Chor collided with Galen and both of them followed Aletha down the river.

Aletha came up against a boulder and briefly clung to it before slipping away again. Galen lunged for her and missed, his arms stiff and heavy with the cold. All three of them were dragged along by a strong current, afraid to lose sight of each other, desperate to reach the shore. He heard Aletha scream in fear and flailed his way toward her. His hand encountered something made of fabric and then he had grasped her belt and pulled her toward himself. He redoubled his efforts to gather up what chi'ro there was, knowing she was doing the same. They used it to conserve their body heat and to remain afloat while fighting their way toward shore. But there was so little of it and he felt it slip away, felt himself going over, his mind forcing his body to move when no strength remained. There were voices nearby, or perhaps he was imagining that, and something brushed past him. It might have been Chor. Then the riverbank was suddenly close and he saw people running along it, waving and shouting. He rasped along a rock and then there were many hands, pulling on his arms and legs to heave him out of the water.

FIFTEEN

"Thank you, whoever you are," Galen wheezed around a lungful of river water. His twin, too, had survived the trip downriver and was struggling to his feet, coughing. Galen groped for Aletha stretched out beside him. He lifted her into his arms and pushed the wet curls from her face, utterly relieved when he saw that she breathed evenly. She was exhausted and frightened but clearly more adept than he when it came to keeping water out of her lungs. He rubbed her arms to return some warmth to them, and at last looked up at their rescuers.

He sighed. Swords and cudgels, greaves and holsters, studs and buckles. Bearded, weathered faces looking down on them, wary stances and brawny forearms ready to deal with the strange intruders. Identical broad belts slung across armored chests hinted that all of these men belonged to the same band of mercenaries or private army.

"By Dazai's moldy beard, what brings you out here?" said the first to recover from their surprise.

Raised voices reached the group at the bank and some of the soldiers stepped aside to let others through. Torches were brought to illuminate the three shivering, dripping travelers. "La'il be merciful! Aletha!"

Aletha had buried her face against Galen's chest and now

pulled back to peer beyond the light of the torches. "Delann?"

"By the Gods!" he cried and rushed toward them with arms extended. "Release her at once," he snapped at Galen who, surprised by the venom in his voice, did just that.

"Delann," Galen said. "I can't believe our luck! We've run into—"

"Not a word from you, Demon!" Delann turned briefly to an armed man at his side. "These are the Descendants we are looking for! Delivered right into our camp!" He took Aletha's arm and tugged her away, toward the tents. "Bring them, don't listen to anything they say. Those two are demons and she is under their spell."

"No, Delann, please…" Aletha began weakly.

"Shh, all is well now, Aletha," Delann said. He removed his short riding cloak and swung it around her shoulders. "I've been sick with worry. You're so cold! Are you hurt? Did they injure you?"

She extricated herself from his loose embrace. "I'm all right, Delann. Why are you doing this? I am in no danger from these two."

Delann nodded. "She knew you'd say that. They've bewitched you, but La'il has sent me to your rescue. She came to me, Aletha! She came and told me what must be done. You have nothing more to fear once these two demons have been delivered to Her." He signaled to his men. "I'll take her with me. We'll move on with the dawn. Tie those two up somewhere, out of my sight."

Chor took a step backward but made no move to defend himself. But Delann's men, eager for action after their monotonous journey along the coast, fell upon them as though Chor had raised a sword. One mercenary struck him senseless with the stock of his crossbow; the others wrestled Galen to the ground.

"Delann, please stop it!" Aletha cried. "Whatever she told you isn't true. The La'il is not who you think. She is…" she faltered. The La'il was what? Not a goddess? "She is evil,

Delann. A demon herself! She is going to harm everyone. She's already doing it! She made the storms and the tides, Delann. You have to believe me!"

Delann regarded her with great worry. "This is my fault. I never should have let you leave Phrar. But I'll help you overcome this! The Goddess is so very concerned about you. You are one of Her favorites. She told me so Herself when She asked me to free you from…" He glanced at Galen and Chor in distaste. "These monsters. They won't hurt you anymore. I would run them through myself if She had not forbidden it." He held up his hands. "No, I won't hear any more of it until you've been restored to your good senses. It's still a few hours to morning. You can sleep in my tent. You're like ice! You must be exhausted!"

But Aletha did not sleep and the dawn found her anxious and weary. Delann had provided her with clean clothing, food, hot water, and an animal to ride. But the twins had spent yet another cold night in chains, hungry and bleeding from re-opened wounds. She was kept away from them while the mercenaries broke their camp and when they at last moved out the twins walked in the middle of the column, bound to each other and surrounded by guards. Troubled, Aletha realized that they were moving toward the launch site where the La'il awaited them.

"You'll soon be well again," Delann said to her after the twentieth time she had turned in her saddle to catch a glimpse of Galen. The coast road, little more than a worn path through rocky terrain, rose steeply now and the march was becoming a chore for the men. "Those two have you completely turned around!"

"Delann, I am perfectly fine. There is nothing wrong with me and no one's put any spell on me." She noted with relief that Galen had captured a tendril of chi'ro from the launch site still some distance ahead and was using it to fortify himself and his twin. Once they were restored it would not take much of the riser's power to break free of their bonds and escape their captors.

Delann smiled and shook his head. "All will be well, you'll see." He closed his eyes to recall his vision of the La'il. "You should see Her, Aletha! If you saw Her you would understand. I have never in my life seen anything so magnificent, so very powerful. I am going to build Her a new shrine when we return. I will spend the rest of my life waiting for Her to appear again!"

She studied him with narrowed eyes, concerned. In spite of his ecstasy, there was something worrisome here. Pale, tense, nearly trembling, Delann seemed not to have slept in days. His eyes twitched nervously, drawn into a squint as if he was plagued by a monstrous headache. "I think it's you who's bewitched, Delann. This isn't like you at all!"

He laughed happily. "You can't understand how I feel. I have looked into the face of the Goddess. She spoke to me. She gave me a quest! You are so privileged to have been singled out by Her. I am not a Descendant but perhaps, by returning you to Her, I will find favor with Her as well. She is so beautiful, Aletha! She glows, She radiates." He held out his arm in a sweeping gesture. "She was floating in front of me, first close to me, then away, then close again. Her hair was like spun ice, but it flowed like silk. Her gown was like glass and everything shimmered. Her skin sparkled, too, like when the sun hits new snow. And Her voice! I felt Her voice inside my heart!"

If Aletha had not been very much worried by her friend's peculiar rapture she would have rolled her eyes skyward. What had the La'il done to him? She could not remember a time when Delann had voiced any deep religious conviction; he was not often seen at the temple. But she knew how easily La'il bent Galen to her will, even while he was completely aware of her intentions. Breaking the gentle Delann to her yoke would have been done in a wink.

"If she is so concerned about me, why doesn't she come after me herself?"

Delann shook his head. "The Gods always work through mortals, Aletha," he lectured. "Perhaps this task is a test of my dedication! And truly," he added with a note of wonder, "it was Her hand that delivered you to us. We've been looking for you for days and then you simply washed up on our shore."

Aletha gave up. "Please, Delann," she said. "I am worried about Galen and Chor. Your people have mistreated them."

His dreamy smile faded. "Mistreated them? And have they not mistreated you?"

"No! That's what I've been trying—"

He dismissed her protest with a wave of his hand. "The La'il showed me what they did to you. Awful things!" He shuddered. "You are still suffering. She will set everything right."

"Fine! Until then I'll just be out of my mind." She swung her leg over the neck of her charger and slid from the saddle. Determined, she marched along the column to where the twins stumbled along. Some of the guards threw baffled glances to Delann, who simply shrugged.

"Let me pass." She glared at the soldiers. "Give me that." She snatched one of the men's water container from his pack, daring him to stop her. When no one did, she fell into step beside Galen and Chor.

Galen smiled tiredly in greeting and took the offered waterskin. He drank deeply and then handed it to Chor. "Are you all right?"

"No worries, but you don't look so good." She examined a long scratch running from his temple to the edge of his jaw. There was blood on his twin's face, too.

His gesture invited her to join her mind to his. When he spoke, his voice was pitched so low that none of those nearby heard him and even Aletha understood his words only by reading the mental images that accompanied them. "I'm a little tired of getting kicked around on this moon, but I'm all right," he murmured. "I look worse than I feel. Chor has a cracked rib that is taking a while to mend but I'll be fine in a while. Let's hope we can do something with the conduit before the La'il does or I'll have more than a rib to worry about."

"I'm not going near that launch!" she whispered urgently. "If you show me what to do, I can try to take us away from here, like I did when I pulled you away from the emissary ship. I don't know how I did that, but with your help I can get us out of here."

He chuckled. "I know you have the power of a hundred adepts, but you almost broke my spines. I don't think we should try tossing all three of us through the air until you've had a few more lessons, Goddess."

"I'm some goddess," she grumbled. "Maybe, instead of pulling splinters, you should have been showing me how to keep my head above water. I'm useless!" She kicked a rock out of her way. "Damn, I can't believe she got Delann into such a state! He's completely down the river for her." She peered up at Galen. "Is she really so dazzling?"

"She is the most beautiful thing I've ever seen." He glanced at her and smiled. "No, wait, she's the second. The absolutely most beautiful thing I've ever seen is that snow vine in the forest near Alarit Dunn. The one you told me not to touch but I just had to, anyway, and it burst open and all those black maggots splattered all over us. We shall rename that flower La'il, since they are so alike."

Aletha hid a giggle behind a fold of her cloak. One of the soldiers walking nearby glared at them until Galen offered him a sunny smile. The man spat and busied himself with watching his feet as they continued to trudge uphill.

"I have no idea how she got to Delann," Galen said. "Maybe she linked to him through me, somehow. He's not difficult to reach, for a non-adept."

Aletha moved to walk between the twins and took Chor's hand. To accommodate the chain binding the twins together, Galen fell back a step. "Ah, that feels good," he said when he felt her healing touch, speaking for Chor who had some trouble catching his breath. "Don't exhaust yourself."

"That riser is more than I need," she replied. She looked along the column of marching men to see Delann watching her anxiously from atop his mount. Everywhere she looked, weapons gleamed and suspicious eyes observed them for some deviant behavior. Tensed muscles were ready for action should the demons attempt an escape. "Can we not get away from this? You are well enough recovered. I know I can help you."

He also studied the column of men, a far more disciplined cadre than the mob aboard the emissaries' ship. Judging from the deference with which they treated Delann, here were not only hired mercenaries but also a good number of his own men, battle-hardened sailors, perhaps pirates. There were too many of them, and too well armed, to attempt an escape. "That riser isn't enough. We'll be killed. Chor and I. We could get past these first dozen or so, maybe, but then what? I'm an easy target for those crossbows and not at all sure how interested Delann is in our survival, no matter what La'il wants."

"I can help! You underestimate me."

"On the contrary! But you don't have the skills to just disable these people. Would you kill them? That's not in you and I'm not putting it there."

"So you'd risk everything just so I don't get my hands dirty?" She pursed her lips and peered up at him with a critical eye. "What's on your mind, Galen? You're thinking something. Out with it."

"Clever girl. There is another way. If we escape now nothing will have changed. She'll just try again. She'll send someone else after you. Eventually she will find a way to get to Chenoweth. I've never known the La'il to give up on anything."

"Please tell me you're not thinking of actually fighting her!"

Both Galen and Chor's eyes fastened on Delann at the head of the column. Another decent person twisted into some other shape by the La'il. Another life ruined, as were those of the people she had pitted against Galen and her other adepts over the years. She had devastated one world and now sent her pawns to destroy another. She would never stop bending people to her will, no matter what the cost. "I can't," he said. "I've failed at that for years. Even spiked on chi'ro I can't beat her and here I have practically none. You cannot fight her by yourself, either. You don't know how. Imagine what would happen if you lost control to her. Her skill and power combined with your potential will give her anything she wants."

"So then what do we do?"

"We appeal to the gods."

She gave him such a look of astonishment that he had to laugh. "I'm serious. We will travel to Chenoweth. If Yobar is right and Chenoweth is not our enemy, then surely they will offer us sanctuary."

"If they don't kill us first, for being Descendants!"

"I don't believe they would."

"You are supposing too much! You don't know anything at all about Chenoweth. For all you know, there isn't even anyone up there to help us!"

"Have some faith, Aletha."

She glared at him and punched his arm. "Don't you mock me, Homeworlder!"

He sobered. "I'm sorry, really," he said, not sounding particularly contrite. "Doesn't matter who's up there. It's an escape for us. And once we're there we will find a way to close the launch sites permanently. There must be a way to destroy them for good."

"What about Thali?"

"It's worthless to her. It's just a way to get to Chenoweth. If we take Chenoweth away Thali won't matter any longer. They'll be left alone." He looked over the train of sweating, cursing men who were far more at home riding the pitching deck of their ships than climbing a mountain at a forced pace. "Everyone here is far better off without us. She's done enough damage."

"And so you think we can just live out our lives in the Garden of the Gods?"

"Isn't that what you wanted? Unfortunately, you will have to let her touch you to get there."

Aletha missed her step and nearly lost her footing on the rough trail. "No! No way, Galen. I am not letting her into my head. Not now. You can't ask this of me."

"It's the only way. You'll have to learn how to open the seals and activate the launch. Something that complex can't just be explained. She needs to show you what she knows. She will use Delann for that."

"Del? Why?"

"Because he won't try to come up with some scheme to stop her. She's not sure about me anymore, about how far I can resist her. She's expecting a knife in the back from me. She'll start by showing you how to open the seal between here and the planet. That's all we want from her. Once you understand how that's done we have to break your link with her. When she's out of your head we'll open the seal to Chenoweth instead, go up there, and then seal it again before she can send anyone to stop us." He saw her glance at the nearby soldiers. "No, not these people. They can't touch us once we have control of the riser. But La'il might send other adepts up here, no matter how much chi'ro it'll cost her.

"Do you really think I can get her out of my head so easily?"

"Not easily, no. But while you and Delann and she are concentrating on the seal, I'll be able to soak up chi'ro without her noticing. Between you and me, we'll be able to separate you two."

"She'll kill you. She'll kill us all."

"What difference does that make, if we don't succeed?"

"And maybe the Chenowans will kill us the moment we do, thinking we're La'il's minions."

He grinned. "I *am* La'il's minion."

Aletha was silent for a long while, confused and worried and torn between trusting him and the urge to convince him to try another way to escape. She chewed on her lower lip to keep it from trembling. "I'm so scared, Galen. I don't know how to do the things you expect of me. I don't know if I'm strong enough. I'm not ready for this and I don't think I ever will be." The corner of her mouth lifted in a weak smile. "I got my wish. It turns out I'm really not like her."

"And I wish I'd never doubted that."

She sighed. "I'm sorry about how things turned out. Yesterday, on the way up the mountain, when you kissed me, I just couldn't stand it. No, don't look at me like that! I meant *I* felt wrong, not you. I knew you were Chor then but everything felt just so damn right! Chor is quiet and moody and lifeless. Chor doesn't kiss like that and I never wanted Chor to touch me like that. But there I was, wanting Chor. Chor isn't Galen!" She looked from one twin to the other, pensive. "I don't believe I can ever think of you two as one person, but that doesn't matter now, does it?"

He shook his head in agreement, waiting for her to continue. But then a shout rose among the men ahead of them. The train of marching soldiers and their captives came to a slow halt and everyone craned their neck to discover the cause. The twins peered over the heads of the others to see who was blocking their way along the narrow trail.

"Emissaries," Galen said, his lip curling in distaste.

She cowered between the twins while the newcomers marched wordlessly past the vanguard toward the three fugitives. Most of Delann's men moved hastily out of the way as they passed, more in aversion than out of respect. The group stopped to face Aletha and the twins, as one glaring at them accusingly.

"Hello again," Galen said to their leader. He studied the man's exhausted and disheveled companions. Likely none of them had rested since he and his twin had disappeared into the night. Stained robes with torn hems, dusty boots and grimed faces along with crude walking sticks and the occasional makeshift bandage added up to rob them of their preeminence. "I thought you had gone fishing. Where is your army?"

Tsingao regarded him with such hatred that even some of

the nearby soldiers exchanged uneasy glances. "You will not escape us again, Descendant." He stepped around Galen to look at Aletha, keeping a measured distance between them. "And you, she-demon," he said. "You've cost me years of my life, given in service to our Gods. None of the other Descendants that I delivered to them would satisfy them. Time after time I failed to capture you and time and time again I stood shamed before the Gods. You will pay for each of those times! You will bleed. You will beg for release before you are purged!"

Chor stepped forward, a wordless growl rising from his chest. Some of the soldiers raised their swords to him, forcing him to stop short of the chief emissary. Aletha huddled behind Galen, unable to look at the monster that had sprung from her nightmares to finally claim her.

Delann had ridden down the path and now stood slightly above the group, politely waiting for a pause in the hateful conversation. "These people are in my charge," he said to the leader of the emissaries once it was clear that Chor wasn't about to break the man's neck. "Please stand down."

Tsingao turned to gape at Delann, taken aback by the heresy he was witnessing. While he had come to terms with the disturbing mutiny of his hired guard in the islands, the man who defied his authority now was no commoner. "These demons are magic-users. Enemies of Chenoweth and therefore enemies of Thali. They escaped our custody only a few days ago. We have come to claim them and their witch. You dare order me to stand down?"

"I do."

"These three are accused of murder, using magic, conspiracy, and escaping justice," Tsingao continued. Unbelievably, he once again found himself at the center of a hostile army. "They must be purged and delivered to the Gods. I will take the woman with me now and you can deliver the other two demons to us upon your return to Phrar."

"They are going nowhere but up there," Delann said

conversationally, pointing his riding crop uphill. "I have my orders."

"Yala!" Aletha suddenly cried, looking past the emissary.

All of them turned to see the last of the straggling emissaries reach the column, a small girl of about ten among them. Seeing her friends, Yala raced downhill and threw herself into Aletha's arms. Aletha stooped to embrace her before looking up at the twins in puzzlement.

"She was on the emissaries' ship," Galen said, relieved to see her unscathed and grudgingly grateful to the emissary for not having left the girl with whatever brutes had remained aboard their ship.

Aletha turned to the chief emissary. "If I hear you've harmed the girl I will turn you into a toad!"

Startled by her rancor, Tsingao took a step backward. Galen placed a cautionary hand onto her shoulder, grimly pleased that she had thrown off her paralyzing fear of the emissary. "Don't tease him. He's mean."

Delann had watched the exchange in silence as if none of this truly affected him. "Come and ride up front with me, Yala," he said at last.

"I'm staying here with them," the girl said defiantly.

Chor nudged her forward. "Do what he says," he said. "You'll be safer."

"Don't want to be safer. And here I'll stay!"

Aletha tugged Yala closer to her. There was something peculiar in Delann's expression. The unpleasant smile had for an instant changed it into something even more unfamiliar, as if someone else was lurking behind Delann's face. Someone with a reason for wanting the girl nearby.

At his leader's impatient gesture, a soldier pulled Yala away from the adepts and heaved her onto Delann's saddle. Delann turned his charger to continue their march up the mountain. "Kill them," he said, pointing at the emissaries.

No one moved for several moments while Delann's words hung in the air like some peculiar object that had just appeared out of nowhere to be examined, discussed perhaps, to see if it would bite. No one in Thali's history had ever given such an order; the very thought of it was profane. Bewildered glances were exchanged before someone, perhaps, remembered a brother or a wife taken away to be purged, or property confiscated, or judgments passed in the name of their gods. The mercenaries surged forward, easily overpowering the untrained priests. Aletha screamed when two of the emissaries, suddenly lifeless, were tossed aside. Before Galen could stop her she leaped forward and scurried through the fray toward Delann. Restrained by his guards and his chains, Galen watched anxiously as she slipped through the mob, certain that at any moment someone's sword would cut her down. She reached up to grasp Delann's arm, shaking it, shouting, begging for him to stop the slaughter. At last, Delann raised a small pipe to his lips and whistled a signal. His men, well trained and well paid, stopped their assault on the emissaries.

Delann surveyed at least a half dozen dead emissaries, his puzzled men, the angry twins, and the small woman still clinging to his saddle. "Dazai…" he breathed, suddenly looking very confused.

"This isn't you, Delann," Aletha cried. "This isn't you!"

Delann ran a hand over his eyes. When he looked again the awful scene before him was still the same. "Bring them along," he snapped at his men, meaning the remaining emissaries. Without another word he turned and rode onward, Yala slouched in front of him, stunned into silence.

* * *

It was past noon when they finally reached the launch site. While Delann had been following some beacon placed in his mind by the La'il, both Galen and Aletha could have found this place blindfolded. Although it was still firmly sealed, both knew that the La'il was standing at the edge of a similar aperture on the Homeworld, her entire being focused on the chi'ro that would shortly enter into it.

The company and their captives came to a halt in an open

area ringed by ancient evergreens. It was an unremarkable patch of rock-strewn hillside offering a dizzying view of the western islands and the vast ocean beyond. No one here failed to look into the distance to see the Homeworld heave over the horizon as though it was rising from the sea, perhaps on its ancient quest to catch up with Chenoweth directly above their heads.

Everyone but Aletha, the twins, and five or six of the emissaries looked about themselves in puzzlement. Why had they come here, to this ordinary place? Here lay simply a slab of smooth, exposed crystal embedded in the rock, partially covered by leaves and rocks and other hillside debris. Yet surely something important was to take place here.

The twins moved ahead of the group toward the riser guarding the launch. "You can feel that," Galen said, half-turning back to the huddled group of emissaries, his words directed at Tsingao. He held up his free hand as if to test the heat of a fire. "Maybe some of you can even see that. Do you not wonder why you can?"

The men looked back at him, some staring in defiance, some curiously waiting for him to continue. Delann had dismounted and now stood nearby, silent, his arms crossed on his chest. The half smile on his face belonged to someone else. Yala slid from his saddle and scurried to Aletha.

"It's called chi'ro. Do you think it's your gods speaking to you when you touch this magic? Does it lead you to your enemies? Are we even your enemies?" Galen and Chor tugged lightly on their shackles and snapped the chain that tied them together. Some startled exclamations and hastily whispered invocations rose from the circle of men around them. "Do you really know what your gods are saying to you?"

"Our duty is to destroy the magic users," Tsingao said. Distracted, his eyes flicked to the riser and back to Galen. "They are abominations in the eyes of our Gods. Chenoweth commands it. Nothing less."

"It is your duty to *stop* the magic users. Not to kill them."

"Our histories are not open to interpretation by the likes of you!"

Galen ignored him and turned to the other emissaries. "Your ancestors were the agents left here by Chenoweth after most other magic users had gone. They were given instructions to prevent the use of chi'ro, of this magic, for needless purposes. But few of us can resist the power it gives us. And so the only way your people found to stop the magic was to punish any violators of Chenoweth's commandment. To lock them away. To kill them, even. Now, generations later, you have forgotten the purpose of your mission. You have made gods of the people who gave you this law, and you use it to enslave all of Thali. You yourselves are Descendants, and your gifts allow you to hunt and destroy your own people."

He moved to Tsingao and reached into his pocket before the emissary had time to react. Holding the small book aloft, he continued. "'None henceforth may draw forth from the ground the essences that belong to the Gods. To do so is death.' That is written. But this is not a promise of what will happen to those who disobey. It is a warning of what will happen to Thali moon." He returned the book to the silently fuming Tsingao before pointing at Aletha, who was as surprised by his words as the priests were. "We are guilty of this. In these past few weeks we have used much of the magic that drifts through this moon. But our crime is not against your gods. It is against Thali. I'd wager my last breath that nowhere in that book are there instructions to kill a magic user, or how this is done. That was not Chenoweth's intent."

"Your blasphemy ends here," Tsingao screamed and charged toward Galen, a thin dagger held aloft. Galen dodged, ready to disarm the man, but before the priest and his ineffective weapon had even crossed the distance between the two, Delann had stepped forward, his own dagger ready. The long blade drove into the emissary's chest and emerged through his back. Tsingao took two more steps before his eyes widened in surprise and disbelief and his hand grasped the hilt of the weapon. When he sank to the ground, Delann shoved him backward to free his blade, his own face empty of any emotion. Aletha held Yala close to her, feeling the child tremble in terror.

"There is work to do," Delann snapped at his guards, his voice strained. After taking a crossbow from his saddle, he slapped the animal to send it away. He gestured at the corpse. "Take this away. Move the emissaries back to that line of trees there. You four start clearing the debris off the crystal."

His company obeyed. The emissaries picked up Tsingao's lifeless body and moved to the edge of the clearing where they gently laid him onto the ground, unsure of how to proceed. The soldiers, ever more confused by the day's events, began to throw aside the deadfall and stones that Delann had pointed out, finally using their hands to sweep pebbles and dust aside to reveal the smooth surface.

At last, Delann ordered the soldiers out of the way. The men were reluctant to leave this place. Few of them felt the power emanating from the riser but they knew of their employer's pilgrimage to bring the three fugitives here and were curious to see who would come to claim them. There was some grumbling when they were forced out of earshot.

Aletha cared nothing for the crystal, or why it was there, or where it led. None of this was real, none of this made sense. In spite of his outward charm, Delann was neither timid nor ill-equipped when confronted by his foes. He didn't shirk the battles into which he ordered his men and was not taken lightly by rival smugglers and pirates. But not ever had she imagined a day when he would defy the authority of the emissaries, no matter how much he loathed their methods. And now he had needlessly killed one of them, the most preeminent of them all, in defense of Galen whom he thought to be the enemy. He did not even look like the gentle, cheerful man she had come to adore over these past few years in Phrar. Armed, tense, scowling at everyone, he was a stranger now, serving only as La'il's voice. "This isn't you doing these things, Delann," she said, as much to convince herself as the frightened child clinging to her. "This isn't you! You can still stop it. This doesn't have to happen."

"I did what I had to," he said resolutely. He did not look at her.

"This seal is ready to open," Galen said, nodding toward the larger crystal. The twins circled it as if it were a snake ready to strike. "I can feel the La'il on the other side. She's already reaching for us. Impatient. Twitchy. And fully powered up."

"So what do we do?" Aletha said, aware that anything she might say to Galen would likely be relayed to the La'il through Delann's link with her. Her suspicion was confirmed when Delann raised his arm to point his crossbow at Galen. "Delann!"

"I'm sorry, Aletha. The La'il is with me now. She said this demon will die if you don't do as She says. She wants him to let Her in so that She can help you with the seal. I don't know what that means, but I know She's sincere. It is Her hand upon this bow, Aletha."

"Need me, after all?" Galen said, realizing what was happening. "You can't use Delann to get to Aletha, can you? You can walk around in his body, but he won't survive with you in his head."

"Weak, like the rest of the squatters up there," Delann said, no longer sounding like Delann. His gentle voice was replaced by something with barbs and edges and other unpleasant things that had never been a part of him. "He's been useful so far, but he's getting a little used up now. Afraid to face me, Galen?"

"I won't do this," Galen said, inwardly cursing. A dash for Chenoweth would be impossible with her in his head, understanding his intentions before he could carry them out. Expecting resistance, she would make sure that their link was not easily broken this time. "You will stay where you are. This launch will remain sealed."

"What are you doing?" Aletha cried. "He'll kill you!"

"So be it."

Delann's hand jerked but he did not let the quarrel fly at either twin. Instead, he strode to Aletha and tore Yala away from her. Casting his bow aside, he drew his dagger again and held it to the girl's throat. "Drama isn't one of your talents, Galen. How about I start with the kid? And then that little jungle town of yours. Who's to stop me from burning demons?"

Galen unleashed a blast of energy intended to knock Delann senseless before his knife could harm the child. Delann turned his head toward him and grinned. The bolt of chi'ro deflected and slammed into the ground, exploding in clods of dirt and splintered rock between the launch and the uneasy spectators. Astounded, Galen tried again and witnessed another demonstration of La'il's control over Delann.

"You're killing her," Delann said. His body trembled under the onslaught of La'il's power and the blade at Yala's throat shook dangerously. He looked to Aletha. "Will the girl live, Aletha? Will your people live? Will Phrar? I will destroy them one by one until you give me what I need. Ask Galen if I'm known to bluff." He winked obscenely at Galen. "This is so easy! You can't even begin to imagine what I'm learning from this little encounter. But now it's your turn, Galen. Let me in or the body count starts with this one."

With a curse, Galen exhaled sharply and dropped his guard against the La'il. Instantly, her explosive presence drove into his mind, the force of her intrusion causing him to drop to the ground, clutching his head. "How nice," she mocked, securing her grip on him. "At last you fall to your knees before me."

Abruptly released by the La'il, Delann staggered backwards with a startled cry. Yala twisted and bravely grasped his forearm with both hands but her captor only gaped at her, his growing grief clearly outlined on his face as he began to understand his deeds of these past hours. "By the Gods," he whispered hoarsely. His fist slowly unclenched and the dagger tipped out of his fingers to fall to the ground. "What… Aletha, I…"

"Go," Aletha snapped. "Now! Get away from this place. Stay away, no matter what happens." Something in her tone and the peculiar expression on Galen's face convinced them to obey. Delann put a hand on Yala's shoulder but none could say who led whom toward the people who stood in slack-jawed wonder at the edge of the trees. Now only Aletha and the twins remained near the crystal and, although a few of the others had taken their chance to flee this fearsome place, none among those who remained dared to come nearer.

Galen came to his feet again, unaware of anything but the La'il visible only in his thoughts. "Yobar told me what you did to Thali," he said. "Don't do this, La'il. Not again."

At the mention of her betrayer, the La'il's eyes narrowed dangerously. "Yes, I heard your speech. But he was absolutely mistaken in all he told you! What a notion! Do you really think me capable of destroying these moons? I've consulted with the others over this matter for years. There is no danger to Thali. Or to Chenoweth."

"You can't possibly believe that! Phrar is one tidal wave away from being dumped into the bay! If things had been like this from the beginning no one in their right mind would have settled here. You made this place what it is!"

"I made the Homeworld what it is, Galen Chor, and I need Chenoweth's power to keep it that way. You're not about to get my way." The La'il waved a hand as if dismissing the matter. "Let's get this done. I know you're trying to hide something from me. Don't get ideas of playing martyr and trading your lives for Thali. I know you better than you do."

"She'd rather die than let you do this. As would I."

"You'll get your turn!" The La'il slammed into his mind with a sickening barrage of images that made clear the extent of suffering Aletha and her people would endure before being allowed to die. Galen moaned, struggling to ward off the visions displayed before him. He knew quite well that bluffing was not part of La'il's strategy. In fact, she would probably enjoy exacting the revenge she promised.

"What is it, Galen?" Aletha asked, disturbed by the torment washing over his faces. "What is she saying to you?"

He shook his head and held his hands out to her. "Let's do this," he said, aware of how unprepared Aletha was for a confrontation with the La'il and unable to warn her. He prayed that she would be able to resist the more experienced adept.

Aletha took his upturned hands and opened her mind to his touch. Instantly, the power of the La'il flowed into her; an immeasurable force fuelled by all of the chi'ro hoarded on the Homeworld. Never had she felt this immense, so incredibly powerful as she did that moment. There was complete clarity of mind, complete understanding of Galen, whose hands she gripped, and a keen awareness of every cell in her body and most living things around her for miles. She smiled at Galen in wordless amazement, momentarily forgetting why they were here.

"The launch, Aletha!" Galen prodded.

Aletha's thoughts returned to the moment and reached for the La'il through Galen. She was met with a blank, solid wall that allowed no glimpse beyond what the La'il was willing to show her. Her presence was so incredibly immense that Aletha felt like a mote of dust caught in the light of the brightest star. "She's so cold…" she whispered. She flinched when she felt the La'il lead her to the key to opening the seals within her vast knowledge of such matters. Nodding to herself, Aletha drew the nearby riser closer and guided it toward the sealed launch behind them. She explored the crystal tentatively, following La'il's instructions until she felt it dissolve into its natural fluid state. The cloudy surface of the seal began to move as something churned in its depth, ready to accept whatever conduits were placed upon it. "I think that's it," she whispered, awed by what she had seen in

La'il's presence. "The launch is active."

Both of them felt the La'il gather up the energy needed to form a conduit, her attention momentarily on her task.

"Now!" Galen shouted. "Cut her off!"

"Huh?" Aletha blinked as if startled out of some pleasant daydream. "What? Uh, I can't. I think…" Aletha fumbled for her link with the woman and was swatted aside like a minor annoyance. He barely caught her when her knees gave out and she collapsed against him. "I can't let go of her, Galen! I can't stop her!"

Steeling himself, he jabbed at the La'il in a desperate attempt to distract her long enough for Aletha to break free. La'il's outraged scream blasted through their skulls when she turned on him and he felt Aletha fade, about to faint under the adept's assault. None of their playful exercises in learning how to control mental intrusions had prepared him for the force of La'il's resistance. "She's getting through, Aletha," he hissed through gritted teeth. He shook her roughly. "Cut her off! Let her go!"

Aletha rallied, fighting desperately to expel the La'il from her mind. "Chi," she gasped. "I'm going over!"

Wasting no time with tapping into the nearby riser, Chor stepped forward and shoved both of them into its center. It whipped through their bodies and minds, its surge too violent to feel pleasurable or even refreshing this time. With a final, tremendous effort, the mental contact between the two women came apart. Before the La'il fully understood that she had underestimated the strength of Galen and Aletha's combined abilities, Aletha pulled out of Galen's grasp to break their physical link. He recoiled, his hands flying to his head, when La'il's wordless outburst of frustration and hatred stabbed into his brain, driving both of him to his knees again.

"She's gone." Aletha put some distance between herself and the riser. "We did it! By Dazai, I've never been so scared."

Galen nodded, still on his knees, gasping for air as though

he had just finished a foot race. "We have to hurry. Can you find the seal on Chenoweth?"

She concentrated on the churning launch. "Yes, I can feel them all. I think. There are ten or so launch sites on Thali, more on the Homeworld. But there is only one on Chenoweth. Hey, you know what? This is the only launch that can actually connect to Chenoweth. Guess that's why she picked this one, huh?" She laughed, still reeling from their success against the La'il. "This is so easy, now that I know what I'm looking for."

Galen heaved himself to his feet.

"Are you all right?" she asked.

"Yes. Open the seal on Chenoweth. Hurry!"

"What about La'il? Shouldn't we wait to make sure she's—"

"There is nothing she can do for now. But we need to get away from here and start working on a way to permanently destroy the launch sites."

Using what she had learned during her encounter with the La'il, Aletha probed the launch and was soon able to touch the crystal on Chenoweth. She probed the seal carefully, using as little chi'ro as she could to make the most of the meager resource even as she felt her own reserves drain along with the riser's power, taxed by the distance to the moon. It took her a little longer than when La'il had been part of this, but eventually she felt the barrier dissolve. "I got it open! The way is clear. Hey, I think I'm good at this! But this riser is pretty much spent. We can probably shape a conduit but it won't be very stable if there isn't any chi on Chenoweth to draw on."

"Now is the time to find that out." Chor joined his twin beside the launch and both men raised their hands to shape the conduit needed to reach Chenoweth's launch site. Soon, a shimmering pillar began to rotate and rise gracefully into the sky. They watched it soar higher, arcing toward the hazy disk hanging in the sky until it thinned and faded from view. They lowered their arms when all of them felt the conduit touch Chenoweth's crystal where the wealth of chi'ro surrounding the place allowed him to anchor it with the barest nudge of his mind. "It's there," Galen whispered. "So damn much of it."

Aletha came to stand beside Chor, marveling at the calmly swirling vortex on the launch, visible only because of the space and light it distorted by its presence. "This is incredible. Now that it's anchored it's hardly using up any chi'ro at all. Do we just step in there?"

Chor shook his head. "No, I'll draw chi through it to this place."

"How do you do that?" She furrowed her brow. "Uh, *why* do you need to do that?"

"So I can send it to the Homeworld, of course. That's what we're here for, after all."

"No, it isn't. What are you talking about?"

Galen grasped the collar of her cloak and pulled her aside when Chor turned his full attention to the launch. "Watch this." Ignoring the weakened riser hovering nearby, he began to siphon chi'ro from Chenoweth at a rate that actually began to feel like a strong wind against their bodies. Soon, he was able to form a second conduit and send it into the sky toward the planet where La'il waited. They could almost feel her reaching out to it, eager to merge it into the open launch on the Homeworld. "She wants to come visit," he said and laughed. "She wants to meet you."

"Have you lost your mind?" Aletha flung her hand toward the new conduit, thinking only of disrupting its supply of energy before it made contact. The conduit obeyed her command and they watched it dissipate like smoke in the wind.

Galen, still gripping her collar and looking only mildly bothered by her antics, gave her a shake. She winced when her head snapped back and her teeth came together on the edge of her tongue. "Being annoying is not going to help you live through this day. Now I'm going to have to start over."

She peered into his face, which was composed and

friendly as always. He might as well have been commenting on the weather. Aletha prodded him cautiously and found herself firmly shut out of his mind. "You can't mean this," she whispered hoarsely.

"I can. And I do." He lifted his hand to her face and wiped a bead of blood from her lip. It was a casual gesture that would not have been out of place during any of the past days and, for the insanity of the moment, felt far worse than the threat he had made. "Sorry about that. Try not to get in the way. It's time to finish this now. This vacation is over; it's time to put the toys away. Unfortunately that means you, Aletha."

She felt something akin to a whimper rise in her throat and fought it back. "What are you saying!"

"Wake up! It's over. The seal is open. You're done here and I'm leaving this place now."

"What? Is this what you had in mind all along? To trick me into opening the seal?"

"Of course not. What do you take me for?" He frowned and gazed beyond her as if to puzzle over something. "I changed my mind, that's all. I'm going home."

"Home? Why? You said you didn't belong there any more. And what about Chenoweth? What about Thali?"

"They belong to La'il. They always have. If the few colonies on these moons must be sacrificed to sustain our planet, our people, then so be it. I've done what I was sent here to do and there is no reason for me to stay here now."

"You can't mean this. You'd help her destroy all of these people? And what about me?"

"What about you?"

"Me and you! What about us?"

"Us?" He scowled. "There is no *us*. You made that quite clear, I think. You've made your choice and now I've made mine."

She swallowed the panic and the tears threatening to rob her of her voice. "Damn you, don't do this! I love you, Galen. You know that!"

"Yes, I know." He caressed her face, his eyes on his fingers. "You are making this too damn hard," he said softly. "I love the way you move, your touch, that sweet smile. The way you feel inside my head." His hand trailed to her throat and closed around it. "I love the way you taste, Goddess, but unfortunately you won't fit into my bed any more. And that's where it counts, doesn't it?" He smiled and briefly closed his eyes as if savoring a pleasant memory. "Going to miss that, I'm sure. Of course I don't want to hurt you. And so maybe, if you want to stay unhurt for a while longer, you can stop the damn hysterics and let me finish here."

His fingers dug into her skin when he pressed his lips to hers in a passionless kiss. When she struggled against him he drew back with a careless laugh. "Not in the mood? Or would you rather have Chor today? He's a little busy right now." Gripping her arms, he turned her to the left and shoved her to the ground. "Someone rather powerful up there is trying to keep all that lovely chi'ro out of Chor's reach. I think they're upset or something. It would take an earthquake to get his attention."

Aletha glanced from him to his twin. Something odd had passed through his eyes when, just for an instant, the flippant tone of his voice had changed as if to add weight to some point he was trying to make. She realized that she had fallen next to the riser.

Galen turned away when an arrow sailed over their heads. In the distance, Delann's frantic gestures suggested that he was ordering more of his men to aim at the demons who were clearly a threat to Aletha now. Shaking his head in amusement, Galen sent a wisp of flame across the clearing to set one of the emissaries ablaze. "Those priests burn so easily. It's those dresses they wear. Impractical, with people like me around."

Aletha looked at the riser beside her. Why hadn't he killed her? Why hadn't he killed them all? He seemed entirely unconcerned when she shifted to put her hand into the faint emanation of chi'ro. "Stop this, please! You can stop her."

"Maybe, but I don't have a good reason to want to. You don't understand any of this, Aletha." He rejoined his twin by the launch to help him regain control of the flow of energy from Chenoweth. "She knows what's best. We need Chenoweth's power or the Homeworld will diminish."

"Then let it!" Aletha directed her energies toward an outcropping high above them on the mountainside, sobbing in dread and exhilaration when a deep rumbling sound echoed among the slopes and the ground began to shake.

Galen and Chor looked up. Huge boulders had shaken loose and, along with currents of smaller rocks and pebbles, began to surge down the mountain on a gray river of stone and loam. The noise blotted out every other sensation, too loud to fit into their ears. Still not shaken out of the eerie calm that possessed them, the twins stood firm by the launch, arms raised, and the wave of rock and debris parted not thirty paces uphill to flow past them on either side, spraying pebbles and dust over the clearing. Aletha cried out when a shard of rock struck her knee, tearing her trousers and slicing into her skin.

Silence returned grudgingly to the mountainside as the avalanche petered out and took its rumble down into the valley. They stood in a changed landscape strewn with sharp-edged boulders and broken trees whose split, shredded limbs looked too much like bones. Anxiously, Aletha looked for Delann and Yala in the distance, finding them safe on the far side of the rubble. Not everyone had been so fortunate and she could see some of the soldiers rush downhill to look for survivors. Dazed, Aletha realized that once again she had misjudged her abilities.

The twins turned toward her, their bodies moving in perfect, disturbing synchronicity. "I thought you were against hurting people," Galen said. "What a waste of energy. I had far too much time to react. You should have just picked up a rock and hit Chor over the head with it. I suppose you wish you'd paid more attention when I wanted to teach you fun things like that. But you wanted to be a healer. What a waste of your talents!" He strode to her and hauled her roughly to her feet. "Never too late, though. Let's start now. Show me what you can do, Goddess. It'll be just you and me." He gestured in a casual sweep to erect an unseen barricade around themselves and the launch. "That'll keep the boys from interrupting us."

Aletha backed away when he circled around her. Chor stood near the conduit to block her way to that escape and prevent her from accessing even a shred of chi'ro from Chenoweth.

Nothing in Galen's expression suggested his murderous intentions. She had seen him react to La'il's torments, controlled by false emotion to boost the adept's own abilities. He never looked like this at such time, never this dispassionate, so devoid of even a hint of anger. Both of him looked like Chor now, as when Galen was too busy with something to give life to his twin's expression.

"Are you in there, Galen?" Aletha said, feeling some hope. He was fighting La'il, she knew now, waging some unimaginable battle to keep her from infusing him with the sort of fury needed to actually harm Aletha. His eyes were flat gray spheres in a bloodless face. "Galen, please wake up. Please don't let her beat you. Not this time."

"How about this," he said, his voice strained as though he had to force himself to speak. "You stop trying to distract me and I'll make this very quick. Not what La'il had in mind, but I guess it's the least I can do."

Aletha glanced about for some way to escape the twins. There was now barely any chi'ro venting from the ground here and Chor had a firm grip on what was arriving from Chenoweth. She crouched as if to stanch the blood flowing into her boot but when she rose again her dagger was in her hand. "Don't make me hurt you," she said, hoping that she sounded braver than she felt.

He rolled his eyes and lifted a hand toward her. The knife flew from her fingers and into his, where he snapped it like a twig. "Silly girl. The knife is nothing. The rocks are nothing.

You're going to have to use your head if you want to get at me. But you're too scared. You're scared because you *know* you can kill me. And you don't want that." He grinned broadly. "You'll want to soon enough. So come on! Break my neck, rip Chor's heart out, burst every vein in my body! Let's have a real battle. It'll be fun."

Aletha stumbled backwards when she realized that his mockery of her was Galen speaking to her. Asking her to kill him to stop this madness. "No," she sobbed.

He scowled. "Well, that's disappointing. Maybe you do need to stick to throwing rocks to see if you can get it right."

"Let him go, bitch," Aletha hissed angrily. Perhaps she could stun him somehow. Perhaps incapacitate him so that La'il would lose her grip on his unconscious mind. At the periphery of her vision, she saw Chor's hand reach for her shoulder. Startled, she projected the precious little energy she had hoarded at the twins and was surprised when they were thrown backward, onto the rocks.

Chor and Galen lurched to their feet, his composure finally cracked. There was only an instant of comprehension before utter darkness descended. Aletha's surprise attack had given La'il the opening she needed. She honed in on his new bruises and whipped this trivial irritation into the mindless rage that allowed her to break through his barriers. Things seemed suddenly much clearer to Galen. He no longer remembered why it had been so important to keep the La'il from taking over completely. A red slash of pain shot through his heads, coloring his vision, obliterating all reason. He seemed to be looking at Aletha through a long tunnel. She was causing this pain; of this he was certain. La'il had said so.

Galen swung a fist at Aletha and missed when she ducked out of his way. His second blow grazed her. When she tried to force him back again with another burst of energy he was ready and diverted it easily. Whatever she was shouting was meaningless. He lunged again. Barely in time, she deflected a blow meant to kill and this time managed to sweep his feet from under him. He came down painfully on his elbow and heard something crack.

"Kill her already and be done," La'il shrieked into his brain. "She's weak now. Finish it and get on with your work!" She laughed spitefully when Chor leaped toward Althea and grasped a fistful of her curls. Whipping her around to face him, he wrapped his hands around her neck. She had little energy left to keep his powerful hands from crushing her. "What did you tell me?" La'il cackled. "You'd rather die than hurt her? Is this killing you now? No? I didn't think so."

Chor laughed. It was a harsh, triumphant, and utterly foreign sound. A terrible sound. Had it even been he who had laughed? He looked down at his hands and then into Aletha's terrified eyes. Seconds skewed to hours as his mental focus shifted to Galen and he suddenly saw Chor like a stranger, someone outside himself carrying out the La'il's murderous commands. Who was that? Galen came to his feet and rushed toward his twin - that alien, soulless monster who wanted Aletha dead. He gripped Chor's wrists to pry him away. La'il shrieked in protest, unable to maintain her control of the two bodies no longer thinking as one. She fought to maintain Chor's iron grip around Aletha's neck while fighting to pull Galen away from his twin but she could not do both. Before she found the means to overpower him again, he severed his mental link to her and gave up his control of the launch. Aletha tumbled away from them, gasping for air.

Something struck hard against his back, just below his shoulder blade. Galen saw the feathered end of a crossbow quarrel protrude from Chor's back and he felt the searing pain that came with it. The surrounding shield of chi'ro had collapsed and now Delann was racing toward them, long dagger raised. He collided heavily with Chor and drove his weapon into his chest. Chor staggered backward and tripped over Aletha onto the launch.

"Galen!" Aletha screamed although no sound escaped her

tortured throat when Chor fell back, arms flailing. Galen flung himself after his twin and gripped his vest with both hands. The current of chi'ro was strong and in an instant both twins were swept into the conduit and disappeared.

SIXTEEN

Galen's momentum catapulted both of his bodies through the instance of nothingness to land on a surface no less jagged and rocky than the battleground they had just left behind. They tumbled once or twice, and lay still. There was someone nearby; he thought he heard voices and there was coughing and a groan that might have originated in himself. The pain in his back and chest was excruciating. When he finally opened his eyes he saw Chor motionless on the ground, the long dagger buried in his chest. Panicked, he reached out to grasp the hilt.

"Don't!" Several hands restrained him. "Let us help him," someone nearby swam into focus. An older man, balding and stout, bent over him with an expression of mixed apprehension and curiosity. "There is much damage."

"Have to get back," Galen moaned, trying to rise. The ground tilted dangerously and he sank back again.

"You're not going anywhere!"

When Galen felt the slow torture of someone pulling Delann's dagger from Chor's body he had to agree. When he was able to breathe again he sat up more slowly, keeping his eyes averted from the slashed body of his twin lying next to him, too much blood trickling over the bare rocks in long rivulets. A quick inventory of his own limbs suggested that he was mostly unharmed, in spite of the pain. It was then that he realized that the La'il was no longer inside his mind. He shook his head, trying to remember. "Gods, I tried to kill her!"

"Kill who?"

Galen looked around. A dozen or more people surrounded him; some were staring at him in wonder, some up at the conduit soaring into the air. Others were bent over the dying man lying beside him, their hands on his injuries. Men and women, tall and lithe, dressed in rich layers of gauzy fabric loosely arranged for modesty rather than the need to shield them from the balmy weather.

"What is going on? Who are you people?" Galen staggered painfully to his feet and as he straightened up he found himself overlooking a vast, shallow valley where open meadows alternated with swathes of forest. Brilliant sunlight flooded the area. From everywhere, Galen perceived the unmistakable presence of risers. But here the chi'ro did not arc through the air in an orderly stream, drawn toward some central collection point to be hoarded, and then meted out where needed most. Here each riser simply rose in an airy column until it spread out high over their heads to form an unseen dome over the valley. In the far distance, behind a gently shimmering veil of chi'ro, the jagged peaks of snowcapped mountains guarded plains of ice and rock. As if to confirm what he saw, both the Homeworld and the small blue and white orb that was Thali hung in the clear sky above him. "Unbelievable," he marveled, drawing the moon's immense power into himself and his twin. "We have to channel this to Thali! Help me!"

"Stop at once!" Galen felt the adept's attempts to restrain him. "The La'il is over there! I've not felt her this strongly in years!"

Galen was surprised that, although powerful, the man's abilities were not what he had expected of the people of Chenoweth. It would take very little effort to elude his mental grasp. "She is still on the Homeworld. But there is only a single, untrained adept between La'il and this little gathering. And she's just about out of chi'ro."

"What is happening down there? I've never felt the La'il so powered up. What is happening on Thali? Why were you drawing chi'ro from here?" Sensing no deceit in Galen's urgency, the man released him. Immediately, some of the adepts began to feed the moon's energy into the conduit and from there to Aletha, who picked it up hungrily.

Galen experimented with a deep breath and found it relatively painless. "We have to get back," he rasped, rubbing his chest. "We need to close that seal again." He staggered against the adept, feeling a new wave of pain as Chor coughed, blood pouring from his mouth and nose.

"Your brother can't go back in this state. This will take more time. His lung is punctured."

Galen cursed. "I can't leave him up here. We have to go back together." Looking at the man's puzzled face, he shrugged. "Complicated. I'm one of the giants. From up there."

"A Homeworlder? How is this possible?"

Galen winced but did not ward off the adept's intrusion when he felt himself scanned far more thoroughly than he imagined possible. This adept's abilities were wielded differently than those of the Homeworld's primes, and far more effectively.

Galen shrugged uncomfortably when the man released him. "I've always been in favor of a little conversation before getting that personal."

"Dazai!"

"What?" Galen looked around to see what had startled the man before realizing that the adept's astounded gaze was fixed upon him.

Suddenly several more people appeared from conduits forming and fading so quickly that Galen wasn't sure he had even seen them. No one but the older adept had spoken aloud, even the healers surrounding Chor did their work silently, evidence of some sort of mental communication among these people.

There was an odd excitement among these newly arrived adepts now and he found himself backing away from their intent, expectant stares.

"Dazai!" the elder adept said again. "Returned after all these years."

"Returned? What are you talking about?"

The adept lifted a hand to cup Galen's chin. "Yes, I see the resemblance." He turned Galen's face to look at his profile. "A good likeness, in fact. And not aged a day!"

Galen felt others now reaching for him, digging into him until he finally had to shut them all out. They looked surprised and even offended at this and, as they exchanged meaningful looks, he was sure they were discussing the uncouthness of this Homeworlder. "What do you people want?" He turned to the older adept. "What are you talking about?"

"You are Dazai! A son, perhaps, or grandson. But there is more than that. Something too familiar, too much like Dazai to be merely progeny. How did you come to be?"

Galen could only stare at the excited adept. Dazai his sire? The Chenowan's discovery answered as many question as it posed and, reluctantly, Galen put it all aside. He sank onto a large boulder, his eyes on the splendor of the valley below. The Garden, Aletha would say. It was everything her people imagined it to be. "How many of these habitats have you built?"

The adept blinked, taken aback by Galen's response. "Five, although we live only in this one, for the most part." The Chenowan shook his head, as if suddenly aware of his lack of manners. "I'm sorry, my name is Bacchias Dwen Neben. We've been watching the seal for weeks now, knowing that the La'il is gathering her forces to break through. The day we've dreaded has come. Three hundred years of peace are at an end."

"I was told you were trying to open the conduit. To invade the Homeworld."

"The Homeworld?" Dwen Neben exclaimed. "Hardly! May La'il choke on it."

"You sealed the apertures," Galen pointed at Thali. "You left them there."

"We did. There was no choice. With so much of the moon's chi'ro removed we feared that it would become uninhabitable within a few centuries, if not sooner. We tried to get them to leave Thali, to come here. Many of their adepts came with us rather than live without chi'ro. But the lesser talents did not want to leave. So Dazai closed the doors in the hopes of keeping the La'il out. We assumed that we would return to Thali later to find out if the moon was restoring itself or if we should try again to evacuate the people. Unfortunately, we did not foresee that we would be unable to activate the launch, nor La'il's determination to succeed in that."

Galen sighed. This man had no inkling about the misery that their well-intentioned advice had brought upon the remaining adepts. "And then Aletha was born and she has the ability to open the gates. You've been trying to stop her ever since the La'il found her and sent me to bring her here."

"Even before then," Neben said. "Any significant use of chi'ro is harming the planet. Over the years she grew steadily more powerful. We hoped our agents on Thali would find her before she caused much more damage. But they've become so weak that their talents barely even register with us and it became difficult to lead them. We started to trifle with the launch again, hoping to bring her here where she could do no harm. Then when you found her the drain of resources became alarming. And today La'il stands at our door, ready to tear it down."

Galen studied the small crowd, easily reading the apprehension with which they regarded the conduit in their midst. Yet no one had attempted to dissipate it. "Come back with me and help us destroy the launch sites that lead to the Homeworld. There must be a way. You'll never have to fear La'il again."

Neben's gaze strayed to the launch. "Destroy the sites? Even if that were possible, surely the La'il and her ambitions will some day cease to be. These links to the planet were here long before our people arrived on the Homeworld. Can we truly know their purpose? Can you say that some day we will not desperately need them? Can we destroy something so singular, so mysterious, without risking damage to ourselves, or these worlds, in the future?"

"She will destroy all of this if we don't find a way to stop her! If you won't take out the launch sites then come with me. Help us fight her."

"Fight her? How?"

"Kill the bitch! You're prime adepts. You have a wealth of chi'ro. Surely you can stand against her."

"I doubt any of us can." His gesture swept across the people now watching them in silence. "We've not raised voice or hand in anger in nearly three hundred years. No, we have not forgotten the La'il, nor what happened on Thali. But we are no longer a part of that. We spend our lives in a dream. What matters is only what we can create in our minds or how we touch the minds of others, to please them and ourselves. Look around you. We have all we need because we need very little. We don't even build cities. Why build castles when anyone can do so? Why own a house when we can be anywhere we wish? If we want to eat we let something grow. If we are cold we change the air around us. If someone upsets us we go away." He shook his head. "The La'il would find no worthy adversary among us. It's beyond us to destroy, even one such as she."

Galen sighed, unaccountably amused by the man's revelations. Then he saw the sickening amount of blood darkening the stone around the launch and was reminded that Chenoweth's philosophies had no part in the matter at hand. That was his blood on the ground and La'il was to blame for it. "We have to go back." Chor was stronger now and able to breathe more easily. The adepts of Chenoweth were able healers. "We'll reseal the launch down there and the one up here. You will have your peace back. At least for a while, until she finds another way."

"Why not return here and seal our launch from here? We have much to talk about."

Galen scrubbed a hand over his face. Did these people not understand? "We can't leave the crystal unguarded. She will try again. She'll never stop trying."

"You would do this for us?" Dwen Neben said, genuinely puzzled.

Galen took a last look at the valley, its bounty made possible only by the shroud of chi'ro separating it from the hostile environs of Chenoweth. It was a vast garden, filled with all that was beautiful, forever waiting for inhabitants who would never arrive. Chenoweth's people, evolved into peaceful, otherworldly creatures, would not even be noticed by the La'il when she came to take their magic away. He doubted that any of them really understood their peril.

"Yes," he said.

"Dazai," someone said, sounding the word like an invocation.

Dwen Neben nodded. "Yes, so it begins again. Dazai stood between these moons and La'il three hundred years ago. They were lovers, once, but her greed drove them apart. He came to Thali when he met Amaya Phrar. She showed him a new way to use chi'ro and the two of them led our people to discover a new existence, a new way of thinking. But then La'il's ambitions and her jealously drove her to nearly destroy Thali. Dazai and she battled for days. It killed him, in the end, but not before he created the seals. And now it's all begun again."

"Yeah," Galen said and pulled his twin to his feet. Both men stifled a pained groan when Chor tested his newly mended injuries. "But this time there are two of us." He glanced at Chor. "Well, three." Taking a deep, shuddering breath, they stepped back onto the launch.

* * *

"Aletha!" he shouted, finding himself inside a maelstrom on the Thali side of the conduit. She was using the energy he had sent from Chenoweth like a stopper on the open seal to the Homeworld. The tornado of chi'ro raged through the clearing, centered on Aletha's small figure hunched between the crystals. She was on the ground, eyes closed, her lips moving silently. The forest debris brought down with the rockslide had been pitched aside by the violence of the storm tearing at her clothes and hair. Delann and the remaining soldiers were pushed back beyond the edges of the storm that also kept their arrows from reaching Galen when he moved toward the woman. Galen heard their shouts and threats but he doubted that, in his present, chi'ro-suffused state, their weapons could injure him even if the chi'ro tempest around them hadn't kept them out. He bent to touch Aletha's shoulder.

She recoiled instantly and launched a missile of chi'ro at him and his blood-soaked twin. He held his hands up to shield himself against her assault and it swept around them in a spray of sparks. "That was pretty."

"Galen? Is that you?" Tears blurred her vision when, in answer to her tentative probe, she felt his familiar, untainted mental touch. "Galen, by the Gods, I thought you were dead!"

He crouched beside her to fold her into his arms, appalled by the purple bruises ringing her neck. A lattice of scratches beaded blood across her forehead; much more of it still seeped from the wound at her knee. She hid her hot, tear-streaked face in the curve of his neck and his throat closed around something like a helpless sob when he felt her tremble with fear and exhaustion.

"I thought the La'il had taken you," she wept. "Or Delann killed you… I thought you were gone! Or… or maybe gone insane. Those awful things you said…"

"I remember," he said, wincing.

"Don't leave me," she said. "I don't care about Chor. I don't care if there are ten of you. Just stay with me."

"I won't leave you," he promised. "Let's close the seals."

She pulled away from him and wiped her face on her sleeve. "I can't. I know how to seal this thing up again but it'll take longer than she'll need to get up here. She's trying to send a conduit so she can get at this chi and I keep having to knock it down. She's so angry!"

"We can do it together. I'll keep her conduit from forming and you slam the seal shut. There are adepts up on Chenoweth. Let them—"

"She's gone!" Aletha cried suddenly. "Disappeared. Let go. I don't know what happened. I can't feel her anymore!"

"Maybe she's out of chi for now. Seal the launch, quick!"

Suddenly the amassed chi'ro rose high into the air and then shot away toward the distant horizon, drawn southward by some unimaginable force, leaving them with nothing but the weakened riser near the crystal. "It's a conduit!" Galen shouted, knowing that nothing within the scope of his talents would let him prevent what was about to happen. "She's making a conduit!" Everyone in the clearing gawked in wonder and disbelief when the La'il appeared in their midst. Not gently floating in midair, not robed in exquisite costume. This was no mirage of herself projected through space. The goddess stood before them in her true shape, towering above them all, dressed in trousers and loose-fitting shirt, her white hair gathered at the nape, unadorned.

"Now you die, all of you," she growled, her voice a low rumble vibrating through the cool mountain air. "Did you think it would take me any longer than this to open the other seal in Phrar? Or did you forget it was there?"

With barely a glance at Aletha, she seized control of the launch. She smiled sweetly as she admired the conduit to Chenoweth with proprietary interest, knowing her power to be absolute now. She had only to reach into that gateway to touch as much chi'ro as she desired. "So it is, dear. And I no longer need either of you. I will miss you, though, Galen Chor."

Galen tried to signal a warning when someone stepped

out of the conduit. But three adepts from Chenoweth had already set their feet upon Thali before the two who followed turned around again and fled. The La'il hammered the three with a fiery burst of energy that catapulted them across the clearing where they were crushed against rocks and boulders. They heard shouts of dismay from where Delann's men watched in horror and fascination.

The La'il turned from her inspection of the dying Chenowan adepts back to the twins and Aletha. "Is that all there is to these creatures? Oh, sorry, were they coming to your rescue? How rude of me not to at least let them try. Well, I'll be nicer to the next ones." She leaned forward a little to squint at Aletha. "You have not introduced me to your friend, Galen. Is that it? She looks a little gone over. Too bad I need all this chi for myself. She's such a little thing! She looks so different in your head! What powers, what talents does she possess to capture your twofold heart?" Amused, she watched Galen and Chor draw together to stand in front of Aletha. "I'm touched, Galen, but I hold the power of three planets. Do you really think you can stop me?" She gestured toward Galen and when she spoke her derisive tone was replaced by the razor edge that usually lined her words. "This body is first, halfling. When it's gone I think I'll let you watch Delann have a little fun with your friend there. A reward of sorts. Won't that be entertaining?"

"Let Aletha be," he pleaded. "You can leave her here once you've got the Homeworld linked to Chenoweth again. Thali is worthless to you."

La'il scrunched up her nose and thought about this for a moment. "You know, that sounds reasonable. Very well, off you go."

Aletha glared at her. "Bitch."

The La'il laughed out loud. "Oh, she's plucky. No wonder you like her." Her expression returned to one of malice. "I had no intention of ever letting her live past this moment. Would I allow such an adept run loose up here? Especially one I can't perceive, even now. She's an abomination! Time to put an end to this nonsense. Come here."

Galen glanced wistfully at Aletha. With a deep sigh, he reached around her waist to pull her close and bent to kiss her. She gasped when she felt his lips move against hers to form a few words, repeating his instruction urgently until La'il wrenched him away from her.

"That's not the show I was looking for," La'il said.

Galen groaned when some invisible fist wrapped around his body and began to squeeze his rib cage with steadily increasing pressure. He was suddenly unable to breathe. The La'il was killing him slowly, enjoying his growing terror.

He lurched away from Chor and Aletha, toward Delann and his company. The La'il turned to watch him with great interest, a gentle smile on her face. "Can't catch your breath, dear?" She shivered with delight when she heard some of his ribs break. "Where are you going? I've got an interesting afternoon planned for us. You won't need those anymore." Both Chor and Galen groaned when some of Galen's fingers snapped.

"Hurry," Chor grunted.

"Now!" Aletha said and Chor launched himself forward. He raced at the La'il to ram his shoulder into her midriff before she had quite turned around again. Utterly taken by surprise, she had no time to react and, although much taller than Chor now, she was no match for his bulk. His momentum carried her backward and onto the launch where both of them instantly disappeared into the conduit that Aletha had released from Chenoweth's terminus.

* * *

The La'il's scream of rage and protest stabbed into his ears, quickly muffled and distorted when the vortex of chi'ro enveloped them. He fought off her attempts to access his mind as they were swept along, each fighting for control of the conduit that no longer led to Chenoweth. Instead of instantly stepping out of the vortex onto some distant launch site, they grappled with its unanchored terminus, desperate to use it to their advantage. Almost frozen to immobility in the non-space and non-time that was called a conduit, they felt neither gravity nor atmosphere inside their cocoon of shifting smears of light and shadow.

La'il forced the conduit toward the Homeworld, laughing out loud when she felt it shape itself to her will. Galen drew on every bit of aptitude and training he had to foil her attempt and succeeded in taking the conduit back. She hissed angrily, doubling her efforts and he felt his control slipping again, unable to match her abilities. When defeat seemed inevitable, he opened his thoughts to her, jabbing at her to get her attention.

"Idiot!" she screamed and reached into him, ready to tear his mind to pieces.

Galen met her without resistance. He offered no mental imagery, no physical confrontation, nothing for her to grasp. When she delved into his brain to once again incite him into unwillingly supply her with the strength of his own talents, he merely ducked playfully and returned a mental sneer. "I'm not in the mood," he grinned, rallying every shred of resilience to remain unmoved by her intrusion, counting on her vanity and arrogance to persist in her attempts instead of simply destroying his mind as she had destroyed Yobar. He continued to taunt her, only dimly aware that there was neither air nor warmth inside the conduit still whipping untethered through space.

She tried again and again, her rage growing with each failed attempt to gain control of him. Taking the mental equivalent of a deep breath, he finally launched his own attack and drove into her mind, aiming for the part of her that she so often controlled within him. He moaned when he felt the force of her fury enter into him, bringing with it all of La'il's strength and abilities.

Never before, even when bathed in the most powerful riser he had ever encountered, had he felt this powerful, so very limitless in all that was possible. Her energies blasted through him and he knew that nothing was beyond him now.

He knew everything she knew and felt everything she had ever touched. He laughed, cradling the La'il in his arms like a lover. Gods? Of course they were gods. Aletha had been right, those pitiful emissaries had been right. But he hadn't seen it. None of his people had. He hadn't believed in gods because he was one of them. Mortal, perhaps, but ultimately supernatural. The thought that he was losing his mind occurred to him. Or perhaps he was dying. That seemed interesting, too.

"Galen?"

He flinched when he perceived the small voice somewhere at the very periphery of his awareness. Aletha was calling to him. Something worried her; she was near the conduit's anchor on Thali and her fear reached him in palpable waves. He had taken care to shut her out of his mind before tackling the La'il, afraid of dragging Aletha into their confrontation. How was she reaching him now?

"Galen, can you hear me?" He realized that he could hear her voice with his ears. Galen's ears. She was speaking to his twin, left behind on Thali. "There's something wrong with you. Where is Chor? Is he still in the conduit? Come back, please!"

He frowned, tempted to ignore that voice and simply float here forever, or for whatever few seconds remained of his life, feeding on La'il's charged state of mind. He looked into her half-closed eyes and suddenly realized that she no longer resisted him. A terrible, watchful intelligence observed him from those hooded eyes, flooding his willing mind with far more than he was able to process. She was healthy and strong and suffused with chi'ro; Chor's body was a catalogue of serious injuries, barely patched by the efforts of Chenoweth's healers, already on the brink of collapse. The icy reality of the conduit slapped him awake when he understood that, if he succumbed to his delirium, she would be free within moments.

* * *

Far below the poorly formed conduit rippling above the trees, Aletha hovered over Galen who had collapsed when his twin and the La'il had vanished. She found it hard to fathom that they were up there somewhere in this conduit leading to nowhere, fighting their never-ending battles, physically unmatched, and this time surely intending a fatal outcome. Galen was whispering something, his breath barely moving the strands of hair that touched his lips when she bent closer.

"Cooking stones," he gasped, each word a tremendous effort. "Above the broken crystal."

She frowned. "Galen? What do you mean? I don't understand."

"Trees fly uphill and we fall. We fall."

"No, Galen," Aletha wailed when the meaning of his hints became clear. "No! Please don't!"

The hand closing around her own felt cold and lifeless. "Do it!"

Aletha bit her lip as she concentrated and traced her way back through the jungle islands until she found the place he was looking for. She did as he had asked, her eyes fixed on Galen's empty face. "I got it. It's done."

The unstable conduit suddenly ceased its aimless undulations and soared into the sky, heading west where it rocketed toward the islands and finally slammed into the boiling lava flow they had found along their journey. Aletha clasped her head in both hands when a flash of immeasurable fury and fear enveloped and infused every living thing able to perceive La'il's terrible power. A few of the others felt it, too, and some fell to ground, unconscious, when all of Thali moon's adepts became witnesses to La'il's final moment. They felt her life wink out in an instant and when Galen cried out in terror Aletha knew that Chor was gone, too.

Minutes passed in silence before Aletha fully understood what had happened. She knelt motionless beside Galen, feeling her way to the other launch, the one hidden inside the volcano, afraid of what she might find. But there was nothing there now. The crystal, briefly opened by her to show him the way into the pool of lava, remained sealed, its guardian riser undisturbed. Whatever living thing had fallen into the fiery depths was no longer recognizable to her touch.

She dissipated the conduit. "They're gone, Galen. Both of them."

"Aletha!" Yala raced across the clearing to throw herself into her arms. She clung to her, apparently willing to remain in her protective embrace indefinitely.

Aletha drew her back to look into the dirt-smudged face. "It's all well now, Yala. It's over." But she wondered if it would ever be over for the child, and what had to be done to heal the wounds she had sustained today, witnessing events that were beyond anything for which even the harshness of her life in the slums had prepared her.

The girl's attention was drawn to something beyond Aletha. She turned to see a new conduit forming on the launch and several of the Chenowan adepts emerge to look cautiously around the clearing. Dwen Neben came first, probing the crystal to assure himself that no link to the Homeworld remained. Some of the newcomers rushed to their fallen companions in the hopes of finding some of them still alive. Seeing Galen on the ground, Neben motioned to another adept to come to his aid. Everyone here moved like one who has just woken from a strange dream, not entirely certain that it is over.

Aletha gaped in awe at Dwen Neben and his people. How often had she wondered about these adepts, these gods, who lived in Chenoweth? She had prayed to them and hoped to join them some day and here they were, looking as confused and astounded as any of the mortals present. True to the tales told of them, these people were handsome and fit, dressed in rich fabrics and enveloped in sheaths of chi'ro that she felt like a warm breeze against her skin. These were truly her people. She could touch each of them, could understand their power, their abilities, and their limits. Nothing lay hidden within these adepts and knowing that they were mortals like herself only deepened her feeling of kinship.

She looked toward the edge of the clearing to Delann and those who had not fled in terror when people began to disappear and reappear, bloodied and murderous, struggling over something that few of them could even perceive. Most of them remained at a distance, cautiously circling closer, and only Delann approached, looking as mystified and fearful as the others. Perhaps it would never be possible to explain to them what had happened here today. Perhaps it wasn't necessary. They had seen enough of the La'il to understand that there had been more to her ungodliness than mere mortality.

"Bacchias," Aletha heard an urgent whisper. "This is wrong."

Both Aletha and the elder adept turned to where the Chenowan healer knelt beside Galen. He still sprawled where he had fallen, his face without life, without expression. The woman's hands were on his temples and then moved to his chest. "I can't get to him!"

"Galen!" Aletha cried and dropped to the ground beside him. "Galen, wake up! Don't do this!" She looked into his eyes, which were not quite closed. Dead, empty eyes that saw nothing. "What's wrong with him?"

Neben reached out to the comatose adept, finding nothing there but an empty shell. The Homeworlder still breathed but his body seemed to be shutting down, barely functioning in his deep trance. Neben shook his head. "Where is his brother?"

"Dead," she said. "They were joined. One mind. And it was centered on the other one."

After a long, silent search the adept's touch withdrew from Galen. "I'm sorry," he said. "I've not encountered this before. He's gone. I can't help him."

Aletha shook her head, unwilling to follow what this man

was telling her. "No!" she whispered. "By the Gods…" Her eyes traveled to the woman beside Dwen Neben and then to the other adepts. "You can't help him," she said, at last understanding the enormity of that fact. She had spent the past few weeks in the company of a man who had no gods and whose accounts of Chenoweth seemed sensible and right. But it was only now that the significance of what he had been trying to tell her became clear. Had she even wanted to listen? Had she ever stopped believing? When all worldly efforts failed what remained but an appeal to the gods? Here were her gods. Tangible evidence of three hundred years of delusion. There was no one left to hear her prayers.

"No!" she said through gritted teeth. "I can do this. He's not dying!" She drew on the power of Chenoweth to aid her in joining her mind to his, calling to him, hoping to find some evidence that his twin had not taken with him the essence that gave life to this man. She felt a ghastly void there, a cold, dead emptiness of such vast proportions that she shivered uncontrollably. It was as if his battle with the La'il and the crushing shock of having witnessed his own death had cast him to the edge of sanity and now his devastated mind refused to comprehend that part of him was still alive. Confused bits of random thought reached her, carrying with them a terrible sense of loss as he moved away from her, ready to follow wherever it was that his twin and the La'il had gone.

Desperately, she tried to catch his attention with the lure of chi'ro, enticing his senses with the promise of well-being until, somewhere in their trance, he recognized her. Images began to swim into view, unfocused and incomplete, but familiar. She felt his panic subside, replaced by a calmer state of mind, as though they had reached deeply into each other and joined in an embrace without boundary between bodies. He accepted her mental touch, responding to her offer of oblivion, willing to follow where she led if only it would erase the last moment of Chor's life from his memory.

Untold minutes, hours, days later a gentle, persistent presence made itself felt, drawing them back to a state of awareness where Dwen Neben was able to wake them. Reality intruded into their dreams and both became aware of the hard ground beneath them, the cold mountain air, and the presence of the people around them. When Galen took a deep breath both of them felt the pain of his broken ribs. "Come back to us now," Neben said softly from somewhere nearby.

When she drew back, Galen's eyes traveled to Aletha's dirty, bloodied and tear-streaked face; it was the most beautiful thing he had ever seen. He tried a smile. "I feel... odd."

"You said my spike could wake a dead man," she said, forcing her tears back to be dealt with another time. "It's done, Galen. She's gone. And you're back!"

He raised an arm to draw her close to him. "I told you I wasn't leaving you." He buried his face in her tousled curls. "I love you," he said for her ears only, knowing that she knew already, that she knew him now like only the La'il had ever seen him, but needing to say it anyway. The constant physical presence that was Chor had been torn away and he felt its absence like the loss of a limb. But he was alive, and his mind intact, because of her. He said it again, unwilling to release her until one of the Chenowan adepts pulled her gently to her feet and another set to work on Galen's broken bones.

Needing to share her joy, Aletha turned to look for Delann and found that he had backed away, eyes wide in shock and incomprehension. She moved toward him. "Delann?"

He took a few more steps, looking from her to the graceful strangers and back at her again. "You're one of them. The... the gods." He pointed at Galen. "You did this. He was dead! I saw it! He was dead and you brought him back!"

"No, not dead. He just needed a little help."

He shook his head, struggling to find words. "I'm so sorry. I... I didn't mean—" His distraught gesture included Galen, the other adepts, the emissaries' dead leader lying on the ground, the blood that smeared her clothes. When she embraced him he fell to his knees, tears streaming unchecked over his face. "Gods, I can't believe I did those things!"

"It will be all right, Delann," Aletha whispered, holding him close. "I promise. You are not to blame. Don't ever blame yourself for any of this!"

Dwen Neben touched her shoulder. "Let me help him," he said.

Aletha did not look up at the adept when she brushed Delann's tears from his face. "No," she said resolutely, helping her friend to his feet. "Would you make him forget what happened? Feel better about this, maybe? We can't just make this go away. We can't keep playing god for these people."

"I sometimes have an overly enthusiastic opinion of my skills, but godhood hasn't occurred to me. I must make a note of that." Neben sobered when no one else here offered even a smile for his little joke. "Come to Chenoweth with us. I think you could use some time of peace and recovery. And bring your friends," he added, observing Yala's pallid face. "You have much to recover from."

Hearing this, Galen struggled against his healer's restraining hands. His determination clear, she supported him when he stood up and both of them swayed like drunken sailors. He was reminded of the queasy hours following his transformation after Chor had been created. Without his extra set of eyes, his vision seemed strangely skewed. "I have a better idea," he said, breathing in shallow gasps around his broken ribs. "Conduit's open now. Let's leave it open. Wouldn't take much energy to bring everybody from here to Chenoweth. This place isn't so wonderful any more. Maybe they'll need less persuasion this time."

Both Aletha and Delann started, stunned by his suggestion.

"I know this comes a little too close to your prophecies, but it's really just something that started a long time ago. Let's finish this now. I don't think anyone will insist that you have to be dead to get to the Garden."

Dwen Neben conferred silently with his people. "It was our original intent to bring them to Chenoweth. Three hundred years ago! It won't be easy now. There are so many more of them, and few adepts among them." His eyes found the group of soldiers and robed emissaries circling them at a distance, mistrustful and afraid of what they had seen here. Some of their number were no doubt already on their way down the mountain to spread the news of whatever they believed had happened here today. "Not everyone will be able to adapt. There is bound to be much suffering before Thali is emptied."

"They already suffer," Galen said. "Their resilience will surprise you, I think. What do you say, Neben? It might give you people something to do up there."

Dwen Neben laughed, rapidly warming to the idea. It would certainly infuse new meaning into the lives of his people. In his mind he saw towns springing up, teams of hosts and mentors working with the new arrivals to create new lives among the vast splendor of Chenoweth. There would be schools, and farms and industry – all of the things remembered now only in historical accounts and certainly destined to be improved upon through Chenoweth's vast resources of chi'ro. He rubbed his hands, ready to start creating this new world at this very instant. "We'll start with settlements along the lakes. They would like that, don't you think? There is probably enough coastline for everyone!"

Galen looked around to find Delann standing pale and uncertain beside Aletha. "Well, Delann." He tipped his head into the direction of the visitors who would soon begin the process of inviting thousands of people to move to Chenoweth. "These people will need your help. You have ships, you have men, you have contacts in every port of call on this moon. How would you like a real job?"

EPILOGUE

"Where else would you be on a day like this?"

Galen looked up from his studies when Aletha stepped out of a conduit to find him perched on the sun-drenched steps leading into Delann's gardens. She crouched behind him to run her hands over his bare shoulders.

"You'll burn," she warned. But a quick glance skyward assured her that the clouds arriving from the west would soon put an end to his sun bath. "What are you reading?"

He put his book aside. "Some incomprehensible tale about someone who is either having an objectionable adventure with a rather large fish or is hunting one for dinner. I'm trying to learn these peculiar scripts so I can make sense of Gynn's writings. Wish he wasn't so long-winded about what's happening at the delta. But if I don't get through those things Delann is awake half the night trying to catch up. He's not sleeping so well, anyway. How are things on Chenoweth?"

"It's a confusing mess but the town is coming along just fine. We're trying to evacuate the barrier islands first, but I forgot to mention that my people won't cut living trees to build new houses. So now we have to disassemble their villages and transport the pieces to Chenoweth. Delann is not very happy about that. It's holding up his ships."

"The new ones are almost ready to sail. But I meant your studies with Dwen Neben."

"Wonderful! I'm learning so much! He's very patient with me and we can use as much chi'ro as we want." She ran her hand through his hair and he smiled when he felt her mental touch. "You should join us."

"We're a little busy down here," he said. "Too much trouble with the priestesses and… and the enclave… and… how about we go upstairs and you do that? I haven't seen you in, uh, days." He grunted and shuddered. "He taught you *that*?"

She laughed. "No, you silly man. His companion did. She's the one with all the truly useful tricks. Oh, speaking of tricks…" She jumped down the steps and turned to face him. "Watch this."

Galen saw the air around her begin to shimmer while she turned, her bottom lip gripped between her teeth in concentration. Gradually, the space around her began to blur and colors merged until she was entirely hidden from view inside a shifting envelope of refracted light. It was not chi'ro that she had drawn to herself, nor had she tapped into the small riser venting by the orchard wall.

"The Chenowans are better at making these things round, or whatever shape or size they want," he heard her voice, as clearly as if she were not utterly invisible. "This is how they go to sleep at night. They just built a house like this when they don't want to be seen."

"Can you see me?"

"Yeah. Sort of."

"Room for two in there?"

Her arm emerged from the shimmering veil surrounding her. He took her hand and stepped through it. "You can make this any size," she said. "This is just ambient chi'ro. I just had to nudge it around a bit. It takes a bit more to make this thing totally dark or quiet or warm, or keep people out, even."

Galen ran his hand along the wall of nothing. "This is

why they don't build towns. I saw a few of these bubbles last time I was up there. Meant to ask about them."

"You can even move them along. It's like wearing your house!"

"You could wear it like clothes to keep warm."

"Or float it over your head like an umbrella when it rains," she laughed and let the mirage fade away. "Oh, good, Delann's back."

They strolled around the house to the courtyard where Delann and Yala were busy with their animals. A broad smile transformed Delann's pale face when Aletha called out to him and, for a fleeting moment, he looked nearly as he had when La'il had been little more to him than a crude image scratched into a cave wall. He had made his peace with Yala and been pardoned by the emissaries for Tsingao's death, but some bits of him had not resurfaced after La'il had left him. Gone were the expensive and flamboyant clothes, replaced by practical gear worn threadbare during his ceaseless travels around Thali. Gone also were the parties and late-night gossiping, the multitudes of guests in his house and his love for wine and exotic foods. He now moved with deliberate care, spoke little and laughed even less. "I hoped I'd see you before we leave," he said when Aletha hugged him.

"You ought to see the harbor, Aletha!" Yala exclaimed, staggering under the weight of a saddle. "Two freighters ready for the trip north and fully loaded with Inlanders! Some brought their animals, too! Not like Inlanders to leave their livestock behind. More waiting on the docks for their turn. Hundreds of them!"

"And you pick pocketing the lot of them," Delann said. After piling a saddlebag on top of Yala's already heavy load and pretending not to hear the girl's complaints, he followed Galen and Aletha into the main building.

"You're going north with this lot?" Galen asked.

"No, I'm taking the brig around the horn. Gynn and some of his emissaries are coming with me. I'm expecting trouble along the way. Moving a village of herdsmen to

Chenoweth is nothing compared to sorting out clans who've been at war for years. We've found places for them, well separated, but I don't think they'll be easily convinced to leave."

"Could take years to sort out," Aletha said. "Take a few adepts with you. Perhaps the gods can do a little convincing."

She was not surprised when both Galen and Delann scowled at her suggestion. Both of them were bitterly opposed to the peculiar conspiracy that had developed between the adepts of Chenoweth and Thali's emissaries. After La'il's demise, Dwen Neben and his people had traveled to the emissaries' main enclave in the delta and simply presented themselves as the ancient gods of Chenoweth, finally returned to continue their work on Thali. Once the clergy had recovered from their dumfounded surprise, they had all sequestered themselves for days, debating and arguing, until their plan had come together.

To Galen's dismay, the adepts had emerged in firm partnership with the emissaries, their strongest allies now in convincing the population of Thali to move to Chenoweth. While he had to admit that perpetuating the ancient legends was a far simpler solution than to rob the people of their beliefs entirely, continuing to masquerade as deities troubled him. When, against his wishes, his own connection to Dazai was exposed, he and Dwen Neben had nearly come to blows. Strangely, Delann was as adamantly opposed to the conspiracy as he was and a bond had developed between the two men of which they themselves seemed scarcely aware. It was as if having been utterly possessed by the La'il, knowing her mind in ways no one else ever had, had forever soured them on the very concept of godhood.

"Well, you can't take soldiers in there with you. They're at war down there and you'll only add water to the rain. Adepts are your only chance to get close to their leaders, and you know it."

"Yeah, I do," Delann sighed. They had walked through

the house and now lounged comfortably in the breezeway leading to the garden. A servant began to bring food and, with a disapproving frown, rearranged everyone on woven mats so that, even if they shunned chairs and couches, her employer and his divine guests would not sit on the bare flagstones. "Can I leave Yala with you while I'm gone? Her father has gone up but we can't get the girl to stay with him. I guess it's just too exciting down here these days."

"I'll be in Phrar for the next few weeks," Galen said. "She can stay here."

"I was hoping you'd come out to the highlands with us. Might get interesting."

Galen shook his head. "There was trouble between some emissaries and a bunch of Descendants who aren't ready to forgive. Not sure how I got into this, since I can't exactly blame them, but they want me to mediate. I think my place is in Phrar for now."

"Not a bad idea. I think we'll have more trouble with Masin and her sect. Much more trouble." Seeing Aletha's puzzled frown, Delann explained, "She's gathering followers. Mostly other priestesses, but now she's taken to preaching her message to larger audiences. I heard there are even emissaries among her people. They're saying the people of Thali are being deceived. The prophecies are true and we are being led to our deaths on Chenoweth. They believe her. They refuse to leave, even when they meet migrants who have been up there and returned to tell others about it."

"I can see why the priestesses would oppose us," Galen said. "The emissaries depend on Chenoweth's goodwill. After centuries of making Thali miserable, the gods are the only thing keeping them in power. Imagine what would happen to them if the truth were known!" He chuckled humorlessly. "But the priestesses are useless now. Pointless rites and prayers, empty temples, no one looking for divine intervention. Why visit a priestess if you can just stop at a god's house for tea?"

Aletha frowned at him. A few weeks earlier, when they

had visited the emissaries' enclave to meet with Gynn, word had spread that Dazai himself was among them and a crowd had mobbed the gate, seeking favors and blessings from the deity. The adepts had finally resorted to using a conduit to escape. Even with the benefit of Delann's tightlipped staff, it was only a matter of time before their presence at Delann's home was known. "You are what you are," she said.

"I am what they think I am."

"We all are!" she retorted. Although she had no interest in the leadership of either Thali or Chenoweth, taking a part in shaping the new world for her people was a consuming passion and much of her time was spent in helping them in making the transition. But she also studied tirelessly with the adepts of Chenoweth to hone her skills and abilities, ravenous in her desire to learn more. She passed much of this new knowledge on to Galen, but he watched her progress with unease. He was glad that Chenoweth had remained adamant about the use of chi'ro on Thali and no adept tapped into the moon's scant resources. Instead, chi'ro was funneled from Chenoweth through the conduit in the mountains to be used when necessary to help with the migration. Little was left for the sort of play that amused adepts and so the people of Thali were spared needless displays of magic.

But it was not possible to obscure the palpable essence exuding from the newcomers. Chenoweth's adepts had not learned or needed to hide their gift from those who might prosecute them for it. Even the least able among Thali's Descendants could feel the power of the gods who walked among them. Rarely a day went by when someone was not overcome by fear, or awe or joy upon meeting one of the strangers. Regrettably, as on the Homeworld, jealousy and suspicion was also a common reaction and so only those Chenowans who helped with the migration came to visit here and none used chi'ro without due consideration.

Galen knew that Aletha and some of the other adepts were frustrated, unable to give their talents free reign. They had argued that it would be far simpler to transport everyone to the mountain launch at once, using conduits shaped with Thali's own risers. Fortunately, Dwen Neben had supported Galen's objection to this scheme. Not only would it harm the balance of chi'ro on Thali, but it would be months, perhaps years, before Chenoweth was ready to receive them all. To Galen, delaying the migration meant that the people of Thali would have time to adjust, form new alliances even as they formed new towns, and perhaps recognize that their gods were as mortal and fallible as they were. Even as his own skills grew through his association with Aletha, he hoped that adepts would not assume privilege and leadership over the lesser talents.

Delann smiled uncertainly. "Uh, are we having an argument?"

"An old one," she sighed. "Dazai over here is afraid we'll recreate La'il and her people."

"That isn't funny," Galen snapped and Aletha cringed when Delann also glared at her.

"Yes, it is," she said. She got up and went to the door when a servant entered. She took his tray and slammed it onto a nearby table before closing the door to the hall. That done, she turned back to Galen and Delann. "What is the matter with you two?" she demanded. "We knew this wasn't going to be easy. Even Dwen knew this from the moment he set foot on Thali. Maybe bringing the gods back isn't the best idea, but it's the way things worked out. You don't like the emissaries and I don't, either. But they could have opposed us and then what? Would we remove them by force? Kill them, maybe? Nonsense! Fortunately, they're making this work. People listen to them, just out of habit. Maybe we'll end up with the adepts ruling these moons, and maybe it'll be the emissaries. So what? Someone will always try to lead and no one," she paused to give emphasis to the words that followed, "including me, compares to the La'il in ambition or power. Right now Dwen Neben is doing a damn fine job of managing the migration, considering that none of the

Chenowans care one bit about leading anything or anyone. You're a god right now, Galen Chor, so deal with that. And you, Delann, you haven't had this much fun since you launched your first pirate ship. I don't know what La'il did to you, but it's done now. She's gone. And I'd like to have the two of you back now. We have work to do and maybe it'll take the rest of our lives to finish. I guarantee you it's going to be whole lot better if you found something funny once in a while!"

Her outburst was followed by a long silence while the others stared at her with a mix of surprise and puzzlement. "She's fierce," Delann said to Galen.

"Agreed."

"I'm right!" she said.

"Agreed." Delann stood up. "I have to get my maps together."

Aletha followed him to the door. "I'm sorry I said that... about the La'il. I know she hurt you. I shouldn't have brought that up."

He looped his arms loosely around her waist. "Yeah, you should have. You're right. About everything. We can only do our share and leave it at that. And, yes, I love my part in this. Walking into a hive of warmongering hillmen is going to be exhilarating. I'll take Jeon and Samnang with me, even if our favorite ex-demon over there disapproves." He kissed her and then waved a farewell to Galen. "Look after my house."

Aletha stared silently at the door he had closed behind him before turning back to Galen. He was looking out into the garden, watching a flock of colorful lizards glide from tree to tree, their webbing holding them aloft for their acrobatics. She sat beside him, leaning into him until he wrapped an arm around her shoulders.

"Mad at me?"

"Of course not," he said, a smile tugging at the corner of his lips when he yielded to her playful mental nudges. She slipped into his mind, easily, pleasurably, and they fell into an odd sort of communication they used whenever alone and at ease. It was a rhythmic combination of whispered words, thoughts and mental images becoming more fluent with each passing day. With practice, their conversation would soon be entirely mental, as it was between Aletha and the adepts of Chenoweth, and then even the distance between moons would no longer separate them as they went about their lives and work.

"You're not happy," she said.

"I'm happy when you're here."

"That's not what I meant. You're thinking about something. This isn't about La'il or gods and emissaries or shipping people to Chenoweth. You said yourself, with so much chi'ro on that moon, within a few generations we'll all wonder what a non-adept is. We won't need gods and emissaries."

He nodded.

"Out with it, then!"

He ruminated for a long while before pointing skyward. "Ever wonder what's happened to the planet?"

She looked up to see the Homeworld hanging in the sky, its features rendered in remarkable detail today. "Yes, I wonder. I can't begin to imagine."

"They'll adapt," he said. "Like Thali adapted and Chenoweth will adapt. Things change. But we made that change. I made that. I killed her."

She turned sharply to look at him. "You regret that?"

"Killing her? I've spent years wanting to kill her. I wanted her dead because of what she was doing to me. Then I wanted her gone because of what she wanted to do to this place. I never wondered how things would be once she was gone. She's always been there. She made the Homeworld work, just like the emissaries made this place work. Who's making it work now? What's happening there now? I have family there, friends. What'll happen to them?"

"Like you said: they'll adapt."

"If they can't control the chi'ro distribution, people will suffer. There will be wars fought over each riser. People rely on their supply. They've not had to live without it. I'm not just talking about keeping the lights on. You know now what it feels like to take a full charge of chi'ro. We need this to be who we are. Without chi'ro, the adepts will diminish. Like the people on this moon did."

"They'll find a way to work things out. Surely, the La'il is not the only one there capable of leading your people."

"I want to talk to them," he said.

"Huh? How? Why?"

"We'll tell them about Chenoweth. What they've done up there. It will help them."

"You can't be thinking of going back there!"

"No. I'm going to find a prime to talk to. With your help." He came to his feet. "Come on, let's go to the mountain. I don't want to create a big chi commotion here in town."

Within moments Aletha had requested and received a quantity of chi'ro from the adepts guarding the way to Chenoweth. They were greeted by a blast of cool air when they stepped out of their conduit onto the rocky surface near the launch. The hillside had been leveled off to accommodate the hundreds of people travelling through here each day so that now the launch to Chenoweth stood slightly elevated with rough steps hewn into the rock to lead to the crystal. A few tents had been set up to shelter those who watched over the launch, alert to any attempts from the Homeworld to send a conduit to Thali. The narrow path leading up to this place, as well as the coast road that brought the migrants here, had been widened by the tramping of many feet and now there were resting places and way stations along it to comfort weary travelers.

There were few people here now. To ease the burden for Chenoweth's welcoming committee, people were sent up in groups, arriving a boatload at a time at the foot of the mountain or guided along the road in unhurried caravans. The next wave of migrants was not due until the ship arrived from Phrar. Galen and Aletha were met by two adepts who were nearly beside themselves to find Dazai's heir among them, accompanied by the legendary adept whose talent surpassed any found on Chenoweth. Galen scowled at them for their subservience and Aletha hustled him into one of the tents before he found cause to snap at them.

"Should we get Dwen Neben to help?" she said when they were alone.

"No," he said quickly. "You can do this."

"Hmm, if you think this is going to work. Are you sure you'll be able to reach someone down there?"

"I think so. There are others of my generation who were bred with these genes. None of us were very good at this but we've made some sort of mental contact now and again. Let's see if we can wake someone up." He grinned and pulled her into a tight embrace. "Spike me, Goddess."

With some misgiving, she reached for a tendril of chi'ro coming from Chenoweth, undiminished by distance. She let it surround them, move through them and, finally, used it to infuse him with the power of her own abilities. He gasped and tensed and then slowly let out a deep breath. "Damn that feels good," he sighed.

"Can you feel them?"

He turned his thoughts to the Homeworld, allowing himself to float farther through nothingness, looking for something, anything, that felt human and conscious. He was only dimly aware of Aletha's body pressed to his, but her thoughts stayed with him, supporting and guiding his attempt. "Nothing," he said, disappointed. "There is no one there."

"Can you take a little more?" she said, now also fascinated by this journey. She channeled more chi'ro to him, holding back only when he winced.

"There!" he said suddenly. Indeed, there was now someone out there, down on the planet, whom they were able to feel. Faintly and bewildered, but someone perceived his touch. "There are others."

They swept over the planet, finding a number of people

who felt their presence, some more distinctly than others, some barely there. Galen learned from these encounters and was soon able to delve more deeply, gauging each adept's mental abilities by the strength of their surprised response. "I know this one," he whispered finally. "Rangii." He moved on, looking more closely at this area. Surely, Rangii was either in the reservoir tower or nearby. Surely, then, other prime adepts were also there.

"Can you talk to that one?"

Galen was certain that he could. Even as children, he and Rangii had been able to connect and doubtlessly he could do so now. He also knew that he carried with him enough of Aletha's strength to seriously damage the man. He had learned about the merciless destruction of Vankrug's enclave during those delirious moments when he had possessed La'il's mind in the conduit. She was to blame for that, but Rangii had been a part of it, no matter how reluctantly, and Galen felt a little lacking in forgiveness. "No," he said.

"Why are there so many of them?" Aletha said. "You told me that not a lot of you had this gift."

"We don't. I think these are mostly children. The next generation of prime adepts. La'il was working on this, trying to breed into them whatever Dazai found was happening on Chenoweth naturally." He smiled as his thoughts moved on. "Ah, there's a friendly face. Caelan. Interesting. He's not a very strong adept but I can feel him more than the others. Maybe we're related somehow."

"You think so? That one?"

"Can you feel him?"

"Yes, and he can feel us. Talk to him!"

"No. I want a higher ranking adept. There, that one is strong, too." Galen honed in on a bright presence not far from where he had felt Caelan, certain now that they were in the tower. He nudged her carefully, feeling Aletha's guarded presence hovering nearby.

"Shai?" They received a startled, frightened reply from the woman. "It's Galen Chor," he said. "Don't worry, all is well." They waited patiently until Shai overcame her surprise and sent a hesitant question. There were no words, but her meaning was clear enough.

"Yes, I'm on Thali. The adept is here with me, but she is not La'il's sister. Chenoweth is no threat to the Homeworld. Tell me what's happening on the planet."

They waited for Shai's response. It was a jumble of emotions and imagery but eventually they were able to piece things together. Yobar had been found dead and the La'il had disappeared in a terrible surge of chi'ro that had left the continent's reserves nearly depleted. The primes had moved quickly to secure all risers, sending any adept capable of it to guard them with their lives, if necessary. But things were coming apart. Without La'il's iron control, some of the more powerful adepts were seeking alliances among lesser talents and the primes were now divided. Chi'ro was still distributed through all major nodes but the reserves were jealously guarded by primes who laid claim to them by virtue of their presence in the area alone. La'il's inner circle had retained possession of the tower but infighting had begun to fray their allegiances.

Galen sighed, his worst fears confirmed. "They'll rip each other apart over this," he said to Aletha. They strained to receive a question from the woman on the planet.

"Yes, we know how to open the seals," he replied. "But I can't come back. La'il tried to destroy Thali. She's dead now. Listen to me, Shai. And then you must get the others to listen." He bit his lip, wondering how to proceed. "Chenoweth understands chi'ro better than any of us. You don't need more chi'ro. You don't need to fight over it. I wish you could meet these people. They've evolved far beyond us. They don't have more chi than we do; they just use it in different ways. They live completely inside their heads. They have nothing because they need nothing. We can all get there, Shai. You have to stop building roads and bridges and wasting chi'ro on digging for ore and on flying planes. You don't need to breed more powerful adepts.

Those will only need more chi'ro. Stop using chi'ro like it was a hammer and start using it to look into your minds. It's already begun on the Homeworld. You, Rangii, Ciela, those kids. Talk to the people who selected our parents. You have to continue what La'il started. You have to breed a different mind. A different talent. You can accomplish much in a few generations. You'll never have to fight over chi'ro again, or ration it, or hold it at ransom. You'll have all you need! Are you hearing me, Shai?"

He shook his head. "She can't possibly understand what I mean. I should go down there, or bring her here, to see for herself."

"No!" Aletha said at once. "Absolutely out of the question. That place is ready to collapse! I won't open the seal again. I won't bring the giants back up here. Not now. Your adepts are far more powerful than anyone we have here and they'll have their hands on Chenoweth in an instant. They'll murder us all just to finish what La'il has started up here. And I'm not letting you go back, either. You'll be a tiny little man there and they'll take you hostage in a moment to get us to open the seal. Or they'll hurt you for killing La'il."

"All right," he said. "All right. I hear you. Tiny little man, indeed!"

"Well, don't frighten me like that!"

"Was just an idea. I just wish we could do more for them, or show her what I mean."

"Hmm, maybe we can." Aletha turned her attention back to Shai. Carefully, gently, she touched the woman's mind, whispering an instruction, instilling an idea, until the adept signaled her understanding and gratitude.

"What was that?" Galen said.

"A little gift. I showed her how to make those bubble houses that I showed you earlier. It takes so little chi'ro. If things go bad down there, at least they won't freeze to death. I remember how you talked about your winters!"

He smiled at her and kissed her face. "You're sweet, but we don't have objections to burning wood down there." He sent a few thoughts of reassurance and affection to Shai before breaking their contact. "She's a bright person. She can get the others to listen. I suppose this is all we can do for them."

"Once those kids grow up we'll be able to talk with them more easily. We can teach them. They'll be fine."

He smiled. "You're right. Let's go home. I'd like to stay in bed until you run off to Chenoweth again."

"I'll be here for a few days."

"Then that's how long we'll stay in bed."

* * *

Shai walked slowly out into the circular aerie that had been La'il's favorite room in the tower. It was still encased in a thin shield of chi'ro allowing only the gentlest breeze to flow through the arcing pillars that carried the roof of the building. Soon, this needless luxury would end, but without La'il this room had lost its meaning, anyway. There were dozens of people here, waiting for Shai to seat herself on the raised couch where no one had dared to sit since La'il's disappearance. Some of them watched this with trepidation, convinced that some sacrilege was being committed here.

Shai did not sit, but she did ascend the two steps to stand above her audience as she addressed them. Most of them were telepaths of varying ability and almost all of them were adepts. There were a number of primes among them while a few had barely any talent at all. All occupations, all ages, many of them children. Three were non-adepts, summoned here because they knew the ancestry of each person in this room and guided the parentage of the next generation. Shai nodded to Fromm and Ciela; both knew why they were here. She saw Caelan, Ciela's daughters, Rangii's brother and many others she now knew to be related, sharing the gene that was to be passed along. Galen Chor's youngest son, already displaying signs of significant talent, played on the tiled floor with something he had found among La'il's things.

"There is no need for preamble here," Shai said. "Many

of you felt Galen Chor's touch on this planet just a few days ago. He sends a message from Chenoweth." She waited until the startled murmur running through the crowd had ebbed again. "Yes, Galen found the moons much like La'il described them. They can break through the seals whenever they choose. La'il is destroyed and Galen cannot return to us. But his is a message of hope. A new breed of adept will rise from this calamity! We are that breed. The years that follow now will be difficult. It will be a time for us to change the way we use our gifts, and to pass them on to the next generation. We need not use chi'ro to create energy. To us, chi'ro *is* energy. It is power." She paused to find Rangii in the crowd. "To demonstrate what lies ahead for us, La'il's sister on Thali has touched my mind and shown me something new. A weapon. I've already passed this knowledge on to some."

Rangii stepped forward, as did Karyana, a strong telepath but one with little talent for wielding chi'ro. They faced each other across the open area at the bottom of the steps on which Shai waited.

"Kill her," Shai said to Rangii.

As expected, the surprised crowd reacted with cries of protest and worried questions. Some voiced their fears loudly; others merely watched in apprehension to see if La'il's policy of unthinking obedience was to continue in this place. Only Karyana seemed entirely indifferent.

"What are you doing, Shai?" Caelan raised his arm across Rangii's chest as if to stop him from physically attacking Karyana. "What's gotten into you?"

"Don't worry, Calie," Rangii grinned. He stepped away from his companion and raised a hand. A shred of chi'ro danced over his fingers which, incendiary or not, would seriously maim anyone less able than he. Few people in this room matched his abilities. "Just watch."

Karyana waved her hand diagonally across the space in front of her to create a shield and did not even blink when Rangii hurled his missile across the small space separating them. Panicked, some of the others surged back. But Rangii's attack failed, its result no more spectacular than the fumbling attempts of the lowliest novice just coming of age. The chi'ro burst struck the shimmering wall in front of Karyana and dissipated. She merely rocked on her feet for a moment and then steadied, her pleasant smile unwavering.

"What happened?" someone shouted. "Where did it go?"

"Absorbed," Shai said. "Thank you, Karyana." She winked at Caelan. "She should have been knocked through that wall. Instead, she took that blow as if her rank was equal to Rangii's. She is not a great talent, but she can be harmed in battle no more easily than he could." Shai looked over the astounded faces surrounding her. "This is just the beginning. Look how that screen of chi'ro obscures her! With shields like this we can hide our numbers and our intentions. We'll learn to talk with each other the way Galen Chor showed me. We'll learn to see into our opponents' thoughts."

"Will this protect us from Chenoweth?" someone else wanted to know.

"This isn't about Chenoweth! Here, on the Homeworld, is where we'll make our stand. We are of a new breed created by La'il and we will continue to grow and evolve." Her gaze moved to Caelan to see him stare open-mouthed in bewilderment and growing, horrified alarm. "We will control every riser, every adept, every wisp of chi'ro on this planet. It will not be long before we can start to replace the old order of prime adepts. We will be the new guard on the Homeworld. This planet is ours."

~ ~ ~ ~ ~ ~
~

ABOUT THE AUTHOR

Chris Reher is a first generation Canadian currently and out of necessity residing on planet Earth (which, in the general and interplanetary scheme of things, could *really* use a catchier name. Imagine heading past Proxima Centauri and someone asks you whence you came and you tell them "dirt". All theological implications aside, that just won't do.)

When not finding ways to defy the laws of physics or torture her subjects or entice them with inter-species hanky-panky, she designs web sites or writes about designing web sites. She enjoys long walks on the beach or, given the local beach shortage, writes about beaches far beyond Proxima Centauri.

www.chrisreher.com

Also by Chris Reher

Sky Hunter

The Catalyst

Only Human

Rebel Alliances

Delphi Promised

Quantum Tangle

Terminus Shift